The
Second
Chance
Tea Shop

FAY KEENAN was born in Surrey and
raised in Hampshire, before finally
settling back in the West Country. When
Fay is not chasing her children around
or writing, she teaches English at a local
secondary school. She lives with her
husband of fourteen years, two daughters,
a cat, two chickens and a Weimaraner
called Bertie in a village in Somerset,
which may or may not have provided the
inspiration for Little Somerby.

The
Second
Chance
Tea Shop

Fay Keenan

ⓐ

First published as an ebook in 2017 by Aria,
an imprint of Head of Zeus, Ltd.

First published in print in the UK in 2017 by Aria.

9 7 5 3 1 2 4 6 8

A catalogue record for this book is available from
the British Library.

ISBN (PB): 9781788541022
ISBN (E): 9781786694881

Typeset by Divaddict Publishing Solutions Ltd.

MIX
Paper from
responsible sources
FSC® C020471

Printed and bound by CPI Group (UK) Ltd,
Croydon, CR0 4YY

Head of Zeus Ltd
First Floor East
5–8 Hardwick Street
London EC1R 4RG

WWW.HEADOFZEUS.COM

To Flora and Roseanna, with all my love.

WINTER

Chapter 1

'Are we nearly there?' A small voice came from the back seat of Anna Hemingway's car.

We're getting there, Anna thought. 'Just a couple more minutes.'

As she drove, she kept half an eye on the scenes that presented themselves. Although she had been a regular visitor to Little Somerby, the Somerset village where she grew up, since she'd left eighteen years ago it had changed little from her last visit, yet as a soon-to-be resident once again she looked about her with fresh eyes.

'Will there be a swing in the garden?' Ellie asked.

'I don't know, darling. We can always get one if you want.' Anna spotted the church on the corner, gravestones covered in a crisp shroud of frost, surrounded by yew trees. On the other side of the road was the village pub, The Stationmaster, site of countless drunken nights and teenage liaisons.

'Tomorrow?'

'Perhaps when we've settled in a bit.'

Continuing on she saw the Post Office and stores, now rather more organic and free range than she remembered. Next to that, the Village Hall, red-bricked and proudly declaiming its Temperance movement heritage. A little further on she passed the garage where she'd bought her first car, and then, the warm, inviting lights of The Little Orchard Tea Shop. She briefly glimpsed a couple of occupied tables through the bay window, and a shiver of anticipation went through her. Of all the decisions she'd made over the past few months, taking on a new job was the one that she'd agonised hardest about. But this move was intended to be a fresh start, a change to nearly every part of her life, and there was no doubt that managing a tea shop would provide plenty of change.

As she drove closer towards her new home, the sprawling land and buildings of the local cider farm – once a shed and a shop, now a thriving multinational business – loomed into view. Apart from the more dominant presence of the cider farm, so little in the village had changed; Anna found it difficult to believe that *she* had. But she was thirty-six years old, with a D-cup bra, a C-section scar and a three-year-old daughter. She was hardly the same hopeful girl who'd left the village to pursue education, a career, and later, love.

Love. Anna swallowed hard. They'd have been married ten years this spring. But she pushed that to the back of her mind; today was about taking the next step in her new life.

She felt a small stirring of excitement as she turned up Flowerdown Lane, which was a pleasant spot a little away from the main part of the village. Pippin Cottage was the last house on the right, one of only four houses. It was painted white with dark beams running from top to bottom. A curved oak door was set into the centre of the front of the cottage, protected from the elements by a slightly rickety porch. Three windows adorned the first floor and two further windows sat either side of the front door. The slate roof had been repaired extensively but still retained its aged charm. The front garden was enclosed by a stone wall with a rusty wrought-iron gate. At the end of the lane was an orchard of neatly ordered apple trees, their branches lying dormant now, but promising new life when the spring arrived.

4

Anna had chosen the cottage because it was close enough to the village to feel connected, but, being the last house on the lane, it also had a pleasantly secluded feel. She'd only viewed it once before putting in an offer, and she'd nearly been put off by the estate agent, who had been brusque to the point of rudeness while he showed her around, but she'd always wanted to own a cottage, and this one was practically the stuff of dreams. The fact that her absolute worst nightmare had come true, and allowed her the freedom to buy the place, was an agonising irony that tormented her, nearly two years on. The sharpness of loss pierced her heart once again and she had to draw in a calming, steadying breath.

'Are you ready, darling?' Opening her car door, she went to the back to get Ellie out. The little girl took approximately half a second to look around before she bounded through the garden gate and raced up the garden path.

'Come on, Mummy!' she called from the porch.

Anna pushed the car door shut and looked at her daughter hopping impatiently from foot to foot on the doorstep. It was time.

*

'Well, as soon as you hear from them please can you get them to give me a ring?' Anna pressed the end call button to the removal company and yet again cursed the fact she'd shoved her mobile phone charger in the last box that had been loaded onto the lorry. Only a few minutes behind her when they'd left, they still hadn't turned up. Chucking the phone down on the lamentably empty kitchen worktop, Anna jumped as a deep bark rent the air, and, almost immediately, fuzzy black and white fur flying, a Border collie erupted from the hall into her kitchen. This was followed by an unmistakably outraged female voice. 'Seffy! Come back here *now!*'

Despite the cold December day, Anna had left the dark oak door open to let in some light and a little fresh air, and as she made an abortive grab for the dog's collar, she noticed its owner silhouetted in the door frame. Dark-haired, pale-skinned and slender, as she turned towards Anna and dropped her hand from the door, Anna saw a generous red-lipped mouth and the most startling blue eyes she'd ever seen. The girl was clad in dark jeans and an oversized striped jumper, combined with ballet pumps that were totally unsuitable for the December weather.

'I'm so sorry,' the girl's voice was low, modulated and hinted at a public school education. 'I tried to get him on the lead before we got to the gate, but he outsmarted me.'

Anna smiled. 'No harm done.' As soon as the collie saw his mistress he trotted obediently back to her.

Looping the dog's lead through his collar, the girl smiled apologetically. 'I'm Meredith. But most people call me Merry.' She glanced back at the dog. 'And this is Sefton.'

'It's nice to meet you,' Anna said, reaching forward to pat the dog. 'I'm Anna, and somewhere in the house is my daughter, Ellie.'

'So you're moving in today?' Merry asked.

'Yup, if the removal company ever get here. I'd offer you a cup of tea, but I don't have my kettle!' She glanced around the kitchen. The Rayburn – something else she'd always wanted in the kitchen of her dreams – squatted dull yellow and imposing against one wall of the kitchen, its top scrubbed clean. Anna was a keen baker and she was looking forward to learning how to cook on it, especially in light of the new job she was going to be taking on in a week or two. She hoped the previous owner had left the instruction manual, as she didn't know where to start with it.

'Thanks for the offer anyway, but I can't stop. Seffy's been bugging me for a walk all day and he needs all the exercise he can get. Whenever he sees an open door he takes it as an invitation! Sorry about that.'

'It's fine,' Anna replied. 'I'm sure he won't be the last visitor!'

'No, definitely not,' Meredith rolled her eyes. 'The local gossips will be on your doorstep in no time, so be careful. I'd install CCTV if I were you, or get a dog yourself to chase them off!'

'Thanks for the warning. I'll keep that in mind.'

'Well, welcome to the village – hopefully catch up with you again soon,' Meredith turned on her heel and wandered back out.

As she stood in the doorway, she saw the girl disappear up to the end of the lane, open the five-bar gate that marked the entrance to the orchard and walk through. If all the teenagers in the village looked like that, Anna reflected, then things really had changed over the time she'd lived away.

A buzz from her mobile interrupted her thoughts. Walking back to the kitchen, she found a message from the movers blaming a pile-up on the M5 for their non-appearance. Anna winced and locked her screen again, willing her thoughts not to wander. In the meantime, she figured she'd look in on her best friend Charlotte, who lived two doors down. Charlotte had texted that morning demanding to know exactly when Anna was arriving. The fact that she would be living so close to her oldest school friend was another reason she'd swiftly put an offer in on Pippin Cottage. Anna had the feeling she was going to need friends and family around her in the next few weeks and months. Guiltily, she realised she'd not texted Charlotte back. She really must get a grip and crack on with things. After all, she'd arranged to meet Ursula Rowbotham, the owner of the tea shop, at six o'clock and it was edging up to three o'clock now.

First, though, she decided to set up the Rayburn, which ran the central heating as well as providing the main source of cooking in the kitchen. There had been some wrangling between solicitors about the Rayburn before the exchange of contracts, but she'd been assured that it would be serviced and fuelled before completion. As she turned knobs and fiddled with switches, however, she quickly realised the huge iron beast wasn't going to work. *That's all I need,* she thought. *No furniture, no broadband and now no bloody central heating!* Biting back her irritation, she punched out the estate agent's number on her mobile. After a brief exchange, one of the agents assured her they'd contact the previous owner and get someone round as soon as possible, so Anna decided to cut her losses.

'Come on, Munchkin,' she called to Ellie, who was spinning around in circles in the empty living room. 'Let's go and find Charlotte and Evan.' Taking the slightly dizzy toddler's hand, she closed the old front door behind her and went in search of her best friend.

Chapter 2

Anna didn't have to look far. Charlotte, auburn hair tied up in a messy bun, a smudge of soot on her cheek from her wood burner and a rip in her jeans so high up her thigh it veered on the indecent, was striding up the lane towards her.

'You made it, then.' Charlotte hugged her warmly and Anna felt a lump rising in her throat. She'd been on autopilot during the moving process, and now she was finally here, about to embark on a new phase of her life, she suddenly felt totally overwhelmed. Charlotte seemed to sense this, and as she released Anna, she took Ellie by the hand. 'Come on,' she said. 'I've left Evan in front of CBeebies and he'll spot I'm gone in a minute. I can see your stuff hasn't arrived yet, and there's no point hanging around an empty house. You've got time for a quick cuppa, or something stronger if you're up to it, before the lorry arrives. That's if you don't mind the usual chaos of my house. Especially this close to Christmas.'

Anna didn't doubt things were hectic at number 2. What she wouldn't have given to be frantic with normal Christmas preparations right now. She felt a sudden, sharp stab of jealousy; Charlotte was doing what she'd always done at this time of year, preparing for a big family Christmas, while Anna, on the other hand, was just trying to keep on an even keel.

'I'm surprised your mum and dad aren't here on moving in

day,' Charlotte said, pushing open the door to her own cottage.

Anna gave a small smile as she stepped over the collapsed coat stand in the porch and noticed the overflowing washing basket in the corner. Charlotte's brand of organised chaos was something she'd got used to over the years; her best friend was far more concerned with people than the practicalities of home life. Hers was a messy, happy house, and Anna envied it, especially now, as it contrasted so starkly with her own very empty new cottage.

'They booked a holiday before I knew what my completion date was – we all thought it wouldn't be until after Christmas, but my solicitor managed to push it through a few days early, and they're away until the twenty-third.'

'That's cutting it fine for Christmas!' Charlotte said, leading Anna and Ellie through to her equally chaotic kitchen. 'But, knowing your mum and dad, they're still going to pull it out of the bag on the day.' She got a jar of instant coffee down from the overflowing kitchen cupboard. 'Sorry I haven't got anything posher, but you'll probably be sick of the smell of ground coffee in a few weeks' time!'

'Mum seemed confident they could manage Christmas dinner at theirs again this year.' Anna moved a pile of shirts off one of the kitchen chairs and sat down at the large wooden table that dominated Charlotte's kitchen. 'My sister's spending the holiday with her in-laws and my brother's staying in Australia this year, so it'll be just Ellie and me.' She swallowed hard, feeling the sharp sting of loss once again, and busied herself with handing Ellie and Evan, Charlotte's little boy, a biscuit from the packet that was open on the table.

'Lucky you, to have Christmas dinner done for you,' Charlotte grimaced good-naturedly. 'Simon's mother's coming so it'll be gritted teeth all round and buckets of Prosecco to ease the pain. What time did the removal company say they were going to turn up?' Charlotte asked, grabbing a third biscuit.

'They didn't,' Anna said gloomily. 'And to cap it all, the Rayburn doesn't seem to be working, so the house is bloody freezing.'

'I thought you'd asked for it to be serviced before completion?' Charlotte said. 'So you could live out your Mary Berry fantasies, instead of doing the sensible thing and ripping it out!'

'I did, but there's something wrong with it, and, being so close to Christmas, I don't fancy my chances of getting anyone out to look at it.'

'Have you tried calling the estate agent?'

'Yup. They said they'd ring the previous owner.'

'Didn't you buy the cottage off some company?' Charlotte said. She furrowed her brow. 'Surely they've got contacts to sort this kind of stuff out.'

'I hope so,' Anna replied. 'And if they can't sort it out immediately, at least I can snuggle up with Ellie. We could both do with an early night.' She sighed. 'It's the last thing I need, though, on top of our stuff not arriving. I wish...' She couldn't go on.

Charlotte reached over and squeezed Anna's hand. 'I know. And I can't imagine how hard it's been to get to this point. But you've done it. Now all you've got to do is settle in and enjoy your new home. Well, until you start at the tea shop, anyway.' For a moment, the friends held each other's gaze.

There was a sudden rumble past the kitchen window. 'Thank goodness for that!' Anna jumped up as the removal lorry pulled up two doors down. 'Let's hope I can find some jumpers and blankets in there.'

'Leave Ellie here for a bit,' Charlotte said, gesturing to the two three-year-olds, who were stalking Charlotte's ancient cat, Gizzy. 'You'll be far more productive without her under your feet, and I'll give her some tea if you like.'

'If you're sure. That would make things a bit easier.'

'No worries.' Charlotte grinned. 'Now get back over there and give those movers some direction, or you'll end up with your crockery in the garden shed!'

Anna smiled, marginally happier. Coming back to the village had been a decision she'd fretted about, but having Charlotte so close definitely made her feel as though it had been the right one. Kissing Ellie goodbye, she hurried back to Pippin Cottage.

*

Once the removal men had left, Anna paced her new kitchen restlessly. The cottage was rapidly getting colder, despite the fact she'd lit the wood burner in the lounge using the small amount of logs left in the store out the back. For the thousandth time since her husband's death, Anna yearned for James beside her to offer her a smile and, in this case, some actual constructive help with the Rayburn. Coupled with the fact that she was now standing amidst piles of her possessions in boxes, she once again felt overwhelmed.

A sharp knock at the back door made her jump. Turning around, she hurried to open it. The man on the doorstep looked familiar, right down to the expression of irritation on his face. Of all the people to have turned up to solve her problem, it had to be the bloody estate agent who had been so rude to her when she'd viewed the cottage.

'Oh. Could you not get hold of the previous owner after all?' Anna said, as the man waited on the back doorstep, presumably to be invited in.

'I am the previous owner,' the man replied. 'Or rather, my father is.'

Anna, flummoxed, tried to recover her wits, which seemed to have fled as she opened the door to this tall, grim-faced stranger. 'Oh. Right. You showed me around when I came to view, and so I just assumed...'

'Well, you assumed wrong. Can I come in?'

Anna nodded and stepped out of the way to allow the man admittance to her kitchen. So tall he had to duck under the doorframe as he walked in, his wavy dark hair was shot through with threads of grey. Hazel eyes sketched with fine lines of crows' feet and a jawline with a brushstroke or two of five o'clock shadow framed a prominent, but obviously once broken, nose. A broad chest wrapped in a dark blue cable knit jumper tapered down to endless, denim-clad legs. He might have been dressed more casually this time, but his expression of irritation at being called out was the same as when he'd showed her around the cottage. Why hadn't he told her he was related to the owner when she'd viewed the place?

'I'm sorry to have bothered you,' Anna said, trying to lighten the mood that he had brought into her kitchen. 'But I didn't know what else to do. The Rayburn doesn't seem to be working, and I was assured when I signed the inventory that it would be serviced and in full working order on completion.'

'My father should have seen to it.'

Anna couldn't help but notice the gruff stranger's pronounced West Country burr.

He knelt down and examined the power panel tucked away behind a small hatch. After a minute or so he stood back up again. 'There's no oil in it. You'll have to order some.'

After a long day full of hassles and irritations, Anna's temper flared. 'The inventory said there was half a tank of oil left. Surely that's enough to run the thing for a little while?'

'Well, there isn't now. Perhaps the time it took for the purchase to go through meant that the tank ran dry. Heaven knows your solicitor took long enough to come back to us.'

'It wasn't my fault the roof needed fixing!' Anna retorted. 'Your solicitor didn't exactly rush back with confirmation that the work had been done, either. I assume that won't be found wanting, like the oil tank.'

'I'm sure the paperwork is all in order on our side. I'd get onto your own solicitor if you have any more queries.' The man seemed to be struggling with a decision, and his eyes flickered from the Rayburn back to Anna. 'In the meantime, I'll give the merchant I use a ring and get him to come and fill up the oil tank as soon as he can.'

Anna exhaled. 'Thank you.'

For a moment they both stood, an awkward silence between them. *If only James were here,* Anna thought.

'I'll be off then.'

His voice broke into her thoughts. Anna glanced up at his face; his mouth was set in a grim line still, but his eyes betrayed a trace of something warmer. 'Right,' she said, her voice quieter than she intended. As she looked at him, something tugged at her memory, something long forgotten that, as soon as she tried to grasp it, slipped away like sand through her fingers. *I've met you before,* she thought. *And not just when you showed me the cottage.*

Before she could ponder further, the man nodded, and then, without another word, he opened the kitchen door and stepped back out of the house. It was only as he closed the door behind him that Anna realised that once again he'd failed to introduce himself. The paperwork on the house had listed Appletree Holdings as the previous owner of the cottage, and she was still none the wiser about who, or what, they actually were. Not that it seemed to matter, after such a long day. Leaning back against the worktop, relieved that Ellie wasn't around to witness them, the tears she'd been holding back all day slid down her cheeks.

Chapter 3

Matthew Carter looked at his watch and picked up his pace. Normally, a walk down the Strawberry Line – a former railway track that had now been converted into a cycle path which ran alongside the village of Little Somerby – would be enough to take his mind off whatever was causing him stress, lined as it was with oak, ash and silver birch trees and bordered by acres of farmland. Holly bushes, laden with berries, thrust forth their prickly hands in a potent reminder of the festive season, and there was the sharp scent of frost, laced with pine balsam in the air. But this afternoon Matthew had entirely too much to do to appreciate the beauty of the countryside.

He'd decided to work from home for most afternoons this week, mindful that his teenage daughter had started her school holiday. His decision in no way reflected a let-up in his considerable workload. The absolute last thing he had needed was to be dragged away from his work to that bloody cottage to fix a problem that wasn't of his making. He should really have driven over, but after hours at his desk he had been almost glad of the chance to stretch his legs.

He couldn't understand why anyone would move house so close to Christmas. Surely her solicitors should have advised against it, being, undoubtedly, in the process of winding down themselves for the holiday? Having had to take a few people around the cottage when the estate agent had double-booked was pushing it, and to be dragged back in there, on the day of the sale, and castigated for an issue that his father should have sorted, was the final straw.

Picking up his pace, he felt his back pocket buzzing. As he pulled his phone out, he recognised his PA's number on the screen. He couldn't even get away from work for half an hour, it seemed. He sighed. 'Hello? Yes, that's fine. Tell them I'll be in touch tomorrow morning. Thanks, Jen.' Yet another thing that needed his attention, he thought. Sometimes he wondered why he bothered employing anyone else when everything clearly still landed on his desk. His daughter would doubtless tell him it was his own lack of delegation skills, but, he thought with a reluctant grin, she'd soon discover it wasn't quite so easy when she took the family business on. If, indeed, she ever did.

As he neared his own house once again, he wondered if she'd be at home. He was sure he wasn't imagining it, but since he'd been working from home, his daughter had seemed to be making herself scarce. Pushing open the back door, which led straight into the kitchen, he saw his border collie, replete from dinner, stretched across the rug by the fireplace.

'Meredith? Are you home?' Matthew heard the muffled sound of the television coming from the sitting room and strolled through the kitchen and hallway.

'In here.'

Matthew pushed open the sitting room door. Stretched out on the battered brown Chesterfield leather sofa, feet propped up on one of its stubby sides, phone in one hand and a slice of Marmite on toast in the other, was his daughter. The television blared, and Matthew automatically reached for the remote to turn it down a notch or two, just as he had when she'd been a viewer of CBeebies, many years ago.

'Have you finished for the day?'

'Nearly,' Matthew replied. 'Just got a few more figures to look at. This close to Christmas, there's a hell of a lot to go through before shutdown.'

'Aren't you ever off duty?' Meredith asked, leaning over to stroke Sefton, who, ever hopeful of a dropped morsel from his mistress' plate, sniffed around.

Matthew grinned at his daughter. 'The boss has told me I can take Christmas Day off.'

'Ha ha,' Meredith grinned. 'The last time I checked, you were the boss.'

'You'd never know it, sometimes,' Matthew said. He glanced down at Sefton. 'I take it, from the way that dog's behaving, that you've walked him already today.'

Meredith ruffled the collie's furry neck affectionately. 'He'd been pacing the kitchen since lunchtime so I thought I should get him out, as I didn't know what time you were going to be back. I took him over the East Orchard.'

'I'm surprised I didn't see you there,' Matthew said.

'Why? What were you doing over there?'

'Some woman rang moaning about the Rayburn in that old cottage that Granddad just sold,' Matthew's brow furrowed as he remembered the rather combative discussion he'd had at Pippin Cottage.

'Her name's Anna,' Meredith said wryly. 'I met her earlier, too. She seems nice.'

'Nice or not, I didn't really have time to go sorting out something your grandfather should have already done. I've got to break the back of what's on my desk before start of business tomorrow or I really will be working on Christmas Day.' He glanced at his daughter, who had been joined on the sofa by the dog. Sefton met his gaze, unrepentant, as Meredith pulled his head onto her lap. 'He's not allowed on the furniture. Do you fancy a curry tonight?'

'No, Dad. Remember I made that casserole for us. I'll stick it in the oven now,' Meredith kissed Sefton's black nose. 'It'll take two hours, I reckon.'

'What would I do without you, daughter of mine?'

'Starve to death, probably. Or die of heart failure. Now get back to work so we can chill out and watch the next episode of *Game of Thrones* together later.'

'All right, all right,' Matthew muttered. Sometimes he wondered who was the parent and who was the child in this relationship; he was lucky to have such a practical and considerate daughter.

Walking back out of the living room and towards his study, where a dozen different bits of paper awaited him, he hoped he'd be able to pick up where he'd been forced to leave off. Before he did, however, he had a couple of calls to make. The one to his father could wait, but he found the number of the oil merchant and rang through.

'All right, John? I was hoping you could sort out some heating oil. No, not for me, for Pippin Cottage. Yes, needs a full tank. Stick it on my account. Can you check the condition of the tank as well; let me know if it needs replacing. Thanks. Merry Christmas to you too.'

As he ended the call, his thoughts wandered back to the new occupant of Pippin Cottage. He couldn't help thinking he'd seen her somewhere before, but he was buggered if he could put his finger on where. Not that it mattered; the cottage was sold. At least he could now, hopefully, put it and his encounter with its new owner behind him. It was a place, for many reasons, he was none too keen to revisit. Shaking his head, he settled back down at his desk and picked up the nearest sheaf of papers.

Chapter 4

Anna didn't have time to be miserable for long. The meeting with Ursula at The Little Orchard Tea Shop was looming. What had possessed her to arrange it on the day she moved in, she now wasn't sure, but at least it would give her something else to focus on other than the packing boxes.

It was about a ten minute walk from the cottage to the tea shop, and as Anna walked up the High Street she was assailed by all things Christmas. Real fir trees, around two feet tall, had been attached high up on the walls of virtually every building, and the festive light panels that were fixed to the lamp posts were shining in the winter darkness. The shops were still open, as this close to Christmas they were encouraging all the trade they could get. As Anna passed The Stationmaster pub, enticing smells from the restaurant drifted on the chilly air. The chill presaged snow, but in this part of the world a white Christmas was hugely unlikely. A few people walked past Anna and smiled or nodded. She found herself smiling back.

The Little Orchard Tea Shop was about to close when she arrived, and as Anna reached the front door of the shop she could see Ursula behind the counter slicing up a rather delectable winter fruitcake. Her head of wild grey curls gave her a bohemian air, but under the crazy hairstyle lay an astute business brain. The Little Orchard Tea Shop had been a joint project with her husband Brian, who worked behind the scenes and kept the finances in order. Ursula herself had been running the shop for nearly twenty years, with the help of Lizzie, her chief waitress, currently sitting on one of the squashy red sofas that were in the far corner of the tea shop, and a troop of teenagers, who passed the baton to younger friends when they either lost interest or moved on to university or permanent employment. Anna herself had done a stint at the tea shop the summer before she went to university.

Over the years she'd kept up to date with the progress of the tea shop, as not only was Ursula a dear friend of her mother's but she was also Anna's godmother. Though neither of them were remotely religious these days, the bond between them had always been strong, and even when Anna had settled on the other side of the country, she'd kept in touch with Ursula by letter and, later, despite Ursula's technophobia, by email. Anna was one of the first to know when, due to worsening health, Ursula was looking for someone to take over the management of the tea shop, and it seemed like the perfect opportunity for both of them to make a fresh start.

The Little Orchard Tea Shop had become a goldmine over the years, converting even the staunchest tea drinkers into aficionados of various types of Italian and Columbian coffee. With the nest egg that they'd accumulated for their retirement, Ursula and Brian had decided to buy a villa in Umbria, where the climate was kinder to Ursula's arthritis.

As Anna crossed the threshold, Ursula looked up from the cake and gave her a welcoming smile. 'You made it in one piece, then,' she said, putting the cake knife down. Stepping out from behind the counter, she enfolded her goddaughter in a warm embrace.

'Just about!' Anna replied. 'My furniture took a bit of a detour, but everything's arrived at last.'

'You could have always rearranged tonight,' Ursula started to walk over to the sofa. 'I mean, you don't officially take over the management of this place until the New Year, so we have a bit of time.'

Anna noticed, with a stab of sympathy, the wooden stick Ursula used, and the stiffness of her movements.

'I wanted to come in and catch up as soon as I could,' Anna sat down on the other end of the sofa, feeling relieved at actually having somewhere comfortable to sit after a very long day. 'And I'll have a bit of time between Christmas and New Year to swot up on how things happen in here.'

Lizzie, who was still wearing her green apron with 'The Little Orchard Tea Shop' embroidered in white on the front, smiled at Anna as she reached for a slice of the fruit cake that Ursula had brought over to the table. In her late forties, with thick dark hair and a friendly smile, she exuded calm. 'Hi there,' she said. 'It's nice to meet you.'

'You too,' Anna replied, sitting down.

Ursula poured Anna a cup of tea from the pot that was already on the table. 'I'll be on hand for a bit while we sort out the final arrangements in Italy. You're still happy to sign the contract for a year?'

'Oh yes,' Anna replied. This move back to Little Somerby was, hopefully, her last major upheaval for a while. 'Managing this place seems like a really good way to get back into village life.' And, she thought, it would hopefully allow her to combat the last of the darkness that her grief over James habitually plunged her into. The tea shop took her back to a time before her 'proper' career had started, when she'd managed a small sandwich shop after university. She hoped the skills needed for retail would come back to her fairly easily, given a week or two behind the counter. And Lizzie would continue to work her own shifts at the tea shop, leaving Anna free to work around Ellie's nursery hours and also to do the baking of the stock. She knew, if she wanted to take any annual leave at any point, that Ursula also had a number of local suppliers who could be called upon to provide stock if needed. This gave her some much needed reassurance, since home baking was one thing, but baking professionally was an entirely new venture.

'This cake is gorgeous,' Anna replied, taking another bite of the slice of fruit cake. Its moistness came from not just the fruit, but a generous addition of cider, which made a nice change from the usual seasonal brandy-soaked recipes.

'I've no doubt you'll be producing things just as good,' Ursula said. 'Those lavender and honey cupcakes you baked for your mother's birthday in the summer were superb. You should add those to the menu when you've taken over. There're a few local honey producers you might want to look up, to give them a real Somerset flavour. I'm sure if you go onto the internet you'll find quite a few you could try.'

Anna was secretly tickled that Ursula referred to the internet with as much affection as she might have a mangy Somerset fox, and as she saw her own amusement reflected in Lizzie's eyes, she had to hide a wider smile. She knew that Ursula had deliberately resisted installing customer Wi-Fi in the tea shop, as she didn't like the idea of customers 'typing into their laptops when they should be making conversation', but it was something that Anna was definitely considering. After all, times were changing.

'And feel free to put your own stamp on the place,' Ursula said as she swallowed another bite of cake. 'If you want to paint it, paint it, and you've got carte blanche to chuck out the tablecloths if you want to, although they're in fairly good nick.'

Anna grinned. 'Thanks, but I won't do anything too outrageous without checking with you first!' She liked the shabby chic look, and the only walls she planned on painting were the ones at Pippin Cottage.

'As you wish,' Ursula said, then gave a sigh. 'I like to think I'll be back in here when your year is up, but to be honest, the Italian climate suits me much better these days, and I do like having the chance to paint.'

Anna glanced at the walls of the coffee shop, where there were several tastefully framed watercolours. She took a guess that they must be Ursula's work. The Italian influence – warm colours, broad landscapes – was clear. 'It sounds great,' she said, her eyes drawn again to the bay window, where the contrasting weather couldn't have been more obvious.

'I'll leave you a folder with all of the important stuff – who we pay the bills to, suppliers, instructions for the oven,' Ursula paused. 'And, of course, the diary, so you two can sort out who's doing what and when.'

'Anything's got to be easier to use than the Rayburn I've just inherited!' Anna gave a wry smile. 'That's going to take a bit of getting used to.'

'You'll probably need some special tins if you've got one of those at home,' Lizzie interjected. 'The kids and I stayed in a cottage in Cornwall a few years ago that had one, and it took me most of the holiday to realise that the baking tray that came with it was a cold shelf. I lost count of the amount of things I burned until one of the girls got on Google!'

'Well, complications aside, if you want to bake at home as well as in the kitchen here, you'll have to get a Health and Safety certificate, but I'm sure that'll be fairly straight-forward.' Ursula smiled. 'And the rest, I'm sure you'll pick up as you go along. Lizzie knows the place inside out, and she's happy to help.'

'Thank you,' Anna said, then finished her coffee. 'And thank you for trusting me with this. It's good to know I'll be getting my teeth into something now I'm back in the village.'

'As if a new house and a toddler weren't enough,' Ursula smiled gently. 'And on your own, too.'

'I need a new challenge,' Anna said softly. Even two years on, the grief would sneak up on her, but she was far more able, now, to deal with the sympathy of others. Initially, in the raw months after, she'd have disintegrated, but now, for the most part, she could manage. Besides, after the Rayburn situation, she was all cried out.

'Well, let's call it a day today, then,' Ursula said, brisk again. 'I'm sure you've got plenty to be getting on with in that new house of yours, and we've got to get this place ready for opening up again tomorrow. So I'll see you bright and early in the New Year.'

As Anna left the tea shop, she once again felt a frisson of excitement. It had been quite a day, but the worst was over. Now all that lay ahead was a mountain of unpacking, Christmas and her first week at work. All a piece of cake, she thought wryly, making her way back to Pippin Cottage.

Chapter 5

As with any upheaval, though, it wasn't all plain sailing in the run-up to Anna's first week in the tea shop. She had made it through Christmas Day, just, spending the night at her parents' house with Ellie, but, from the moment she'd opened Pippin Cottage's front door late on Boxing Day morning, she'd felt the grief hit her once again. Finding a box of James' old love letters to her that had been soaked by a broken bottle of Scotch whisky in the move had been the final straw. Beyond saving, they were now in the ugly black wheelie bin outside the back door. That was where Charlotte had found her when she'd popped round with the hat that Ellie had left behind on the day they'd moved in. Helping Anna into the house, she sat her in a kitchen chair and put the kettle on.

'It's not fair!' Anna howled. 'James should be here, in this house, sharing it with me and Ellie. It's not fucking fair!' Breaking down into helpless sobs, she put her head in her hands on the kitchen table.

'I'm so sorry, hon,' Charlotte said. Putting her arms around her, she let Anna cry, stroking her hair and muttering soothing nonsense until Anna's sobs turned to hiccoughs.

Eventually, Anna looked up. 'No. I'm sorry,' she said. 'You've got enough to do without me dumping all over you.'

'Don't worry about it,' Charlotte grinned ruefully. 'I've left Simon's mother with a bottle of sherry and a pile of Simon's socks to darn, since she's always so scandalised I won't sew them up myself. That'll keep the old bat busy for hours!'

Wiping her eyes on her sleeve, Anna smiled. 'That's what I've always loved about you – your optimism.'

Charlotte rolled her eyes. 'Oh please; don't go all mushy on me now.'

'What time is it?' Anna asked.

'About elevenish.'

'Good. At least I can get my face back to normal before Ellie sees me.' She'd left Ellie for a little while longer at her parents' house, taking up their offer of childcare while she sorted out the last few boxes.

'It's OK to cry, you know,' Charlotte said gently. 'You lost your husband not even two years ago. It's to be expected.'

'Two years last week,' Anna replied. 'The day we – I – completed on this place.'

'Christ, talk about timing.'

'I still wake up thinking he's alive,' Anna said. 'And I question everything I do, thinking whether or not James would approve of my choices. I could be buying milk or a house, or sending Ellie to time out, and I still have to think for a minute.'

'I remember your wedding,' Charlotte said. 'The church, the flowers, your little cousin Emily kicking off halfway down the aisle and having to be escorted off to her mother's lap...'

'Dad getting plastered on whisky before his speech, James' mum being all sniffy we hadn't got her Aunt Maureen to make the cake, despite the fact Maureen was eighty-five and half blind...'

'James and Simon playing skittles on the lawn with all of the empty champagne bottles and a random football...'

Anna laughed. 'It was a good day. Not quite so many people came to the funeral.'

'They didn't know what to say,' Charlotte offered.

'People crossed the road to avoid me after he died.'

Charlotte smiled ruefully.

'And sometimes I feel so lost without him.'

'Anna,' Charlotte put a refreshed mug of tea down in front of her friend. 'It's you and Ellie who matter now. James would want you to be happy. I know it's not like having him here with you, but he's left you in a pretty fair position. He'd want you to do what feels right for you, and your gorgeous little girl.'

Anna blinked back tears again. Charlotte wasn't her best friend for nothing. 'You're right,' she conceded, taking a sip of her tea.

'When am I ever wrong?'

There was a pause while the two friends munched on their biscuits.

'I keep meaning to ask,' Charlotte said between mouthfuls. 'What was Matthew Carter doing knocking on your door the day you moved in?' Despite living two doors away, the friends hadn't really caught up since before Christmas Day as they'd had so much going on.

'Oh, is that his name?' Anna said. 'He was so off with me, I didn't even bother to ask.'

'Well, off with you or not, he's still bloody good-looking. I would, if I wasn't already married to the love of my life, of course!'

'If you like that sort of thing.'

'What's not to like?' Charlotte replied. 'Tall, dark – well, badgery now, to be fair, but he is a bit over forty – outdoorsy, tanned, muscular and happens to be filthy rich.' She sighed, then, at Anna's quizzical look. 'You know... Carter's Cider? *That* Matthew Carter?'

The penny dropped. 'Oh, of course! I thought I recognised him from somewhere. Didn't he show us round the farm about a million years ago when we were helping out with the village Girl Guide company?'

Charlotte laughed. 'You tripped up the gantry steps in the barn and he had to pick you up off the floor. And those bloody kids wouldn't stop talking all the way round. Thank God we went off to uni soon after.'

Anna laughed. 'Well, he obviously wasn't keen on letting the cottage go, because when he came round on the day I moved in, and also when he showed me around on the viewing, all he could do was scowl.'

'Really?' Charlotte looked shocked. 'I thought you said it was the estate agent who behaved like an arsehole when you viewed the place.'

'I thought he *was* the agent,' Anna frowned. 'But it turns out he was stepping in, for some reason. I didn't put two and two together until he came round the other day. The deeds to the cottage were in the name of a holding company.'

'Canny old Jack,' Charlotte replied. 'Keeping the property as a business investment all these years.' She finished her mug of tea. 'I can't think why Matthew would have been so off with you when you viewed the place, though. Perhaps Jack went over Matthew's head and, control freak that Matthew is, his nose was put out of joint because his dad made a decision without him. Matthew's brother Jonathan lived in the cottage for a while and it's been rented out ever since. Perhaps Matthew was hoping to rent it out again.'

'Oh, that's right,' Anna said. 'I forgot there was another Carter brother. I suppose because they were both a bit older than us we didn't really move in the same circles, did we?'

'Speak for yourself,' Charlotte said wryly. 'But Jonathan's just as gorgeous, in a kind of model-like, unattainable way. Pity he doesn't live here anymore.' Charlotte grinned. 'I hear some flaky single mother's taken over the cottage instead!'

Anna snorted. 'Charming as ever, cow!' She slapped Charlotte on the arm playfully. 'So where did he go? This even more gorgeous brother?'

'No one really knows,' Charlotte replied. 'He still keeps in touch with Jack, so I hear, but he hasn't been back to the village in years.'

Anna looked at her watch. 'I'd better get going – Mum and Dad are cooking lunch.'

'So I'll be ogling Matthew Carter from afar, alone, as always, then, Merry Widow?' Charlotte teased, draining her teacup.

Anna winced. 'Not interested, Charlotte. And I do wish you'd stop calling me that.'

'Would you prefer I went all tea, sympathy and patronising pats on the hand?' Charlotte said. 'You and I have never minced our words with each other – and I'm not about to start now.'

'Point taken,' Anna said, smiling a little. There were worse nicknames to have, she supposed. 'But as for the other thing, don't hold your breath.'

We'll see.' Charlotte grinned. 'A few months living back here and you'll realise eye candy is rather thin on the ground. Matthew's the best we've got by a long way, unless you're into geriatric dairy farmers!'

Standing up and crossing the kitchen to get her coat and keys, Anna didn't even grace that with a response.

*

'Bye Mum, thanks for looking after Ellie.' Anna kissed her mother goodbye and took her little daughter's hand.

'Are you sure you don't want Dad to run you home?' Julia Clarke looked at her daughter, furrowing her brow in concern.

'Nah – thought we'd have a wander down the Strawberry Line as it's such a nice day.' Anna appreciated her mother's lack of probing. The delicate maternal balance was something she relied on, especially at the moment. If her mother had noticed Anna's still slightly bloodshot eyes when she'd arrived for lunch, she hadn't mentioned it.

'Well, enjoy – I hope Ellie lasts the distance!' Julia kissed her daughter and granddaughter and walked them down the drive.

'We will – it'll be good to get some fresh air.' Anna hugged her mother again and set off down the path. The winter light streamed through the bare branches of the trees as she and Ellie walked down the Strawberry Line. It was a relaxing walk and she felt rejuvenated by the cold winter air.

Looking down the path, Anna could make out the old bridleways that led to places she remembered walking, alone and with the odd boyfriend, during the hazy summer days of her adolescence. She'd spent a lot of time roaming the countryside as a teenager; growing up in a village allowed her certain freedoms that she'd taken for granted back then, but was appreciating with new eyes now. As she looked around her, taking in the sights and smells of a sunny winter's day, she felt as though she was starting to come home.

Ellie ran a little ahead of her, also enjoying being outside. The passing of time made Anna wistful; her toddler was almost gone and in the blink of an eye would be old enough to take on her own life.

Full of restless energy from being inside for too long, when Ellie caught sight of a black and white dog about a hundred metres further down the line, she took off. Not for the first time, Anna wished she'd put the reins on her little daughter as she grabbed, a second too late, at the hood of Ellie's pink coat.

'Eleanor Mary Hemingway, come back here this minute!'

Anna shouted at her daughter's receding back. Forgetting all vestiges of dignity, Anna raced after the little girl, hoping Ellie would have the sense to stop within a reasonable distance of the dog.

Thankfully, at that moment, the dog's owner came into view. Lead in hand, he picked up his own pace slightly as he caught sight of the little girl. By the time Anna reached Ellie, she was stroking the dog and chatting animatedly to its owner.

'Is it a girl or a boy?' Ellie's high-pitched voice rang in the wintry air.

'He's a boy,' the owner responded. His back was turned away from Anna as he stooped beside Ellie, but she noticed a curtain of tousled dark hair and a tweed flat cap.

'Ellie, what have I told you about running off like that?' Anna was breathing heavily and cursing the extra Christmas pounds.

'No harm done,' the dog's owner replied, 'He's good with children.'

As the man stood and turned to face her, Anna realised she had strayed again into Matthew Carter's path.

'Oh. Hello,' Anna said. She wasn't quite sure what else to say. Their first encounters hadn't exactly been friendly.

'Look,' Matthew said, once Anna had straightened up again. 'I'm sorry I was rude to you about the problem with your Rayburn. It wasn't your fault the oil tank was empty; it was a rotten welcome to your new home, wasn't it?' He took his tweed cap off and ran a hand absently through his hair.

Anna was surprised, not just by the apology, but by the fact he seemed so nervous about giving it. This was a man who presided over a successful business empire. Why should he care about apologising to her? She decided to give him the break he asked for.

'Apology accepted,' she said, smiling. 'No harm done.' She stuck out her hand. 'Shall we try again? I'm Anna Hemingway.'

Matthew grinned and took her hand. 'Matthew Carter.' He gave her a quizzical look. 'You look familiar... have we met before? I mean, before this whole cottage business?'

Try as she might, Anna couldn't stop the laugh that escaped. 'Did you *really* just say that?'

'No, honestly! I'm not pulling your leg, I promise.' He looked at her thoughtfully. 'Did you... did you come for a tour of the farm?'

Anna smiled. 'Funnily enough, I was talking to my friend Charlotte about that earlier on. She saw you coming to the cottage the day I moved in and reminded me.' As she looked at Matthew, more memories of that night came back to her. It was a less than brief encounter at a tender age; a pair of sparkling eyes in a very public setting; a whiff of chemistry that was commented upon by others, but never to be repeated; the one that wasn't even there long enough to get away. The scent of fermenting apples on an autumn night; a gentle, understanding smile and a slight, gossamer-light connection.

'I did the tour – you spent most of the evening trying to get the Guides to stop giggling! And was it you, or your friend, who tripped on the steps to the gantry in the barn?'

Anna's face turned red as if it was yesterday. 'It was me,' she admitted. 'You were very patient, under the circumstances!'

'There were far worse ways to spend an evening back then.'

'Well... it's good to see you,' Anna said, as the conversation paused. Suddenly, Anna remembered the oil tank. 'I don't suppose you could give me the number of the oil merchant so I can chase up an invoice for the tank?'

Matthew smiled again, and Anna found herself thinking how attractive he was when he did. It was such a contrast from the surly expression he'd had when she'd seen him at the cottage. 'Don't worry about that. It was our mistake; we'll pay for it.'

'You don't have to do that, honestly.'

'I want to.'

Anna smiled. 'If you're sure. Thank you.'

They regarded each other for a moment, unsure how to proceed. Anna was almost grateful to her small daughter when Ellie broke the small silence, hopping on one leg. 'Wee wee, Mummy!'

'I'm thankful my daughter Meredith's well past that stage!'

Anna was surprised for the second time in as many minutes. 'You're Meredith's dad?' Glancing at him again, she noticed the same dark hair, the height, and, she thought unguardedly, the same smile. Matthew's eyes were a deep hazel brown, though, whereas Meredith's were ice blue.

Matthew nodded. 'She did say she'd met you. I hope she didn't make a nuisance of herself.'

'Not at all.' Anna took Ellie's hand as her little girl started jumping up and down on the spot. 'Come on then, Munchkin, let's go and find a loo.'

'See you soon,' Matthew said as he put Sefton back on the lead.

Saying their goodbyes, Anna began the walk back home. Imagine Matthew Carter remembering that tour, after all these years, not to mention footing the bill for the oil tank. It was probably pocket money to him, but it was still a nice gesture. When she got home she was surprised, looking in the mirror in the hallway, to see the colour in her cheeks and a sparkle in her eyes. The walk must have done her some good, after all.

Chapter 6

Before she took over The Little Orchard Tea Shop, Anna concentrated on getting Pippin Cottage as she and Ellie needed it. She was amazed at how little furniture she had, in the end, brought with her. Finding homes for things became a peculiar kind of therapy, and Anna found herself to be, if not exactly happy, then at least content in this new home and life.

Meredith Carter popped over once more before her term started again. She formed an instant rapport with Ellie, and spent a couple of hours entertaining her while Anna continued to get the cottage into some kind of order. Meredith, as Anna had surmised from her accent the first time they had met, was indeed a student at a public school. She was a day girl, returning home at varying times in the evening depending on the activities she was taking part in, and although the school gave her the option to board, she felt more suited to living at home with her father.

'Dad would die of a coronary in weeks if I left him to live up at St Jude's,' Meredith said, by way of explanation. 'He never cooks for himself, and barely eats during the day, so I need to make sure he doesn't end up at the chippy every night.'

'But don't you miss something by not living on site?' Anna asked. She was fascinated by the idea of life at a private school, and imagined hours of lacrosse and sticky, heavy puddings for tea.

'Not really,' Meredith replied. 'I'd rather not spend my nights there as well as my days.'

'But you enjoy it?' Anna asked.

'Oh sure!' Meredith replied. 'But I like coming home to my own space, too.'

Anna smiled to herself. As Meredith was an only child, she wondered how she had so much patience with Ellie.

'I've always wanted a little sister,' Meredith said. 'And she's sweet.'

'When she's behaving herself, or asleep!' Anna replied.

'Why don't you bring her to the wassail on Saturday?' Meredith asked. 'She'll love it. Singing, dancing, shotguns—' she laughed at Anna's panicked expression. 'Don't worry, they're only fired into the air!'

'What exactly does it involve?' Anna asked, curious.

'Well, Dad's arranged it every year since he took over the business full time. The Morris Men dance around a bit, everyone drinks mulled cider and eats a hog roast, and the trees get blessed.'

'Sounds like fun. Is it an open invite?'

Meredith looked thoughtful. 'Well, sort of. It's a kind of friend-of-a-friend invite, if you see what I mean. And you're my friend, so I thought I'd invite you.'

'Are you sure your dad won't mind me coming along?'

'Not at all – after all, you practically live in one of the orchards, so why shouldn't you come and celebrate?'

Anna smiled. 'That's kind of you, Merry – we'll certainly think about it.'

'And you'll need something to do to wind down after your first full week at the tea shop,' Meredith said. 'If you want, I can take some flyers up to St Jude's for you and leave them around.'

'I don't know if me, or the tea shop, could handle an

invasion from St Jude's!' Anna laughed. 'Although, I'm surprised some of the students at least haven't been in before.'

Meredith grinned. 'Ursula can be pretty scary. After a group of kids in the year above me started a food fight, she barred them.'

'Perhaps I'll hold off on the leaflets for now, then,' Anna said, 'and just rely on you bringing in some rather more sensible students.'

'Fair enough, but one bite of your lush cakes and you'll have a riot on your hands, I reckon.'

'I'll bear that in mind,' Anna said wryly, as Meredith reached for another slice of vanilla and orange carrot cake.

Chapter 7

Anna woke early on the Monday morning of her first shift at The Little Orchard Tea Shop. Her stomach fluttered, not just for herself but for Ellie. She had been to a couple of sessions at the village nursery the previous week in order to settle her in, but Anna still felt a little bit nervous. She hoped her friendly and outgoing little girl would soon settle in the environment where she was going to be spending so much time.

That morning, Lizzie would be opening up, giving Anna plenty of time to drop Ellie off. Then, Lizzie would work alongside her for the day. This would be the pattern for the first week, while Anna familiarised herself with the premises and its equipment. Ursula had also arranged a crossover period with the cake supplier so that Anna could find her feet before taking on the baking.

As it was, Ellie ran straight into nursery, without a backward glance, so Anna got to the tea shop as Lizzie was unlocking the door.

'Hi there,' Lizzie was softly spoken, with a distinct Somerset accent, long on the vowel sounds. Her smile was equally welcoming. 'I wasn't expecting to see you for at least another hour.' She turned back to the door. 'Couldn't wait to start?'

Anna smiled back. 'Something like that.'

As they walked into the tea shop, Anna took another look around. The tables, dressed in varying combinations of floral and polka-dotted oilcloth, were all clean and tidy. Lizzie had brought some fresh flowers in to put in the small vases that would adorn each table by the time the shop opened. The coffee machine lay gleaming and silent off to the left of the high counter, which had a wooden top and a glass cabinet to display the cakes and scones.

Seeing it all this time felt different to when she'd met Ursula here a fortnight ago. Now, she was the one who would be making the day-to-day decisions, making sure the business not just stayed afloat but thrived for the next year. It was a huge responsibility, but one she suddenly knew she was ready to take on.

'Everything OK?' Lizzie asked as she came back through from the small kitchen that led from behind the counter.

Anna smiled. 'Just getting used to the layout, and psyching myself up to actually doing this job.'

Lizzie smiled back. 'Don't worry,' she said, putting out the first of the small vases that she'd brought back from the kitchen and starting to arrange the flowers. 'You'll get the hang of it in no time. I'm glad you're going to be the one taking care of the baking and the books. For a while there, when Ursula told me she was going to look for another manager, I thought she was going to ask me to take it all on, and I really don't have a head for figures. Or baking!'

Anna felt relieved; she was worried Lizzie would feel resentful about a newcomer taking over, but clearly this wasn't the case. She wandered over to the set of hooks behind the counter, took one of the dark green aprons with 'The Little Orchard Tea Shop' embroidered on them, and popped it over her head. Glancing somewhat nervously at the chrome coffee machine again, she prepared to go on her steepest learning curve since university.

By Friday morning, Anna was finally starting to get the hang of the Italian coffee machine, as well as the infinitely more complex task of preparing Miss Pinkham's pot of Earl Grey. On her first day, Anna had made four pots before the old bat was satisfied, but by now it was down to two. Luckily, the other customers weren't so fussy. She'd mastered slicing the exquisite cakes into perfect portions, and got a few tips added to the jar on the front of the counter. She'd even exchanged a bit of banter with the vicar and his wife when they'd come in for a cuppa after matins.

'Morning, Sid,' she called as Sid Porter, who Pat Davis, her next-door neighbour, had informed her was a renowned breeder of Gloucester Old Spots and would be supplying the hog roast for the wassail that evening, walked through the front door. 'A cup of your usual?' Sid came in every day at the same time, and sat at the same table with the same order of a large Americano.

'Ta, love,' Sid replied. 'But can you put it into one of those takeaway cups today? Got a consignment of feed coming in at ten so I need to be back down the yard ASAP.'

Anna smiled. 'No worries. Fancy a slice of apple tart to take with you?' Upselling was, of course, the key to a successful business, even a village tea shop.

'Not this morning, but I might pop back in later.'

Anna busied herself with wrestling the coffee machine to produce Sid's Americano. Taking the proffered cash, she handed Sid his coffee and his change, and with a smile, bid him farewell. Then, she went out to the kitchen to grab a cloth to wipe down the tables and check the oven to see when the next batch of scones was due out. Although the current supplier was still providing the more extravagant cakes and confections, Anna had managed to whip up a batch or two of scones for the cream teas.

The brass bell over the door of the tea shop jangled as she finished wiping the last table. Her stomach fluttered as she realised it was Matthew Carter, dressed in a smart pinstriped suit and white shirt. As he approached the counter, Anna smiled. Ever since their encounter on the Strawberry Line, she'd seemed to see Matthew everywhere; on the High Street, at the local pub when she'd gone for a meal with Ellie and her parents, and now, here in the tea shop. She figured it was inevitable that their paths would cross, but she was still surprised by how often she'd noticed him. They'd not spoken since the Strawberry Line, but he'd been there, on the edge of her vision, and every time they'd seen each other in passing, they'd exchanged friendly smiles.

'Good morning,' she said. 'What can I get you?'

'What would you recommend?' Matthew asked. 'It's been a long time since I've actually bought coffee in a shop, I'm at a loss as to what to have.'

'The Americanos are good,' Anna said. Actually, all of the coffee was good, but she was most comfortable making that particular one at the moment.

'I'll have one of those, then,' Matthew said. 'I wanted to pop in earlier this week to wish you luck but I've been frantic at work. If there's anything I can do to help you to settle in, let me know.'

'Thanks,' Anna said, touched by the offer. 'It's a bit of a learning curve, but I'm getting the hang of things slowly.' She glanced at the price list by the till. 'That'll be two seventy-five, please.' She was about to ask if Matthew fancied some of the apple tart, but then remembered she was serving a man who made a living growing apples. He was probably sick of the sight of them.

'Well, good luck,' Matthew said as he picked up his coffee from the counter. He paused for a moment, and Anna wasn't sure what he was waiting for. 'Any chance of my change?'

Anna's cheeks started to flame. 'Oh God, sorry. I'm still learning!' Hurriedly, she opened the till again and fumbled out Matthew's change for the fiver he'd handed over. Passing it to him too quickly, she dropped the coins all over the counter. Scrabbling for them, her hand brushed Matthew's. 'Sorry. I'm not usually this clumsy, I promise!'

Matthew laughed. 'Don't worry. It must take a bit of getting used to. I grew up in the family business; you're taking this all on new.'

'Have a good day,' she said as he pocketed his change.

'You too. See you soon.'

As the bell swung again to signal Matthew's exit from the shop, Lizzie came out of the kitchen, from where she'd been washing up. 'Well that's a turn-up for the books.'

'What do you mean?' Anna asked, grabbing a cloth from under the counter and wiping the small spills from the coffee machine.

'I can't remember the last time Matthew Carter came in. He's certainly not been through the door since before his marriage went up the spout.' She gave Anna an appraising look. 'Something must have caught his interest.'

Anna felt her cheeks getting warmer for the second time in as many minutes. 'He probably wanted to make sure I'm not turning the place into a speakeasy or something.'

'Hmmm,' Lizzie said, before she turned away to check the tables over for stray crockery. 'I'm sure you're right.'

Anna didn't know her well enough yet to be sure if Lizzie

was implying anything, but she was sure she hadn't imagined the knowing tone in her voice. She dismissed the thought, though; she had enough to think about without adding cider farmers to the mix, no matter how attractive they were when they smiled.

*

That evening, Anna and Ellie wrapped up warmly and set off for Carter's Cider. As they reached the farm, Meredith raced up to Ellie and pulled something out of the bag she was carrying. 'Here, squirt, these are for you.'

Ellie squealed in excitement as Meredith popped a pair of pink Hello Kitty earmuffs over the toddler's woolly hat.

'They used to be mine,' Meredith said. 'I thought you might like them.'

Anna smiled. 'Say thank you, Ellie.'

'Fank you,' Ellie chorused.

'You're welcome. I've got to go and get ready for the anointing of the trees, but I'll see you later, OK?' Grinning at the toddler, Meredith wandered off.

Anna looked around and realised, thanks to her first week at the tea shop, she was beginning to recognise a fair few people. By the main barn there was a group of mothers and children, all wrapped up against the chilly January air, and a little further down the courtyard there were the fathers, all sipping pints of Carter's and chatting. Off to her left she heard the fizz and crackle of the hog roast cooking, and she could smell its delicious aroma. Then the assembled bunch of Morris Men caught her eye. Resplendent in their whites, with bells attached to their elbows and knees, they were warming up ready for the main event. In the midst of the group was the Green Man in a ribbon-bedecked hat. Later on in the evening he would present a slice of toasted bread to the Wassail Queen, who would place it in the branches of one of the slumbering apple trees as a gift to the gods for a good harvest in the coming year. Meredith, whose turn it was this year to be Wassail Queen, was across the yard, putting on a headdress of holly and ivy leaves. The colours stood out beautifully against her long dark hair.

The cold seemed to lessen as Anna watched the centuries' old ceremony take place. Row upon row of cider apple trees, bare and spindly-fingered in the fast descending frost reached out into the blue-black of the night sky. They gave the impression of slumber, the hushing of a vibrant life force under the soil. The troop of Morris dancers, headed by the Green Man, jingled and sang their way down the rows of trees. With one hand Anna clutched Ellie's gloved fingers, and with the other she held her own glass of sweet mulled cider.

She was somewhere in the middle of the group, and Matthew was standing off to her right-hand side, chatting to locals and applauding the singers and dancers. Still in his customary dark blue cable knit jumper, tonight he was also wearing a Barbour jacket that was somewhat the worse for wear, and had a soft, dove grey scarf wrapped around his neck. Anna knew that the scarf had been a present from Meredith for his birthday a week ago, and while it looked vaguely incongruous, he had obviously been touched enough by his daughter's effort to wear it tonight. As she was musing on this, she heard the singers start up with the traditional song.

> *Wassaile the trees, that they may beare*
> *You many a Plum and many a Peare:*
> *For more or lesse fruits they will bring,*
> *As you do give them Wassailing.*

The song was hearty, and the villagers joined in on the second chorus. As the dancers and singers passed, there was much cheering and laughing. The Green Man paused as he reached Meredith, and, dipping a slice of toast into the wassail cup, he handed it to her. Then, the Morris Men gathered her up and, smiling gamely, she speared the toast onto one of the spiked branches of the nearest apple tree. Adjusting her crown as her feet touched the ground once more, she grinned at her audience. 'Thank the gods, or whoever, that's over!'

Eventually, the singers and dancers paused, and Matthew stepped forward.

'Ladies and gentlemen, thank you for coming out on this very cold January night to help us in our celebration of the apple crops for the coming year. As many of you will know, there has been wassailing on this site for well over four hundred years, and my family's celebration of the custom is just the most recent in a long succession of celebrants of the land, its power and its ability to give us the crops we so desire.' Matthew paused and looked around at the assembled villagers. The polite smile turned to one of delight and surprise when his gaze lingered on Anna for a moment.

'We at Carter's Cider are thankful to the forces that provide us with such bountiful apple crops year after year, and we are equally thankful for the help and support of the village of Little Somerby. As a gesture of our appreciation, please feel free to partake of some more of our famous mulled cider, and a slice or two of the hog roast Joel and the boys are cooking up for us. May the apple crop be plentiful once again this year. Wassail!' The wassailers had reached Matthew now, and he took the proffered wassail cup and poured it onto one of the sleeping apple trees. Another cheer went up from the villagers and then they gratefully retreated to the warmth of the hog roast and another glass of mulled cider.

'Thanks for coming tonight,' Matthew said, once he'd got through the many locals who wanted a chat and a gossip and reached Anna's side.

'I enjoyed it,' Anna replied. 'There's something very... elemental... about it.'

Matthew smiled. 'Well, I'm more of a believer in science and reason as techniques for growing good apples, but who am I to argue with the Morris Men? And it does make for a good party.'

'It does,' Anna agreed. 'Thanks again for hosting it.'

Matthew smiled. 'Well, it's lovely to see you here.' He paused. 'I should probably...'

'Yes – well, see you then.' Anna smiled back, and for a moment they both stood, thinking, assessing. Anna found she was holding her breath. She laughed nervously.

Matthew seemed reluctant to break the moment. Eventually, clearing his throat, he spoke once more. 'Um... look, Anna... I'm not sure if you'd fancy it, but... do you think you might have a think about...'

Just then, Meredith bounded back up to her father. 'Have you asked her yet, Dad?'

Matthew glared at his daughter, and for a moment their roles seemed reversed.

Anna couldn't help laughing. 'Asked me what?'

Meredith rolled her eyes. 'Dad wanted to ask you if you fancied going out to dinner next Friday, but it looks like, as usual, he's taking forever to get his act together.'

'Well, I – um – I don't know what to say!' Anna stalled for time. Meredith marching up and dropping a bombshell like that was one thing, but, judging from the look on Matthew's face, she couldn't be sure if he was outraged with his daughter or horrified to be put on the spot like that.

Was she imagining things, Anna thought, or was Matthew

Carter actually blushing? He certainly looked like he wanted the orchard to open up and swallow him along with the tree roots.

'Say yes, obviously!' Meredith replied. 'God, you two are so pathetic.'

'Thank you, Meredith!' Matthew growled. 'I'm more than capable of arranging my own social life, if you don't mind.'

'That's not what Granddad said,' Meredith quipped. 'He said you couldn't find your own backside if you were sitting on it!' She turned back to Anna, smiling down at Ellie first, who had started to giggle at the mention of the word 'backside'. 'So, anyway, what my dad is trying to say, is would you like to go out for dinner next Friday? In Bath? At The Priory?'

'Well, I – er—'

'That's quite enough, Meredith,' said Matthew, taking back control of his senses, and his daughter. 'Go and make yourself useful handing round some of the hog roast.'

'Yes, sir!' Meredith beat a hasty retreat, giving her father a mock salute and grinning at Ellie.

There was a brief, uncomfortable silence, before Matthew laughed nervously. 'I'm going to kill that girl... or at least dock her pocket money for life.'

Anna joined in the tentative laughter. 'No harm done.'

'But she does have a point,' Matthew conceded. 'I had intended to ask you if you wanted to come out for dinner with me.'

Anna's heart turned over. It had been a long time since anyone had asked her out, and despite Meredith's crashing approach, she felt terrified. It still felt so soon after James. She opened her mouth, then closed it again.

'It's all right, it was just a thought,' Matthew said hurriedly, misreading her hesitation. 'I didn't mean to put you under any pressure. Meredith's too direct for her own good sometimes.

Don't worry about it.' He went to turn away.

'No, wait, please!' Anna stammered. 'That is… thank you. I would like to come out with you.'

The relief on Matthew's face took years off him, and Anna was suddenly reminded of that night, all those years ago, when they'd met so briefly.

His eyes sparkled, and he gave a broad smile. 'Great. Shall I pick you up at seven?'

'That would be lovely. Thank you.' Anna smiled. 'Meredith's not afraid to say what she thinks, is she?'

'Never let it be said she's backwards in coming forward. I think she gets it from having to deal with me for all these years!'

'Well, I'd better get this one home and into a warm bed,' Anna said, gathering a very tired Ellie up into her arms. 'And hadn't you better go and do the Lord of the Manor thing?' She grinned at Matthew, feeling a sudden relief that the potentially embarrassing moment seemed to have passed.

'I suppose I should,' Matthew grinned back. 'Although my dad can't quite get used to being out of that role – he's far better at it than me, anyway.'

'He certainly seems to be enjoying himself,' Anna observed.

Jack Carter was, indeed, holding court a little further away, chatting up some of the maiden ladies of the parish and keeping them in gales of girlish laughter. For a man of nearly eighty, he had a twinkly-eyed look that women of all ages found appealing. Leaning on his shooting stick, dressed in his Harris Tweed, his charisma and enthusiasm were infectious.

'Well, he always was a ladies' man,' Matthew replied lightly. Then a shadow seemed to cross his face. 'I'd better go and retrieve him before he says something unforgivable to old Miss Pinkham.'

As Matthew moved away from Anna, she wondered at

his sudden change of expression. She still felt like a relative outsider, and there were undertones and subtleties in the village relationships she still couldn't fathom. Sooner or later she hoped she'd be able to read the emotional crosscurrents a little better. At the moment she spent half of her time feeling emotionally illiterate.

As she watched Matthew approach his father, Anna was sure she didn't imagine a slight stiffening of Matthew's back. She wondered why. But that would have to wait for another time. She was in dire need of her best friend's counsel, wise or otherwise, on what exactly you did when you were asked out as a thirty-six-year-old widow by a man you barely knew, but found decidedly attractive. Of all the situations she thought she would encounter when she moved back to Little Somerby, this was one she never would have anticipated.

Chapter 8

'So you're not interested in him at all then?' Charlotte rolled her eyes over her mug of coffee the next morning. 'You've got a funny way of showing it!'

Anna grimaced. 'Look, can we get the piss-taking out of the way quickly, please? I haven't been on a date in well over twelve years; I need advice, not wisecracks.'

'Point taken. But you do realise I've been married nearly as long as you were, don't you?'

'I know.' Anna groaned and put her head down on Charlotte's kitchen table, narrowly missing the slice of Victoria sponge she'd brought along for the coffee date. After a few weeks of only cooking on top of her Rayburn, she'd finally taken the plunge and started using the ovens. There had been a few less than pleasant results, before she'd remembered what Lizzie had said about the cold shelf, but she was, at last, getting the hang of baking cakes. Charlotte had been only too happy to help test the ever-better results. But cake was the last thing on Anna's mind at the moment. 'What the hell am I supposed to do?' she muttered into the tabletop.

'Well... let's look at this logically. Do you fancy him?'

Anna raised her head. 'What am I? Fifteen?'

'It's a perfectly valid question,' Charlotte said primly. 'After all, at your age, you shouldn't hang about.'

'Gee, thanks.'

'What I mean is, there's not much point in going out with him if you don't at least think you can tolerate spending an evening alone with the guy. You're hardly footloose and fancy-free any more, but you don't exactly *need* a man, either – so you've got to be brutal about these things.' Charlotte gently disentangled Evan from the ball of wool he'd stolen from her knitting bag, the contents of which had been entertaining the little boy and Ellie for the past twenty minutes.

'Well... he is pretty OK-looking,' Anna conceded. 'And it was kind of sweet the way Merry had to intervene to make him get the words out. Although that does worry me a bit – he seems so alpha male in all other areas, especially from what you've told me.'

'Where's he taking you?'

'Well, Merry mentioned The Priory in Bath when she shotgunned us, but that could be her having a laugh.'

Charlotte gave a low whistle. 'That place is hotter than David Beckham's boxers!'

'Really?'

'I'm *so* not joking – mere mortals like me would have to sell the family silver, if we hadn't already, to get a table there. It's worth going out with him just for the grub!'

'I'll keep that in mind,' Anna replied, simultaneously unnerved and tickled by the reference to English football's erstwhile best-looking midfielder and his nether regions.

'So what does one wear to a place like The Priory?' She continued. 'I'm assuming it's pretty posh?'

'Oh, casual chic – you know,' Charlotte tossed her head. 'Own any Boden or Jigsaw?'

Anna laughed out loud. 'Have you forgotten that, as the parent of a toddler, anything that isn't instantly washable is out of the wardrobe? I haven't dressed in anything but Matalan for the past three years. And a jigsaw is—'

'I know, I know, something more suited to a small child.'

'Now I wish he'd just asked me out to the local pub!'

'Wouldn't that all be a bit close to home?' Charlotte replied, giving Evan back the now detangled and reballed wool. 'After all, the local gossips are going to have a field day anyway without subjecting yourself to their intimate scrutiny all the way through the actual date!'

'I suppose. I mean, I'm not even sure I *want* to go on a date yet. Whether I should, even.' Anna swallowed hard, awash, suddenly, with memories.

'No one expects you to just jump from loving James to walking down the aisle with someone else,' Charlotte said gently. 'Matthew's just asked you out for dinner. Take it slowly.'

'You're right, of course,' Anna said. 'It all just seems so complicated. Back in the day, there weren't any kids to consider, I was fairly confident my boobs didn't sag and small talk was something that happened over a glass of wine. Now, I need candlelight to look halfway decent and I can't talk about anything much other than CBeebies!'

'And you'll have to warn him about that C-section scar or he'll really freak out!'

Anna nearly dropped her mug. 'Wh-what? You think he'll want to... on the first date?'

Charlotte laughed. 'Relax! I'm joking. He's been married before, remember, and goodness knows that didn't end well. I don't think he's going to want to rip your clothes off before he's completely sure you're not a psycho.'

'Was his ex-wife really that bad?' Anna was intrigued.

'Believe me, hon, you don't want to know. Rumour has it a lot more went down than even I managed to pick up.'

'Such as?'

'Well, the village gossips think they know what happened between Tara and Matthew, but not many people actually know the full story. The rest of us are just left guessing.' She sighed. 'Such a waste, that he's been on his own so long... but you never know...'

'Hang on a minute. It's one date. And we might hate each other.'

Charlotte laughed. 'Methinks the lady doth protest too much!'

'Stop getting vicarious thrills, Charlotte, and start being helpful, please.' Anna drained her coffee cup. 'I'm already on the verge of ringing him and backing out.'

'OK, OK – let's stick the kids in front of the telly and get online. You haven't got the time, or the patience, to drag Ellie shopping with you, so we might as well see what options there are frock-wise on the internet.'

'Charlotte, I am *not* going to buy a whole new outfit for the sake of one night out.'

Scrolling through the website of a more expensive high street chain, though, Anna did concede she had very little sitting in her wardrobe she could actually wear. In the end, she bought a simple shift dress in a subtle yet colourful print – 'no black allowed, darling, you don't want to remind him of your Merry Widow status' – and paired it with a darker cardigan and a pair of medium-heeled strappy shoes. With next day delivery, she should, at least, be able to send it all back if it didn't fit or, worse, she bottled out.

'Now that wasn't so hard, was it?' Charlotte said. 'And it beats slobbing around in your jeans.'

'I don't want to look like I've made too much effort,' grumbled Anna.

'Yes, but you also don't want to look like you haven't made any! He *is* taking you somewhere nice, remember?'

'I'll be lucky if I don't drop off over the main course; it's been so long since I've been up past ten o'clock.'

'Well, for god's sake don't drink too much or you'll be dribbling into the lemon parfait!' Charlotte said, which didn't do much to quell Anna's nerves.

'Why am I doing this?' Anna groaned. 'I don't even know if I like him. I mean, he's been perfectly fine the past couple of times I've seen him, but I still can't get those first encounters out of my head. What if he goes all mean and moody on me again? I'm not sure I can cope with a split personality for my first date since James.' She swallowed hard, fighting against the sadness.

'Chill,' Charlotte said. 'It's dinner. You wouldn't have said yes if you didn't at least think you'd get some decent grub out of it, and you *have* said yes, so suck it up and get on with shaving your legs and all that.' She grinned. 'I was only half joking about the C-section scar, you know.'

Anna only just restrained herself from throwing her half-eaten piece of cake at her best friend.

Chapter 9

Anna didn't have much time to fret in the days leading up to her date. Although it wasn't exactly peak time, the tea shop still did steady business in the off-season. Word had got around that it was under new management, and a stream of customers came through the doors, as much to check its new manager out as to sample the cakes. In one of her quieter periods, Anna had also managed to set up Wi-Fi, so alongside the post-school-run parents, who often popped in for a latte and a chat, the odd laptop surfer showed up to eat cake and drink coffee.

Anna, who was a keen observer of people, couldn't help but be intrigued by the snatches of conversation she heard as she brought drinks and cakes to each table. The village school's Parent Teacher Association seemed to be a hotbed of scandal and intrigue. This, Anna surmised from what she'd overheard so far, was down to the fact that the Chair of the PTA had a charming smile and a roving eye, as well as an infinity pool in his back garden.

'Jenna was over at Duncan and Maria's house for four hours the other Friday night,' stage-whispered a woman across the table to her friend as they sipped their lattes. Between them, a toddler munched on a vanilla cupcake, scattering crumbs happily over the tabletop.

'Maria had taken the kids to stay with her mother while Duncan oversaw the renovations to their kitchen that weekend.

Home alone, and he invites Jenna round to, er, do the PTA last quarter accounts. What are we all supposed to think?'

Anna was torn between helpless laughter and irritation. She'd forgotten how easily gossip spread in a small village. 'Can I get you anything else?' she asked the two women, as they came to a natural pause in their conversation.

'Oh, go on then,' the woman who was sitting with her back to the window said. 'I'll have another coffee. And another small slice of that amazing honey flapjack, too, please.' She glanced at her companion. 'What about you, Sarah?'

'Just the coffee, thanks.' Sarah turned and smiled at Anna. 'You're brave, taking on this place. I've never seen it so busy.'

Anna smiled back. 'It's been pretty hectic, but good fun so far.'

'I've seen you at nursery,' Sarah said. 'I think Flora does a couple of the same mornings. Are you here every day?'

'Four days a week,' Anna said, 'although the baking takes up a bit of that.'

'Bloody hell, you're cooking too? You must be mad.' Sarah grinned. 'If you do have any free time, make sure you join the Facebook group for the nursery parents. It's a bit of a giggle and we have the odd night out occasionally.'

'Thanks, I will,' Anna said. 'I'm not sure I'll make the nights out, but it would be good to meet some new people.'

'A lot of them are just a few drinks down the pub, so you and your other half are more than welcome to come and join us,' Sarah said.

Anna's stomach lurched; there were obviously some people who hadn't heard all about her circumstances. 'Thanks,' she said quickly. 'I'll be sure to look it up.'

As she picked up the now empty mugs and turned away, she heard Sarah's friend muttering, 'Well done. Hadn't you heard her husband died?'

Anna was surprised that she didn't feel the prickle of tears, the lump in her throat that such conversations could still invoke. However, the tea shop was her territory, and these women were her customers; that seemed to override everything else at the moment. And it wasn't as if they'd actually set out to insult or upset her, anyway. Loading the dirty mugs into the dishwasher, she pondered. Goodness knew how long it would be until word of her first date with Matthew Carter got out; she had the feeling it was impossible to keep anything quiet around the village.

*

Matthew cursed as the heavy metal bonnet of the Land Rover fell for the umpteenth time. Chucking the spanner down on the ground, he reached for the errant prop and opened it again.

'Anything I can do to help?' Jack Carter's voice broke into another of Matthew's expletive-filled rants as he straightened his ominously creaking back.

'Not unless you know how to replace a carburettor,' Matthew growled, rubbing the back of his head.

'I don't know why you don't just scrap that unreliable heap of junk and invest in something more sensible,' Jack said, passing Matthew the cloth that had also fallen to the ground.

'It's not quite ready to be condemned yet,' Matthew said. 'And I'm not the leather interiors and air-conditioning type.'

'*You* might not be, but from the sounds of it it's not just yourself you need to think about,' Jack replied. 'Aren't you taking a young lady out tonight?'

'Meredith's been sneaking, has she?' Matthew said. 'I asked her to be discreet about it. I don't want the whole village jabbering.'

Jack looked offended. 'I am hardly the whole village.'

Matthew put the cloth down and leaned against the wing of the Land Rover. 'I'm sorry, Dad. I just don't want myself, or Anna for that matter, to be the subject of a load of salacious speculation.'

'You're flattering yourself a bit,' Jack said. 'Do you really think anyone's that concerned about what you get up to, or with whom?'

Looking sheepish, Matthew ran a grubby hand through his hair. 'Probably not, but you know how people talk.'

'They will if you end up broken down half a mile from the village boundary!' Jack dug into his pocket. 'You'd better take these.' Chucking a key fob towards Matthew, he smiled to himself as his son caught it one-handed.

'If anything, aren't I more likely to need to call the RAC if I take this?'

'She's been serviced recently and garaged all winter. She's all yours if you want her.'

Somehow, Matthew knew he wasn't going to be able to say no. Smiling in resignation, he turned and put the bonnet of the Land Rover down again. 'Thanks. I don't think this is going anywhere for a while.'

'Just be careful with her,' Jack said. 'Your mother, God rest her, would never forgive either of us if you wrote that one off.'

'I'll treat her like my own,' Matthew said. 'Does she need a fill-up?'

'Did it on the way over,' Jack replied. 'Should get you to Bath and back.'

'Can I give you a lift home?'

Jack shook his head. 'Walk'll do me good. It's fairly mild today. Now call Patrick Flanagan and get him to pick up that heap, if you insist on getting it fixed. And go and sort yourself out for tonight.'

'Anything else?' Matthew said tartly.

'You *have* bought her some flowers, I presume?'

'Goodbye, Dad!'

As his father turned, waving a jovial hand, Matthew cast an eye over the other vehicle in the drive. Grinning slightly, he realised his father had left him something else on a hanger on the passenger seat grab rail. He shook his head. Something told him Jack and Meredith had done more than converse politely about his dinner date and he had the feeling if he wasn't careful he was going to be outmanoeuvred.

Chapter 10

'You should have seen Dad before I left!' Meredith said as Anna buzzed around the cottage, grabbing her keys, money and a slightly toothless comb to put in her bag. 'It's been so long since he's been on a date, he's in a right tizzy.'

Anna's smile came out as more of a grimace, lock-jawed as she was through nerves. 'I can't believe I'm doing this.' As soon as the words were out, she looked apologetically in Meredith's direction. 'I mean, not that your dad's not a lovely man, he is – I mean—'

Meredith rolled her eyes. 'Pur-leeze. I've got this far without a sick bag, don't make me vom now.' Giving a grin, she added, 'Besides, as far as wicked stepmothers go, I could do worse!'

Anna felt another wave of nausea rush over her. 'We're having dinner, Merry, not eloping, remember?'

Meredith tossed her a knowing glance. 'We'll see.' Then, suddenly serious. 'I'm glad it's you he's going out with tonight. It's been a long time since I've seen him so excited. About anything.'

Anna went very still. The expectation, yearning even, in Meredith's voice was almost enough to make her call a halt to the evening. In her nervousness about meeting Matthew she'd almost completely forgotten there were children in the picture too. Putting down her bag on the scrubbed kitchen table, she walked over to where Meredith was sitting.

'Whatever happens with your dad and me, I'll still be here for you,' she said gently. 'After all, I'm not exactly going anywhere, and you've been a good friend to me.'

'Thanks, Anna. I just can't help hoping...'

'Let's just concentrate on getting through tonight, shall we?'

'It's a deal.' Meredith put out her hand. 'Shake on it?'

'Only if you promise not to tell your dad how much my hands are actually shaking!'

As the doorbell clanked, Anna nearly went through the roof.

'You really ought to get that fixed!' Meredith laughed.

Anna smiled back, more confidently this time. 'It gives the place character.'

'Uncle Jonno said the same when he lived here.' Meredith started towards the door. 'Do you want me to answer it?'

'Could you?' I just want to check on Ellie one more time. And then you'd really better head home yourself.' Despite Meredith's offer to babysit, Anna had decided that since it was her first date with Matthew she should ask her parents to look after Ellie instead. After all, while returning home to face her parents if things went pear-shaped would be awkward; coming face to face with your date's daughter in that same situation would be even worse. Meredith, while disappointed, had understood, but couldn't resist dropping in to help Anna get ready.

As Anna climbed the stairs, she heard Meredith greet her mum and dad and show them through to the living room. Their polite chatter drifted upwards and Anna smiled. Breathing a sigh of relief that they'd made it in plenty of time, she crossed the landing to Ellie's room. Slipping quietly inside, she saw Ellie's shock of blonde hair, so like her father's, and resisted the temptation to stroke it. Planting a gentle kiss on the girl's forehead and breathing in her sweet, childish scent, Anna felt some semblance of calm returning. She closed Ellie's bedroom door, then turned and looked briefly at her reflection in the landing mirror. She'd clipped her dark hair away from her face in a loose chignon, and although she looked a little pale and her large green eyes just that little bit too serious, the lipstick, borrowed from Charlotte, was a flattering shade. *Not too bad,* she conceded. James had always said she scrubbed up well. The stab of grief was nearly enough to make her back out of dinner, but she steeled herself.

From the lounge below she could hear muffled voices, and then the doorbell clanked again. She took a deep breath. *Breathe*, Anna thought. *It's dinner. It's not like he'll expect to rip your clothes off on the first date.*

Meredith, hanging around to spectate, opened the front door once more.

As Anna descended the stairs, she was momentarily at an advantage. She saw the top of Matthew's head, hair still pleasingly tousled despite his obvious best efforts with a hairbrush. He was wearing a smart tweed jacket that looked suspiciously like the one Jack Carter had worn to the wassail. The thought of Matthew borrowing Jack's clothes for a dinner date made her smile and relax a little more.

'Tell her she looks gorgeous,' hissed Merry as Anna came into view.

Matthew looked up, the kitchen light casting a glow on his face. 'No need to remind me, Meredith,' he said mildly. 'I do sort of remember how it goes.' In two long strides he crossed the kitchen and met Anna at the bottom of the stairs. 'And though my daughter has obviously pre-empted me, I will say she's right. You do look lovely. That's a great dress.'

'Thanks. You look great, too.' Anna looked up into Matthew's open, smiling face and caught her breath as a familiar, but long-dormant, flutter began in her stomach. She had realised when she first saw him that Matthew was an attractive man, but here, in the warm light of her kitchen, his dark hair already starting to spring back and curl, a waft of an old-fashioned but nonetheless desirable cologne and the faintest trace of five o'clock shadow, he seemed all the more so. The pause between them seemed to go on for an eternity, until Meredith took matters into her own hands.

'So don't forget to have her back before midnight or she'll turn into a pumpkin. And don't forget I've got to ride out tomorrow, so no sudden bunks to France or anything. And don't forget—'

'If you tell me to hold doors and pay the bill, I'll dock your pocket money for the next three years!' Matthew growled.

'I don't expect I'll be getting any pocket money for that long, anyway, given you're blowing so much cash on dinner tonight!' Meredith replied tartly. 'But you need to get going – I booked… I mean *you* booked the table for eight o'clock and it's gone seven already.'

'And you ought to get off home, too,' Matthew said. 'Sefton'll be wondering where you are.'

Meredith gave Anna a quick hug, then dutifully kissed her father's cheek. 'Have a great time. And don't do anything I—'

'We won't!' Matthew and Anna responded immediately. Their laughter seemed to break the tension.

'Did you want me to run you home, Meredith?' Anna's father, Richard, walked through from the lounge to greet Matthew, and Anna suddenly felt as self-conscious as a teenager on her first date. 'It's getting pretty chilly out there.'

Meredith smiled. 'Thank you, Mr Clarke, that would be lovely.' Her grin widened as she regarded Anna and Matthew once more. 'I'll see you later, Dad?' Mischievous as a kitten, the implication was in the question.

Matthew nodded firmly. 'You will.' He turned to Anna's father and held out his hand. 'It's nice to see you again, Mr Clarke.'

From the tone of Matthew's voice, Anna could tell he was also feeling somewhat teenagerish, but as her father shook Matthew's hand, Richard Clarke grinned. 'You too, Matthew. And call me Richard. At least I don't have to ask the usual questions about what you do for a living!' He paused, before adding, 'But I will ask you to take care of my daughter tonight.'

Anna flushed with mortification. 'Dad...'

Matthew laughed. 'That does it, now I really do feel nervous! But I promise I'll get her home at a reasonable time.'

'Shall we go?' Anna asked, suddenly desperate to get out of her own kitchen.

Matthew nodded. Anna kissed her father goodbye, and hugged her mother, who'd entered the kitchen after sneaking upstairs to check on her granddaughter. As Anna put her arms around her, she was sure she didn't imagine her mother's eyes brimming slightly. Not trusting herself to speak, they held one another's gaze as they broke apart. There were too many emotions running too close to the surface, and tonight Anna needed to focus on the here and now.

'Thanks for running Meredith back, Richard,' Matthew said as they left the cottage. 'If it was up to her, she'd probably stay and keep you company, but she really ought to get home.'

'No problem. See you later. Come on, Meredith.'

Following them, Anna was surprised to see a smart, clean, dove grey vintage Jaguar XJS parked outside. In answer to her unspoken question, Matthew grinned.

'Dad's pride and joy. I've had a bit of trouble with the Land Rover, so he insisted I take the Jag. He reliably informs me it'll manage the run to Bath in better time.'

'Does he lend it to you for all of your dates?' Anna teased.

Matthew grinned. 'Only the ones with the girls he approves of!'

Anna was charmed when Matthew hurried to the passenger door to open it for her. She slid into the car, which was so low she momentarily feared for her modesty, even though her skirt was an inch above her knees. Settling back against the tan leather, she took a breath to steady her nerves. As Matthew climbed in beside her, she couldn't help noticing the length of his thighs across the seat, and the way the tweed jacket rode up and exposed his wrists as he started the car. The throaty purr of the engine opened out into a controlled roar as he pulled out of the lane, and Anna sat back to enjoy the ride, silently thanking Jack Carter.

*

The Jaguar seemed to eat up the distance between Little Somerby and Bath, and in less than forty minutes they arrived at their venue for the evening, The Priory. Anna was both nervous and flattered that Matthew should take her to such a place for their first evening alone.

'I hope I can remember which set of cutlery to use when!' Anna said as they pulled up, then cursed herself for sounding so gauche.

But Matthew grinned. 'You're telling me! Meredith was the driving force behind this choice – although I've heard the food is very good.'

'Not a regular, then?' Anna asked.

'As Meredith has no doubt informed you, I'm more of a regular down the local fish and chip shop, but it will be nice to try something different – and with some grown-up company!'

'I hear you!' Anna replied. 'Ellie makes for a cute dinner companion, but conversation can be limited.'

'Seriously, though, Anna,' Matthew said, turning to her suddenly. 'In case I forget to say this later, thank you for agreeing to come out with me tonight. I know it can't have been easy, with Meredith haranguing you.' His dark eyes met hers intently. 'I'm looking forward to getting to know you a bit better.'

Anna's stomach turned over. 'I'd like that, too,' she stammered. 'But I'm a bit out of practice... at going out with someone, I mean.' She blushed.

'I don't exactly make a habit of it, either,' Matthew replied wryly. 'Believe it or not, my daughter doesn't proposition every woman under forty on my behalf!' He unclipped his seatbelt. 'But enough nattering in the car, people will start to talk. Shall we?'

It was Anna's turn to grin, now. Matthew had put her at ease and she was pleased to find she was actually looking forward to getting to know him over a decent dinner. She had the feeling there was much to know.

The maître d' settled them quickly at a table that looked out over the terrace.

'This is lovely,' Anna said.

'Isn't it? In fact...' Matthew looked deep into her eyes for a moment, as if he was going to say something serious. Then, a grin split his features. 'I can't quite believe they've let me in!'

Anna laughed. 'So it's not just me, then?'

'These kinds of places must make their money from hopeful first daters,' Matthew replied. 'I wonder how many married couples come back once the first flush of optimism has faded.'

'Well, let's make the most of it, then,' Anna said. 'Before

we both wonder what the heck it is we're doing!'

'Merry will chuck me back out if I get home before she deems fit,' Matthew said.

'That's all right, we can pop down the chippy if you like!' Anna gave a little smile.

'I like your style, Mrs Hemingway,' Matthew said.

Anna flinched.

'I'm sorry,' Matthew said immediately. 'That was tactless of me. 'Sometimes I speak before I think.'

'It's all right – after all, it is my name.' Anna smiled again. 'I should be used to it by now!'

'Doesn't make it any easier, I'm sure,' he smiled gently. 'This must be very difficult for you.'

'It's been pretty scary getting this far,' Anna replied. 'But then everyone has things to face that they'd rather not. Not that this date is something I'd rather not do,' she added quickly.

'I know,' Matthew said. 'And although I couldn't possibly understand what it's like to lose someone you love in the way you did, I think you're incredibly brave for making a fresh start in a new place.'

'Not *exactly* new,' Anna said. 'I did grow up in Little Somerby.' She paused and took a sip of the water Matthew had poured into a tumbler for her. 'And having the tea shop to focus on helps. It's only been a few weeks, but I really feel as though I'm settling into the place. I always fantasised about running something like that, although I hadn't quite anticipated going it alone.' She paused, mentally stepping off the path she was nearly going down. 'But what about you? Meredith says her mum lives in the States now.'

'That's right.' Matthew said. 'She left.'

'I'm sorry,' Anna replied. 'That must have been hard for you both.' She took the menu the maître d' offered and started to scan down it. The food sounded exquisite, and expensive.

'Let's just say we had different ideas about what married life should be,' Matthew said.

Anna smiled sympathetically. 'Sounds… intriguing.'

'Not really.' Abruptly Matthew shut the menu he was holding and without waiting to double-check with her, he motioned to the waiter.

Anna felt momentarily stung. Former partners were a touchy subject, to be sure, but she couldn't quite fathom Matthew's sudden reaction. Things must have been *very* bitter at the end of his marriage for him to allow it to infringe on first date territory.

'Are you ready to order?' the waiter asked.

'Um… yes, I'd like the scallops to start and then the beef.' Anna chose hastily, aware of the sudden shift in mood.

After the waiter had left the table, Matthew turned back to Anna. His gaze was apologetic. 'I'm sorry,' he said. 'Meredith spent months after her mother left crying herself to sleep, and I was too hurt and angry to be of much use to her, I'm afraid. I suppose I never really forgave myself for it.'

Anna felt a stab of pity. 'I understand.'

Matthew smiled sadly. 'It's not something I talk about, even now. But if you want to know, I'm sure the local gossips will be only too happy to fill you in on all the lurid details at some point.'

'I get the feeling it's impossible to keep anything quiet around the village,' Anna replied. 'The day I moved in, Mrs Ashton walked past the cottage at least fifteen times, making sure she got a look at every last box and bit of furniture she could. She probably assumed I was one of "those blooming single mothers" she reads so much about in the local rag.' Despite her cheerful start, she heard the bitterness in her own voice as she finished.

Matthew immediately picked up on the change of tone. 'What happened to James?' he asked gently.

Anna felt a sudden, sharp stab of pain. 'You mean the gossips haven't told you?'

'I don't listen to them, having been the subject of so much of their hot air time myself.' Matthew's expression was calm, compassionate, but there was still a trace of anger in his tone.

The silence between them seemed to extend past the table and cover the whole restaurant. Anna was taken back in time to when her whole world changed. The sound of the doorbell at ten o'clock on that icy winter's night would never leave her. Nor would the tone of careful compassion in the police officer's voice as he broke the news. Swallowing hard, she spoke.

'He was working late. It was Christmas party season. He'd driven the road a thousand times, but the other car came out of nowhere. A teenager who'd passed his test barely a week before. Over the brow of the hill on the wrong side of the road, ice everywhere. He was overtaking a tractor. James didn't stand a chance. The teenager was in his father's Range Rover, something far too powerful for him to handle in the road conditions. He survived. James was killed outright. That was my only comfort. If he'd lived, his injuries would have been horrific. Ellie has no real memories of him, except from the photos and videos we have, and what I tell her.'

If the matter-of-fact tone of Anna's voice shocked him, Matthew didn't show it. He put his hand over hers, where it rested on the table. 'I'm sorry,' he said softly. 'I can't imagine how hard it's been for you.'

'In the end, I wanted to settle back here. Mum and Dad are in the village, and although my grandfather lives about five miles away from our old house in Hampshire, I couldn't stay where I was any more.' As she spoke she found herself turning her hand to hold Matthew's on the table. 'But sometimes it gets so tiring being both mother and father to Ellie. And even though the tea shop is exactly what I wanted to do, I fall into bed absolutely shattered each night.'

'Now *that* I can identify with!' Matthew smiled. 'Cider's not quite as seasonal as people imagine; the work goes on all year, in one form or another, and after Tara left, I had to re-evaluate what I knew about parenting, and girls in particular. While Meredith has plenty of women around her, she misses a mother in her life to navigate some of the more girly things.'

'Does she see Tara at all?' Anna asked.

'She used to fly out to the States during the school holidays and spend time with Tara and her new man, but since she hit puberty she's been clashing with her mother more and more. She seems to prefer being here, with me.'

'You've done a great job,' said Anna warmly. 'She's a lovely girl.'

Matthew blushed. 'Thank you. She's had a tough time and it's a miracle she's turned out as sensible as she is. Although I'm dreading when she brings her first boyfriend home. I'm a bit unreconstructed in that regard.'

'My dad wasn't exactly friendly to James when he first met him!' Anna said, surprising herself with the ease at which she was able to mention her husband's name. 'It took eighteen months for Dad to speak properly to him. I'm amazed he graced you with a conversation tonight!'

'I like your dad's style.' Realising he was still holding Anna's hand, he disentangled his own gently. For a moment there was silence between them again, broken eventually by the waiter returning with a very decent Chablis.

*

The food, when it arrived, was excellent. Matthew, doing the driving, had barely half a glass of wine, which left Anna feeling relaxed on most of the bottle of Chablis, although the heavenly scallop dish, followed by a cut of local beef, did a great deal to mop up the wine. Conversation flowed freely between them during the meal, and as Matthew called for coffee and the bill, Anna couldn't quite believe they'd been out for so long.

'I hope Mum and Dad don't mind me being out this late,' Anna said as they walked back to the car.

'Should I ready my apologies?' Matthew asked. 'Is your dad likely to meet me at the door with a shotgun?'

Anna laughed. 'Hopefully not, but they're still a little bit protective, after... everything.'

'As well they might be.' Matthew's tone was gentle. After the briefest of pauses, he headed round to the passenger side of the Jaguar and opened the door. 'Let's get you back before they start to worry.'

Matthew was a fast but careful driver, and the Jaguar was, it had to be said, an elegant method of conveyance. Anna leaned back against the comfortable leather upholstery and settled in for the ride back to Little Somerby.

'Would you like some music?' Matthew asked.

'That would be lovely,' Anna replied, wondering what he would choose.

There was a pause as Matthew fiddled with the CD player. As the music filled the air between them, Anna smiled in the darkness.

'Everything all right?' Matthew asked, taking his eyes off the road for a second to glance over at her.

Anna hesitated, then nodded. 'I was just thinking that Ed Sheeran's a pretty cool choice for people our age. I'm impressed. Is he one of your favourites?'

Matthew grinned, partly in relief and partly in amusement.

'Actually, I can't say I'm familiar with him, although I am enjoying it. Meredith chose it for me. My music taste kind of stopped evolving when Kim Wilde was better known for her singing than her gardening!'

'So what would you have chosen?' Anna asked.

Matthew laughed, a rich, deep sound that made Anna's stomach flutter. 'Shall we save that for our second date? If you'd like to see me again, that is!' Anna paused just long enough for Matthew to qualify his comment. 'You... do want to see me again?'

She glanced at him. 'That would be lovely,' she said softly.

A companionable silence extended between them for the remaining few miles back to Little Somerby. Eventually, Flowerdown Lane came into view.

'I hope Ellie's slept through OK,' Anna said as they drew up outside Pippin Cottage.

'I'm sure we'd have heard if there'd been a problem,' Matthew turned off the Jaguar's engine and paused for a moment. He shifted in his seat to face Anna. 'I had a really lovely time tonight. Thank you for coming out with me.'

'I'm the one who's supposed to thank you first!' Anna laughed nervously. 'Thank you for inviting me.'

There was an expectant pause. Neither of them moved. Then, slowly, tentatively, Matthew leaned towards Anna. Her heart started to beat faster.

'You're welcome...' Matthew replied. 'But I have to warn you...'

'W-what?' Anna said softly.

'My dad told me that the interior passenger door is very sticky in the cold weather, so I'd better open it for you!' Playfully, he leaned further across her and grabbed the handle. As he opened the door, the cool night air rushed in.

Anna grabbed her handbag from the footwell and stepped

out of the car. They headed up the garden path together. As they got to the front door, Matthew put his hand on Anna's arm and turned her to face him. His face was cast in the soft glow of the outside light, his eyes slightly in shadow.

'Look, Anna...' Matthew hesitated, looking painfully uncertain. 'It's been a long time since I've done this...' he cleared his throat. 'But... I like you.'

Anna blushed under his suddenly intense scrutiny. 'I like you too, Matthew.'

Another pause. Then, slowly, gently, Matthew leaned forward and kissed Anna's cheek. 'I'm glad.' He laughed nervously.

'I'll see you soon,' Anna said as Matthew hovered on the doorstep.

'Definitely.'

To break the tension, Anna scrabbled in her bag to find her door key, hoping against hope her mum or dad wouldn't open the door before she found it. As she located it, she looked back up at Matthew. 'Thank goodness, here it is.'

Matthew smiled. 'Well, goodnight then.' He hesitated, then, as if coming to a decision, he leaned forward and touched Anna's lips very, very gently with his own. The electrical charge between them made both of them draw breath.

'Goodnight,' Anna murmured as they broke apart. Matthew just smiled.

Closing the door, she wasn't surprised to feel that her knees were shaking. It had been a brief kiss, but she was stunned by how good it had felt. Taking another deep breath, she opened her front door and prayed her parents didn't give her the third degree.

Chapter 11

'I couldn't, like, get a thing out of Dad when I asked him how it went last night, so I thought I'd come round and bug you about it instead!' This was in lieu of a greeting when Anna opened the door to a very cheery Meredith on Saturday morning.

'And what makes you think *I'm* going to spill the beans about anything?' Anna smiled.

'Because I saw Charlotte come round about ten minutes ago, when I was walking Seffy in the orchard, so I thought it would be worth a shot.' Meredith went to tie Sefton up on one of the porch struts, but Anna was well used to the dog by now and beckoned them both inside. Lizzie worked three Saturdays out of four, which meant Anna could catch up on the books from home. There seemed scant chance of that, with Charlotte and now Meredith in situ.

'OK, well shall we start with what an *utterly amazing* snog we had?'

Meredith made retching noises. 'Well, OK, perhaps I don't want to know *everything*!'

Anna grinned and led Meredith through to the kitchen. 'Guess who's here?'

Charlotte looked up. 'Good luck, Merry. She won't tell me anything, either!'

Meredith raised a sceptical eyebrow and helped herself to a freshly baked cupcake from the plate on the table. 'These look lush. You'd better start selling them in the tea shop soon.'

'I'm just waiting for the Health and Safety assessment,' Anna replied. 'But I'm glad they meet with your approval,' she added wryly, watching Meredith demolish the cupcake and reach for another one.

Meredith paused before her next mouthful and grinned. 'They're well nice. But anyway, tell me about your date with my dad!'

'I wouldn't bother. The Merry Widow is playing things very close to her D-cup.' Charlotte scrunched up the cake case she was holding and threw it across the room, where it missed the bin by a mile. Sefton ambled over and hoovered it up.

'Don't call me that,' Anna muttered. 'And why *should* I tell you everything? Or *anything* for that matter? There's nothing *to tell*.'

Meredith and Charlotte's 'pull the other one' was unstated, but extremely obvious. Anna was about to chuck them out when her phone beeped. Grabbing it from the table, she turned away from them both and read the screen.

I had a great time last night. When can I see you again?
BTW, is Merry with you?

Anna tried to stop the smile that tickled at her lips as she read, but before she could reply, Charlotte had snatched the phone.

'Ooh! Nothing to tell, eh?' Pressing the reply key, she started to type.

'You can see as much of me as you like, you gorgeous stud-muffin wink-smiley face,' she cackled.

'Don't you dare, Charlotte, I'm warning you!' Anna tried to grab the phone back, but Charlotte chucked it to Meredith, who ran into the hall.

'Send it, Merry, go on!'

'What's it worth?' Merry dashed for the front door.

'Meredith Carter if you send that text you will never eat another one of my cakes!' Anna hollered at the girl's rapidly disappearing back.

'Dad can take a joke, I'm sure he'll see the funny side.'

'Funny side of *what*?'

Anna froze in horror as Matthew ducked through the door, holding his daughter by the arm. He had Anna's phone in the other hand.

'I believe this is yours,' he said mildly, handing Anna back the phone. His expression didn't give away whether he'd read the screen or not.

'Thanks,' Anna gasped, puce with embarrassment.

'Meredith, that dog needs more than a quick jog to Anna's cottage,' Matthew said, as his daughter tried to slink away. 'Get him back into the orchard and give him a proper run.'

'Yes, sir!' Meredith grinned, sticking her tongue out at her father's back as she made her way out of the front door with Sefton.

'I'd better get back, too.' Charlotte drained her mug and scuttled for the door, although her expression as she left definitely had something of the *call me when he's gone or I'll disown you* about it.

'I take it you got my text,' Matthew, looking rather sheepish, turned to Anna. 'I'm sorry to just descend on you. My feet sort of left the house before my brain did, so I texted you on the way.'

'Yes,' the corners of her mouth twitched in amusement at Matthew's demeanour. 'Thank you. I was about to reply when... well, you saw.'

'I meant it,' Matthew replied. 'I had a great time.'

'Me too,' Anna said. There was a pause. 'Can I, um, get you some coffee?'

'Thanks,' he sounded relieved. 'Look, I'm sorry to burst in on you. I suspected Meredith might have gatecrashed you again, and I wanted to make sure she wasn't making a nuisance of herself and putting you on the spot.' He followed Anna through to the kitchen and took the mug of coffee she poured him from the cafetière.

'Not at all,' Anna said. 'Although she did try to cross-question me. Oddly enough, though, the thought of us kissing seemed to put her off knowing anything else!'

'Really?' Matthew raised an eyebrow. 'Then perhaps we should put her off some more.' Putting his coffee down on the kitchen table, Matthew closed the short distance between them.

Suddenly, the kitchen seemed entirely too small. Anna's head started to swim as Matthew drew closer. She drew a shaky breath, and jumped as his hand slid around her waist. He pulled her to him, and Anna closed her eyes in anticipation of the touch of his lips.

The kiss deepened in intensity. Matthew's mouth tasted of coffee and sweetness, and Anna felt herself going under in the waves of sensation that were being unleashed by his presence. It had been so long since she'd been kissed like that. He was the first man since James who had kissed her, and though he was still being incredibly gentle, there was an undercurrent of hunger. The feeling of being adrift on a sea that was intent on taking her breath away was absolute, and she hovered between wanting to surrender entirely and feeling completely overwhelmed. His hand reached up to run through her hair, and she found herself doing the same, pulling him closer so they were body to body, pressed against one another, until her heart was beating wildly in her chest and the speed of her pulse made her feel weak.

'I can't... I just can't... I'm sorry.' Breaking away, lips

bruised, head hanging, Anna couldn't meet his gaze.

Matthew's eyes, half closed and dark with desire, softened as he dropped his hand from her cheek. 'I understand.' He took a step back from her. 'I'm sorry. I shouldn't have rushed you.'

'It's not you.' It was barely a whisper. She covered her face with her hands. 'I just can't seem to let go.'

Wordlessly, Matthew stepped forward again and enfolded her in his arms. He smelt of apples and woodsmoke, and the comforting scratch of his cable wool jumper made Anna want to cling to him for safety. Her tears soaked into his chest, in a rush of sorrow. His long fingers stroked her hair, his arms gently rocking her, and a sense of peace came over her that had been absent since James' death.

Sometime later they broke apart. Anna wiped her nose on her sleeve.

'It's never pretty, is it?' she hiccoughed.

Matthew reached into the pocket of his jeans. 'Here.' He gave her a rather crumpled cotton handkerchief.

'I didn't think people carried these any more,' Anna's smile was cracked.

'What can I say? I'm old-fashioned.'

'I'll return it to you – washed and ironed of course.'

'Any time.'

'Matthew...'

'Anna, I—'

They both laughed nervously.

'Shall we take a rain check?' Matthew's smile faltered only slightly.

'Let's. I... I want to see you again. Really I do.'

Matthew brushed a stray lock of hair out of Anna's eyes. 'Meredith would have us walking down the aisle by next Sunday if it was up to her. She likes you, Anna.' He paused, as if considering his words before he spoke. 'So do I. Very much.

But if anything happens it has to be in your own time, Anna, and if it doesn't happen... it's OK.'

'Thank you.' Standing on tiptoe, she kissed him on the cheek. She felt him tremble slightly and closed her eyes as the sensations threatened to overwhelm her again.

'Perhaps it was fate, all those years ago on that night we first met. But it was the wrong time, the wrong place.' He paused. 'I know you think I don't remember, but you've drifted in and out of my mind ever since, like a summer breeze.'

Anna's knees went weak again. 'You don't mean that, surely? It was such a long time ago.'

'Of course I do. I'll see you soon. Take care of yourself.'

As he walked out of the door, Anna sagged back against the kitchen worktop, completely confused by what had just happened. Last night she had felt more normal than she had in a long time, but this morning, in the cold light of day, the twin bonds of obligation to the past and desire for the future were at war in her head and her heart. And the more she tried to untie the tangled skeins of her emotions, the more she found herself caught up in them.

Before Anna had a chance to mull over the kiss in the kitchen, however, Charlotte, desperate for information but now stuck in waiting for a delivery from the supermarket, had broken the silence by phoning her.

'I'll talk to you later, Charlotte – I'm taking Ellie to the park in a couple of minutes. Yes, yes, OK, I'll pop round later.' Anna pressed the end call button on her mobile. In her current state of mind she couldn't bear to be interrogated. She turned the phone off, and walked briskly upstairs to hurry Ellie along.

'Come on sweetheart, get your shoes on, and find a jumper.'

'Can I wear my Hello Kitty shoes?' Ellie asked, holding up a pair of silver sparkling slip-ons that were completely inappropriate for the wintry weather conditions.

'Not today.' Popping a jumper on over her distracted daughter's head, she fished out a pair of red wellies and helped Ellie into them. 'Go and have a wee, then we'll get going.'

As she went to leave Ellie's room, Anna took a brief glance around it. It was still early days, but the cottage was finally starting to look like it had an owner. She'd made a start on painting Ellie's room first, a soft rose pink that hopefully should last a few years before whatever consumer-driven fad took over her daughter next, and she'd hung some cream waffle blackout curtains at the small window. The floor was still bare as Jack Carter had had all of the boards in the cottage varnished a year or two previously, but Anna had decided Ellie needed a carpet to ward off the chilly winter mornings. While she had a moment, Anna thought she might as well measure the room and get the carpet ordered. Grabbing the tape measure from the windowsill, she went to the corner of the room and knelt down beside the built in cupboard.

It was then that she saw it.

Right in the corner of Ellie's room, inside the cupboard and tucked between the skirting and the first wooden board, almost out of sight in the crack, was the corner of a piece of paper. Anna figured it was probably an old newspaper – after all, there had been several occupants of this cottage over the years, but she never could resist an ancient news story, so she gently pulled on the corner.

It was immediately obvious that this was no newspaper, but it did, nonetheless, provide very interesting reading. Tape measure forgotten, Anna sat on the floor of her daughter's room, a sense of shock and then comprehension gradually taking over her.

After she'd read it, she folded it neatly and stuck it in the back pocket of her jeans.

Descending the stairs, she saw Ellie was now playing with her toy house and village.

'Are you ready to go?' she said.

'Can I take Bunny with me?' Ellie held up her rather worse for wear comforter by one of its ripped ears.

'Yes, of course,' Anna murmured. Forgetting the park for the moment, Anna locked her front door. There was one person she knew would be able to shed some light on the piece of paper she'd just found, and it wasn't Charlotte.

Chapter 12

'Now I'm not one for gossip,' Pat, Anna's next-door neighbour, said, pouring a cup of tea and then settling in at the kitchen table, 'but the whole village knew about Matthew and his wife Tara splitting up almost before Matthew himself did. She was so brazen about it all.'

'What happened?' Anna asked. She sipped her mug of tea, and waited for Pat to enlighten her. Ellie was playing contentedly with a jigsaw puzzle that Pat had unearthed for her from a basket of toys she kept for when her grand-children visited.

'Well, Matthew was working all hours on the business. Ten years ago it was at serious risk of going under, and he had fifty employees all depending on him to pull it through. Jack was still at the helm but he was leaving more and more of the legwork to Matthew. Matthew was away from home a lot, and when he was here he was chained to his desk in the office. Some nights he barely made it home before the birds started up again. Tara and Meredith were lucky if they saw him in daylight. It got so bad that Meredith knew her grandfather better than her own dad, and Matthew was at breaking point. Jack tried his best to help, but he wasn't in the best of health and his wife Cecily, Matthew and Jonathan's mother, was in the late stages of cancer so he had enough on his plate.'

'Sounds terrible,' Anna shuddered. 'Poor Matthew, and Jack. How did they get through it?'

'Matthew put his head down and carried on working. He's never been one for confiding things, or sharing responsibility. When Jack handed him the keys to the firm, he opened the door and made the place his own. For well over ten years he's driven it forward, and no one was going to get in the way.'

'So what did Tara do?' Anna asked. 'She can't have been very happy.'

'That's an understatement,' Pat sighed. 'She was bored out of her mind, by all accounts. She was already stuck at home with a four-year-old, didn't have a job and was starting to look around for other entertainment. There were rumours their marriage was starting to fall apart, even as the business was beginning to pick up. Jonathan had finished university about a year previously and was lounging about the place, spending time with Tara when Matthew was busy slaving away to keep a roof over their heads. Things happened.'

'Tara and Jonathan?' Anna gasped, although the note she'd found had been pretty self-explanatory. 'How could he do that to his own brother? Matthew must have been devastated.'

'More angry than anything,' Pat refilled their cups from the teapot on the table. 'He'd sacrificed his own ambitions to run the family business – he'd really wanted to practise law, studied it at university and completed an internship, but when Jack asked him to take over the business he couldn't refuse. Left the offer of a plum job at a top firm just like that and came home. Cider's in his blood, he's a fourth-generation brewer.'

'Couldn't Jonathan have done it?'

Pat snorted. 'You've as much chance of getting angels to come down from the sky as you would getting Jonathan to have any hand in the cider business.' She took a biscuit from the plate in front of her. 'Oh, he was more than happy to spend the profits, when there were any, but he didn't give a fig about how they were made. He's a businessman all right, got the brains to do really well, but he didn't want the family business. Jack, ever the indulgent father, let him make his own way. Unfortunately, Jonathan's focus wasn't on his career when he came home. He and Tara started carrying on, and... well, you know the rest.'

'Are they still together?'

Pat shook her head. 'No. They split up, apparently, quite soon after they left. I don't really know the details. So it was all for nothing, really.'

'What did Matthew do? How did he manage after Tara left him?'

'Bottled it up, ploughed all of his energy into the business, tried to do the best he could with Meredith, but she missed her mother terribly. Now she wants a woman around – and Matthew's worried about having to have "the talk" with her, although, frankly, he's left that a bit late and she's probably better informed than him in certain regards.' Pat sipped her tea. 'Not that she's given her dad any cause for concern as yet,' she added hastily. 'But you know how they are at that age. Curious. Reckless.'

Anna's heart turned over at the thought of Matthew dealing with both daughter and business without help, although she knew Pat, in addition to cleaning for the Carters, had obviously been of some emotional support, too. She told her so.

'Well, I do what I can, but I'm getting on a bit, now,' Pat said. 'He needs someone in his life.'

Hating herself for asking, but compelled to anyway, Anna did. 'Has there been anyone?'

Pat's eyes twinkled. 'One or two women have cast their nets in his direction over the years. After all, with Carter's

Cider the way it is now, he'd be a good catch. But no one's turned his head in the way Tara did. Until recently.' She gave Anna a brief, knowing look.

Anna looked away, embarrassed. 'It was just dinner. And besides, I've got a long way to go myself before I can think about anyone in that way. After James...' She swallowed hard.

'There there, love, don't go down that road,' Pat said sympathetically. 'Enjoy things for what they are. Matthew's a good man. Having been burned once himself, he's not minded to jump feet first into the fire again. Give yourselves time.'

Anna felt the lump in her throat, both for Matthew and herself, and took a gulp of her tea to try to dislodge it. She nodded at Pat. 'I can forget, sometimes, for a moment, that James isn't here. The moment I wake up, before I'm fully awake, and as I drift off to sleep. But then my brain kicks in and I realise I'm on my own bringing Ellie up, and it's very unlikely she'll ever remember what a kind, wonderful man her father was. I don't think it'll ever go away.'

Pat smiled sadly. 'It won't,' she said. 'But it'll gradually get easier to bear.'

'What happened to Jonathan?' Anna asked.

'Oh, he checks in with his dad from time to time. Jack's always trying to convince him to come home, but he's understandably reluctant. Jack hasn't got a clue what really happened between them, so he misses his younger son dreadfully.'

'Why hasn't Matthew told him?' Anna was shocked.

Pat sighed. 'If there's one thing Matthew's good at, it's sticking his head in the sand. Take Meredith for example. She's nearly fifteen but he still thinks she's a little girl. He's still angry, but he won't drag his father into what he sees as his own personal business. Deep down, he couldn't bear to ruin Jack and Jonathan's relationship, and he still mourns the loss of the brother he loved so much. It was only Matthew's insistence that Jack be kept in the dark that denied Tara that last act of revenge.'

'But surely the village gossip would have worked its way back to Jack eventually?' Anna had already realised from listening in to customers' conversations in the tea shop that it was virtually impossible to keep anything quiet.

'Only a couple of us really knew what had happened, and we weren't minded to fill Jack in, either. It's no less humiliating for Matthew, of course, but at least he spared Jack some of the pain of having to choose between his boys.'

'But surely Jonathan should have known better?' Anna said. 'How could he have done that to Matthew?'

'I'm not excusing Jonathan,' Pat said, 'but Matthew was never right for Tara. We all knew it. He was blinded by her. You only have to look at Meredith to get an idea of how beautiful she was. Matthew wasn't ever the type to fall head over heels, but Tara enchanted him from the start. When she turned that charm on Jonathan, who was far less responsible and far more susceptible, that was that.'

'So what happened to her?'

'The last I heard, she'd moved back to America with the latest in rather a long line of lovers. ' Pat sniffed.

'Is that where she was from, then?'

Pat nodded. 'She looked like the typical all-American girl when Matthew brought her home, but I always thought she was harder than that underneath. She'd have to have been, to have walked out on Meredith.'

Anna felt a lurch of sympathy for Matthew's daughter. She knew all too well the pain that losing a parent could cause, having seen Ellie in the early days after James. 'And Jonathan?' She asked, to take her mind away from such things.

'He's spent the past few years sporadically trying to reconcile with his brother, but Matthew won't have it. Matthew can't do anything about Jonathan's share in the business, and he's still on the board of directors in name, but he's kept Jonathan at arm's length. Perhaps one day they'll be reconciled, but, as the Americans say, they've got an awful lot to work through first.'

'That explains why Matthew was so snappy with me when he had to come over the day I moved in,' Anna said. 'It must be hell for him, knowing his wife and brother were at it on his own doorstep.'

'And to add insult to injury, Jack was out of the country for three months during the time the cottage was on the market, so Matthew was the point of contact for interested buyers. He even had to take a few around himself when the estate agent double-booked.'

Anna looked aghast. 'One of them was me.' She remembered how short he'd also been with her that day; how, when he'd left her to look around upstairs, she'd had to swallow back tears, knowing he was waiting impatiently downstairs for her to make a decision. She couldn't read him that day, but now it all made sense.

'It probably wasn't his finest hour,' Pat agreed. 'But now that you've got the cottage, perhaps he can let things go a bit.'

'Poor Matthew,' Anna murmured. 'No wonder he didn't want to talk about it last night.'

'Give him time, love,' Pat replied. 'It's early days, like you say.'

'Well, thank you for trusting me with it,' Anna said. 'And don't worry, I won't say a thing.'

'I know you won't,' Pat replied. 'He's a good man, and he deserves some happiness. I hope you might be the one to give it to him.'

Anna smiled. 'Early days, Pat, remember?'

Chapter 13

Anna soon got into the rhythm of village life. She and Lizzie had worked out the shift rota at The Little Orchard Tea Shop so that Anna could work around Ellie's nursery provision, but downtime was limited. Meredith and a few of her friends started popping into The Little Orchard Tea Shop a couple of times a week after school and wolfed down their cake with such enthusiasm that Anna found herself increasing the numbers she was baking to compensate.

One drizzly Thursday afternoon in early February, when her netball practice had finished, Meredith, on her own for once, was sitting on one of the tea shop sofas, about to embark on a slice of treacle tart. She was still in her sports kit, and her hair was tied in a messy plait that reached down her back. Looking at her, Anna couldn't stop the *Mallory Towers* comparisons from running through her head, although she doubted modern public school life was anything like Enid Blyton's portrayal of it. As if to dispel Anna's imaginings further, Meredith reached into the pocket of her hoody and pulled out her mobile phone. Texting furiously, she then put it away again.

'Tart all right?' Anna asked, noticing the empty plate.

'Great,' Meredith replied. 'Any chance of another slice?' She held her plate up for Anna to take.

'I thought teenage girls survived on fresh air and bottled

water, these days!' Anna quipped, taking the plate.

'Oh, please.' Meredith looked down at her own, enviably slim, thighs.

'No danger of you getting an eating disorder then!' Anna said.

'I'm blessed with a good constitution,' Meredith said piously. 'I get it from my dad. There's no way he could chug the amount of chips he does and still look halfway decent without some great genetics going on, don't you think?'

'No comment,' Anna said lightly, knowing she was being led.

'Anyway, no point in obsessing about weight – there're plenty of other things to worry about.'

'Such as?' Anna was intrigued. She could just about remember being a teenager, but she did wonder whether the things she remembered worrying about were the same as the twenty-first century breed.

'Oh, you know,' Meredith went vague. 'Stuff.'

Anna smiled to herself and went to cut Meredith another piece of treacle tart. On her return, a giggle from the sofa got Anna's attention. Meredith was staring at her phone, thumbs furiously working once more.

'Something funny?' Anna asked.

'Oh, just Flynn,' Meredith grinned. 'He makes me laugh.'

'What's he like?'

'Lush,' Meredith replied. 'And funny.'

Anna smiled. 'And more specifically?'

'Well, Dad doesn't like him, obviously, but then he's always been a bit funny about stuff like that. I only have to mention a boy's name in passing and he threatens to pack me off to a nunnery.' Meredith rolled her eyes. 'I mean, it's not even as if I've been out on a proper date with anyone, yet!'

'He just wants to keep you safe,' Anna replied. 'My dad

wasn't exactly that fond of my husband James at first, so I wouldn't worry too much!'

'I just wish he wouldn't be so moody about me seeing boys,' Meredith grumbled. 'I mean, he doesn't have to worry about any of *that* kind of stuff – I do know the facts of life and I'm not likely to do anything dodgy. It's not as if we don't get all of that shoved down our throats at school enough.'

'I know, Merry, but in the heat of the moment, things can happen.' Anna forced herself to suppress some of her fruitier teenage memories. She'd spent enough afternoons with boyfriends in the long grass off the Strawberry Line to know what teenage hormones were like.

'Flynn's not like that,' Meredith said. She sighed. 'He's sensitive. And musical. And he can drive... well, he's taking lessons.'

'So he's not in your year, then?'

Meredith laughed. 'No, he's older. In the Sixth Form. Taking A-Levels.'

Anna nodded. So far, so harmless.

'He wants us to go out sometime,' Meredith said. 'To the cinema.'

'What does your dad say?'

'I haven't told him yet.' Meredith looked speculatively at Anna. 'I was wondering if maybe you could... like... put in a good word with Dad.'

Anna's brow furrowed. 'Don't you think it'd be better coming from you?'

Meredith sighed. 'Every time I try and talk to Dad about it, he shuts me down straight away. There's no way he'll listen to me. When he found out I'd snogged Joel at the wassail last year, he went apeshit and tried to sack him on the spot.'

Anna smiled inwardly. Joel was eighteen and a packer at Carter's Cider with dubious personal hygiene and an equally dubious reputation with the teenage girls of Little Somerby. In that particular instance, she could sympathise with Matthew.

'He's just trying to protect you,' Anna said reasonably. 'He probably feels like he has to be mum and dad to you, and believe me, that's not the easiest thing in the world to do by yourself.'

'He can't protect me from the whole world,' Meredith said, jumping as her phone beeped again.

'It'll take time for him to get used to the fact you're growing up,' Anna replied, but she'd lost her audience. Meredith was furiously texting again. 'Do you want another drink?' Anna asked, having cleared two tables and bid farewell to another group of customers by the time Meredith finally put her phone back down.

'Thanks, but Dad's actually promised he's going to be home a bit earlier tonight so I'd better get back and do some dinner for him.'

'What's on the menu?' Anna asked, wondering just how able Meredith was in the kitchen.

'Chicken chasseur and roast potatoes.'

Anna whistled. 'There I was thinking you were strictly a fish fingers and beans kind of girl.'

Meredith laughed. 'It was either learn to cook or starve after Mum left. Luckily, Pat taught me a lot!'

'Well, enjoy it,' Anna replied. 'And don't worry about your dad. If you're honest with him, he'll give you a bit more freedom.'

'Sure, Anna, and were you ever, like, a teenager?'

'Go home!' Anna playfully pushed her out of the tea shop door.

'You'll have trouble on your hands if this place gets popular with that school,' Miss Pinkham, who was sitting at her usual table, sniffed. 'Rowdy buggers they are up there, considering how much their parents pay to send 'em.'

'Oh, I don't know,' Anna said, picking up the now empty teapot on the old bat's table. 'The ones I've met so far seem all right.'

'Ursula barred them.' Miss Pinkham paused meaningfully. 'I hope you're not going to let standards slip, now you're in charge.'

Anna was tempted to snap back that so long as they all paid their bills and were polite they were welcome, but since Miss Pinkham was as regular as clockwork with her custom, she merely smiled and went to refill her teapot.

Chapter 14

During the second week of February, working around her shifts at the tea shop, Anna busied herself with finishing painting Ellie's bedroom. She buried herself in the task, listening to the local radio station, which played a comforting mix of older tunes and the more middle of the road current hits. On the third evening, Charlotte volunteered to give her a hand.

'So how many coats do you reckon we need?' Charlotte said as she merrily slapped the paint on the far wall.

'I hope we'll get away with two.' Anna replied. She pulled her ponytail a little tighter. 'I'd like her to be back in here by the end of the week.'

'How is she as a bedfellow?'

'Wriggly.'

'But I guess you could do with the company over the next few days, right?' Charlotte paused her painting and turned to look over at Anna, who was taping the windowsill before tackling the wall.

'You remembered,' she said softly.

Charlotte crossed the small room and gave Anna a hug. 'Of course. He'd have been forty this year, wouldn't he?'

Anna nodded. 'We always joked about arranging his midlife crisis for midnight on his birthday. I'd have liked to have seen it happen!'

'Did he want sports cars and fast women?' Charlotte asked,

putting her paintbrush down before she accidentally daubed Anna with it.

'Hardly!' Anna gave a shaky smile. 'He was rather partial to the idea of a motorbike, though.'

'Really?' Charlotte smothered a snort of laughter. 'Sorry, darling, but I just can't see you as a biker's chick somehow!'

'Meaning what?'

'Well, you wussed out of go-karting on the Upper Sixth night out because you were such a scaredy-pants. I can hardly see you riding pillion on James' back seat.'

'Any cracks about throbbing engines between my legs and I'll bloody well paint you a new hair colour!'

They continued for a while in companionable silence. Eventually, Charlotte spoke. 'So have you and Matthew made any plans for Valentine's? It's only a couple of days away, you know.'

Anna nearly dropped her paintbrush. 'Me and Matthew? You make it sound like we're actually a couple!'

'Sorry, darling – didn't mean to freak you out. I wondered if he was going to whisk you off to Paris or something.'

'We've had one date, Charlotte. I hardly think that qualifies me for a trip that requires a passport.'

'So he hasn't mentioned anything to you?'

Anna shook her head. 'I'd be surprised if he had, to be honest. I haven't been out with him since our date few weeks back. He's been busy at work and I've been busy here and at the tea shop. Plus, we're taking things slowly. One date does not a marriage make!'

'Ah well, since Meredith Carter seems to be the arbiter of her father's love life lately, perhaps I'll just have to ask her next time I see her!' Charlotte rested her brush on the top of the can of paint. 'Now can we *please* stop for a cuppa before I die of thirst?'

As if on cue, Anna's mobile buzzed. Wiping her hands on the old shirt she was wearing over her top, she picked the phone up and retrieved the message. She couldn't help the grin that spread over her features.

'What? Who's it from? Is it from lover boy?' Charlotte tried to grab the phone, but Anna locked the screen and put it back in her pocket. 'Come on, what did it say? Don't leave me in suspense!'

Anna gave her friend the benefit of her grin. 'Let's just say I might actually have plans for February 14th after all!'

*

'This place is so much bigger than I remember it!' Anna exclaimed as, two days later, on a chilly St Valentine's evening, she and Matthew walked across the yard between the brand new bottling plant and the older part of the business.

'I bet you say that to all the guys,' Matthew said, a twinkle in his eye.

Anna laughed. 'What, you mean the millions of men who've been queuing up to ask me out since I got back on the market?'

'Don't flatter me and tell me I'm the first,' Matthew said. 'I'll never believe it.'

'Well, James' sister did try to get me to join an internet dating agency a few months back but I bottled out after the trial period and never actually went out with anyone.'

'I don't blame you,' Matthew shuddered. 'Meredith did the same to me about eighteen months ago; said I was turning into a sad old man who didn't know how to have any fun anymore. I was so outraged she'd signed me up without my consent, I stopped her allowance for a month.'

'Evil dad,' Anna laughed. 'Besides, I'm hardly a great

prospect with a three-year-old in tow – tends to put potential dates off.'

'Evidently,' Matthew raised a wry eyebrow.

Anna grinned back. 'Well, maybe you just need your head examined!'

They crossed the main part of the farm and were soon at the door of the on-site shop. Matthew produced a key from his pocket and unlocked the door, then reached for the light to the left of the door frame. They stepped into the shop, which had closed for the evening about an hour previously.

'I remember coming in here as a kid,' Anna said. 'And seeing all these old men filling up their tankards and plastic bottles, then, heaven forbid, driving home.'

'Ah yes,' Matthew shifted uneasily. 'That was before the drink-driving laws thankfully put paid to most of that. We had a regular troupe of local farmers who'd spend more time in the shop than in their fields during the summer, but they were good old boys. Most of them are no longer with us now.'

As Anna came fully into the shop, Matthew led her to the wooden counter. She smiled when she saw he'd set up glasses, two plates and a few small bottles of different varieties of cider. Next to the bottles were several types of cheese, all locally produced.

'I thought this might be a bit of a corny thing to do for our second date, but Meredith convinced me it would be fun to give you another tour, just you and me this time. And I hope you might have worked up an appetite,' Matthew said.

In truth, Anna had been too nervous to be hungry, but when she saw the effort Matthew had gone to, she decided she should at least taste some of what he'd put out.

'See what you think of this first.' Matthew poured a snifter from the first bottle.

Anna took a sip. It was perfectly chilled, sweet, with a

slight fizz and very agreeable. 'That's nice. Very refreshing. Not sure I'd have it with cheese, though – rather sweet to wash down a slab of Cheddar's finest.'

'Very good,' Matthew smiled approvingly. 'That is actually one we'd recommend as a dessert drink. Goes rather well with Yeo Valley Vanilla ice cream.' He poured another small glass. 'This one should taste a little different.'

Anna took the glass. This time the cider was earthier, drier, with an undercurrent of cognac. 'Now that *would* be good with cheese,' she said. Immediately, Matthew handed her a small piece. The cider brought out the tangy undertones of the cheddar, and she suddenly found she was hungry after all.

Sometime later, Anna was starting to feel the effects of the fizz, and even Matthew's eyes were sparkling a little more in the lamplight. 'So how does this compare to Valentines past?'

Anna smiled. 'Well, I suppose with every relationship there are memorable ones, and not so memorable ones. James and I tended to treat ourselves to a takeaway and a bottle of wine most years. I can't say I've ever spent Valentine's night in a cider shop, though!' She took another sip. 'How about you?'

Matthew looked thoughtful for a moment. 'It was always a big deal for Tara, even long after we were married. Perhaps it comes with being American – she and her family always seemed to do things bigger, better, more extravagantly. I remember one year she stopped speaking to me because I forgot to get her a card and she'd cooked me a five course dinner. I got quite familiar with the spare bed, that week!' He smiled ruefully, but, Anna noticed, without any particular chagrin. 'That sums up why we split, really,' Matthew said. 'We always came from two different places, on everything.' He pushed back in his chair and stretched long arms out above his head. 'I can't believe I'm telling you this,' he said wonderingly. 'I don't talk about it, to anyone. And it's hardly the most tactful thing in the world, is it? Forgive me.'

Anna shook her head. 'Nothing to forgive. We're not teenagers, Matthew – we both come with rather a lot of history.' She finished the glass of cider she'd been cradling. 'Like a second-hand car...'

'Or a library book!' Matthew laughed.

'Or a cider farm...' Anna mused. 'Plenty of history in here.'

'Like you wouldn't believe,' Matthew said. 'Sometimes it's helpful and sometimes it's a total bloody hindrance. I spend my working life struggling to modernise while staying true to the old principles, and finding the balance between the two can be more hassle than it's worth sometimes. And don't get me started on Dad...'

'I can imagine,' Anna said. 'But, like everything, it's a case of holding on to the best bits of the past while trying to work out a direction for the future, isn't it?'

'Sounds like a mantra for life!' Matthew replied. Finishing his own glass, he stood suddenly. 'Can I show you something?'

Anna's immediate thoughts must have registered in her expression, because Matthew threw back his head and laughed.

'Relax! I'm not going to jump on you.'

Anna blushed. 'Sorry – was I that obvious?'

Matthew's eyes twinkled. 'Follow me.'

'Where are we going?' Anna trailed out of the shop in his wake.

'Come and see,' he said playfully, and grabbed her hand.

Anna felt like a teenager as he pulled her across the court-yard to the large central barn that was the oldest part of the farm. Laughing breathlessly, Anna tried to match Matthew's longer stride but found herself trotting behind him. As they drew closer to the barn's main door, Matthew let go of her hand.

'Wait here,' he said.

It was dark on this side of the yard, and Anna could barely see her hand in front of her face. After thirty seconds or so, she began to wonder whether Matthew was having a laugh at her expense. Just as she opened her mouth to call out to him, there was a click, and a soft orange glow suffused where she was standing.

'OK?' Matthew asked, coming back to her.

'I think so,' Anna replied.

Matthew took her hand once again, and led her through the large double doors of the barn. A slight draught whispered through the air, and Anna felt a tingle go down her spine. There was history in the building, softly weaving its spell around her like the motes of dust in the atmosphere.

Anna looked around as she walked into the dimly lit main barn. To her left and right, enormous wooden vats stood sentinel, reaching thirty feet up towards the roof of the barn. The concrete floor was slightly uneven, and the only light came from two orange roof bulbs that cast a glow over the barn. Particles of dust glittered and danced, and Anna's shadow loomed long in front of her. 'I remember seeing this place, years ago... of course it wasn't quite the same with the Guides in tow!'

'Ah yes,' Matthew said. 'The night you actually did fall for me... or over the steps, at least!' He grinned at her.

'Oh, haha,' Anna muttered, feeling again like a mutinous teenager.

'Come on,' Matthew said. 'I won't let you trip this time.' He took her hand and led her to the stainless steel steps that were attached to the gantry overlooking the top of the vats. In the air was the earthy scent of fermenting apples. Underlying the sweet, fruit smell was the faintest whiff of cognac from the barrels themselves.

'Wow!' Anna breathed as they reached the top. 'That's quite something.'

'It's certainly quieter up here,' Matthew replied. 'I'm not often the last person on site, these days – we work through the night most of the time, so there's nearly always someone here, but every so often I like to sneak in when everyone else has knocked off and just spend a few minutes up here. It's a good place to think.' He looked around. 'This was where I came the night Tara left me. It was also where I made the decision to take Carter's to the USA.' Gesturing to the vats, he smiled. 'It's like they're the guardians of this place – patient, watchful, making sure we do the right thing. They'll be here for another hundred years, I would think, long after the next few Managing Directors have moved to pastures new.'

'It's quite a contrast to the rest of the site,' Anna said. 'Everything else is so high tech – so scientific.'

'I like to think of this barn as the beating heart of the farm,' Matthew replied, turning to look at Anna in the low light. 'Everything reaches out from here and touches everything else.' Slowly, deliberately, he took her right hand in his and placed it on his chest. 'It's all linked, connected, alive,' he kept her hand covered with his. 'A living, breathing, thing…'

Anna felt the roughness of his thick jumper under her palm, and below that, his heart beating, the heart of a man steeped in the tradition that surrounded them, shaped by the land and the fruit of four generations. A man who'd put his own dreams on hold to take the business to the next level, but who had suffered for that choice. A man who was now sharing this moment with her. Cider might have been in Matthew Carter's blood, but life and passion was in his veins, and Anna could sense it burning.

'Matthew,' she whispered.

'Sssh…' His lips were a breath away.

This time, there was no doubt, no hesitation and no lingering worry. Anna yearned for the kiss, ached for it, and when Matthew's beautiful mouth met hers, she didn't just taste cider—she tasted desire. She slid her hand from his chest up to caress the back of his neck, where his hair curled over his shirt collar. Entwining her fingers in his dark, wavy locks, she felt him shift closer to her, pulling her more tightly into his embrace. Her mouth opened to taste him further, and the kiss deepened. His arms slid around her, his fit, hard body against hers, and, not for the first time she realised that while his job title might suggest sitting behind a desk all day, this was a man who was still very much in touch with his physical side. As his right hand moved to rest in the small of her back, her head swam with the sensations their contact was unleashing. She pushed herself against him, never wanting it to end.

Eventually they broke apart. Matthew's eyes looked almost black in the low light.

Anna drew in a slightly shaky breath. 'Wow,' she said softly.

Matthew gave a broad smile. 'That's a better reaction than the last time I kissed you! You're not crying, that's a start.'

Anna grinned back. 'I think we both know your timing wasn't great on that last occasion.'

'Well, it seems the cider barrels are magical, after all!' Matthew replied. 'I must remember to tell the Green Man next year at the wassail.'

'Thank you for bringing me here,' Anna said softly. 'It means a lot to me.'

'I wanted to share it with you,' Matthew said. 'I don't expect anything of you, Anna. I know we both have a long way to go but maybe we can help each other get there.'

Anna smiled. She felt both touched and absurdly flattered. 'I'd like that. But tonight we should get home.'

'Agreed.' And with that, Matthew turned out the barn lights.

SPRING

Chapter 15

March dawned chilly but full of sunshine. Anna found herself very busy as she was due a visit from Ursula's accountant at the end of the month, which was also the end of the tax year. When she wasn't serving in the tea shop, or out in the back kitchen baking up a storm for the next day's trade, she was poring over the books for the last financial quarter. Thankfully, she'd always had a head for figures and found the spreadsheets strangely therapeutic. This was mostly due to the fact that takings were up on the previous year, which she put down to an increase in the number of people taking up cycling as a New Year's resolution. By the time most of them reached Little Somerby's stop on the Strawberry Line, they were in urgent need of sustenance, and her home-baked apple and rosewater cupcakes had hit the spot for many of them.

Just as she was saving the most recent version of the spreadsheet, and wondering whether the accountant had a sweet enough tooth to be distracted from the rather garish colour coding she'd used by a large slice of carrot and orange cake, there was a quiet tap on the window pane.

'Sorry,' Matthew said as he walked in the front door a moment later. 'Didn't mean to frighten you, but if you won't get that damned doorbell fixed, what else am I supposed to do?'

Anna raised an eyebrow. 'Well, some bloke did say he

was going to fix it for me, but he's not made good on his promise yet!'

'Bugger, I'd forgotten about that – things have been a bit mad at my end.'

'Mine too,' Anna wandered through to the kitchen and put the kettle on. 'Tea or coffee?'

'Oh, sod the tea, just come here!' Matthew said, pulling her to him.

Since their first proper encounter on the barn gantry, kissing Matthew, Anna decided, was definitely her new favourite pastime.

'So how's Merry?' she asked, once she'd got her breath back.

'Not bad,' he said carefully. 'I take it she's not popped in this week, then?'

'Haven't seen her since last Thursday,' Anna replied. 'She must have been busy with her schoolwork.'

'Hmmm...'

'Is that a note of scepticism in your voice?' Anna teased.

Matthew looked troubled. 'She's been singularly elusive lately, and even when she has graced me with her presence, she's spent most of her time texting or in her room. If I didn't know better...'

Anna passed him a mug of tea and joined him at the kitchen table. 'What would you think?' she asked gently.

'Well, I know she's not doing drugs or drinking – growing up around a cider farm has been enough to put her off the latter, and she's too savvy to do the former. That only leaves the opposite sex as enough of a distraction to keep her at school and texting at all hours.' He looked directly at Anna with an inquisitor's stare she found distinctly unnerving. 'Has she said anything to you?'

'Well,' Anna hedged, wondering how to put it without

dropping Meredith into something she couldn't get out of. 'She did mention she was quite keen on a boy.'

'I knew it!' Matthew grimaced. 'I've been dreading this.'

'It's nothing serious,' Anna replied. 'He's just asked her to go out with him next week. I'm sure it's all above board.'

'And I suppose he's the real reason she's been staying late at school as well.'

Anna grinned. 'I would suspect you're onto something there, Sherlock! But, you know, she might be learning something, too.'

'So long as it's only world politics she's getting acquainted with.' Matthew frowned. 'She's not expressed any interest in boys before.'

'She's fifteen,' Anna said, mindful that she was speaking to a very overprotective father. 'In teenage girl terms, she's a late starter.'

'You mean I've got off lightly so far?' Matthew shook his head.

'Let's just say that if Flynn's the first boy she's shown an interest in, she's likely to be taking things rather cautiously. Despite the inevitable hormones.'

'Sounds like the voice of experience.'

'No comment,' Anna said wryly. 'After all, you must remember being that age?'

'That's what worries me!' Matthew said. 'If this Flynn boy is anywhere near as – er, teenaged as I was, I'm going to lock Meredith up until she's twenty-one!'

'Perhaps it's time to give her a little freedom,' Anna said. 'She might surprise you. She's a responsible girl, and far too sensible to take any chances.'

'So what do you suggest?' Matthew asked.

'Let her go out with him,' Anna said. She placed a hand over one of Matthew's on the kitchen table. 'I mean, if you don't, she's likely to see it as a challenge.'

'It's just so hard to let go of the reins,' Matthew said. 'She's still a baby.'

'She's halfway through her teens, Matthew,' Anna said. 'And if you give her a little bit of freedom now, she'll respect you more for it. Trust me.'

'The voice of experience again?'

'Well, let's just say I kissed a few boys before I got married, and I think I turned out all right!' Anna smiled.

Matthew stood up and pulled Anna up from her chair and into his arms. 'What did I do to be blessed with such a paragon of good sense?'

'Something terrible,' Anna murmured, leaning upwards to kiss him. 'Now, you'd better get going – she'll be expecting you for dinner, and probably an answer about this date.'

'Yes, Boss!' Matthew grinned. 'But you do know I'm holding you personally responsible if she elopes with him?'

'It's a deal,' Anna said, ushering Matthew to the door.

'I'll agree to it on one condition,' Matthew said before he left.

'What's that?'

'Will you hold my hand on the night she goes out with him, and take my mind off it all?' He turned serious brown eyes on her.

'Of course. I'll even cook you some dinner if you like.' Still grinning as she closed the door behind him, she wished she could be a fly on the wall for the dinner table discussion at the Carters' house that night.

*

'So did she get off alright?' Anna asked as Matthew came through the front door the following Friday evening. Having put Ellie to bed half an hour earlier, she was at her desk working out a potential new menu for the summer months. There were so many amazing local food producers around, she was desperate to include as many as possible on her 'Flavours of Somerset' light lunch menu. She'd already contacted an apiary just outside Taunton which sold the most exquisite local honey, an artisan charcuterie manufacturer in nearby Wrington that made juniper infused hams and, of course, there was plenty of cheese down the road in Cheddar, not to mention strawberries that were regularly supplied to Wimbledon. Even for a menu that was essentially sandwiches and cakes, there was so much to choose from, and to innovate with.

'Apparently,' Matthew muttered. 'His mother's acting as a taxi service for tonight, so at least I don't have to worry about him hurtling down the back lanes with her in some death trap car.' Matthew must have seen the shadow that passed over Anna's face as the words came out. In a flash, he was apologetic.

'It's OK,' Anna said softly. Despite her reaction, she'd never wanted people to feel they had to mind their language around her because of what had happened to James. She leaned into him and gave him a quick hug to break the tension. 'Dinner'll be ready in about ten minutes, so pour yourself a drink and come and sit at the table.'

'Ought I to drink?' Matthew worried. 'I mean, what if she calls me and wants picking up?'

'Don't panic,' Anna replied. 'I've bought us some elder-flower fizz for tonight – strictly non-alcoholic.'

'Just in case he messes her about?' Matthew frowned.

'I'm sure he won't,' Anna said soothingly. 'But something tells me you don't want to take any risks.' She put a hand on his shoulder as she passed him to stir the bolognese sauce that was simmering on the stove top.

Matthew sighed. 'You're right, of course. And I've told her

to be home by eleven. Or she's never going out again.'

'Eleven?' Anna asked.

'Well, the first curfew was nine-thirty but she told me I was being *so nineteenth century, Dad*, that I had to negotiate. She wanted midnight!' Matthew shook his head. 'Even when she left, she still looked entirely too young to be going out alone with a young man.'

'She'll be fine, Matthew, trust me,' Anna said. 'Now, can you do me a favour and get the garlic bread out of the oven?'

After a hearty meal and a glass or two of the elderflower cordial, despite the lack of booze, Matthew was starting to relax. As the two of them settled down on the sofa, Anna broke the companionable silence.

'So who was your first date with, and where did you go?'

Matthew smiled. 'You're asking me to think back a long time. Let me see. I was about sixteen, I think. She was the same age. We spent an afternoon walking around the village fete, and then a couple of hours snogging behind the tithe barn.'

'How very quaint!' Anna laughed. 'What happened to her?'

Settling back onto the sofa, and putting an arm around Anna, Matthew grinned ruefully. 'Well, we went out for a few weeks, and then she decided my best mate was more her cup of tea and that was that.'

'What a rat! What did you do?'

'Took it on the chin,' Matthew replied. 'Mates are difficult to replace, whereas women...' he winked.

'I'll pretend you never said that,' Anna said, swatting at his arm. She was secretly relieved he made so light of it, given his rather more recent experiences. She hadn't said anything to him about what Pat had told her about Tara, and hoped he'd tell her in his own time.

'So what about you? Come on, it's only fair!'

'Oh, I was a bit of an early starter,' Anna said. 'I was thirteen and he was fifteen. We went to a school disco together. We kissed on the climbing bars in the gym and got a round of applause from the entire year!'

'Exhibitionist!' Matthew chided. 'I didn't know you had it in you.'

'I was young and carefree back then,' Anna sighed.

'So what happened to him?'

'Oh, the usual – he snogged some other girl. You trust, and forgive, so much more easily at that age, don't you? Before life throws a whole load of baggage at you.'

'Definitely true,' Matthew said. 'But I wouldn't want to go back there.'

'Me neither,' Anna agreed. 'The highs are so much higher, but the lows...'

'All of those teenage hormones flying around – far too much hassle.'

Anna looked thoughtful. 'You know, you might have to do a bit of mopping up if and when Flynn and Meredith come to an end. Are you prepared for that?'

'Oh, yes,' Matthew said lightly. 'I'll put him in one of the cider vats if he messes her about.' He paused, giving a wicked, irresistible grin. 'Head first.'

'Seriously,' Anna said. 'She might need you to be... tactful. It could be worth filling one of those vats with Chew Moo ice cream in the eventuality of a split.'

Matthew sighed. 'This is why she really needs a woman around. Not that I'm suggesting you take that role, or any-thing,' he added hastily.

'I'm happy to be a sounding board for her, don't worry,' Anna said. 'But you might want to keep the lines of communi-cation open with her – that way she'll keep you in the loop.'

'You are wise beyond your years,' Matthew said, kissing

the top of her head. 'Now how long have I got left before I can stop worrying?'

Anna looked at her watch. 'An hour and a half. What can we do in that time to take your mind off things?'

'What do you suggest?' Matthew asked, pulling her towards him.

'Well, there's an episode of *Midsomer Murders* on the hard drive recorder!' Anna teased.

Matthew didn't grace that with a vocal response. Anna quickly found out it wasn't just teenagers who enjoyed kissing in quiet places.

Chapter 16

'Now before you start, please think about what you tell me,' Anna said, semi-seriously, as she placed a plate of hot buttered doorstep toast on the coffee table in front of the tea shop sofas the following Monday afternoon. 'I can promise discretion, but not complete confidentiality when it comes to your father!'

'Oh, chillax!' Meredith rolled her eyes. 'We went to see a film and then got some food at Nando's. Nothing my dad would freak over.'

'Glad to hear it!' Anna said. 'Right, now that's done, do you want a drink with that toast?'

'You're not going to ask me *anything?*'

Anna grinned. 'Oh, go on then. Did you get on OK?'

Meredith sighed dramatically. 'He's lush. He paid for the cinema tickets, and the food afterwards. And walked me back to my door, although his mum was watching so he just kissed me on the cheek.'

All good signs, Anna thought. Perhaps Matthew didn't need to worry quite yet.

'And he got you back on time?'

'Well, his mum *was* doing the driving, so really she did!' Meredith tucked her long legs underneath her on the sofa. Anna thought about reminding her that she wasn't in her own home, but, mindful of the other customers, merely swatted the teenager's knees and, with a grimace, Meredith lowered them again. 'But he's hoping to have passed his driving test in a few weeks so I guess then I'll be able to tell you about his timekeeping.'

'That'll be one more thing for your dad to worry about!' Anna quipped, although her own alarm bells were ringing faintly. She didn't want to think too much about teen drivers.

'Add it to the list!' Meredith replied. 'He's already given me the third degree about Flynn's A Levels, what his mum and dad do, is he a hard worker, has he had any previous girlfriends. I think I spent more time finding out the answers to Dad's questions than the ones I wanted to ask him!'

'So what film did you see?'

'I can't remember... didn't see much of it!' Meredith gave a wicked grin.

Anna raised an eyebrow.

'Oh, OK, I'm joking! It was some vampire teen thing.'

Anna felt secretly glad that particular trend had passed her by. 'So are you going to see him again?'

'I should think so – he's persuaded me to join some political group at school – the Model United Nations or something, so I daresay we'll get the odd evening together.'

Anna suppressed a smile. 'Well, your dad'll be pleased you're learning something, as well as seeing vampire teen films!'

'I hadn't, like, realised how interesting world politics was until I met Flynn,' Meredith sighed again. 'He's so clever. But not a geek,' she added hastily.

Turning away to hide her smile, Anna busied herself clearing away the plates and teacups from the adjacent table. She remembered all too well how love made everything more seductive when you were a teenager; even, it seemed, world policies on hunger and war.

'So you think you might be learning something, then?'

'Oh yeah!' Meredith said. 'And Granddad has promised to

fill me in on some of the finer points of the functions of the UN committees, so I don't look like a complete twonk during the first meetings of the group.'

Good for Granddad, Anna thought. Jack Carter was clearly an erudite man, which made it all the more surprising he'd never clocked what had happened right under his nose between his beloved sons. She wondered if she'd ever be present at a gathering of all three around the table, and how, if she ever was, it would be likely to end.

After Meredith had left, Anna remembered that she'd intended to put up a poster in the front window. In an attempt to broaden the appeal of the tea shop, she'd decided to draw on her former career as a librarian and start a book exchange. On holiday in Cornwall a few years back, she'd been tickled by the contents of an old red phone box in the village where they'd been staying. It was filled to the roof with shelves and shelves of books; everything from mainstream fiction to tomes on history and biography. She'd been particularly amused by the juxtaposition of a novel by Katie Price and Margaret Thatcher's autobiography, and wondered what the two formidable women would have made of each other. Since she'd never got around to buying new shelving for the books she couldn't accommodate at Pippin Cottage, she'd decided to bring them into the tea shop and convert the Welsh dresser, which had hitherto been filled with a wide variety of somewhat garishly flowered crockery, into a bookshelf.

During a quiet spell the previous week, she'd taken down the plates and cups and had brought the cardboard boxes of her books from home over. After a moment's deliberation about how to arrange them, she decided to throw caution to the wind – not to mention her considerable training – and arrange them by colour. Somehow, in the world of the tea shop, this seemed to make more sense than by genre or surname. The colours of the countryside; deep, luscious greens of fielded hills, pearlescent whites of the new elderflowers that frothed and fizzed over the hedges like sparkling wine, the heavenly scented lilac that spilled down to the Strawberry Line and filled the air around it with such a gorgeous aroma, all seemed to have worked their way into her subconscious.

As she worked, she heard the tea shop's door open again and smiled at the two women who'd come in with their children, dressed in the colours of the local primary school. 'I won't be a minute,' she called as they settled themselves at the table nearest the counter. Anna smiled as she heard the children, two girls, requesting one each of her rose-pink cupcakes. The tea shop was becoming more and more her haven every day.

*

Matthew had taken to popping into the cottage after he'd had dinner with Merry and during Sefton's evening walk. The collie seemed to appreciate it, too, and he was rather at home on Anna's red poppy embroidered rug in front of the wood burner. The March weather was gradually warming during the day, but there was still a chill in the air at night, so Anna was still lighting it most evenings. They would sit on her battered leather sofa and talk, sometimes sharing a glass of wine.

'This is nice,' Anna snuggled closer to Matthew. A warmth and relaxation gradually spread through her, down to her bones.

'I'd forgotten how good it is to relax,' Matthew murmured into Anna's hair. 'Things are getting really busy at work. I'm lucky to be getting home at all.'

'Does Merry mind?' Anna asked, tilting her head up to look at Matthew. He had dark rings around his eyes, and although his body was relaxed, she sensed his mind was still racing.

'She's been doing a lot of stuff herself,' Matthew said. 'Model United Nations or something. I keep meaning to ask her a bit more about it, but either she's late back or I am, and then we're both too shattered to do anything other than eat off our knees. She's gone back up to school tonight for some meeting or other.'

'She did mention she'd joined the Model UN,' Anna said.

'And Ellie's fine?' Matthew asked. He'd grown as fond of the toddler as Anna was of Meredith.

'Oh yes – she's still agitating for a dog, though – I might have to borrow Seffy!'

'Feel free,' Matthew smiled. 'He'd probably enjoy a change of scene.' As if in agreement, Sefton stretched out his front paws, sighed and put his long nose between them.

A comfortable silence descended. Matthew leaned towards her and touched her lips with his. He tasted of wine and coffee, and Anna could feel the stubble on his face. As his mouth explored hers, she responded to the kiss, and she wrapped an arm around his neck, pulling him towards her. They stretched out, Matthew's long, jeans-clad legs intertwining with hers, the soft leather of the sofa under her back creaking gently.

'You feel so good,' Matthew murmured, kissing his way down her neck.

'You too,' Anna replied. She was getting rather fond of this stage of their relationship, where they necked like teenagers for hours. It was taking her back to some very interesting places – exciting places, where the thrill of the sensation was enhanced by the fear of discovery. Of course, back in the day, it was parents who would do the discovering, whereas now it was more likely to be her own daughter coming down the stairs. It was fun to lose herself in the moment, but at the back of her mind was the awareness that this would, inevitably, lead to more.

Teasingly, Matthew's hands wandered towards the buttons of Anna's cardigan. He began to undo the small mother of pearl buttons until he was able to slide a hand up inside the jersey top she was wearing underneath. This wasn't new territory, and Anna relaxed, enjoying the feeling of his warm hands on her bare flesh. She pulled Matthew's checked shirt out from where it had caught in the back of his jeans. Running her hands up the inside, she caressed his back. Their kisses deepened in intensity and as Matthew's hands began to work their way back down her body, Anna tensed. Immediately, Matthew moved his hands away and broke the kiss.

'I'm sorry,' he said. 'Am I pushing my luck?' His eyes were dark with desire.

'There's something you should know.' Anna's face grew hot.

Matthew smiled. 'You're not going to tell me you're actually a man, or an alien from outer space?'

Anna laughed. 'No...' she shifted awkwardly. 'It's just that...'

Matthew looked concerned. 'You know you can tell me anything, don't you? I want you to be comfortable, Anna.'

Squirming, Anna dropped her eyes. 'I feel so stupid.' She took a deep breath. 'I guess I'm frightened that if you get my clothes off, you won't fancy me anymore.'

Matthew did his best to smother his bark of laughter.

'Oh, god,' Anna groaned. 'Did I really just say that?' She buried her face in Matthew's shoulder, her cheeks flaming.

'I'm afraid you did!' Still laughing, Matthew shifted position so Anna had no choice but to look at him. Gently, he placed a kiss on each cheek, and one on her lips. 'You are so adorable when you're embarrassed.'

'Don't!' Anna tried to wriggle away. 'I feel like a total muppet.'

Matthew composed his features into a more sensible

expression. 'Anna Hemingway,' he said softly. 'In case you hadn't noticed, and frankly, I'd be the one who should be embarrassed if you hadn't, you only have to get within ten feet of me and I'm standing to attention.' He took her hand and placed it on the fly of his jeans. 'See?'

Anna nodded. There was very little doubt he spoke the truth, if what was now under her palm was anything to go by.

'But what if that all changes when...' Anna swallowed. Even to her ears it sounded ridiculous.

In answer, Matthew kissed her again.

Some moments later, both were breathing more than a little heavily.

Anna spoke again. 'Fair enough,' she said. 'But you should know... when I had Ellie... she didn't exactly come out the normal route.'

'And this should worry me why, exactly?' Matthew looked genuinely affronted.

'Well, it's just that... I've got quite a large scar, and I thought it might come as a bit of a shock.'

Matthew shook his head, and brushed a lock of hair out of Anna's eyes. 'You're forgetting I grew up in the country, so there's very little that shocks me about procreation and childbirth.'

'What did I do to deserve you?' Anna said, starting to calm down.

'Something terrible,' Matthew muttered, as he dipped his head to kiss her neck again. And, suddenly, Anna knew everything was going to be all right.

Stretching back against the sofa, she began to relax, and when Matthew's warm hands reached the button of her jeans, this time she didn't hesitate.

He shuffled down the sofa until he was level with the top of Anna's jeans. He undid the button and pulled the zip down.

Instinctively, Anna sucked in her stomach, but Matthew ran a hand over her exposed flesh. 'No cheating.' He sighed. 'You are, as my daughter might say, well lush.'

Anna couldn't help laughing, but that laugh turned into a sigh as Matthew replaced his hands with his warm mouth. He kissed her stomach, and lower, until he reached the horizontal line of her caesarean section scar. He ran his tongue along it, all the time stroking her waist with his warm hands.

'As battle scars go, I've seen worse,' he murmured, raising his head, a twinkle in his eye, before continuing the route with his tongue.

Anna squirmed, growing warmer. Her thighs parted; she wanted to wrap herself around Matthew, to feel him inside her. 'Oh, you're good at that,' she whispered. She felt the warmth of his breath as he kissed her, and his fingers slid under the waistband of her knickers.

And then, on cue, from upstairs. 'Mummy!'

Anna groaned. 'Coming, darling.' She wriggled off the sofa and rebuttoned her jeans. Then, she walked on not entirely steady legs up the stairs.

Ellie had had a nightmare, and was nearly inconsolable. By the time Anna had settled her back down again, Matthew had fastened his shirt and was finishing a cup of tea.

'Sorry,' Anna said, returning to the lounge.

'No problem,' Matthew replied. 'It wasn't meant to be.' He put his phone away. 'Besides, while you were upstairs, Merry texted me. She wants picking up from school, so whatever way you look at it, we're destined to sleep frustrated and alone tonight!' Putting his arms around her, he pulled her close. 'If nothing else, I hope I've dispelled any worries you might have in regard to how much I fancy you – clothes on or off!'

'Message received loud and clear,' Anna replied. She felt herself responding to Matthew again, and it was obvious he was feeling the same way. She groaned. 'Bloody kids!'

'Now now, we'll get our time,' Matthew grinned. 'But for tonight, I'll have to love you and leave you.' He leaned down to kiss her, and his mouth was warm and insistent on hers. Anna very nearly buckled on the spot. 'I'll see you soon. And no more worrying!'

'Agreed,' Anna's voice had the barest quiver in it. 'Now get out of here before I drag you to my bedchamber and make you finish what you started!'

Matthew groaned. 'I am about a hair's breadth away from telling Meredith to bloody well walk home!'

'Better not – it's a fair way, especially at this time of night.' Reluctantly, Anna let Matthew go and they walked to her front door.

'Later – and that is a promise,' Matthew said, kissing her one more time.

'I'll hold you to that,' Anna replied. As she shut the door, Anna closed her eyes and took a deep breath. She couldn't believe how close they'd come tonight; and she could barely wait for another opportunity.

Chapter 17

Frustratingly, for most of April Matthew was overseas trying to work out the finer points of an international distribution deal with a firm in the USA. He and Anna kept in touch via Skype, and Anna was busy with the increasing numbers of customers at the tea shop since the weather had warmed up. She'd also started mulling over possible cake recipes for the stall at the May Fair that Lizzie usually ran. She wanted to bake something that would represent the village, but a concept was proving difficult. She'd lost count of the amount of nights she'd fallen asleep with a notebook in her hand, jotting down possible ideas.

On his return, Matthew invited Anna and Ellie to Sunday lunch at Cowslip Barn, the Carter family home. Anna greeted this invitation with pleasure, but also a kind of trepidation. Matthew might have been a successful businessman but his cooking left a lot to be desired. While she'd shared the odd meal of beans on toast at Matthew's place, they'd eaten together more regularly at Pippin Cottage. But, Meredith seemed confident Matthew could pull it off, and so it was that Anna found herself in the cosy living room on the last Sunday in April.

'I never thought I'd see the day Dad actually got his apron on!' Meredith giggled and passed Anna a glass of chilled Chardonnay. 'But he was determined the four of us should have a proper Sunday lunch together, and wouldn't accept any of my help in cooking it.'

Anna raised an eyebrow. 'None at all?' Meredith's love for promoting her father was one thing, but she couldn't quite visualise Matthew doing a Jamie Oliver.

'Well, Pat did come in last night and help him get the casserole ready... and she might have helped a bit with the dessert, too.'

That was more like it, Anna thought. She couldn't help feeling relieved; both that she wouldn't be made to eat something Matthew had cooked without assistance, and that there appeared to be something he wasn't instinctively good at.

'I bet Dad's not shown you this place at all, has he?' Meredith said. 'And it's, like, so full of history, it seems a shame not to.'

Anna smiled. Of necessity Matthew had tended to visit her more, simply because of Ellie's earlier bedtime. She let Meredith take Ellie's hand, and looked forward to learning a little bit more about the house.

'This used to be the farmhouse when the family had a dairy herd,' Meredith said as she led Anna out of the living room and through the dark interior corridor. 'Hence the cheesy name.' She wrinkled her nose at the unintended pun. 'Cowslip was, apparently, one of my great-great-grandfather's favourite Friesians. The Carters switched from cows to cider in about 1900, I think.' Meredith led Anna through the stone-flagged hallway and past the kitchen to a room with a closed, oak-panelled door. 'This is the formal dining room, but don't worry, we're not eating in here!' Meredith pushed open the door to an austere-looking chamber, with a long, dark table running down the centre. 'I don't think Dad's used this room since before Mum left. I certainly can't remember ever sitting in here, but apparently Nan and Granddad used to have wicked dinner parties, millions of years ago!'

Closing the door, Meredith then led Anna and Ellie into a smaller room at the back of the house. 'This is Dad's study,' she said. 'Oh, no, don't worry, he won't mind you taking a look.' She opened the heavy wooden door and escorted Anna through. 'He retreats in here with Seffy when my girl stuff gets too much for him!'

Anna looked around the room, appreciating the floor to ceiling bookshelves and the large, leather-topped mahogany desk. Browsing the shelves, she was unsurprised to see Matthew still had his legal textbooks, a relic of his university days, but tickled to see them buffered up against a set of John Grisham crime thrillers. There were several books on English history, and quite a few volumes of political memoirs, as well as a few pulp fiction titles that looked rather more well-thumbed.

On one of the walls not covered by shelving was a kind of rogues' gallery. Meredith fell silent as Anna perused the framed photographs, some black and white, some in colour, that represented various aspects of Matthew's past and present. Two young boys looked out from a faded colour photograph, tinted with age. The elder boy was around nine or ten; serious brown eyes staring directly at the camera, framed by a messy dark fringe. The younger boy looked about six, the grey flannel shorts coming almost past his knees, the blazer looking a size too big for him. He, unlike his older brother, was grinning, his face dimpled and soft.

'That's Dad and Uncle Jonathan,' Meredith said. 'Dad says it was Uncle Jonathan's first day of school.'

'He doesn't look scared enough!' Anna replied, looking at the confident, open face of the younger boy. Matthew, already tall for his age, was the one who looked pensive. The contrast in skin tone and hair colour between the two brothers was striking, but there was no denying they were siblings; it was like looking at an image painted in two distinct palettes.

'And this one's Dad being all sporting at university,' Meredith pointed to a slightly larger photograph, obviously professionally taken this time. Matthew, all solid muscle and lean legs, was frozen in time, mid-run, cradling a rugby ball. His blue and white shirt was splattered with mud, his hair, worn a little longer in his early twenties than it was now, was as black as a raven's wing. The look of concentration on his face was intense.

'Shortly after that was taken he destroyed his knee, so, even though he's typically modest about his sporting achievements, he likes to keep that photo on the wall as a reminder that he once played rather well.' Meredith shot a wry glance at Anna. 'He even had a trial for England, apparently.'

Chalk another one up on Matthew Carter's list, Anna thought. Had he ever failed at anything?

Seeming to anticipate Anna's thoughts, Meredith pointed to another photo. 'And that's Mum and Dad and the rest of the family on their wedding day.'

Once again, Anna drew breath, her eyes pulled, inexorably, past the clan like presence of three generations of Carters to the woman in the picture. Tara was tall, blonde, all-American. Her dress, while simple, seemed to dance on her lithe, willowy frame, and Matthew, resplendent in frock coat and striped trousers, looked like a Regency hero; they could have been on the cover of *Hello!* magazine. How could something that looked so perfect have been destroyed so totally? And how could that little, smiling boy in the first photo have played such an enormous part in its destruction?

Anna shook her head. Time changed so much; photographs were a reminder that, no matter how happy or sad you were, those moments were fleeting. She tore her eyes away and looked briefly at some of the others; Jack and Cecily Carter on their wedding day; Matthew graduating, an echo of that serious schoolboy still present in his features despite the ridiculousness of the mortarboard and gown; and further back, to the first Carter who brewed cider on the farm. Off to one side of the wall was another picture of Matthew and Jonathan; Matthew must have been in his very early twenties, and Jonathan no more than seventeen or eighteen. They had their arms around each other's shoulders and looked completely at ease. And, finally, there were several photos of Meredith herself. One was of Matthew and Meredith by a young apple tree. Matthew was kneeling next to his daughter, and both were smiling, though Anna detected Matthew's expression was rather more careworn than happy. Meredith must have been around Ellie's age. She wondered if Tara had been the photographer.

'Look, Munchkin, that's me,' Meredith pointed to the picture Anna had been observing.

Ellie grinned. 'You're pretty.'

Meredith beamed and picked Ellie up so she could get a better look at the photograph. 'But not as pretty as you! Shall we go and explore the rest of the house? We've probably got time to go and see my pony, Rosa, before lunch, too. And you'd better go and chivvy Dad along, Anna, or we'll never eat.'

'Yes, Ma'am!' Anna gave a mock salute, secretly relieved she wasn't going to be dragged through Cowslip Barn's bedrooms.

She wandered back through to the large, cosy country kitchen. Although, like the rest of the house, it looked rather shabby, the russet-coloured walls and large scrubbed pine kitchen table lent it a homely air. There was a pile of newspapers shoved into the corner of one of the kitchen units, and Anna got the impression the whole room had been hastily tidied recently. She felt touched by the effort.

Matthew, dressed in jeans and a rugby shirt, was basting some roast potatoes and checking on the vegetables that were steaming on the hob. Wiping his hands on the front of his jeans, he turned as she entered the kitchen.

'I'm impressed, Mr Carter!' Anna said, sipping her wine and wandering over to him. 'Can I do anything to help?'

'All under control,' Matthew replied. 'Although, much like a duck, I'm paddling frantically beneath the surface.'

'So... is this all your own work?' Anna asked slyly. She sniffed the air appreciatively. 'Smells great.'

'Of course,' Matthew replied, a twinkle in his eye. 'I'm a man of many talents, apparently.'

'Apparently.'

'Hold that thought, Anna Hemingway,' Matthew crossed the kitchen and picked her up. 'Or I'll throw you in the pond.'

Squealing, Anna marvelled at Matthew's ability to, quite literally, sweep her off her feet. Contained in his arms, she felt like the archetypal damsel. 'OK, OK, I'll say no more. But I'll be sure to thank Pat when I see her next!'

'I warned you,' Matthew grinned, heading for the back door.

'Put her down, Dad, Munchkin and I are starving.' Meredith appeared at the kitchen door, Ellie in tow and began to set the table. 'You did say it'd be ready by one?'

'It'll be about five minutes,' Matthew said, surreptitiously checking Pat's instructions, that were taped none too subtly onto the front of the fridge.

'This isn't half bad, Dad,' Meredith conceded a few minutes later, spearing another roast potato from the bowl in the centre of the table. 'You should definitely, like, do this more often.'

Anna nodded, mouth full of the rather delicious casserole. 'Agreed,' she said, swallowing.

'Perhaps we *should* make this a more regular thing,' Matthew said, smiling at Ellie, who was busy hoovering up her vegetables, in anticipation of the promised chocolate cake to come.

'So I was showing Anna some of the photos in your study,' Meredith said as she put her knife and fork together. Ellie, imitating, did the same.

'Oh, yes?' Matthew raised an eyebrow. He went to fill Anna's wine glass again but she shook her head.

'She was particularly impressed by your –er– rugby passes!' Anna blushed. Had it really been that obvious?

Matthew grinned. 'That was a long time ago. I don't think I'd be capable of such feats these days, not even down the park.'

'What happened to your knee?' Anna asked, hoping the heat in her cheeks wasn't obvious.

'I was in my last year at university,' Matthew said. 'A needle match during the Roses tournament. I got tackled badly and ruined my anterior cruciate ligament. Six months of R&R and another year of physio, and then they told me I'd never play seriously again.'

'Does it still bother you?' she asked.

'Only when I run, which I try not to do these days!' Matthew grinned. 'And, much as it would have been fun to have played for my country...'

'Mum would have *loved* that,' Meredith said dryly. 'Being a rugby widow as well as a cider one.' She clapped a hand over her mouth, horrified. 'Anna, I'm so, so sorry. I didn't mean it that way.' Her eyes filled with tears and she dropped her gaze to the kitchen table.

'Hey,' Anna said gently. 'It's all right. I don't break down every time someone mentions the "w" word.' She reached out and gave Meredith's hand a squeeze, where it lay clenched on her lap.

Meredith looked up timidly. 'But it's not all right, is it? I'm such an idiot.'

'I know you didn't mean it,' Anna replied. 'Now let's get on with sorting out this chocolate cake, shall we?'

Meredith nodded and jumped up from the table to find the bowls. As she did so, Anna glanced at Matthew. His expression wavered between darkness and light; as if he couldn't quite decide which way to go. When she caught his eye, however, a grateful and tender smile lifted his features and Anna's stomach disappeared. 'Thank you,' he mouthed, over Ellie's head and when he was sure Meredith's back was turned. Anna smiled back. There were bound to be bumps in the road when two families collided; it was getting over them safely that mattered the most. Turning to help Meredith with the dessert, she mused for a moment on this seemingly normal, and yet emotionally charged, family scene, and wondered if she'd ever get used to it.

*

'You were really good with Meredith, earlier,' Matthew said, putting his arm around Anna as they meandered down the Strawberry Line back to Pippin Cottage. Meredith and Ellie were further ahead, Ellie hanging off one of Meredith's hands. Sefton gambolled along, trotting off intermittently to check on the two girls and present them with a drool-encrusted tennis ball that Meredith threw down the footpath for him.

'She didn't mean anything by it,' Anna said. 'And I'd rather people didn't have to consider *everything* they say around me before they say it. A lot of people were like that straight after James died – it was as if they were so desperate not to upset me they would rather explode with the stress of trying to say the right thing all the time than risk saying something wrong. Of course, my bereavement counsellor warned me to expect it, but even so it got quite wearing after a while.'

'I hear you,' Matthew said. 'I can't imagine what it's like to lose someone the way you did, but people's reaction to divorce sounds similar. When Tara left, people pussyfooted around me for weeks, months even. Everywhere I went there were sympathetic stares, people thinking they were being oh so careful and skirting around the subject when I'd far rather they'd just said "I'm sorry" and moved on. Although I have to admit, some of the casseroles that got left on my doorstep were nice!'

Anna grimaced. 'I wish I could say the same, but I ended up with some truly terrible contributions to my kitchen. Not that I wasn't grateful, but at the time, and for quite a while afterwards, I couldn't eat very much.'

'To be honest, Meredith got most of the ones made for us, but at least I didn't have to worry about learning to cook for her. And then Pat sort of took over and filled up our freezer from time to time. Thank goodness Meredith took an interest when she got older, or I've no idea how we'd have survived!' He gave his famous, face-splitting grin, and Anna grinned back, relieved they were moving on to lighter subjects.

'Well, today was lovely,' she said. 'And I know Ellie loved it, too. Especially having a quick sit on Rosa's back. Talk about every little girl's dream!'

'And you? Did you enjoy it?' Matthew's voice was suddenly husky. He glanced up the footpath to check on the girls, then stopped walking and pulled Anna closer to him.

'I did,' Anna replied softly. 'I really did. Thank you.'

The air seemed full of life and sound. Sleepy insects buzzed around the blossoming hedgerows, and the scent of early philadelphus and late primroses made the air sweet and potent.

Matthew raised a warm hand to caress Anna's cheek and slid the other one around her waist. He kissed her, increasing the pressure as Anna's lips parted. She could feel every contour of his body as she pressed up against him, and for a moment she forgot everything else around them.

Matthew's eyes were dark with desire. 'We never did carry on where we left off a few weeks ago, did we?'

Anna shook her head, incapable of speech.

'Promise me we will… soon.'

'You've no idea how much I want that,' she replied. 'Any more kisses like that and I'll expire like a Jane Austen heroine!'

Matthew grinned and released her. 'We can't have that… as Ellie pointed out, I'd probably never be able to carry you home!'

'Oi, you two, stop snogging on the path and get a move on!' Meredith, thankfully, interrupted before Anna could phrase a suitably pithy response.

'Message received and understood,' Matthew replied, taking Anna's hand. 'Let's get moving before Sefton decides he wants to spend the night with you.'

'He's welcome any time,' Anna replied, glancing up at Matthew from under her lashes. 'As long as you walk him in the morning.'

Matthew looked pleasantly surprised, and then gave Anna's hand a squeeze. 'I do believe you're propositioning me, Anna Hemingway!'

'Perhaps,' Anna replied, running her index finger lightly over the inside of Matthew's wrist. She felt him tremble slightly.

'We need to get this sorted out, and quickly,' Matthew said, reaching for her again. 'Or I'll go mad, knowing you're a short walk away.'

'Dad, put her down!'

'We've been told… again,' Matthew groaned. 'But, my god, when we get the timing right, you'd better watch out!'

'I look forward to it!' Anna murmured, feeling a shiver of excitement. No matter how complicated the logistics, she hoped it wouldn't be too long before they made good on their promises.

Chapter 18

It wasn't long before the day of the Little Somerby May Fair dawned, the sun rising sleepily over the hills at the back of Anna's cottage and warming the morning air. For once Anna woke before Ellie, and she spent a few minutes enjoying the rosy glow from the sunrise as it made its way over the brow of the hill. Moments like these were precious now she had become a parent. More often than not, Ellie would bounce through from her bedroom at some ridiculous hour and insist on CBeebies. Anna was beginning to recognise the voices of the different presenters on the children's channel without even opening her eyes.

Today felt different. Anna's parents were going to stop in at the May Fair on their way down to visit Anna's grandfather in Hampshire, and they were taking Ellie with them. Much as she would miss her, it would be nice not to be woken up by the excitable voice of her three-year-old daughter for two whole mornings. That didn't necessarily mean she would wake in the cottage alone, though. With a flutter of anticipation, she considered the possibilities.

Over recent weeks, she and Matthew had been spending increasing amounts of time together, but between her commitments at the tea shop and his as Managing Director of the cider firm it was difficult to get more than an hour or two, and then it was often in the company of Meredith and Ellie. When

Anna's parents had offered to take Ellie away for a couple of days, Anna's mind had immediately drawn the obvious conclusion; her relationship with Matthew was heavy with promise, but they had not yet taken the next step. Two days alone would appear to be a blessing.

It had been so long since she'd shared a bed with anyone though, and she was hardly prepared for a night of passion. She had grown so accustomed to James lying beside her that for months after his death she would reach out at night, forgetting he was no longer there. She missed him in other, more elemental ways, too. The loneliness she felt often took a very physical turn, and the craving for touch at times consumed her. She'd been with James for twelve years; his absence was a physical as well as emotional affliction.

There was no getting away from the fact that she and Matthew were heading in a very physical direction. The current between them had been strong from the start, and now the sparks were flying every time they were near each other. There had been kisses – many, many kisses – but there always seemed to be something that made them stop short of spending the night together. Sometimes it was practical; both had children and, despite Meredith's insistence she was almost an adult, Matthew wasn't prepared to leave her alone in the house all night. Ellie, of course, was a huge consideration for them both too. Ellie liked Matthew, that much was clear, but Anna was loath to confuse her by inviting Matthew to stay over at the cottage too soon. So they'd prowled, light-footed, around each other until they were granted an opportunity.

Tonight, it seemed, would be that opportunity. Meredith was away for the night, and from Monday she was on a school trip to Belfast for her first Model United Nations conference. But there was the fair to go to first.

A tradition in Little Somerby that went back generations,

on the first Saturday in May the village held a fair on the green, in the shadow of the largest of the barrows that stood sentinel over the village boundary. Little Somerby had a long and proud archaeological heritage, and, as religions came, intertwined and evolved, so the barrows still held a significance. The village turned out in force for the fair, and from the afternoon onwards the sound of children playing, music of all kinds and singing rang around the grounds. In the evening there was a ceilidh with several local bands that went on until the sunrise the following day. Few had the stamina to see the whole night through, and those with children usually retired before the sun had even set, but for the steadfast, there was a barbecue breakfast to greet the dawn of the new day.

Ellie would be with Anna for part of the day, but Anna's parents wanted to get going before the holiday traffic kicked off, so they would be taking her with them around lunchtime. That left her and Matthew with two and a half days, and, more significantly, two nights, to themselves.

Just as she was contemplating getting into the shower, Ellie at last woke up. Bounding through to Anna's bedroom, she jumped right in the middle of the bed.

'Morning, Munchkin,' Anna said, pulling her into a tight embrace. 'Ready to go with Nan and Grampy for the night?'

'I take my swimbling costume?' Ellie asked. It took Anna half a second to realise Ellie was already wearing it.

'I should think so, but you'll have to put it in your suitcase!'

After Anna had packed Ellie's suitcase and managed to squeeze in a quick shower, there was a knock at the door and, before Anna could get to it, it had swung open.

'Are you ready?' Charlotte said.

'Yup, just got to grab my keys,' Anna replied, searching for the house keys in the bowl by the door. It didn't help that her hands had started to shake.

This wasn't unnoticed by Charlotte. Stepping towards her best friend, she put her hands on her shoulders. 'Relax, darling. It's not like he's going to impale you on top of the barrow for everyone to see!'

'Thanks for that wonderful image!'

Charlotte grinned, but her smile faded as she saw the look on Anna's face. 'You don't have to do anything you don't want to. You're not seventeen any more. No one's putting peer pressure on you. Matthew's a grown man, not some oversexed teenager.'

'I know,' Anna sighed. 'I think I'm putting pressure on myself. What if, after all this anticipation, it's all a massive let down?'

'Then, being the mature and sensible adults that you are, you'll probably just laugh it off and try again some other time!' Charlotte gave her friend a quick hug. 'Don't you think he's worrying about the same stuff? After all, you know what they say about forty over forty and all that?' She grinned. 'I bet he's already been trawling through his spam email folder frantically trying to find those ads for Viagra.'

Despite herself, Anna grinned back. 'Somehow he doesn't strike me as the anxious type.'

'You say that, but he's not exactly been Mr Stud Muffin, you know. I can't remember the last time I saw him with a woman on his arm, and, he might be cautious and discreet, but no one's that subtle.' Charlotte tucked a stray lock of hair out of Anna's eyes. 'Just relax and take it as it, er, comes. So to speak.'

'Let's get going then,' Anna said finally, taking Ellie's hand. 'I said I'd meet him there at twelve, and it's quarter to already.' Grabbing a cardigan to sling over her summer dress in case it chilled off later, she smiled at her friend. 'You're right, as usual.'

'I know,' Charlotte said smugly. 'But promise me one thing...'

'What?'

'I want details. After the fact. If there is a fact, that is. I've been dying to know if Mr Moody Breeches Carter is as well hung as his jeans have been suggesting all these years!'

'Out!' Shutting the front door behind them, Anna pretended to clap her hands over her ears.

'Work's picking up again for Simon now it's the summer,' Charlotte said as they made their way to the fair. 'Thank goodness. People tend to want to make home improvements when the weather's warm, so he's had a lot of quotes for kitchens, bathrooms and even the odd loft conversion! Had to pass that one onto a mate, of course – he'd struggle to do that single-handed.'

'I'm glad,' Anna said, also glad they were off the subject of her and Matthew.

Charlotte and Simon had had their fair share of hard times financially; Charlotte's decision to stay at home and look after Evan had put the squeeze on them, but, ever resourceful Charlotte had managed to keep the family's heads above water.

'I was thinking about going back to work at some point, though,' Charlotte continued. 'Evan'll be at school in a year or so, and it would be nice to stretch my academic muscles again and get back to the classroom.'

'Well, goodness knows they're crying out for decent teachers – I'm sure a school will snap you up.'

'Here's hoping – and that my brain hasn't turned to total cauliflower in the time I've been off!'

They'd made it to the village green by this time. Ahead of them was a variety of stalls, including the obligatory hog roast and burger stands, bouncy castle and inflatable death slide. There were also concessions from local businesses and craft makers, including a multitude of handmade crafts that reflected the strong pagan tradition of the village barrows. That these were nestled comfortably against the stall run by the Salvation Army charity shop and the church was testament to how much easy cooperation had sprung up over the years between the different religious groups of the parish.

Anna scanned the stalls and the crowd, searching for where Lizzie had set up the tea shop's cake stall. In a flash of inspiration a few nights ago, Anna had decided on the theme for the cakes, and she'd spent the last two frantic evenings baking and icing over a hundred cupcakes. The resulting bakes were a twist on the cupcakes she'd first baked for Ursula; a delicate blend of local honey, sourced from the Sedgemoor hives in Taunton, enhanced with cinnamon and topped with frosted apple blossom. Despite her aching back and tired fingers, she knew they looked amazing, and summed up the spirit of the village and the fair. Lizzie had assured her that she and her daughter would run the stall as they always had, so all Anna had to do was check in with her and then the rest of the afternoon would be hers. She smiled as she located the stall, and recognised the vicar and his wife hovering over the cakes.

'Everything OK?' Anna asked as she, Ellie and Charlotte approached.

Lizzie grinned. 'At this rate, we'll have sold out by lunchtime and Gina and I can take the afternoon off! These lavender ones are selling like hot, well you know!'

Anna smiled back. 'I'm so relieved.' Half the takings would be going to the charities supported by the event, and the other half, minus the stall pitching fee, to the tea shop. She was glad she wouldn't be taking any cakes home either; if she never saw another frosted apple blossom again, it would be too soon.

'Let me know if you need me to step in at any point,' Anna said.

'Don't worry about that,' Lizzie replied, handing over four more cupcakes to the vicar and his wife. 'This is your first May Fair in a while. Enjoy it.' She glanced towards the Carter's Cider concession and then gave Anna a gentle smile. 'Besides, I think someone's looking for you.'

Anna's cheeks started to burn as she followed the direction of Lizzie's gaze. Standing near to the Carter's Cider concession was Matthew. She had the advantage for the moment, as, though he was scanning the crowd, he was still unaware of her arrival. He was wearing his customary blue jeans, and his grey T-shirt showed off tanned muscular arms. His hair was reassuringly unkempt, falling in locks over his forehead, dark waves and silver grey streaks highlighted by the sun. He was laughing at something, and the crows' feet around his eyes deepened as he threw back his head, that miraculous grin lifting his normally serious features. Anna's heart gave a painful thump. The physical impact of him was incredible, even at this distance. She could only imagine what it would be like when there was no more space between them. They'd had so many fumbles, so many near misses; tonight, there would be nothing to keep them apart.

'Earth to Anna, come in, Anna!' Charlotte's voice snapped her out of her reverie and very much into the present. 'Are you going to stand there all day ogling Mr Carter, or are you actually going to go over there and save him from the village gargoyles?'

Anna jumped back into the present. 'Um, yeah, right. Come on Ellie.' Taking her daughter's hand again, she strolled in Matthew's direction. When she was about fifteen yards away, Ellie spotted Matthew and broke free of Anna, sprinting the short distance towards him.

'Hey, titch!' Matthew picked Ellie up and gave her a kiss on the forehead. 'How are you doing?'

'Good,' Ellie squeaked.

'And did you bring your mother with you today or are you here alone?'

Ellie giggled and pointed. 'Mummy's over there.'

With Ellie still in his arms, Matthew turned to where the little girl was pointing and Anna's heart skipped yet another beat. They were standing in sunlight, both smiling, and for a moment Anna was torn between love and heartbreak. It wasn't that she hadn't seen Matthew pick Ellie up before, indeed, he'd carried the little girl to bed a few times, but watching them together, the past and the present collided. Ellie's evident pleasure in Matthew's company reminded her unbearably of what the little girl had lost when James had been taken from them, and despite her desire to greet Matthew, she stood frozen, unable to reconcile her feelings of hope and loss.

'Are you OK?' Charlotte said gently.

Anna swallowed. 'Fine.'

'Hello, stranger,' Matthew's smile softened as he grew nearer. 'Glad you could make it.'

'Hi,' Anna said, raising onto her tiptoes for the proffered kiss. She hoped her face didn't betray how unsettled she was.

'Looks like a good crowd here,' Matthew said. 'I'd better give Andy a ring and get him to bring down a few more kegs.'

Anna looked around again. Trade was picking up at the Carter's stand, due to the already warm temperature. 'Half the village'll be horizontal in the exhibition tent at this rate!'

'As will I, potentially,' Matthew grimaced good-naturedly. 'I've been asked to judge the best homemade wine entries.'

'Christ!' Charlotte said. 'The vicar had that dubious honour last year and he ended up wearing Miss Pinkham's prize begonias as a toupee!'

'And hello to you too, Charlotte,' Matthew grinned back at her. 'I hope you'll be on hand to help Anna carry me home in the event of too much homemade hooch.'

'Don't count on it,' Charlotte replied. 'I've got Simon to keep on the straight and narrow, and that's no easy task, especially if he gets near your concession.'

She searched the crowd for her husband and son, who'd come along earlier to try to beat the inevitable crowds near the rides. 'I think I can see Evan on the death slide,' she said. 'I'd better go and show some motherly support.' And with that, she headed off into the crowd.

'She's on good form,' Matthew remarked, putting a fidgeting Ellie back on her feet.

'When is she not?' Anna said. 'She ought to go on the comedy circuit.'

'Want to see the ponies,' Ellie said, taking Anna's hand and trying to drag her towards the pony rides. With a jolt, Anna realised Matthew had taken Ellie's other hand.

'Everything OK?' Matthew asked, seeing Anna's brief hesitation.

Anna gave herself a mental shake and smiled. 'Fine. Shall we go and see these ponies?'

Matthew smiled back. 'Meredith's been roped into helping with the pony rides, so it wouldn't be a bad idea to check in. But hang on a minute.' He let go of Ellie's hand and walked back up to the Carter's concession. Rummaging in his pocket for a five pound note, he grabbed two bottles of Carter's Vintage Cider and popped the tops on the bottle opener by the stall.

'Aren't you entitled to a freebie?' Anna asked as he came back to her.

'Not in public!' Matthew replied. 'Excuse the presumption, but I really wanted you to try this current vintage blend, and, as you say, it's getting warm.'

Keeping hold of the other bottle, he drew closer to Anna and gently placed the neck of it to her lips. Automatically, she closed a hand around his as he tilted it so that the sweet, earthy liquid fizzed over her tongue. It tasted of summer, warmth and promises, and as Anna swallowed, her eyes never wavering from Matthew's, the hair rose on the back of her neck.

'What do you think?' Matthew said softly, eyes suddenly burning with intensity.

Anna licked her lips as she drew away from the bottle. 'Wonderful.'

'Want to see the ponies, Mummy!' Ellie repeated, taking matters very much into her own hands.

Anna tore her gaze from Matthew's and smiled down at her little daughter. 'Come on then,' she said. But the taste of Matthew's cider still lingered on her lips.

The three of them headed over the village green to where three plump Shetlands and a Welsh Cob were tethered.

'Hey, Dad, Anna, Munchkin!' Meredith greeted the three as they approached. 'I wouldn't go for a ride on Spotty, she's being a real bit— um, naughty pony today.' She shook the angry looking Shetland pony's halter in admonishment as it attempted to bite her jodhpur-clad thigh.

'Which would you suggest?' Anna asked. She eyed the dozy-looking bay cob that was tied up next to the fence.

'I'd put her on Bilbo if I were you,' Meredith replied. 'Quick, bring her over and I'll sneak her on before Katy collars you for the three quid!'

Anna grinned. 'It is all for charity, Merry, I don't mind paying.'

Meredith rolled her eyes. 'True, but Katy has a habit of pocketing the change when no one's looking.' She took the coins from Anna and popped them into the leather pouch across her hip.

Ellie was hopping with excitement as Meredith popped a hard hat on the little girl's head, and by the time she was on the dozy pony's back, she was virtually squealing.

As Meredith led the pony off for a gentle walk, Anna smiled. 'I think it's love at first sight.'

Matthew smiled down at her. 'Meredith was the same the day I put her up on Custard, her first pony. She was about the same age as Ellie. I don't think she's been as smitten with anything since, except perhaps this Flynn character.' His face clouded briefly. 'But so far he's been behaving himself.'

'He'll take care of her,' Anna said.

'He'll have me to answer to if he doesn't.'

With Ellie momentarily occupied, Anna felt Matthew's warm right hand slipping into hers. The jolt of electricity as they touched made her breath quicken. Yet again she thought about the next few hours, and a shiver went down her spine. It wasn't just the contact that made her jump; Matthew had been cautious about showing any kind of affection in public, even when they both knew word of their relationship was starting to spread, so his hand holding hers was a huge step.

As if aware of her thoughts, Matthew ducked his head and whispered in her ear. 'I think it's about time we gave those old trouts a thrill, don't you?'

'Why, Mr Carter, I don't know what you mean,' Anna teased, although the sensation of his lips brushing her ear and the side of her neck was distracting.

'Oh, I think you do,' Matthew's tone was light, but the words were loaded with promise.

'Dad, put her down, will you? You'll put me off my lunch!' Meredith's voice broke into their separate world.

Matthew laughed. 'Watch it, Meredith – you're not too old to be grounded.'

'Where *is* Merry going to be tonight?' Anna asked, suddenly aware that, in her preoccupation with Matthew spending the night at her cottage, she hadn't asked.

'She's spending the night with a mate of hers – Roseanna,' Matthew replied. 'And before you question the veracity of that assertion, I did phone Rosie's mother and father to make sure that was where she was *really* going to be.'

'Sneaky Dad!' Anna laughed, a little shocked by his forward thinking. 'Does Meredith know you did that?'

Matthew looked affronted. 'Are you suggesting I'd check out my daughter's whereabouts without telling her?'

'Well...'

'Well, you'd be right. But I can't be too careful. She's at that age.' Matthew grinned. 'Although, if she *had* been lying to me, it might have put a spanner in the works for us, of course.'

Anna's mouth went dry.

At that moment, Meredith returned with Ellie. 'Again, again!' Ellie squealed as Meredith helped her down from the saddle.

'Sorry, sweetheart, but Katy's looking over and she'll have my guts for garters if I take you round again,' Meredith said. 'But don't worry, you can come and have a ride on my pony when you next come round.'

Anna smiled. 'You're very kind, Merry. Say thank you, Ellie.' But before Ellie responded, Anna's parents emerged from the crowd, and Ellie shot off to give her granddad a cuddle.

'I'll see you later,' Anna said to the teenager. 'Thanks for being so good with her.'

''Twern't nothing, Ma'am,' Meredith doffed an imaginary cap. 'Have a good afternoon.'

As Anna turned, she saw her father chatting with Matthew.

'Very well thanks, Richard,' Matthew was saying. 'Are you all set for the weekend?'

'Absolutely,' Anna's father replied. 'It'll be good to get away for a couple of days. We'd better push on, though, beat the traffic.'

'Oh, bugger!' Anna said, clapping a hand to her mouth. 'I forgot to bring Ellie's overnight bag with me. It's still in the hallway.'

'Must have had something else on your mind,' Charlotte, who'd just arrived back with Evan, muttered.

'Don't worry,' Anna's mother smiled. 'I've got my copy of your house key. We'll pop in on the way through and get it.'

'Thanks, Mum,' Anna sighed. 'It must have been all the worry about the cupcakes for the stall.' She didn't dare look in Charlotte's direction. Charlotte, thankfully, seemed preoccupied with keeping Evan away from Spotty's restless hooves.

'See you soon,' Matthew said, smiling.

And with that, Matthew and Anna were alone, albeit in a crowd of villagers, well-wishers and May Fair revellers.

Chapter 19

'I still can't believe you made it through the homemade wine competition!' Anna said. 'Your fellow judge was looking decidedly unsteady on her feet by the end of it.'

'Ah yes, the Lady Mayor,' Matthew grinned. 'She, unlike myself, made the mistake of actually swallowing the stuff.'

'What?' Anna nearly spat out the contents of her own glass. 'You mean you were *faking* trying all that parsnip and elderflower home brew?'

Matthew raised an eyebrow and poured them both another glass of red. 'If I'd actually drunk any of it, I certainly wouldn't be sitting here now. You'd have been digging me out of one of the barrows.'

'Isn't that a little dishonest?' Anna said, taking a sip of her newly replenished wine. 'After all, how do you know Sid Porter's bottle was the best?'

Matthew leaned forward. 'I had the dubious honour of tasting it at the village Christmas party last year. Believe me, he has the monopoly on home brewing – tries everything out on his Old Spots before bottling it. It's what gives the pork its unique flavour.' His eyes twinkled in the candlelight.

'You're awful,' Anna scolded gently.

'I know, but that dinner was fantastic,' Matthew said. He leaned back in his chair again and gave a satisfied sigh.

'Merry's always telling me how you keep forgetting to eat.'

'Well, I'm glad, for once, that she did, if it gets me some more meals like that!' Matthew chuckled. He pushed back the chair. 'Can I help you with the washing up?'

'It's fine,' Anna replied. 'There's not much to do.' Standing up, she leaned over Matthew to grab his plate. Before she could take it, his hand closed around her wrist. As his fingers traced a pattern on her palm, Anna shivered.

'Then leave it,' he said huskily.

Anna laughed nervously. 'I can't bear to face it in the morning.'

Matthew sighed and released her wrist. 'Oh, all right then, but you can at least allow me to make you some coffee.'

'It's a deal,' Anna replied, pointing him in the direction of the right cupboard.

A weighty, suggestive silence descended, interrupted only by the clink of plates in the sink, and the rattle of coffee cups. As the seconds passed, Anna's stomach fluttered nervously. She could feel Matthew's eyes boring into her back as she glanced up from washing the dishes. Her hands started to tremble.

'Matthew...'

'Are you OK?' he asked, seeing her odd expression.

'I... I *think* so. It's just...'

In a heartbeat, Matthew was next to her. 'It's all right. We go at your pace, as always. I promise you, if you want me to leave now, or to stay just for a little while... whatever you want is fine by me.'

Anna smiled. 'What right have I to have been blessed with someone so patient?' She took a step towards him. 'It's been a long time...' Gently she ran a fingertip down Matthew's cheek, over his lips and down his neck.

Softly, Matthew took hold of her hand and brought it to his cheek. He took a step towards her, so close she could smell the intoxicating scent of his English Fern cologne. Her heart began to beat faster, breath shortening, eyes widening.

'I'm not used to this,' Anna whispered. 'You're the first since...'

'I know,' Matthew replied softly. 'And believe me when I say I will be very, very gentle with you. If you want me to be.'

Matthew's proximity, the quiver in his voice, the warmth radiating from his skin was making Anna yearn for him to be anything but gentle. She stared at his large, long-fingered hands, tanned from all of the time he'd spent outside, and trembled. The words spoken by the pagans at the May Fair that afternoon suddenly came back to her:

> *Let all things live with loving intent*
> *And to fulfil their truest destiny*

Was this her destiny? she wondered. Was *he* her destiny? If looking at Matthew's hands was enough to make her pulse beat, she could only imagine what it would be like to have him touch her. She was reminded of warm things, dark things, anything but gentle things.

They were within a breath of each other. He'd backed her up against the kitchen units so there was nowhere else she could go, not that she wanted to. He filled her vision and intoxicated her senses. As his mouth hovered over hers, for a split second she savoured the anticipation of his kiss, until their lips met.

In one fluid gesture, Matthew pulled her to him. She felt eggshell fragile as he crushed her to his hard, rugged body. As he slid a thigh between hers, she felt herself melting, her senses awakening and responding. He kissed her like a man dying of thirst, as if he would never get enough of her. She realised then he was as parched as she was.

They made it to her bedroom in a tangle of limbs and discarded clothing, stumbling through the door and onto Anna's generous king-sized bed. In very little time they were naked. Waves of building pleasure washed over Anna as, in the half-light, she felt the solid weight of Matthew's body. Between fevered kisses, he murmured sweet nonsense in her ears, none of which made much sense but sounded core-achingly erotic in the heat of the moment.

Anna's hands traced feathery lines down Matthew's back, her fingertips delighting in the warmth and heat of his skin. Matthew moaned, and when her fingers ventured across his thighs and between his legs, his sharp intake of breath made her dizzy with her own desire. Exploring, stroking and teasing, he shuddered under her touch, hips rising to give her further freedom to discover him. For a time she could see him luxuriating in her intimate touches.

But Matthew was not a man to surrender so soon. With a gentle firmness, he pushed Anna back against the deep white pillows of her bed, and began to explore her. His tanned hands against her pale skin danced and caressed, stroking her breasts and moving slowly downwards. While his mouth was still upon hers, the attentions of his hands made her gasp into the kiss. The gentle, circling pleasure of his fingertips made her ache, and move her body even closer to allow him to feel her warmth and heat. The pleasure of sensation, so long dormant, created by months of tension and moments of touch, was nearly overwhelming, and as the tingling throb of desire became more insistent, her thighs parted further.

'Come here... now,' she whispered, her voice dark with passion.

Matthew needed no further encouragement. He slid a warm hand under her and wrapped one of her thighs around his waist. Slowly, despite the heat of their desire, mindful of the occasion, Matthew looked into Anna's eyes, waiting for her final assent.

Breathing a gentle 'Yes...' that whispered across the hollow of Matthew's throat, Anna felt him shift slightly, until he was directly above her. Gently at first, but with growing ardour, he slid inside her. The pleasure as he moved was almost unbearable. She had been on the brink, hovering on the threshold and as his movements became harder, more driven, she felt herself rising and pulsing, until the steady, rhythmic beat of her climax encapsulated all of her senses. Within moments, Matthew had reached his own peak, and as his release made him shudder, so he cried out, burying his face into Anna's shoulder as his powerful thrusts subsided.

Afterwards they lay joined, covered in sweat and enjoying the afterglow. Anna ran a hand through Matthew's dishevelled hair, caressing the back of his neck.

'Are you all right?' Matthew asked, seeing a strange expression on Anna's face.

Anna smiled. 'It's been a long time...'

'And was it worth the wait?' he said, an indulgent yet slightly roguish smile on his face.

'What do you think?' Anna tilted her head and kissed Matthew's lips again, but this time it was a tender, sated kiss. After the passion, she felt peace, and safer than she had for a long time.

As Matthew moved to lie beside her, she snuggled into his chest and felt the old, familiar drowsiness overcome her.

'You don't have to go anywhere, do you?' she asked sleepily.

'Not if you don't want me to,' he replied, placing a kiss on the top of her head.

Anna's sleep was long, uninterrupted, and the best she'd had in over two years.

Chapter 20

By Sunday lunchtime, they were still in bed. They seemed to unleash something in each other. Perhaps it was the knowledge that time was limited, but last night's intensity gave way to a much more playful mood, which left them sated and giggly.

Stretching out his long frame in Anna's bed, Matthew let out a satisfied sigh. 'Why did we not get round to this sooner?' He pulled Anna closer.

'Oh, I think we're making up for lost time now!' Anna smiled, listening to the mesmeric beat of Matthew's heart. Idly, her fingers played with the dark curls on his chest.

'You can say that again.' Matthew dropped a kiss on the top of her head. 'I haven't felt this relaxed in ages.'

'What time's Merry due back?' Anna asked, unable, quite, to shrug off all parental responsibility.

'She texted me earlier, saying Rosie's parents are taking them both out to lunch, so I expect she'll be back home mid-afternoon.'

'Do you think she'll mind that you spent the night here?'

Matthew gazed up at the whitewashed ceiling of Anna's bedroom, watching the shadows from the horse chestnut tree outside the window dappling the paintwork. 'I shouldn't think so,' he said mildly. 'She's been positively encouraging it.'

Anna giggled. 'She keeps making jokes about me being her wicked stepmother!'

'Well, you're most certainly wicked, my darling, but are you sure you're ready to be thrust into the role of stepmother just yet?'

Propping herself up on one elbow, Anna met his gaze. 'I think we both might need a bit of time to think that one through!'

'Perhaps you're right,' Matthew said. 'As I'm singularly unable to think about anything else at the moment than the feel of your gorgeous body against mine, we'll leave more weighty discussion for another time, shall we?' He shifted so he was looking down at her, and Anna yet again marvelled at the way he was able to turn her insides to liquid just by being close to her. It took her another half a second to realise that Matthew was also proving more than ready to resume where they'd left off.

Sometime later, drifting in and out of sleep, Anna lay thinking, again, about how much her life had altered over the past year. After the immediate pain of James' death had begun to subside, she'd been left with a kind of all-pervading numbness. Now, lying in bed with Matthew, she realised that since she'd met him, she was reawakening. She had no idea what the future held, but for once in her life, she didn't care. This moment was all that mattered. As Matthew's breathing became more regular, she wished she could stop the march of time.

*

That week, with Meredith away at the Model UN conference, Matthew became a regular feature at Pippin Cottage. He dropped in, with Sefton at his heels, after he'd finished work. For the first three nights, the customary glass of wine had extended into the night, with Matthew falling into Anna's bed and both of them giggling like teenagers. He'd risen before Ellie and sneaked out of the door in last night's clothes, heading back home for a shower and a change before starting work once again.

On the third morning, Ellie had looked her mother in the eye and asked point blank why Matthew never had breakfast with them.

'Would you like him to?' Anna had asked, trying to hide her astonishment.

'Yes,' Ellie had replied instantly. 'And want breakfast with Merry, too.'

*

'I think she must have spotted you without us realising it,' Anna said that evening. She grinned ruefully. 'And there I was, thinking we were being so careful and clever.'

'Well, she's obviously not worried,' Matthew smiled. 'Or she wouldn't have been so matter of fact about it.' He shook his head and refilled their wine glasses. 'Sometimes these daughters of ours are two steps ahead of us, aren't they?'

'I suppose I didn't want to confuse her,' Anna said. 'I mean, if things don't work out between us…'

Matthew put his wine glass down and took Anna's from her. Very gently, he took her face in his hands, and placed a kiss on her lips, so feather-light she was unsure she'd even felt it. As the kiss deepened, she was lost, yet again, in the moment.

'Sometimes I think we worry too much,' he said. 'Ellie's seeing things in very black and white terms; perhaps we should do the same.' He smoothed a lock of hair back from Anna's eyes. 'Let's take each day as it comes, shall we?'

Anna was surprised at his lack of circumspection; he'd

been cautious for so long, and now he seemed prepared to take risks in the name of their relationship. 'OK. But she does ask a lot of questions when she first wakes up, and we might get invaded at an ungodly hour of the morning at times!'

Matthew grinned. 'I can deal with that,' he said. 'In fact, it makes me a bit nostalgic for when Meredith was that age and still wanted to curl up in bed with me. Tara could never tolerate it, but Meredith spent quite a few mornings snuggled up next to me when it was just the two of us.'

'You might regret saying that when she's kicking you in the back!' Anna laughed.

'Oh, I think I'll cope,' Matthew put an arm around Anna.

The next morning, Matthew poured Ellie some cornflakes as Anna made him a cup of tea.

Chapter 21

May progressed sultry and humid. On the Sunday of the second Bank Holiday weekend, much to Meredith's amusement and Anna's concern, and despite his previous assertions to the contrary about the state of his knee, Matthew had committed himself to playing for Carter's in a charity rugby match against the local bitter producer, Framptons. As the morning of the match dawned, the weather was bright, breezy and warm. The match was taking place at a club two villages away, situated equidistantly between the two businesses. Weeks of dry weather had flattened out the pitch, but a last minute deluge of rain had made the top of it like glass.

As Matthew pulled into the club's car park, Anna, Meredith and Ellie were in the now fixed Land Rover with him in rising apprehension and anticipation. Seeing several of the Framptons players already warming up on the sidelines, Anna's stomach lurched. Apart from one or two old dogs, with slight paunches and battle scars, they all looked in remarkably good shape.

Quite a few supporters had already massed behind the lines as well, and Anna spotted the friends and families of some of Matthew's employees who had signed up to play. She wished Charlotte had been able to come, but she, Simon and Evan had gone to Simon's parents for the weekend.

'Are you quite sure about this?' she asked Matthew for the hundredth time.

Matthew laughed. 'You make it sound like I'm going to be facing a firing squad. I might be deluded but I'm not daft! I'll be on for twenty minutes, max.'

'You'd better be,' Meredith replied. 'Apart from the social embarrassment of seeing my dad in shorts, I don't really want to end up hanging around A and E this afternoon.'

Anna, who actually rather relished the prospect of seeing Matthew in his rugby kit, suppressed a grin.

'Looks like you can get a drink in the clubhouse if you want one,' Matthew said as he slammed the door of the Land Rover. 'I'd better go and rally the troops, if you three will be OK by yourselves.' Giving Anna and Meredith quick kisses, and ruffling Ellie's hair, he strode off to meet his teammates.

'He's such a saddo,' Meredith gave Anna a sidelong glance. 'You know he's only doing this to impress you, don't you?'

'Don't be daft,' Anna replied. 'At our age, we're a bit beyond putting ourselves in physical danger to impress each other.'

'Whatever you say, but according to Jen, his PA, since he agreed to do this game he's been jogging between buildings at work – so it's either a midlife crisis or *someone's* having an influence.'

'Is Flynn coming over today?' Anna asked, desperate to change the subject.

'You know he is,' Meredith said. 'You asked me that yesterday, and the day before, and the day before that...'

'Oh, OK!' Anna grinned. 'I guess I'm just a bit nervous for your dad, that's all!'

'In fact, I think I can see him over by the goal line,' Meredith scanned the crowds. 'Do you mind if I...'

'Not at all,' Anna was secretly relieved. She was far more worried about Matthew than she was letting on, and she needed a moment or two to collect her own thoughts, Ellie excluded. 'I'll see if I can get a place under the canopy in the shade.'

'Fair enough, see you later.' Meredith bounded off, leggy and gazelle-like across the field.

'Want to go with Merry,' Ellie grumbled.

'You'll see her later, darling,' Anna replied. 'Shall we go and get something to drink?' Taking her daughter's hand, she strolled across to the clubhouse, smiling at Patrick Flanagan as she passed him. Patrick was the coach for the Carters team, and was taking things very seriously, checking off each player's name on a piece of paper on his clipboard.

'Joel, is Kev on his way?' Anna heard Patrick ask as the young packer sidled past him.

'Yeah Paddy, chill, man. He was stuck on the M5 when I rang him but he reckoned he was near the exit.'

Patrick shook his head. 'Should've got that minibus sorted,' he muttered. 'Bloody boy racers wanting to bring their own motors everywhere.'

Anna found a place under the canopy by the bar, and sipped a bottle of Carters own Eloise variety cider in an attempt to calm her nerves as she waited for the kick-off.

First came the Framptons team. They were a variety of shapes and sizes, ranging in age from around twenty to forty. Their orange shirts showed up vibrantly against the stinging green of the cut grass, and, for one member of the team at least, clashed with his hangover red face. They were laughing and joking together, kicking out their legs and talking last minute strategy. Then came the opposition from Carters, dressed in royal blue and forest green shirts, reflecting the corporate colours. Anna spotted Joel the packer, and one or two other young players, a smattering in their mid-thirties, and then one or two older men, including, somewhere in the middle of the team but head and shoulders above most of them, Matthew.

Anna couldn't help staring. For a man over forty, he knew how to work a rugby shirt, and his white shorts showed off tanned, muscular legs. Feeling a tingle of lust, Anna momentarily forgot her concerns for Matthew's safety and simply enjoyed the view.

After the obligatory pleasantries, the match kicked off. Not being entirely familiar with the game, Anna couldn't work out what was going on for a lot of it, but she could see Matthew was getting well into the fray, and was fairly certain he managed to set up a few of the points being scored. After the first fifteen minutes or so, she started to relax, knowing his stint would be over soon.

About fifteen minutes into the first half, it was clear that the Framptons players were taking things more seriously than their cider-producing counterparts; far more blue and green shirts seemed to be hitting the deck than orange ones. As Anna felt the first prickle of unease on the back of her neck, Meredith slid up beside her, hand in hand with Flynn.

'Hey, you two,' Anna smiled, to hide her concern. 'Looks like it's going to be an exciting match, even if I don't have a clue what's going on!'

Flynn nodded. 'It's pretty full on.'

'Flynn plays on the wing for the school seniors,' Meredith said proudly. 'I've seen him play once or twice.'

Anna nodded. 'Matthew's quite impressed with that, I think!'

Meredith rolled her eyes. 'Not that you'd know it. He's barely spoken to Flynn yet!'

'He looks pretty knackered out there,' Flynn was scanning the players on the pitch. 'He can't have much longer, surely?'

'Patrick agreed to take him off after twenty minutes,'

Anna replied. 'He'll be back on the bench soon.'

At that moment, there was a shrill peep from the referee's whistle and a collective groan from the assembled Carters supporters. Gradually, players stopped running and collected around a crumpled figure. The course medic jogged onto the pitch.

'What's happened? Who is it?' Anna strained to see.

'Can't see at the moment. Oh, hang on, they're getting back to give the medic a bit of room.' Flynn had his arm around Meredith now, trying to stop her from racing onto the pitch.

Heart in her mouth, Anna peered through the crowd of players. She could see the injured man lying on the ground, but still couldn't make out who it was. Then, as the players got back to their places, she saw Matthew. He was on the ground next to the injured player, chatting to him, obviously trying to keep him calm as the medic performed his assessment. Anna felt weak with relief.

'It's Joel,' Meredith said, filling in the last piece of the puzzle. 'God, his leg looks bad.'

Joel was still on the ground, knee twisted at a hideous angle, face green with pain.

'Well, it was a bit of a hospital pass,' Flynn replied. 'It's a wonder his leg's not broken.'

As they watched, the medic beckoned to his colleague, and with brisk efficiency they stretchered Joel off to the sidelines. After a quick, reassuring word with Joel, Patrick Flanagan strode out onto the pitch and conferred with the rest of his players. There were one or two nods of assent, including one from Matthew, and then they were in play again.

*

Some minutes later, the knot of anxiety tightened in Anna's stomach even further as Matthew, sweating profusely in his rugby top, jogged back up to the home end.

'Isn't it about time he came off?'

'You know Dad,' Meredith said, biting her lip.

They both watched as Matthew picked up a bottle of water that was thrown from the sidelines and took a deep pull. He was breathing heavily, wiping the sweat from his face with a grubby forearm.

'Do you think I should go and talk to him?' Anna asked.

'I think he'll probably tell you where to go if you do!' Meredith forced a smile. 'You know how stubborn he is. With Joel out, he's going to want to stay on.'

'But this is insane! You said he hasn't played for over twenty years. Some of those guys on the other team are half his age!' Anna made to move away to the other end of the pitch, but Meredith's hand on her arm stopped her.

'Seriously, Anna, we have to let him do this. He signed up for it. If he messes up, we can pick up the pieces later.'

The seconds were ticking down, and Anna and Meredith knew Matthew only had to get through ten more minutes more at most. He'd covered the pitch end to end countless times; even managed to convert one or two tries. But he was spent, and from his gait they could tell his knee was giving him hell. Jogging back up the pitch, Matthew was faced with a scrum of younger, fitter players. Somehow he got the ball out, began to run for goal. Anna and Meredith willed him on, along with the collective yells of the Carters supporters.

'He's going to do it!' Meredith screamed. 'He's going to do it! Come on, Dad!' Jumping up and down, she clutched Anna, both of them caught up in the excitement of the scene unfolding before them.

Matthew thundered up the pitch, racing for the try that

would put his team ahead. Seeming to summon every last shred of willpower he had, he strained towards the line. And then, suddenly, inexplicably, ten feet from victory he hit a wall. Going down, tackled by a young whelp from Framptons, his knee finally gave in. With a roar that screamed of pain and frustration, he met the ground hard, breaking his fall with his right wrist and surrendering the ball. Anna and Meredith held onto each other, united in panic.

The Framptons defender shoved the ball back down the line, and play moved on for a few seconds, until the ref blew his whistle. Jogging over to where Matthew was struggling to his feet, the player responsible for the tackle thrust out a hand and helped Matthew up.

'Are you all right, mate?'

Matthew, disoriented, looked at the younger man. Then he grinned. 'Great tackle, well done! Wish I still had the nerve, and the energy to take someone out like that.'

The defender looked relieved. 'Thanks. If you're sure you're OK?'

'Just wait a few months before you come and ask me for a job, all right?' Matthew began to move away, but his knee creaked in protest. Limping to the sidelines, he beckoned to Patrick. 'Think I'm done here, Paddy.'

Patrick nodded, partly in relief, partly in exasperation. 'Is your knee OK?'

'Yeah, but my wrist is fucked.'

'We'll get the medic to look you over. Get to the First Aid van before you get in the shower.'

Meredith, Anna and Ellie, with Flynn trailing diplomatically in their wake, had raced up the sidelines, ready to escort Matthew, kicking and screaming if necessary, down to the First Aider.

'Dad!' Meredith careered into Matthew.

'I'm all right, don't be so melodramatic,' Matthew murmured, kissing the top of her head. Reaching out his good arm, he put it around his daughter. Anna stood back a little, unsure how to react.

'You promised me you'd only do a bit of it, and you've been on for virtually the whole game!' Meredith's voice was trembling with anger and relief.

'I know, sweetheart, but it seemed the right thing to do,' he shook his head. 'I'd have made it, too, if I'd been a bit quicker!'

'You did great,' Anna found her voice. 'But I think someone needs to look at that wrist.'

Matthew nodded and, very carefully, reached out and wrapped his injured arm around her shoulders. 'Let's get it over and done with, and then you can stretcher me off to die in a corner somewhere!'

After a quick check in with the medic, who confirmed a bad sprain and thankfully not a break, Matthew chucked on a hooded top and waited for the presentation.

*

'You nearly gave Meredith a coronary, you know,' Anna chided that evening.

'I thought she was more worried about me having one,' Matthew winced as he picked up his glass of red. 'But she must have been a little bit proud of me, too.'

'Maybe,' Anna said. 'But you might need to make that your last game, if you want to spare us all further injury!'

Matthew sighed. 'I think I just wanted to prove to everyone I wasn't past it. Some hope!'

'To everyone, or to yourself?' Anna asked gently. 'You don't have to prove anything to Meredith. Or me.' She turned so

Matthew could see her expression. 'We think you're amazing, just the way you are.'

Matthew leaned forward and placed a gentle kiss on her lips. 'You are very, very good for an old man's bruised ego,' he said huskily. 'Why did you wait so long to come back into my life?'

Anna smiled. 'Perhaps timing is everything.' She snuggled back against him.

'Christ, I'm going to be a wreck tomorrow,' Matthew muttered, shifting on the sofa. 'I'd better get off to bed soon and lick my wounds.'

'I'd offer to do it for you, but Meredith's expecting you back tonight at some point. She'll only worry if you don't come home.'

Matthew sighed. 'You're right, as always. I guess I'd better get an extra grovelling session in with her before she goes to sleep.' He checked his watch. 'But she won't be expecting me back for a while yet.' His eyes met Anna's, and he gave a school-boyish, suggestive grin.

'Are you sure you're up to it?' Anna asked. 'After all, you've been in the wars a bit today.'

'Oh, I wouldn't worry about that,' Matthew murmured. 'I can assure you that all necessary parts are unscathed and in perfect working order.' Taking Anna's wine glass out of her hand, he put both glasses safely down on the table beside the sofa.

'I'll be the judge of that,' Anna said playfully. She moved off the sofa and positioned herself in front of Matthew, sliding in between his legs. She ran her hands underneath Matthew's untucked blue T-shirt, raising it slightly so she could see the full extent of the damage he'd inflicted on himself. A variety of lividly coloured bruises dappled his torso, dotted from ribcage to waist, with a smattering of circular red stud marks for good measure.

'I'll never understand the attraction of rugby,' she murmured. Exchanging hands for lips, she very gently began to kiss Matthew's exposed and sore flesh, working her way from the highest point of the first bruise downwards. Matthew shifted on the sofa, his breathing becoming shallower. Teasingly, she ran her tongue over the stud marks on his abdomen, feeling the roughness of the lacerated skin. 'Let me know if I hurt you,' she said.

Increasing the pressure of her mouth on one particularly nasty bruise, he flinched.

'That's a little tender,' he murmured.

'Consider that a reminder not to rush back to the pitch,' Anna looked up.

'Harlot.'

Running her hands back down Matthew's abdomen, Anna's mouth hovered suggestively over the exposed skin by the waistband of his jeans. Placing one hand on each of his thighs, she slid her hands up the inside seams of his jeans, and further upwards, feeling Matthew raise his hips in response.

'Now this is the kind of medical attention I like,' Matthew said, a tremor of desire in his voice.

'So you're in full working order, are you?' Anna teased. She began to unbutton the fly of his jeans, the sting of her own desire becoming deep-rooted as she breathed in his scent. Her warm hands soon found what they were looking for, and Matthew shifted back in his seat, legs parting. Her lips quickly joined her hands in their explorations, and as she stroked, tasted and teased, Matthew's left, uninjured hand ran slowly through her hair.

'Yes,' he sighed, 'Very much yes...'

As Anna caressed and stroked with hands, lips and tongue,

Matthew lay back and surrendered to the sensations.

'I see what you mean,' she said as she paused for a moment in her ministrations. 'Nothing injured here.'

'You have no idea how good you are at that...' Matthew trailed off again as Anna resumed her caresses. Soon he was drawing deep, ragged breaths, hips thrusting upwards, guiding Anna towards where he desperately needed to go. Anna moved with him, their rhythm driving him on until he shuddered, gave a throaty moan and came.

Kneeling between his thighs, Anna looked up at him from under her lashes. Matthew's head was thrown back, his eyes were closed and sweat glistened on his forehead. Anna felt a rush of pure, unadulterated lust. She'd never have admitted it in a million years, but bringing such a man to a shuddering climax, tasting him on her lips, gave her an unbelievable erotic charge.

After a long, delicious, self-indulgent moment of observation, Anna got up and took a deep pull from her wine glass. 'You were right,' she said mischievously. 'You're clearly fine where it counts!' She sat back on the sofa beside him, luxuriating in their closeness as Matthew put an arm around her. 'I could get used to this,' she said softly.

'So could I.'

'Which part?'

'All of it.' Suddenly serious, Matthew leaned down and kissed Anna's lips. 'You are the best treatment for bruises I know.'

Anna smiled. She might not have any physical scars, but there was no doubt her emotional ones were healing. 'You're not so bad yourself.' Breaking away from his kiss, she pulled back to look him in the eye. 'And much as I'd love you to stay the night, you really should get going.'

Matthew kissed her again, then, heaving himself up from

the sofa, he groaned. 'I might need you to walk me home, after all.'

'No can do, Mike Tindall!' Anna laughed. 'Sefton'll have to be your guide dog tonight.'

'I'll see you soon,' Matthew said as they walked to the door.

Standing on the doorstep, watching him amble out into the night, Anna knew for sure something she had suspected for a little while. Seeing Matthew injured on the rugby pitch that afternoon had made it fall into place even more. As he turned the corner and headed back to his house, and his daughter, Anna knew she couldn't deny it any longer. She was falling in love with him.

SUMMER

Chapter 22

The apple blossom in the orchards was already fluttering to the grass as May turned to June. Anna had been successful in sorting out the tea shop's accounts, and she was already wondering if Brian and Ursula would consider extending her appointment beyond the year she'd signed on for. She was finding the routine of the tea shop, and the baking, really therapeutic, and it already felt as though she'd been doing it far longer than she had. Lizzie was a capable and dependable waitress, and their shift patterns had, so far, worked out very smoothly. There had been one minor hiccup when the electricity had gone off after Western Power had drilled through an underground cable line, but with the help of the gas kettle and the patience of her regulars, she'd got through it. The same couldn't be said of the batch of gooseberry and elderflower cupcakes she'd had in the oven at the time, but Lizzie's pet bantams had enjoyed them the next day.

After a particularly hectic shift, Anna decided she would take a chance and pop in on Matthew on the way back home. A month ago she wouldn't have dreamed of infringing on his workspace, but since the May Fair, she felt a little more comfortable with testing the old, established barriers. Gathering up a couple of the remaining slices of fruited tea loaf that wouldn't survive until the next day, at five o'clock she did her final check around the tables, hung up her green apron on the hook by the kitchen door, cashed up and locked the tea shop. She had to pick Ellie up from nursery in twenty minutes, but she figured she had just about enough time to walk down to the Carter's Cider offices first, if she picked up her pace.

Jen, Matthew's PA, smiled as Anna entered the outer office. About to go home, she handed Anna Matthew's cup of coffee that he'd requested, with a smile and an efficient apology. Anna knocked on Matthew's door and then pushed it open.

'Thanks, Jen – can you just stick it on my desk?'

'Hey,' Anna said softly. 'Isn't it about time you took a break?'

Matthew looked up in surprise. 'I don't know which I'm happier to see more, you or that coffee you're holding.' He got up from his desk, took the coffee out of Anna's hands, popped it down on the windowsill and took her in his arms.

'I'll take that as a compliment,' Anna said as Matthew pulled her close to him. He was dressed in dark pinstriped trousers and a white shirt, the sleeves of which were rolled up. On some men, the smart attire would have seemed incongruous, given his propensity to dress in jeans and a jumper, but Matthew had the stature and grace to carry off the suit beautifully. Anna felt the crispness of his shirt under her fingers as she placed a hand on his chest.

'God, I've missed you,' Matthew murmured into her hair.

'It's only been a day or two,' Anna replied, surprised by his admission.

'Has it? It feels like years.' He planted a kiss on her lips. It was brief, but enough to set her heart racing. 'This American deal is making my eyes bleed. I can't believe how much detail there is to go through.'

'Anything I can do to help?' Anna asked.

'I don't think so,' Matthew replied. 'One of the benefits of my legal studies is that I can interpret the jargon myself, without having to pay some hotshot legal team to do it for me. Although, of course, I do have a *proper* solicitor on board to make sure I'm not getting too out of touch!' He gave a laugh that wasn't entirely one of levity.

'Do you regret not practising?' Anna asked, surprised Matthew had made reference to his past career choice.

'Sometimes,' he said. 'But it couldn't be helped. Life has a habit of dealing the cards in the way you least expect.' He shook his head. 'But that's a conversation for another time.' He paused, then brightened. 'Meredith's away tonight; Duke of Edinburgh Award overnight expedition, I think. Perhaps I could...' he dropped his head and started to kiss Anna's neck.

Anna groaned, partly in pleasure and partly in frustration. 'I'd love that, but no can do. It's Charlotte and Simon's wedding anniversary and I'm having Evan for the night.'

'Understood,' Matthew replied. 'Just try not to think of me all alone, lying in my bed, wanting you...' He kissed her lips again, slowly, teasingly.

Anna pressed herself against Matthew and felt him harden in response to her. He ran a hand down her back, drawing her closer. She pulled his shirt tails out and touched the bare flesh of his chest.

'Do you have any... idea... what you do to me?' Matthew groaned.

'I'm getting the picture,' Anna murmured. She stood on tiptoe and kissed Matthew's neck, delighted as he arched closer to her. She gasped as Matthew manoeuvred her so her back was against the wall, his hands running all over her, seeking entrance through her clothes to the warmth of her body. One thigh either side of hers, he kissed her, making both of them gasp. For a moment Anna luxuriated in the sensations, pulling him closer and stroking the bare skin under his shirt. She could feel how aroused he was through the lambswool pinstripe of his trousers, and allowed herself to push back against him, meeting his hardness with her own soft, yielding body.

'Steady on,' Anna murmured, pulling back regretfully after a moment or two. 'I've got to go and get Ellie from nursery in a minute.'

Matthew groaned again, in frustration and amusement. 'So you've just come here to inflame my lust and then leave me.' He ran a hand through his dishevelled hair. 'And it's no good, anyway, I've got at least three more hours chained to my desk before I can get away.' He grinned. 'It would be a whole lot easier if you didn't make me feel like a horny teenager every time you came near me!'

Anna laughed. 'I'm flattered I have that effect on you.' Buttoning up her cardigan, which Matthew had managed to pull open, she kissed the tip of his nose. 'Don't work too late.'

'I'll be lucky if I can concentrate at all after that!'

'See you soon,' Anna said, handing Matthew his coffee from the windowsill.

'I'd better,' he replied, tucking his shirt back in. He raised a hand to Anna's cheek. 'Now go home before I lock the door and don't let you out until you've made good on your teasing!'

*

Anna was just about to turn in for the night, safe in the knowledge that Ellie and Evan were fast asleep when there was a tap at the living room window. Jumping in fright, she relaxed when she saw Matthew's amused face on the other side of the glass.

'What are you doing here?' she hissed as she opened the window.

'I've been thinking about you all evening,' Matthew said huskily. 'Thanks to that little stunt you pulled in my office,

I've been craving either a cold shower or a roll in the hay for hours now. And I blame you entirely!'

'Well, you'll have to go for the cold shower,' Anna said. 'Evan's a light sleeper and it would traumatise him for life if he walked in on the two of us in flagrante.'

'Then lock the living room door, and bloody well let me in!' Matthew said. He started to open the window further.

'You're not seriously going to come through that window, are you?' Anna laughed. 'Are you insane?'

'Absolutely mad,' Matthew replied. 'Mostly with lust, so get over there and lock that door.'

Somehow, Matthew made it through the window in one piece and hastily pulled the curtains. Anna padded out to the hallway and listened. Hearing nothing out of the ordinary from the children upstairs, she crept back into the lounge. No sooner had she turned the key than Matthew had grabbed hold of her and was kissing the life out of her.

'You are entirely too delicious to be legal,' Matthew murmured between kisses. 'And all I've been able to think about, when I should have been concentrating on the US distribution, is ripping off your clothes and having you on your living room rug.'

'I can see how that might be a problem,' Anna replied, hastily unbuttoning Matthew's dishevelled white shirt. 'After all, you need to give that deal your full... ah... attention.'

'Damned right I do,' Matthew said, kissing Anna's neck and then pulling her jersey over her head. 'And yet I find I'm thinking more about what I'd like to do to you, how I'd like to part your thighs and get between them... aah... than the most recent... sales... projections... oh God...'

'So really... you were duty-bound to come over here and... focus on one thing at a time.' Anna whispered. She wriggled out of her jeans and then reached for the fly of Matthew's trousers. Hastily he stepped out of them and they collapsed on the rug by the fireside. Anna pushed Matthew back against the hearth rug and wrapped her legs around him. She began to move, arching her back as he slid into her.

'How can I ever concentrate on anything when all I can think of is this?' Matthew groaned. 'You make work impossible.' He grabbed her hips and ground her down closer to him, thrusting further and deeper. As he began to quicken his pace, he rocked her backwards and forwards, until with a stifled cry, he came.

For a moment, neither spoke. Then, Anna raised her head to look at him. She brushed a lock of silvery black hair from his sweaty forehead.

'I'm sorry,' Matthew said. 'That was selfish of me. Come down here.' He began to caress her, until the circling motions of his fingers were driving her towards the edge of her own orgasm. His feather-light touches increased in pressure until the pleasure within her reached a peak, and as the throbbing warmth gave way to a shuddering climax, Anna lay back and rode the waves, thrusting her hips towards his expert fingers.

A little time later, when they'd both come back down to earth, Anna grinned. 'I think we were quiet enough.'

Matthew grinned back. 'Let's hope so.' He grabbed his clothes and started to pull them back on.

'I'm not sure what it's customary to offer after your lover has climbed in through your living room window and had you, but I'll go with a cup of tea, if you want one?' Anna pulled her jersey back over her head and reached for her knickers and jeans.

Matthew grinned. 'You are lovely, but I'm parched in another way, now. Can I trouble you for a glass of water, and then I'll go back from whence I came.'

'Love me and leave me tonight, is it?' Anna quipped.

'You're the one who said Evan was a light sleeper!'

'You're right, of course. But are you sure you don't want anything else?'

Matthew gave her a knowing look. 'Nothing you can find in the kitchen, I'm afraid!'

Anna stifled a giggle and crept up the stairs to see if the children were still sleeping. Evan was snoozing peacefully, and Ellie was doing the same. Sneaking back down the stairs, she filled a glass of water and padded back to the living room. Opening the door, she could only see the top of Matthew's head just above the back of the sofa.

'Here's your water,' she said softly. As Anna approached the sofa, she could see in the firelight that Matthew was slumped, fast asleep. His face was calm, although the recent work stresses had etched deeper lines around his eyes and mouth. A lock of hair fell forward onto his forehead, but Anna resisted the urge to brush it away. She toyed with the idea of waking him, but he looked as if he needed the rest. Grabbing a blanket that was slung over the armchair by the fire, she sat on the sofa and wrapped it around them both.

Matthew stirred slightly. 'Just a couple more minutes,' he said sleepily, putting an arm around her. But within moments, he was fast asleep again.

Anna stayed awake a little while longer, but eventually she could feel her eyelids growing heavy before she, too, drifted off.

Chapter 23

'No, that's fine, Matt, there's no need for you to make another trip until we're all ready to sign the final drafts.' Chris McIvor, Head of International Distribution for FastStream, was wrapping up the conversation. The deal had been a long time coming, and Matthew was relieved.

'I'll have the contracts looked over and sent onto you by the end of the week,' Matthew said, glancing down at the paperwork on his desk, checking that the amendments he required were clearly indicated. Once again, he felt grateful he had at least spent time studying contract law, if not, in the event, practising it.

As Matthew was mulling this over, he realised that McIvor was still speaking. 'You know, Matt, I have to say, eleventh hour as his involvement was, it sure is nice to have your brother on board, too. Kind of underlines the fact that we're dealing with a family business here.'

'*What?*' Matthew nearly dropped the phone. Scrambling to keep it close to his ear, he managed to lose the pen he was holding in his other hand and heard it clatter onto the flagstones. 'I mean, yes, of course.'

'Yeah, Jonathan's a real operator, isn't he? Charmed the pants off the board when he met them.'

I'll bet he did, Matthew thought. 'I'm sure,' he managed.

'And it really impressed them, knowing the two of you had

been working so closely together behind the scenes to make this collaboration a success. I mean, you've played your cards so close to your chest on this one, it was nice to find out a little more about what really goes on on your side of the pond!'

'Great.' Matthew laughed weakly. 'I'm glad they felt that way.' He ducked under his desk to retrieve his pen. 'I'll speak to you at the end of the week, then.'

'Sure. Speak soon.'

Not for the first time, Matthew was relieved they weren't conducting the meeting by Skype. He'd really have struggled to explain how shocked he'd looked. Picking up the phone again, he dialled, took a deep breath and waited.

'It's Matthew. Come to the office. We need to talk.'

*

Anna, while grateful of the influx of students from St Jude's after school ended in the afternoon, could really have done with a breather at times. Meredith was a popular student, and since she and Flynn had got together, they had started to drop into the tea shop when their lessons ended, holding hands over 'their' table, or giggling together on one of the sofas in the corner. Inevitably, their friends had started to accompany them, and Anna found the levels of mess on the tables and floor of the shop increasing in direct proportion to her turnover.

While Meredith would often help to clear tables, she was so swept up in her newfound love for Flynn that she was just as likely to trail off after him when they'd finished their post-school snacks, leaving Anna or Lizzie, who both had children, albeit of contrasting ages, to wonder in exasperation about the state of her bedroom. On a few occasions, Matthew had, rather sheepishly, had to foot the bill for Meredith's gargantuan appetite, which, unlike Anna's, seemed in no way diminished by being in love, bringing over the cash for her purchases to Pippin Cottage later. Anna didn't mind this arrangement, although it played havoc with the cashing up, but she did wonder if her takings were likely to dive if and when Flynn and Meredith broke up.

Hearing the bell above the front door clanging, Anna braced herself for the St Jude's invasion. Sure enough, Meredith, Flynn and a troupe of their friends barrelled through the door, blue striped shirts untucked, trailing school bags and folders and chattering non-stop.

'It was so, like, not like that!' said Meredith, simultaneously smiling at Flynn and waving at Anna. 'I was only talking to Jess to tell her the best way to answer the question, wasn't I, Jess? And Ms Bradshaw gave me a behaviour log for it.' Flumping down on the sofa in the corner of the tea shop, she slung her bag onto the low table and let out a melodramatic sigh. 'Dad'll ground me until the end of term if he finds out about it.'

'How's he going to know?' Flynn asked.

Two pairs of eyes swivelled simultaneously in Anna's direction. She grinned. 'I didn't hear anything. But you need to pay your own bill this time.'

Meredith grinned back. 'Fair enough. Although it is my first ever behaviour log, so perhaps I should make a point of telling him. He might even be a little bit proud of me!'

Anna's grin broadened. 'I wouldn't count on it. Now what can I get you?'

'Well, we're celebrating,' Meredith said. 'Flynn passed his driving test this afternoon.' She grinned at her boyfriend. 'Although he's not getting his car for a few weeks, so we'll be relying on his mum for a little while yet.'

Anna felt a prickle of unease. Trying to write it off as maternal instinct, she forced a smile. 'Congratulations,' she said, turning to Flynn. 'Have a seat and I'll bring you over some cake.'

Some slices of Strawberry Line Gateau and a couple of glasses of elderflower cordial later, Meredith had almost forgotten her behaviour log. She and Flynn were cuddled up on the sofa, chatting amiably with their friends. Anna looked at them, and tried to dismiss her earlier feelings. Given what had happened to James, she was bound to find teenage drivers a tricky subject, but she had to remember that Flynn had proven himself to be nothing but responsible so far, as far as Meredith was concerned. Focussing on the here and now, Anna glanced at the cake crumbs on the floor and sighed inwardly. It was a far cry from the infamous food fight, thankfully, but she'd definitely need her dustpan and brush this evening.

*

'Why the hell didn't you tell me Jonathan was back as an active partner on the board? I've been up to my bollocks in the American distribution deal, I couldn't wade out if I was drowning, and now I find he's swanned in and virtually closed it single-handed? What the fuck have you two been playing at?'

'Look, just calm down.' Jack took off his jacket and threw it over the chair opposite Matthew's desk.

'This had better be good,' Matthew muttered. He resented, still, how his father could make him feel like a naughty schoolboy.

'Jonathan rang me a while back,' Jack began. 'He'd heard through the grapevine we were courting FastStream, and wanted to offer some inside knowledge. He's had some dealings with them before, and thought he could be of assistance.'

'And you didn't think to tell me?' Matthew couldn't sit down, instead, prowling the office like a caged tiger.

'We didn't want to say anything until we knew it would be of benefit,' Jack replied. 'He wanted to keep things low-key until he was sure he could be of help. I promised him I'd keep it under my hat until the right moment.'

'So you've kept quiet about this for quite a while then?' Matthew could feel his temper rising. 'And now I've found out, purely by accident, you're coming clean? Jesus, I must have sounded like the biggest twat on the phone to FastStream.'

'Jonathan wanted to surprise you with it,' Jack replied. 'He feels he's not been as... helpful as he should have been over the years.'

'Surprise me?' Matthew said bleakly. 'Well, if nothing else, he's done that.' He came around the front of his desk. 'Dad, when are you going to learn? *I* run this company now, not you. It's been my blood, sweat and tears that have built this business into what it is over the past decade. *Mine*. I've put everything I had into it, and now you're swanning in here and telling me you've made a unilateral decision to get Jonathan back in?'

'Matthew, son,' Jack stood up again, 'Jonathan still holds a stake in the business. I thought it would be a chance to bring the two of you back together. You've been so far apart for so many years now. I'm sorry. But he has done well.'

'Of course he has,' Matthew said bitterly. 'He could have gone over there, pissed in a bottle and got them to drink it and you'd still think the sun shone out of his arse.'

'Look,' Jack tried again, 'I know this has come as a bit of a shock, but surely anything that proves we're pulling together can only be a good thing. You know how these Americans are. And Jonathan's got the gift of the gab. With his talk and your brains, this could be a really big thing for us.'

'I was handling it, Dad,' Matthew ran a hand over his eyes. 'A few more days and it would have been in the bag. I make the decisions.'

'You've barely seen your brother in years. For the first time in his life he's shown a real interest in the business. He wants to be involved again. What's so wrong with that?' Jack retorted.

Hesitating for a moment longer, Matthew finally spoke. 'OK, Dad. We'll do it your way. Let Jonathan have a part in it. But if he fucks this up, I want him off the board. Permanently.'

'Understood,' Jack said quietly. 'But give Jonathan a chance. Let him prove to you he can help to close this deal.' He stood up from the chair, still tall, spare and elegant, even in his eightieth year. 'Your mother would have been so sad to see the two of you still so far apart after all these years.'

Matthew felt a jolt of compassion for the man in front of him. 'Mum would have understood,' he said gruffly. 'Just don't keep me in the dark any more, all right?'

As Jack left his office, Matthew sank back into the chair behind his desk, head swimming. Jonathan's hand in the deal was a huge risk and all of Matthew's anger and bitterness threatened to come back to the fore. He had no idea how he was going to face his brother, and now Jonathan was, evidently, back on the board of the business as an active partner, Matthew couldn't see how he could avoid that. Grabbing his mobile phone, he texted Anna and said he couldn't see her that evening. This was one set of problems he couldn't burden her with until he had it all straight in his own mind. Opening his bottom drawer, he pulled out a bottle of whisky and poured a slug into his coffee cup.

Chapter 24

It was late in the evening when Meredith wandered into the living room. Matthew was slumped on the Chesterfield sofa, watching a repeat of the last international rugby game, recorded a few weeks back. She slid next to him and he put his arm around her.

'Homework done?' he asked.

'Yup.'

'Even that history essay?'

'Did that one first.'

Matthew looked surprised. 'Well done.'

'Wikipedia's well useful!' Meredith grinned.

Matthew smiled. Meredith always managed to lift his spirits. Once again, as he had many times in the past, he thanked god she'd stayed with him.

For a few minutes they watched the match in companionable silence. Then, as the referee called for half time and Matthew went to skip the recording forward, Meredith spoke.

'I've had a few emails from Mum lately,' she said.

Matthew stopped fiddling with the remote. 'Oh, yes? How is she?'

'Fine, I think. She's got a role in a new play, but rehearsals don't start until September.'

'That's nice.' Matthew kept his voice carefully neutral.

'The thing is, Dad,' Meredith started to pick at the hem of

her dark blue school skirt. 'She's kind of, like, asked if I want to fly out to Florida and spend the summer holiday with her.'

Matthew went very still. Putting down the remote, he turned around to face his daughter. Seeing the apprehension on her face, his heart skipped a beat. 'And would you like to go?'

'I don't know,' Meredith said carefully. 'I mean, I'd love to go to America again, and I thought I might go with you when you sort out this deal thing. But she seems really keen to see me.'

'Well, you haven't seen each other for a little while,' Matthew replied, relieved that his voice didn't betray the churning that had started in his stomach at the thought of Meredith going away. 'Perhaps she wants to get to know you a bit better. And if you go with me, you'll just be stuck in hotel rooms the whole time while I'm in meetings, so it won't be much fun.'

'Oh, I don't know – I quite like room service! But seriously, Dad. What do you think? Should I go?'

'It's entirely up to you, my darling. If you want to go, then you should go.'

'But what about you? How will you manage without me?'

Matthew smiled. 'I'll cope. Pat can come in for an extra hour or two a week to stop me being buried in dirty washing and takeaway wrappers!'

'And you'll have Anna to keep an eye on you,' Meredith mused. 'Dad, are you blushing?'

'What? No, don't be daft!' Matthew cleared his throat and busied himself with cueing up the second half of the rugby match.

'Well, Mum did say Todd's villa in Florida has a pool and stables,' Meredith said. 'So if she gets too heavy, I can get out of her hair.'

'Todd?' Matthew said.

'Oh, come on, Dad, you know very well Todd's her boyfriend.'

'Oh. Right. Well then.'

There was a small silence again.

'So... you don't mind if I go?' Meredith sounded much younger than her years.

Putting an arm back around his daughter's shoulders, Matthew pulled her close. He breathed in the scent of coconut shampoo as she snuggled against him, remembering how her hair used to smell when she was a fraction of the age she was now.

'If you want to, Meredith, then you go,' he said gruffly. 'I'll be fine, and you've worked hard all year at school, that one behaviour log aside. You deserve a break. And if it all gets a bit too much, I can always fly over and collect you. I'll be back in the US at some point to finish some things.' *That's if Jonathan doesn't get there first,* he thought grimly.

'Thanks, Dad.' Her voice was muffled against the fabric of his rugby shirt.

'What date does she suggest you go over?'

'A couple of days after term ends – back at the start of September.'

Matthew fought a wave of desolation. 'That's quite a long time,' he said guardedly. 'What about your holiday work?'

'Perhaps I could go for a month or so, and then see how I feel about staying.'

'And Flynn would no doubt miss you,' Matthew said, managing a wry smile.

'That's the other reason I'm a bit meh about going, to be honest, Dad. I mean, what if he dumps me while I'm away?'

This time, Matthew had to fight back a grin. 'If he really likes you, he'll wait for you,' he said. Secretly, he hoped by the time Meredith came back, perhaps it would be the other way round.

'And there's always Skype and Instagram,' Meredith conceded. 'So it won't be that bad.'

'Sounds like you've made a decision,' Matthew said, trying to hold back the disappointment. He knew he had to let her go, but it didn't make the decision any easier.

Meredith smiled. 'If you're *sure* you'll be OK.'

'I *did* manage to take care of myself for quite a few years before you came along, daughter of mine,' Matthew said, poking her in the ribs playfully.

Meredith looked thoughtful. 'It'll be good to catch up with Mum, and this place of Todd's sounds awesome. But if I don't like it, I can still come back early, can't I?'

'Of course,' Matthew said. 'Just keep in touch and let me know.'

'You're the best!' Meredith gave him a quick hug. 'I'll email Mum tomorrow and let her know.' Bouncing off the sofa, she leaned over and kissed Matthew goodnight. 'See you in the morning.'

'I'll probably take Sefton out for a last run in a bit,' Matthew said. 'Will you be OK by yourself?'

Meredith rolled her eyes. 'Sure, Dad. Don't spend too long round Anna's – you've got work tomorrow, remember.'

'I don't know what you mean,' Matthew said. 'Sefton's particularly fond of the walk through the East Orchard at this time of night.'

'Say hi to Anna for me!' Meredith laughed. 'And tell her I'll pop over tomorrow.'

'Will do.' As he settled down to watch the rest of the rugby, Matthew's thoughts veered between amusement his daughter was cross-questioning him about his love life and a sense of creeping unease about this renewal of relations with Tara.

Chapter 25

The soft chime of the grandfather clock in the downstairs hall reminded Anna that she hadn't eaten a proper meal all day. She'd grazed at the tea shop, but the lunchtime rush had put paid to actually sitting down and eating a proper sandwich, and she hadn't felt like cooking for herself after being around food all day. Ellie had had tea at nursery so Anna had settled for a cup of tea and a biscuit and was putting the mug in the dishwasher when there was a soft tap at the back door.

'Hey,' she said as she opened the door. 'I wasn't sure I'd see you tonight.'

Matthew stepped in out of the rain, which had begun abruptly and showed no sign of ceasing.

'Just wondered if you fancied company,' he said.

'And what makes you think I don't have some wild night planned?' Anna teased.

'I've just heard Charlotte telling Simon off for getting home too late to pick Evan up from nursery, so I'm guessing she's not going to be dragging you out for a night on the tiles tonight!' Matthew quipped.

Anna grinned. 'But I might have had a date with someone!'

Matthew crossed the kitchen and put his arms around Anna's waist. 'I'd soon see him off!'

Anna's knees weakened. His merest touch was always enough to make her senses reel. She brushed her lips against his, but although he returned the kiss, his mind seemed elsewhere.

'What is it?' Anna asked as they broke apart.

Matthew sighed. 'I'm sorry. I didn't mean to come round here just to chew your ear.'

'Hey,' Anna said gently. 'Isn't that part of the deal?' Turning back to her kitchen worktop, she grabbed the bottle of Chablis she'd bought at the supermarket earlier that day. 'As it happens, Charlotte was going to come over tonight for a glass or two but Simon's blotted his copybook and she's stayed at home to give him a piece of her mind. So there's a drink going begging if you want it.' She reached up to the top shelf of the cupboard to get two wine glasses down.

'Let me get those.' Matthew edged closer to Anna and she felt the warmth of his body. Steeling herself against the urge to melt against him again, she busied herself by taking the cork out of the bottle.

'So what's new?' she asked when they were finally sat at the kitchen table.

Matthew hesitated. He didn't like the idea of dragging Anna into the situation with Tara and Meredith, and he still couldn't bring himself to discuss Jonathan at all, but he suddenly felt the urge to unburden himself of at least some of it. Gradually, the story of Tara's latest plan came out.

'It feels like she's taking Meredith away from me,' Matthew said. 'And part of me knows I need to let Meredith make this decision for herself, but the bigger part of me wants to lock her in her room and throw away the key.' He gave a small smile.

Anna moved from the table to stand behind Matthew at the kitchen table. She put her hands on his shoulders and felt the knots of tension under her fingers.

Matthew let out a long sigh. 'You are *so* good at that.' He lifted his head and leaned back into Anna's soothing hands. Surrendering, he allowed himself to forget all about Tara and her plans. The ache in his head ebbed away as she continued massaging his neck and shoulders, and an overwhelming sense of calm and rightness washed over him. 'God, I wish I didn't have to go home tonight.'

'The course of true love... or parenting, never did run smooth,' quipped Anna. She froze. Had she really just said that out loud? Her hands seemed glued to Matthew's shoulders.

'Is that what you think this is?' Matthew said softly. Carefully, mindful that she was behind him, he stood up and turned to face her.

'Um, well, er, I – I don't – that's not what I meant...' Anna stuttered. Her arms flapped helplessly at her sides.

Matthew's eyes were deep, dark and unreadable. Just as Anna thought she would die of mortification, he took her hands in his.

'You're a breath of fresh air in my life,' he said. 'And it's been such a long time... for both of us. This thing with Tara... it's throwing me off balance.' Tenderly, he tucked a stray strand of Anna's hair behind her ear. 'Give me time, OK?'

Anna nodded, unable to speak for embarrassment. She felt Matthew's lips on her cheek, the warmth of his breath as he kissed her flaming face.

'I should go,' he said, stepping back from her slightly.

'Matthew...' Anna was relieved her voice, if not her thoughts, was at least under her control. 'I didn't mean to put pressure on you. I, of all people need to take things slowly.'

Matthew's smile held just a trace of sadness. 'Goodnight, Anna.'

As his broad back disappeared out of the door, it was Anna's turn to put her head in her hands. Just when things were starting to go well, she'd had to put her foot in it.

Even when she went to bed that night, she couldn't help replaying the scene over and over again in her head, cursing her own stupidity at letting slip her true feelings. Curling up in total mortification in the darkness, she eventually fell asleep.

*

'Shit, Charlotte, I really messed up last night.'

'You didn't dump him, did you?' Charlotte was instantly alert. 'Or fart in front of him? Belch? Scratch your arse? No? Well, it can't be that bad, then!'

Anna laughed despite herself. 'Worse. I might possibly have mentioned the "L" word.'

'Darling,' Charlotte admonished, 'just because you go to bed with someone, doesn't mean you have to tell them you love them. Have I taught you nothing by my example over the years?'

'Calm down. I said I mentioned it, not that I got down on one knee and proposed.'

'So what's the problem, then?'

Anna heard a thump in the background and a wail. 'Everything OK at your end?'

'Yup – Evan's just pulled out the contents of my saucepan cupboard and is wearing a colander as a hat. Carry on.'

'I made some stupid joke about true love, and he totally freaked out. I feel like such an idiot.' Anna could feel her face growing hot again as she relived the previous night for the thousandth time.

'Wait, wait. When you say "freaked out", what exactly do you mean?'

Another thump. A louder wail.

'Are you *sure* you're all right?'

'Yes, don't worry – he's just discovered the knife block.'

'What?'

'I'm joking. Now get on with it, will you.'

Anna slumped back in her chair and sighed. 'He told me to give him time. The thing with Tara is throwing him off balance.'

'Well, there you go then. Believe me, darling, the less you have to do with Lady East Coast Bitch Face the better – she's utterly poisonous.' There was a muffled scratching sound at Charlotte's end of the phone and suddenly Anna heard a small, shrill voice.

'Off the fucky phone, Auntie Anna – we going out soon!'

'*EVAN!* Naughty step!' Charlotte snatched the phone back from her foul-mouthed offspring.

'Sorry about that – he's obviously been listening to his father a little too much. Listen, I've got to go and wash this child's mouth out with coal tar soap, but don't panic – it sounds like Matthew's just trying to keep you out of what could potentially be a very sticky situation. And you know what men are like – even suggest that they might be feeling something and they get all tetchy. Simon used to run a mile when I told him I loved him until he finally twigged he felt the same about me. Don't get your knickers in a twist.'

'I hope you're right,' Anna muttered. 'It was all starting to go so well. And now I've come off as some needy cow who can't even shag someone without going all mushy on them.'

'On the contrary, you've been the epitome of patience and understanding, considering there are two children in the equation. Not to mention Matthew's tendency to go all Mr Darcy on you when you least expect it. Keep calm and carry on, darling, that's what I say.'

'And don't ever mention the dreaded "L" word again?' Anna said.

'Just go with the flow, babe, and don't let it get you down. Now I really must go and sort out this child of mine. I'll brain Simon when he gets home.'

Despite herself, Anna grinned. 'Go easy on them – you never know when they might come in useful!' As Anna ended the call, she heard the beginnings of Charlotte's scolding of her errant son. Talking to her best friend always made her feel better, but she still couldn't help the continuing feelings of unease.

Chapter 26

After a couple of days of alternately wishing Matthew would call and then praying he wouldn't, and generally hiding in the tea shop kitchen when she'd seen to her customers' needs, Anna decided something had to be done. Punching out the number to Matthew's private office line, she prayed he'd answer quickly before she bottled out.

'Carter's Cider, how may I help you?' Jen's clipped, efficient tone made Anna's heart sink.

'Oh, hi Jen, it's Anna. Hemingway.' She cursed herself for sounding so gauche. Jen was sleek, composed and ever so slightly frightening, even with the phone line between them.

'Hi, Anna,' Jen replied. 'What can I do for you?'

'Is… um… is Matthew around?' Anna cursed. Why hadn't she just phoned his bloody mobile?

'He's out at the moment, said something about checking over the keggery.' Anna heard a rustle of papers at Jen's end and wondered if she was the one shifting them, or whether Matthew was actually standing right next to her in the office, shaking his head.

'Oh, OK. Well, would you mind asking him to call me when he gets back?'

'Sure thing. Any message?'

Yes, I'm sorry I suggested that I might be falling in love with you. 'Um… no, I don't think so. Thanks.'

Anna ended the call, and as she pressed the button to turn her phone off, she wandered over to the tea shop's kitchen window. Staring blankly out at the small back yard, she got the fright of her life when the back door of the shop creaked open and Matthew stepped into the room.

'Christ!' Anna squeaked. 'You could have warned me you were coming!'

'Sorry,' Matthew glanced at the empty worktop, the cold oven and then looked quizzically at her. 'Were you in the middle of something?'

'Only torturing myself,' Anna muttered. 'And being a complete idiot on the phone to Jen.'

Matthew grinned. 'I wouldn't worry about the latter, Jen's worked for me for years so knows how to fend off any idiotic behaviour, especially from me. And as for the former...' Drawing closer, Matthew placed a tender kiss on her lips. 'I should be apologising to you.' He pulled back to look at her again. 'I don't know why I got so worried by what you said.'

'I might be out of practise at this dating game, but even I know the signs that someone's freaking out,' Anna replied.

'Anna,' Matthew cocked his head to one side, 'I'm not freaking out. I promise. And you're so sweet when you're flustered.' Grinning at her, he reached forward and tucked her ponytail back over her shoulder. 'Just because you mention your feelings for me it doesn't mean I'm going to run screaming to the hills. You just happened to mention it when my head was so full of other things, I didn't quite know what to do.'

'So we can forget it? What I said?' Anna still felt foolish, but was prepared to let it go, if at all possible.

'On the contrary,' he said gravely. 'That's the last thing I want to do.'

'Wh-what?' Anna started to tremble. 'What do you want to do, then?'

Matthew fell silent.

'Are you dumping me? Because of that? Oh god, I'm such an idiot, can't we just forget it...'

Matthew pulled Anna closer to him and cut her off by planting a firm kiss on her lips. 'For goodness sake, just listen to me,' he said as he released her.

'I'm listening,' Anna said in a small voice.

'What I was going to say, before you started wittering on and interrupting me, is that you totally pre-empted me. I've been trying not to admit it to myself, let alone you, but the truth is, Anna...' he ran a hand through his hair, playing a little for time. 'The truth is... I'm falling in love with you. And I don't know if you feel the same way, although I'm assuming from the way you've been reacting that you might go some way to feeling the same, but even if you don't, I just thought you should know.'

Anna took a step back, stunned. 'You know what,' she said slowly, a smile beginning to play over the lips that Matthew had kissed so fervently, 'I was always told solicitors had an awfully roundabout way of putting things.'

'Should have started seeing a barrister, then,' Matthew replied. 'Or perhaps... a cider maker?'

Anna's smile turned into a grin. Matthew's uncertainty was irresistible. 'Well,' she said softly. 'I'd certainly like that.' She knew he was giving her control over this moment. She brushed a stray lock of silvery black hair from his eyes. Matthew, enthralled, leaned into her touch as her fingers stroked back from his forehead and tangled slightly in his unkempt locks. 'I'd like that very much. Because the truth is... I think I'm falling in love with you too.'

With that, Anna found herself swept off her feet again as Matthew gathered her up in a tight embrace. 'I'm glad,' he whispered.

When they parted again, Anna felt a touch unsteady on her feet. 'This is so weird,' she said wonderingly. 'If anyone had told me a year ago I'd be standing in a tea shop with a man I'd met once, eighteen years ago, and kissing him, I'd have laughed them out of the door.'

They stood for a while, just holding each other, surprised, delighted and mildly unsettled by the revelations. Then, with an air of reluctance, Matthew disentangled himself from Anna's arms. 'I really have to get going,' he said. 'I snuck out of the office and told Jen some rubbish about going to check on the kegging plant. Knowing my luck, she's called the floor and knows I've gone AWOL.'

'Will I see you later?' Anna asked.

'I should think Sefton might be making a detour tonight, if you're OK with that?' Matthew grinned. 'He seems to like lying by your fire, even when it's too hot to light it!' Kissing the tip of her nose, he turned for the door.

'I'll save him a biscuit,' Anna replied. 'Send Jen my regards... and my apologies!'

'Will do!' And with that, he was gone.

For a moment, Anna just stood in the kitchen, still slightly stunned by the speed by which her emotions could be so conclusively turned upside down. Matthew loved her. He *loved* her. And she loved him. Half of her wanted to lock up the tea shop, race around to Charlotte's house and squeal like a teenager; the other half wanted to run screaming for the hills in terror. Somewhere, in the intervening years between adolescence and maturity, in the comfortable, homely years of marriage, she'd forgotten the spontaneity and scariness of a new relationship. It was with a not entirely steady hand that she turned on the cold tap and drew herself off a long glass of water, before choking on it as the imperious tones of Miss Pinkham echoed through the space between the tea shop and the kitchen, enquiring if she was *ever* going to get the second pot of tea she'd requested. Jumping guiltily, Anna bleated the affirmative, and set to brewing.

After an afternoon spent thinking more about Anna than his work, Matthew admitted defeat and decided to be at home for once when Meredith came strolling through the door. As sod's law would dictate, he found a note on the kitchen table from his daughter, saying she was going to be eating dinner at school, and staying later to meet with the other Model UN team members.

Smiling ruefully, Matthew poured himself a glass of early evening Scotch and ruminated on the day's events. Telling Anna how he felt had been a huge risk; one he never thought he'd take, but when faced with her serious green eyes, his heart had had no option. He felt like a teenager again, and just for a while he'd forgotten all about Tara, Jonathan and the FastStream deal. He knew it would all encroach back onto him in time, but for now he was content to wallow in the waves of wellbeing and rightness that had washed over him the minute he'd declared himself to Anna.

Just as he was about to sit down and allow himself the luxury of a few minutes' peace and quiet, there was a knock at the front door. For a split second he was tempted to ignore it; it was bound to be Jehovah's Witnesses or someone of that ilk, and he was in too good a mood with earthly delights to consider the heavens.

The knock came again.

Sighing, he ambled to the door, hoping whoever it was would be brief. For the umpteenth time he wished he'd had a window put into it, or at the very least a spyhole. Opening the door, blinking in the early evening light, for a second he couldn't make out who it was. Then, as his vision cleared and his eyes came back into focus, his whisky glass slipped from his fingers and crashed on the flagstones.

Standing there, an unfathomable expression on his face, was his brother Jonathan.

Chapter 27

*Promise I'm not going cold on you, but something's
come up. See you tomorrow? M xxx*

Anna smiled and put her phone back down on the coffee
table. Although she was rather disappointed Matthew wasn't
going to be dropping by on a late evening visit, it did give her
the chance to mull over the afternoon's revelations in peace.
Ellie had crashed out in bed, exhausted from nursery, and so
Anna opened a bottle of Chardonnay, brought it to the sofa
and switched on the television.

Just as she was about to settle in for the evening, her phone
buzzed again.

*Heard a rumour that might interest you. Can I come
over? C x*

Texting a quick reply, Anna went to get another glass from
the kitchen.

Five minutes later, Charlotte took the glass that Anna had
poured for her. 'So, Jen, Matthew's oh-so-efficient PA, let slip
to Vern the pub landlord that Matthew's not going to be the
only Carter brother in the cider business very soon.'

'Really?'

'Yes. Apparently, Matthew asked her to pencil in a few

provisional dates for an extraordinary general meeting of the Carter's board for some time next month. Looks like the prodigal son is returning to the flock!' Charlotte leaned back against the cushions of Anna's leather sofa, and closed her eyes. 'Christ, it's been a hard day.'

Anna winced at Charlotte's mashed metaphors. 'Evan playing up again?'

'Not particularly, but he will keep asking "why" all the time and even my infinite patience is waning.' Charlotte grinned.

'Ellie's doing that, too,' Anna replied. 'And it's not so much the pointlessness of the questions, but the worry that one day I'm not going to come up with a creative enough answer! I mean, why *is* the sky blue, for goodness' sake?'

'But back to the notorious JC,' Charlotte said. 'Has Matthew mentioned anything to you about his little brother getting involved in the family firm?'

Anna shook her head. 'He hasn't. But that doesn't mean it's not happening; Matthew can be a little... parsimonious... with information when he doesn't want to talk about something.'

'John Thornton as well as Mr Darcy, eh?' Charlotte gave a snort. 'Only not as talkative.'

'Something like that.' Anna sipped her wine contemplatively.

'People deal with things in different ways,' Charlotte said.

'When you start a relationship, you're so concerned with getting the other person to talk all the time. It's like everything they say is infinitely interesting and you just want to know every last thing about them.' Anna grinned ruefully. 'Well, at least that's how it happened the first time round. This time, I'm not so sure!'

'You have to remember that you and Matthew both have a lot more history,' Charlotte said. 'That's going to make you both much more cautious. Laying yourself bare can be frightening.'

'I know,' Anna said. 'And I suppose it's not surprising he doesn't want to talk about Jonathan. I mean, it's not like they parted on great terms.'

'So the rumours are true then?' Charlotte's eyes sparkled. 'Jonathan did have something to do with Matthew's marriage breaking up?'

Anna grimaced. 'I don't want to go into specifics.'

'Oh, come on, who am I going to tell? Just satisfy my curiosity, please. Did Jonathan have something to do with it?'

'Let's just say Tara didn't stray far from home,' Anna said heavily. 'And no, I don't know the gory details. All I know is she couldn't have chosen anyone worse to have a fling with.'

'Except perhaps Jack,' Charlotte grinned. 'The old fox has been known to pull a few lovelies in his time.'

'Like father like son,' Anna said sardonically.

'Doesn't Matthew find it weird, you living here?' Charlotte gazed around the lounge. 'I mean, it was Jonathan's place for a long time before he left. He and Tara must have been at it under this very roof.'

'He struggled a bit, at first,' Anna admitted. 'But that's not surprising, really.'

'I'm sure he's laid a few ghosts... and other things... by now,' Charlotte gave Anna a knowing look.

'Trust you to lower the tone,' Anna muttered.

'Well, you never did tell me if I was right about him!'

Anna could feel her face growing hot. 'No comment.'

'Not even a little comeback?' Charlotte raised a sceptical eyebrow. 'Although perhaps *little* isn't the operative word.'

'Bugger off.'

'Well look, if you're not going to divulge any specifics, can you at least tell me if things are back on track between you?'

Anna couldn't help the sudden, silly smile that painted itself across her face. 'You could say that.'

'So do you think you might be seeing in the harvest with him and dancing round some apple trees next January?'

Anna laughed. 'For a moment I thought you were going to make another Maypole-related gag!'

'Too obvious, darling; give me some credit.'

'It's going fine,' Anna said simply. 'And mentioning the "L" word wasn't as bad as I'd thought, thankfully.'

Charlotte let out a low whistle. 'You've really got it bad, haven't you?'

Anna shrugged.

'So do you think he is?'

'Is what?'

'In love with you, you berk!'

'Well, he told me he was.' Anna suddenly felt like a fifteen-year-old again as Charlotte squealed and grabbed her.

'I knew it! Summer wedding, I bet you!'

'Steady on, it's still early days.' Once Charlotte had released her, she topped up both their glasses.

Charlotte grabbed hers back and took another sip. 'I'm so pleased for you, Anna. No, really, I am. Joking aside, you deserve a bit of happiness.'

Anna's eyes filled with tears. 'Thanks. I can't believe all this, sometimes. I feel like at any minute I'm going to wake up back in our old house with my husband by my side, and all this has been some sort of weird dream. And you know what? I really don't know how I feel about that.'

'Falling in love again must be confusing,' Charlotte said. 'I know I'd be petrified if I was in your shoes. Dates are one thing, but this is getting serious.' She looked at Anna. 'Are you ready for that?'

'Sometimes I think I am, that it could be so right for us, but then other times I get caught up in the fear of it all. What if I'm on the rebound? What if he is? What if we let our children get used to a situation that's going to come crashing down around our ears and leaves them even more confused and hurt than we are?' She sighed. 'I just wish I knew more of the answers.'

'If you did, it wouldn't be half so much fun,' Charlotte said wryly. 'If you don't take the risks, you'll never experience the exhilaration.'

'I just wish I didn't feel quite so much like a teenager again. I could do without the angst.'

'Yeah, but one of the joys of being a teenager was the mind-blowing hormonal surge!' Charlotte grinned lasciviously. 'And you can't tell me you're not enjoying that. I can see from your body language whenever Matthew's around that he's pushing your buttons.'

'Whatever,' Anna muttered, gulping down her wine.

'And you're certainly pushing his,' Charlotte said. 'I know you don't believe me, but he's a totally different man since you moved back here.'

'How so?'

'Well, don't get me wrong, he was always pretty high profile in the village; I mean, you can't keep the locals on side without kissing a few babies and putting your name to a few events, kind of a quid pro quo for the villagers not kicking off about a larger than anticipated bottling plant or twenty-four-hour loading, but he's been a lot more approachable since you've been around.'

'Oh, come on, we've only been seeing each other a few months!'

'No, seriously. He's thawed out a lot lately. I can't remember the last time he actually spent more than a token half hour at the May Fair, for instance. And yet there he was with you for virtually the whole afternoon.'

'I'm sure there's more to it than that,' Anna said, but she felt a warm glow of pleasure.

'Anyway, whatever the reason, something's changed. So I'd stop worrying for a bit about whether or not it's going to last, and just enjoy it.' Charlotte drained her wine glass. 'Oh, and give me all the details, of course! And if you do hear anything about Jonathan, do let me know,' Charlotte continued. 'Believe me, darling, if he's half as hot as I remember him being, he's worth viewing!'

'I'll keep you posted,' Anna said dryly, although she doubted she'd find anything out before Charlotte did. Her best friend had an uncanny ability to sniff out a scandal before most people even sensed there was one brewing.

As they parted company that night, Anna reflected on the changes in her life. Yet again, she found herself thinking about how bizarre her new situation seemed, and still couldn't answer whether or not she'd change it for her old life.

Chapter 28

'What the fuck are you doing here?' Matthew growled.

'That's a nice welcome.'

'And you were expecting what?' Matthew moved to close the front door, but Jonathan put a hand up to block him.

'Look, I know this is a bit of a surprise, but we need to talk. I've just got in from New York. Can I come in?'

Shambling Irish Wolfhound grace met whippet slim elegance as Matthew opened the front door to admit his brother. 'I suppose we should do this in private, rather than give more food to the local vultures.'

Time had been kind to Jonathan. Four years his brother's junior, he almost matched him in height, and as he'd grown older his features had matured from a kind of beauty to a more masculine attractiveness. Light chestnut hair framed clear cerulean eyes. The bone structure was unquestionably Carter, but, always naturally slighter than Matthew, he still retained his rather louche good looks and elegant physique. He was wearing a lightweight cream suit with a blue shirt that, to Matthew's irritation, perfectly matched his eyes.

'Don't get too comfortable,' Matthew said. 'You won't be staying long.'

'I'll bear that in mind.'

'Why are you here?' Matthew said wearily. 'What couldn't be done over the phone?'

'Dad rang me,' Jonathan replied. 'He said you weren't too happy about us going behind your back.'

That's a fucking understatement, Matthew thought. 'It wasn't the best news I'd ever had.'

'He suggested that, as FastStream wants us both present when we sign on the dotted line, we ought to meet beforehand and clear the air.' Raising his hands in anticipation of Matthew's objections, he continued, 'Look, I know it's going to be... uncomfortable, but for the sake of the company, I think we need to grit our teeth and get on with it. You can punch me afterwards if you need to.'

Matthew shook his head. 'You really have no idea, do you? You swan back in here, having charmed the pants off the FastStream board, and you somehow convince Dad you can handle this deal better than me. And let's face it, I've only been running this company for over a decade, so what would I know?' He started to pace the short distance between the parlour fireplace and the large window that looked out onto the back garden. 'Dad just goes with it, trusts you have our best interests at heart, even though you couldn't give a shit about the business the last time I checked, and says all right then, Jonathan, you take care of it.' The pacing got more agitated. 'And somehow, against all my better judgement, I have to accept this, despite the fact that the last time you had anything to do with the business, you were actually too busy sleeping with my wife to take much notice of it.' He turned back to Jonathan. 'How am I doing so far?'

Jonathan took a deep breath. 'I know this looks bad. I know I shouldn't have gone anywhere near FastStream without making contact with you first, but I also know these guys. They're big on family values and even bigger on British produce. They pulled out of a deal with Thornbury's Cider two years ago because they weren't convinced it was the right product to suit their ethos. But you got in there, and you convinced them that Carters is the one. They were wavering for quite a while before they agreed, weren't they?'

'So what rabbit did you pull out of whose hat to make them see sense?' Matthew's voice was heavy with sarcasm.

'Don't get me wrong, they loved you, but they found you a touch unapproachable at times. They could see the sense in the deal, and it stacked up financially, but you didn't exactly open up to them, did you?'

'What? You expect me to bare my soul in the boardroom to secure this thing? That's not my style.'

'I know, I know, which is where I came in, as your wingman, if you like.' Jonathan smiled sardonically. 'I played up some of the struggles the business has had, tried to make the board more sympathetic to you as a quality, local producer. They lapped up all the historical stuff, but they wanted to know more about its human face. I stepped in, filled a few gaps with some sentimental bullshit about the bad times, your single dad status, how it nearly all went down the swanny until you saved the day. The Yanks loved it.'

'So you aired my dirty laundry?' Matthew, aghast, took a large slug of his whisky. 'There I was, thinking that my integrity, professionalism and sound business sense would be enough, and all along they wanted a sob story? This is international business, Jonathan, not the fucking *X Factor*. I suppose you left out that you were one of the reasons I became a single father in the first place.'

Jonathan flinched. 'Look, I only told them what they wanted to hear.'

'So, going forward, we need to put on a so-called united front, do we? The deal's only done if we sign together.' Matthew, tired of pacing, slumped in the armchair by the fireplace.

'Don't say you couldn't use the help,' Jonathan said quietly. 'You've done nothing but work for the past fifteen years, Matthew. I want to help, and properly this time. I know you don't believe me, but I want to make things up to you. This deal with FastStream was my way of taking that first step.'

'That's as maybe, but if you're back on board, you do things my way,' Matthew said bluntly. 'I'm in charge, not Dad, and certainly not you.'

'I mean it. I do want to help.'

An uneasy silence descended between the two.

'I should get going,' Jonathan said at last. 'If you need me, I'll be at Dad's for a few days until I can get something more permanent sorted. He's given me the box room.'

'Christ, could you even get in there? Last time I looked, it was chock-full of Mum's old novels.'

Jonathan smiled ruefully. 'It took a while to navigate past the piles, but I got to the bed in the end.'

'So you're going to be hanging around, then?'

'Well, I can hardly be a board member from five thousand miles across the water, can I?'

Matthew let a small smile play over his features. 'You might live to regret saying that.'

'I'll see you soon,' Jonathan replied. 'And we'll make arrangements to fly out at the end of next week, shall we?'

'I'll get Jen onto it,' Matthew said. 'And Jonathan?'

'Yes?'

'You're not off the hook.' Matthew's face was grim again. 'Just because I've let you back on board with this deal, it doesn't mean all's forgiven. I'm doing this because Dad asked me to. Are we clear?'

'As the crystal that's all over your hallway floor,' Jonathan replied. 'Don't worry, big brother, 1 won't be presuming any sense of intimacy.' Without pausing to shake his brother's hand, Jonathan walked out of the parlour and the front door.

Matthew just stood for a long time after Jonathan left. How was it possible to go from adolescent excitement to adult trepidation in the space of half an hour? Shaking his head in bewilderment, he went to get the dustpan and brush.

Chapter 29

Anna's days at the tea shop started early. She'd drop Ellie off at nursery at quarter to eight, and be through the shop door by eight o'clock. Over the last months she'd established an efficient routine of checking the dates on the stock left overnight and the milk in the fridge, giving the tables their first spray down and checking the cutlery, before setting out the newer stock, getting the till sorted out and then opening the doors for eight thirty. This ensured the tea shop caught any passing trade from the other shop owners in the village, and then a group of post-school-run parents would be in at around nine o'clock for their morning lattes and, more often than not, a slice or two of whatever cake took their fancy that day. Then it would be all go until about two o'clock, when she'd have a breather and a sandwich before the afternoon rush. The shop usually closed its door at quarter to five, giving her time to tot up the takings before she left to pick Ellie up at five thirty.

After the first few weeks, she'd grown accustomed to the chats with her regulars, and definitely enjoyed listening in to her customers' conversations; discreetly, of course. She'd learned a great deal of the extramarital frolickings of one particular couple from the gossip of their neighbours, and was stunned to find out that the hitherto rather popular local Member of Parliament was definitely not flavour of the month with his constituents after installing a huge and unsightly wooden building in his generous back garden to house both his sauna and his hot tub. The thought of that particular honourable member stripping for either activity was enough to put anyone off their cake, Anna thought.

The regulars, along with the steady stream of tourists who topped up the tea shop's early summer income, kept Anna busy enough through the day, to the point where customers often waited for tables. Today was no exception, and as Anna took some cash off the table by the bay window to put into the till, she heard the tea shop door open. Surmising she had a minute or two before whoever it was would want to order, she nipped into the kitchen to check on the batch of scones she'd put in the oven. She often prepared the mixtures the night before, at home, since her Health and Safety Certificate had come through, and then baked them to order the next day. It seemed a more efficient use of her time than getting floury during business hours. Ellie, kitted out with her own pair of protective gloves and a hairnet, liked to assist her from time to time, although more scones seemed to get eaten than made when Ellie was involved.

On her return to the restaurant area, she noticed the customer had taken a seat at the newly vacated table by the window. The early summer sunlight, bright and increasingly warm as June started to flame, was casting him in silhouette. Wavy hair tumbled over his forehead; tanned arms were revealed by a light blue polo shirt, and long legs were shown off by tailored shorts, feet in a pair of Dunlop Green Flash trainers. The effect was attractive but a little contrived. Anna assumed he must be a tourist. As if to confirm this, he was tapping away at a MacBook, and his mobile phone, also from the ubiquitous brand, was lying on the table.

'Hello,' she said, wandering over to the table. 'What can I get you?'

It was only when he turned away from the sunlight and faced her squarely that Anna made the connection. The bone structure was unmistakeable, as was the uncanny mannerism of brushing a hand through his hair before speaking. Irrationally, Anna wondered why neither of them had ever bothered getting their hair cut shorter.

'Hi, lovely, can you get me an espresso and a slice of doorstep toast?' Jonathan Carter gave her a winning smile.

'No problem. Would you like any jam with that?' Anna scribbled down the order, taking a moment to observe Matthew's younger brother from under her lashes. She wondered if she ought to introduce herself; it was always so difficult to know what to call herself in relation to Matthew. *Girlfriend* sounded too juvenile, *partner* too serious, and as for *lover...* She blushed at the thought.

'No thanks, just butter it up. You're Anna, aren't you?' Jonathan said, saving her the decision. 'My father's told me all about you.'

Anna smiled. 'Yes. It's – er – nice to meet you, Jonathan.'

'Kind of you to be so polite,' Jonathan replied with a mischievous smile. 'Yes, that's me. Black sheep, prodigal son and all-round bad penny, but attempting to reform my wicked ways these days.' He extended a long fingered hand. 'So you're quite safe.'

Despite herself, in the face so such easy charm, Anna smiled. 'I like to make up my own mind about people,' she said. 'Even the more... notorious ones.'

Jonathan's smile turned into a grin. 'Glad to hear it. And so nice to meet the woman who's been reminding my brother that there is life outside of his office. It's about time he remembered he has a heart as well as a brain.'

'It's early days,' Anna said, blushing. 'We've only known each other a few months.'

'And, before you say it, absolutely none of my business!' Jonathan said, his smile slightly gentler. 'You don't need to worry; I won't be probing you for further details.' He turned briefly back to his computer screen. 'Even though I've decided to use this place as a kind of virtual office for a day or two. If that's all right with you, naturally.'

'I shouldn't think it'll be a problem, provided you buy a few cups of coffee, of course. Speaking of which, I'd better get this one sorted out.' Table space was limited in the tea shop, though, and she might have to kick him out if things got really hectic. She also wondered how Matthew was likely to react if he got wind of the arrangement, but Jonathan was a paying customer and she had no quarrel with him personally, so for the moment she tried not to dwell on it.

Anna, despite the hours of practice since she'd taken on the tea shop, still found the big Italian coffee machine a touch intimidating. She fiddled and steamed until she'd got the perfect espresso, then busied herself with the toast. Sneaking a look in Jonathan's direction while she waited for the toast to pop up, she grudgingly admitted that, while absolutely not her type, Jonathan was decidedly attractive. Although she was more than aware of his hugely questionable past, her initial impression of him was not altogether bad. Buttering the toast, and taking that and the coffee over to his table, she set them both down.

'Thanks, darling,' Jonathan said, looking up from his screen. 'Much appreciated.'

'Let me know if you need anything else,' Anna replied, making to turn away.

'Aren't you going to ask?' Jonathan said, eyes now having returned to his laptop.

'Ask what?'

'Why I'm choosing to work in the local tea shop rather than

212

at a desk at the organisation I will eventually own half of?'

'Given your... history with Matthew, I assume he's banned you from site.'

Jonathan gave a rueful smile. 'On the contrary, he actually offered me use of my old office; he's nothing if not accommodating. But let's just say I thought it more tactful to conduct my end of the business elsewhere for the moment.'

'Not into bridge building, then?' Anna asked, before she could stop herself.

'Any bridge I chose to build at the moment, Matthew would doubtless chuck a Molotov cocktail at, but who knows, given time...' he trailed off. 'For now, though, I think I prefer the rather more chilled atmosphere here.' Turning back to the laptop screen, he began typing again. Anna busied herself with preparing some sandwiches for the lunchtime rush.

*

After a busy shift, Anna finished work and wandered down to collect Ellie from nursery. Jonathan had worked at the table he'd chosen for most of the morning, and Anna had tried not to make it obvious she'd been observing him, but, knowing both his genetic closeness to Matthew, and the brothers' tangled history, she found it difficult to ignore him completely.

Despite the casual clothing, Jonathan had spent his time either tapping on his laptop or making phone calls. He seemed completely engrossed in his work, and as she'd walked past him, seeing to customers and clearing tables, she'd realised it wasn't all about FastStream and Carter's. Quite a few calls were to people unconnected with the cider business. Anna came to realise that Jonathan had quite a few irons in the fire. Was that in case it really didn't work out back in the family business, and he had to make a sharp exit again? She couldn't help making the inevitable comparison; Matthew had devoted his life to the familial concern, hadn't ever deviated from that course once he was set on it. Jonathan, on the other hand, had a wheeler-dealer's ability to have his fingers in several pies. She wondered how the two would mesh in the running of the family trade; if, indeed, they ever would.

Ellie was pleased to see Anna when she picked her up from nursery, and spent the walk home chattering nineteen to the dozen about the things she'd see, done and eaten that day. Anna was relieved she'd taken to nursery so well; she'd been concerned that the little girl would struggle to fit in, or that her naturally sunny nature would be compromised by encounters with other children, but, so far, she'd adapted well. Her rather matter of fact 'Daddy's died' response to other children's questions was as good as any, although it made Anna's throat ache whenever she heard it.

Just as she was burrowing in her bag for her house keys, her phone buzzed.

Dad promising to get home early tonight. BBQ @ours?
Ellie too! xxx

Smiling, Anna replied to Meredith in the affirmative. That was tea sorted, then. She made a mental note to take over some of the vanilla and orange cupcakes she'd been experimenting with for the tea shop; she'd not tried them out on anyone other than Ellie yet, and she knew that Meredith, as well as her father, would be more than willing taste testers. Grabbing her spotted cake tin from the top of the kitchen cupboards, she loaded up four from the plate on the counter where they lay. The action made her stomach flutter; would she and Ellie soon be a more permanent fixture in Matthew and Meredith's lives? Would her family of two, and Matthew's family of two, soon be one coherent whole? Cursing inwardly for her unguarded thoughts, she cut them off. *One day at a time*, she reminded herself firmly.

*

'So you met Uncle Jonno today?' Meredith whispered, when Matthew was out of earshot refreshing Anna's glass. Matthew had brought home a few bottles of a new variety of cider that the firm was currently trialling. Sweet and light with the colour of summer roses, the company was trying to decide on a name. It was the kind of cider you could easily drink a lot of, and, already one glass down, Anna had to keep reminding herself that she had to work in the morning.

How did that get out so quickly? she wondered. 'You could say that,' Anna replied carefully. 'He was doing some work in the tea shop and introduced himself.'

'He's funny, isn't he? I'm glad he's come back.'

'He seems nice.' Anna passed Ellie her cup of squash. 'I bet your granddad's glad of the company in the cottage.'

'Yup, although he said Uncle Jonno's about as messy as he was as a teenager! I just wish Dad would be a bit more pleased to see him,' Meredith sighed. 'Granddad said they used to be really close when they were kids, but not for years now.'

Careful, Anna thought. She knew Meredith hadn't made the link between Jonathan and Tara, and she didn't want to be the one to enlighten her. 'I'm sure they'll work it all out eventually,' she said.

'Why did he stay away so long? Has Dad said anything to you?'

'Not really,' Anna hedged. Then, with some relief, she saw Matthew coming back out of the kitchen with the barbecue provisions. 'Those look good,' she said, taking the tray from him.

'Some of Sid's sausages, and couple of steaks from Maurice's,' Matthew said. 'He assures me they'll only take a couple of minutes each side.'

'Thank god we've got a gas barbecue,' Meredith hissed as Matthew walked over to light the fire, all thoughts of interrogating Anna further temporarily forgotten. 'Not even Dad can mess this up.'

Anna laughed. 'Your faith in your father is touching.'

'You haven't had to live with ten years of burnt bangers and chicken crawling off the plate!' Meredith grimaced. 'Granddad eventually convinced him to get a gas one, and we've not had food poisoning since.'

Good for Granddad, Anna thought, not for the first time. Settling back with her glass, she looked forward to dinner.

*

Sometime later, Anna and Matthew sat watching Meredith pushing Ellie on the swing in the garden.

'They get on well, don't they?' Matthew observed. 'One of the unforeseen consequences of the divorce was the guilt that I was denying Meredith any siblings. I think she'd have been a great big sister.'

'It's not too late,' Anna said. 'You're hardly on your Zimmer frame. Who knows what the future holds.'

Matthew smiled. 'Are you trying to tell me something?'

Anna smiled back. 'Not exactly, but I felt the same way when James died. It seemed terribly unfair to be deprived of the choice whether or not to have another child.'

'You never think, when you're standing there at the altar, that there will ever be a time when you won't love that person; when you'll be without them.' He laughed, but there was a trace of bitterness in his tone. 'How wrong can you be?'

'No one really knows what the future holds,' Anna said softly. 'But we can try to make the most of the chances we get.' She slid a hand across the gap between their chairs and into his.

Playfully, Matthew turned Anna's hand upwards and tickled her palm with his fingertips. 'All too true,' he said softly. Lifting her hand, he kissed her wrist. 'How I wish you could stay with me tonight.'

Anna shivered as Matthew's lips hovered a fraction longer on the pulse point in her wrist. 'Me too.'

'Maybe one day soon we won't have to keep parting at the end of the evening,' Matthew murmured.

'That would be nice,' Anna said guardedly. She glanced back over to where Meredith was now spinning Ellie round and round on the grass. 'Although I don't know what those two would make of it.'

'Meredith's already asked why I keep coming back home every evening after seeing you. She seems to think she'll be perfectly fine by herself.'

'But you're not quite ready to leave her alone all night,' Anna finished the thought. She shivered as she thought back to the blissful nights they'd spent together when Meredith was in Belfast.

'Not yet. But soon. I promise.' He stared at her for a moment, as if considering whether or not to ask a question. 'Does Ellie talk about her father?' he asked, eventually.

'She acts as though she remembers,' Anna said. 'But I think, actually, her memories are just the things I've told her. I used to worry about keeping them alive for her; that we needed to talk about James every single day to keep him real and in her life, but it all felt too forced. We have our pictures, and I have the memories.'

'What are you two gassing about?' Meredith asked as she

sauntered back up to them, Ellie wrapped around her neck. 'And can we join in?'

Anna smiled. 'Nothing important.' Looking at her watch, she realised it was already an hour past Ellie's usual bedtime. 'We'd better get going.'

'Do you want me to run you home?' Matthew asked, wondering for a second where he'd put the keys to the Land Rover, then remembering that it was, yet again, in pieces at Patrick's.

'No, it's fine,' Anna replied. 'It's still light, we'll be OK walking.'

'Sefton could do with a run,' Meredith said, 'so I'll come out that way with you if you like.'

'Merry sleep in my bed?' Ellie asked as Meredith gently disentangled her from her waist.

Anna blushed, recalling the conversation she'd just had. 'Not tonight, darling; Merry's got school in the morning, and you've got nursery. Perhaps some other time.'

'Merry and Mathew stay at our house soon!' Ellie squeaked. 'Please?'

Matthew laughed. 'We'll see, Munchkin. But for tonight we'll have to say goodnight.' Kissing Anna briefly, he turned to Meredith. 'No loitering on the way home, daughter of mine. If you want to phone that boy, do it when you're back home.'

'All right, all right, as long as you don't, like, listen in on me,' Meredith grumbled. 'I'll just go and get Seffy's lead.'

'I hold him?' Ellie asked.

'I should think so,' Meredith replied, smiling. 'He's pretty tired from racing around with us all night so you should be able to handle him.'

'Yay!' Ellie jumped up and down on the spot.

The collie might have been tired, but Ellie showed no such

signs as she bounced home holding Sefton's extendable lead. Anna watched her fondly; yet again she marvelled at how adaptable her daughter was. Could she, should she, dare hope for a future that included both Matthew and Meredith?

Chapter 30

Monday lunchtime came, and Matthew, who had had no breakfast and a long morning, decided, much against his usual routine, to take a proper lunch break. He emerged into the sunlight, feeling markedly lifted as the warmth enveloped him.

As Matthew strolled along the village main street, he was hailed by several people, including Patrick Flanagan, who told him the Land Rover would be ready to pick back up by the end of the day. It had seen the inside of Patrick's workshop more often than its own driveway of late, and Matthew was reluctantly coming to the conclusion he'd have to get rid of the old vehicle soon. He shuddered at the thought of buying something more sensible and reliable, but, time, it seemed, was pretty much up for the Land Rover, unless he intended to keep pouring good money after bad.

It truly was a gorgeous day, and he had no need of his suit jacket. Shrugging out of it, he slung it over his arm. He felt a teenagerish excitement at seeing Anna, however briefly. He'd sworn to himself he wasn't going to encroach on her; she needed some space for her own life; the tea shop was her territory; but, after a hard morning poring over contracts for the FastStream deal and other strategic plans, he yearned for a quick word with her, and a sandwich.

It constantly amazed him how much he was enjoying laying himself bare to Anna; how she'd appeared in his life and cast a charmed glow over it. When he knew he was going to see her, he counted the minutes, and saying farewell of an evening was a wrench, even though he only lived a short walk away.

His destination came into view, a little way up the High Street on the other side of the road, and his heart began to beat faster. It was a heart he'd guarded fiercely over the years since his marriage had ended, and that Anna had managed to break through the barriers and reach it was a source of constant wonder, and occasional terror, for him. Today, inexplicably, he felt as carefree as the teenagers on a leave out from St Jude's as they queued for pizza at the takeaway right at the top of the high street.

As he passed the village butcher, its proprietor waved a cheery hand. Brown's had been part of Little Somerby for almost as long as Carter's, and the two families had often collaborated on village projects and events. The current incumbent, Maurice, he of the delectable steaks, was a cheerful man with a keen eye and a biting wit. Fond of a pint of cider at the local pub after closing up shop, he was a well-known and well-loved figure. Matthew raised a hand back in greeting.

Next to the butcher's was the local wine shop, catering for the more extravagant tastes of the Little Somerby residents. Amy, the proprietor, had been treated with mild suspicion by the locals at first, but her open and friendly manner had won around the most hardened of supermarket plonk buyers, and now she had a steady stream of 'regular occasion' customers, who fancied a change from their usual Côtes du Rhône and Chardonnay. He might have been a producer of a rival beverage, but still drank plenty of wine to make her acquaintance. Perhaps, on his way back, he'd nip in and grab a bottle to take over to Anna's tonight.

And finally, near the top of the street, was The Little Orchard Tea Shop. Suddenly hungry, and wanting to see Anna, he quickened his pace. The High Street was busy with cars, and for a few moments he continued walking on the opposite side of the road, thwarted from crossing. Eagerly, feeling as foolish as a teenager on his first date, he tried to catch a glimpse of Anna as he walked, but the sunlight was too strong, reflecting off the spotless glass of the tea shop's windows. Peering even more closely as he wandered towards the tea shop, he eventually made out two figures by the window table. As he looked on he took in the broad shoulders and confident demeanour of the man sat at the table and Anna, smiling prettily down at him as she took his order.

Suddenly, he lost his appetite. Turning on his heel, all thoughts of lunch forgotten, he walked briskly back towards his office.

*

Anna's morning had been a busy one. As she'd hoped, the book exchange idea had brought in a few more regular customers, and she'd played host this morning to a group of local readers who, with a little cake-based encouragement, were keen to swap books and talk about their reading. This had been the result of a small promotional campaign, nicknamed 'Fudge Cake and Fiction', that Anna had launched when she'd set up the Welsh dresser book exchange. Itching to capitalise on customers who were also avid readers, she'd converted the area of the tea shop with the sofas into an impromptu reading corner, and advertised a free sample of the day's cake to customers who came in and either exchanged or bought a book from the shelf. So far, she'd had a few takers. She'd had to smother a grin the previous week when the vicar's wife had come in and swapped a biography of Emily Bronte for the copy of *Fifty Shades of Grey* that Charlotte had shoved onto the Welsh dresser's shelf as a joke. The next time the vicar came in for his habitual post matins latte, she couldn't help wondering if his unusually cheerful demeanour was down to his wife's new choice of reading matter.

In fact, things were ticking along so nicely that she was toying with the idea of adding a book reviews section to the Facebook page she'd set up for the tea shop. In all the years Ursula had owned the place, she'd resolutely ignored the march of new technology, but in her last email to Anna she'd complimented her new manager on The Little Orchard Tea Shop's social media presence. Anna, glowing with pleasure that Ursula seemed so approving, had printed out a couple of the photos that Ursula had sent of her new Umbrian home, and pinned them to the noticeboard behind the counter. She knew many of her regulars would be pleased to see Ursula and Brian looking so well and so settled. She was just pondering whether she'd have time to get around to this before the weekend when Jonathan Carter had walked in.

'Afternoon, lovely lady. How's life in my favourite tea shop this fine day?' He took a seat at what Anna had begun to call his usual table, the one that allowed him to observe all the comings and goings of the village High Street, and dug around in his leather messenger bag for his laptop.

'Not bad, thanks. I'll be with you in a tick.'

Walking over to the elderly couple who sat at one of the tables by the wall, underneath one of Ursula's more prominent Italian themed water colours, she took their order for a pot of Earl Grey and two rounds of Somerset cider prosciutto and pickle sandwiches before heading over to where Jonathan sat.

'What can I get you?' she said, noting with interest the appearance on Jonathan's laptop screen of a presentation to FastStream.

'What would you recommend for brainpower?' Jonathan

asked. 'Matthew's given me this blasted PowerPoint presentation to spruce up, and while my brother's knowledge about the cider business is extensive, his ability to paint attractive pictures with prose that would appeal to our friends across the water is somewhat lacking.'

Anna grinned. 'Well, I don't know how good it would be for your brain, but this week's toastie has some glorious Wookey Hole cheddar and a few early spring onions from one of the local allotment holders. Meredith and a couple of friends have been coming in most days after school to have one.'

'Oh, darling, you had me at Wookey Hole!' Jonathan's smile could melt the stalactites that clung to the cheese's namesake caves as he reached a lazy hand out to Anna's forearm for emphasis. 'That'll do for starters, with a glass of sparking water on the side, please.'

Anna smiled back, but, ever mindful of the village's proven gossip machine, took a step back to break the contact he'd made. Jonathan's tactility was in stark contrast to his brother's rather more reserved nature, and while it didn't feel invasive to her, Anna was suddenly aware of the power of such a presumed intimate gesture. 'Coming right up,' she said, walking back to the kitchen.

Chapter 31

The next evening, Matthew stood on the patio in Anna's small back garden, looking over the lawn and into the distance. He could see lines and lines of apple trees, *his* trees, wrapping themselves around the cottage as if in an embrace. Anna's house was at the centre of land that belonged to him, but Pippin Cottage was like the heart within the body of the landscape, and he could feel his own heart beating as she approached him. Hearing the clunk of the glasses as she set them down on the wooden patio table, he drew a slightly shaky breath as she slid her arms around him from the back, resting her cheek against his broad shoulders. Cursing the reflex, he stiffened.

'I missed you last night,' Anna said. 'Were you late at the office?'

'Something like that.'

'Are you OK?'

Anna's voice was gentle, concerned, and it made Matthew want to weep. Turning, after a moment's hesitation, he took her in his arms and kissed her.

'Crikey!' Anna breathed, when he'd released her. 'What did I do to deserve that?'

'Be you,' Matthew said gruffly. 'Isn't that enough?'

'I'd like to think so,' Anna replied, raising a hand to brush a stray lock of hair out of Matthew's eyes, 'but something tells me there's more to it than that.'

Matthew pulled her close again. 'Only that I am a prat, and I don't know what I've done to deserve *you.*'

'That sounds serious,' Anna gave a nervous laugh.

'Not really.' Matthew released her, and they both reached for their glasses. 'I just forget how out of practice I am sometimes, at this relationship stuff.'

'Want to talk about it?'

'Let's just say that every so often, and I'm only admitting to this once, I need a little reminder that just because I see the woman I—' he coughed.

'The woman you...' Anna prompted.

'Oh, all right, the woman I *love* talking to another man, it doesn't mean she's going to run off and leave me.' He shook his head.

Anna smiled softly. 'And would this other man have been Sid Porter, by any chance, or are we talking about someone a little closer to home?'

Matthew groaned. 'I told you I was a prat.'

Putting her glass back down again, and taking Matthew's out of his hand, Anna reached up on tiptoe and very gently kissed Matthew's lips. 'You're not,' she whispered. 'You are the most wonderful, desirable, slightly overly possessive, gorgeous man I've met for a very, very long time.' She kissed him again. 'And even if I wasn't in love with you, I'd still never, ever, fancy your brother!'

'Is it selfish of me to feel complete relief you said that?' Matthew said gruffly as they broke apart.

'Given your – er – past, not at all. I think you said to me once that we all come with a little history. Yours just happens to be a bit more... local... these days, than it was.' Anna put her arms around Matthew again. 'But that doesn't mean it's going to encroach on our present. Or our future.'

'You are wise beyond your years, my love,' Matthew finally

smiled. 'I guess Jonathan's getting to me again.'

'Well, let me show you how much you needn't worry,' Anna pressed a little closer to Matthew.

'What about Ellie?' Matthew asked.

'Asleep. Hours ago.'

'Out here? Pat would have a coronary.'

'Not to mention Charlotte,' Anna replied. 'Evan's got a telescope he's quite keen on using at the moment.'

'So by the unlit fireside it is, then?'

'Or we could risk it and sneak upstairs,' Anna grinned. 'And perhaps you'd fall asleep by my side.' She brushed his lips playfully with her own. 'I've missed you since you spent those few nights here when Merry was away.'

Regretfully breaking away, Matthew spoke. 'When you kiss me like that, there is nothing that would please me more than sneaking upstairs with you, and, almost as wonderful, waking up beside you in the morning. But not tonight. Meredith's got an early start in the morning, some art trip or something, and I'm being the taxi service.'

'Fair enough.' Anna conceded. 'But consider it a standing invitation.'

'Oh, believe me, I will.' Breaking away from her to take a last mouthful of his wine, he smiled. 'I love you. And nothing's going to change that. And I'm sorry for... the other thing. Don't hold it against me?'

'I understand,' Anna replied. 'I love you too. Don't give it another thought.'

As Anna walked Matthew to the gate, she thought about all that had happened over the past few days. When she went to bed that night, alone, she spent a long time trying to work out the tangled branches of the dysfunctional Carter relationships. Something told her it was going to take more than one night of lost sleep to get her head around it all.

Chapter 32

'So are you near to agreement on the FastStream thing, then?' Anna asked on Friday evening as she poured them both a glass of wine.

'Pretty much,' Matthew sighed in appreciation of the wine and also the view of Anna's legs beneath the hem of her short summer dress. 'Just a few more things to iron out and then it'll be official.'

'I'm glad it's going to be sorted soon,' Anna said. She paused in her preparation of their dinner and wandered round to where Matthew was sitting at the kitchen table. Sliding her hands underneath the collar of his polo shirt, she kneaded his taut shoulders and neck, feeling the tension he'd been carrying with him for weeks. 'You deserve a break from it all.'

Matthew exhaled and leaned back into her touch. It would be a while before he felt completely relaxed again, but she had a good way of getting him to forget about things. Grabbing hold of her hands, he pulled her onto his lap, capturing her mouth in a hard kiss and sliding his hands down her body and over her hips.

'You are the best break from it all,' he murmured. 'You always feel so good.' He ran one hand up her bare thigh and underneath the skirt of her dress, feeling the softness of her skin against his palm. 'Every single warm, sexy inch of you...'

'I thought you were starving,' Anna teased, pressing closer to Matthew as she straddled his thighs.

'Oh, but I am,' he replied, his other hand slipping down the straps of her dress to find a breast and a tautening nipple. Leaning forward, he kissed her neck and progressed downwards, until Anna was arching her back in enjoyment.

'Will dinner keep for a little while?' Matthew murmured.

'From where I'm sitting, it feels like it'll have to,' Anna replied. She reached down and unbuckled Matthew's chunky leather belt, and then fumbled with the button on his jeans, until he stepped in to help her.

'Isn't this the most deliciously decadent thing?' Matthew released Anna so she could wriggle out of her knickers.

'I don't think I've ever straddled a man on a kitchen chair before!' Anna gave a slightly nervous giggle. 'I hope my furniture can take it.' She gasped as she lowered herself back down onto Matthew's lap, feeling him rock-hard and rampant. 'I hope *I* can take it...' Then, as she began to move, and their breathing became synchronised, she temporarily lost the power of speech. Matthew's expert fingers pressed, caressed and stroked Anna into panting, helpless ecstasy before he abandoned himself to her, thrusting deeply until, head thrown back, he came.

Sweaty and sated, they stayed joined for a few minutes afterwards, relishing their closeness despite the summer evening heat.

Matthew rested his head on Anna's shoulder. 'I think you should just move in with me and be done with it,' he said gruffly. 'Then we can do this a whole lot more often.'

'I think the girls might have something to say about it if we made this a regular occurrence at the dinner table.' Touched as Anna was, she knew all too well the ramblings of a post-coital male were not to be taken seriously.

Matthew grinned back. 'Perhaps it would be entirely too tantalising to have you in the same house all the time with me. I'd never get anything done!'

'One step at a time, my Romeo,' Anna replied. 'And for now, that step had better be dinner.' She climbed gingerly off Matthew's lap. 'And perhaps another glass of wine?'

'I'd better not,' Matthew replied. 'Flynn picked up his new car this afternoon, and it would be sod's law if it broke down and they needed a lift back from the ski slope.'

'Fair enough.' Anna cast an eye around her kitchen; at least the lasagne she'd cooked wouldn't have been harmed by a little extra time in the oven. Slotting the garlic bread in beside it, she poured them both large glasses of water and put the cork back into the bottle of red. A few minutes later they were tucking into dinner.

'So Meredith's flying out with you when school ends, and then you're going on to Florida the day after the contracts are signed?' Anna asked.

'Yup. She's going to spend six weeks with Tara and her bloke, Todd, I think his name is, and then come back in time for the start of the new term.'

'You're going to miss her, aren't you?' Anna said gently.

'Apart from the odd week or two when she was younger, she's been with me pretty much permanently since Tara and I split, so yes, I will miss her.' Matthew shook his head. 'But it's good for her and Tara to spend some time together. There's been precious little of that, and hopefully it'll allow them to build some bridges.'

'And what about you?' Anna asked. 'How are you at bridge building?'

Matthew shook his head ruefully. 'I guess I walked into that one, didn't I?' He took a sip of his water. 'Let's just say I've got some way to go before I'm ready to start laying foundations, let along building any bridge that has Jonathan on the other side of it.'

'But he *is* going to be back on board permanently, and on *the* board, isn't he?'

'According to Dad, yes.' Matthew raised his eyes from where they had been fixed on his plate. 'But there's a huge part of me that is wishing Jonathan will completely fuck this deal up, and then get back to where he came from, leaving us all alone again. That's completely stupid, isn't it?'

Anna said nothing, sensing it was better to let Matthew talk.

'Even though the FastStream deal is the absolute best thing to happen to the business in years, I'd chuck it all away in a heartbeat if it meant I didn't ever have to see my brother again.' He could feel the tension seeping back into him, as quickly as it had begun to dissipate, and battled against it. 'But that's not a discussion for tonight. I swore I was going to leave it all at work this evening. There's plenty of time tomorrow to start fretting again.'

'You know I'm here if you need me, don't you?' Anna smiled gently at him. 'I like to think we know each other well enough now to offload occasionally.'

Matthew nodded. 'I know. But anyone who knows me will tell you that I'm a stubborn old bastard, and it's best to let me deal with these things in my own time. You do understand, don't you?'

'Of course.' But Anna still felt a prickle of unease. She'd seen the exhaustion on Matthew's face over the past few weeks, more prominent since Jonathan had returned to the village. And she was well aware that the common consensus on Matthew's failed marriage, apart from the obvious, was his inability to share his burdens with those who loved him. Putting her knife and fork together, she looked at the clock on the wall behind Matthew. It was half past ten already.

'Everything all right?' Matthew asked.

'Yes, just wondering if you could switch off worried-dad mode yet!' It was a weak joke, but, thankfully, it seemed to do the trick.

'I told him to get her back by eleven,' Matthew replied. 'Perhaps I should get on home soon. Much as it pains me to eat and run, especially away from you.'

'I understand,' Anna said. 'I've got an early morning tomorrow, anyway – Lizzie usually does most Saturdays but she's off to see her daughter at uni for the weekend so I said I'd cover. Thankfully we shut at two so Mum and Dad are keeping Ellie until I knock off.'

'Picking apples for me would be less stressful, if you fancy a career change,' Matthew grinned. 'We could always do with a few extra pairs of hands in the autumn.'

'Thanks, but I wouldn't want you to be accused of favouritism,' Anna replied. 'And as you can't lay claim to the tea shop, as far as I know, it might be a safer bet.'

'Well, my mother did once make the scones for the cream teas there, but that was before Ursula's time,' Matthew said, picking up his plate and taking it to the dishwasher along with Anna's, 'and seeing as that was also long before I was born, I think you'll be safe enough from claims of nepotism!'

'And as for picking your apples, I wouldn't want you to think you could claim *droit de seigneur* whenever you felt like it,' Anna laughed. 'Let's keep things purely personal rather than business, shall we?'

Matthew gave his heartbreaking grin. 'Agreed. Although I wish I'd thought of that years ago... we've had some comely wenches working in the orchards over the years...'

Anna didn't grace that with a response, but picked up the last of the dishes and turned to put them in the dishwasher. As she did so, she heard Matthew's phone buzzing. It had been stationed on the table next to the salt and pepper mills during dinner, and he was just about to move it as he cleared the plates away. Glancing at the screen, he frowned.

'Number unknown,' he said. 'Probably a nuisance call.' He looked apologetically at Anna and pressed the end call button. Almost immediately it rang again. 'Well, they're persistent, I'll give them that!'

Anna saw the bottle of red wine sitting on the kitchen worktop and wondered if she dared risk another glass. After all, her mum and dad had Ellie for the night. She turned back around to gesture to Matthew for the water glasses and saw that he was ashen, all colour draining from his face as he listened intently to the call.

'Yes. I see. I'll be there right away. Thank you.' As Anna watched, she saw his hand start to shake so badly he had trouble pressing the button to end the call.

'What's wrong?' Crossing the kitchen, she went immediately to his side. 'Was it someone from work?'

Matthew shook his head, unable to speak for a moment. 'I have to get to the hospital,' he said hoarsely.

Chapter 33

Anna clung onto the front seat as Matthew took the corners of the winding roads at increasing speed between Little Somerby and the hospital in Bristol where Meredith had been airlifted.

'I knew I should never have let her go out with that idiot boy!' Matthew smacked the steering wheel in frustration as yet another slow driver pulled out from a side road. 'If she dies... Christ, Anna...'

'Just try to stay calm,' Anna said. 'It won't help anyone if you end up in an ambulance too.'

Ignoring her, he swerved out to pass the meandering Fiat in front of him and cut back in without bothering to indicate.

'She's all I've got. What if...'

'She's in the best hands.' Seeing his desperation, she was transported back to the night when James had been taken to hospital. Only then, there was no need for her to rush; he was past helping. She prayed they'd be at the hospital soon. Not only was she terrified about Meredith, she couldn't wait to get out of Matthew's car.

'And that boy... crashing his car and walking away virtually unscathed. If he's there, I swear I'll put him in a hospital bed myself.'

'You don't know if it was his fault,' Anna said. 'We don't know anything, yet. Please, just try to keep calm.'

The turning for the hospital was up ahead. Making the

Land Rover's engine squawk with rage, Matthew slammed on the brakes and turned down the road that led up to one of the best neurology units in the country. Its setting was rather incongruous, based as it was on the outskirts of the well-to-do village of Frenchay, but Matthew was never going to heed a village speed limit under these circumstances. Tearing up the road, he spun into the hospital car park, found the first space he could and was out of the car before Anna had even got her seatbelt off. As she slammed her car door, all she saw was his retreating back as he sprinted through the hospital's main entrance.

Maddeningly, there was a queue at the front desk, and, as an inebriated teenager with blood on his face was guided to a wheelchair by his concerned father, and a painfully thin old lady on a walking frame and in a nightgown was manoeuvred to a seat overlooking the car park, Anna could sense Matthew's tension reaching breaking point. His fists were tightly clenched at his sides, his back ramrod straight.

'Meredith. Meredith Carter.' He'd got his breath back by the time the patients in front of him had been redirected. The administrator nodded and turned to look at her computer screen. As she typed in the password for her screen saver, Anna could see Matthew's set face, jaw almost locked with tension. Eventually, she located the correct window.

'Ah yes. Brought in by air ambulance from an RTA. And you are?'

'Her father.'

'Go up to floor twelve, ward fifty-seven. Someone will meet you.'

'Do you have any other... I mean... can you tell me...' Matthew shook his head in frustration at his increasing inability to speak.

The receptionist smiled sympathetically. 'Someone will be

there to meet you and answer all your questions.'

Matthew tried to open his mouth but couldn't speak. Anna nodded at the receptionist. 'Thank you.' Taking Matthew's arm, as for a second he seemed frozen to the spot, she led him to the lift. 'Come on.'

The lift journey was interminable. As the doors opened, Matthew seemed to recover his senses. Striding from the lift, he accosted the first white coat he saw.

'Excuse me. My daughter Meredith was brought in?'

The doctor consulted her clipboard. 'Ah yes. She's in surgery at the moment. The surgeon, Ms Burke, will be down to see you shortly. Would you like to take a seat in Room 73?'

'Surgery?' Matthew's face went from white to grey. 'Please, can you tell me what they're operating for?'

The medic shook her head. 'I'm sorry. I don't have that information. If you go to Room 73, the surgeon will be with you as soon as she can.'

'Come on, Matthew,' Anna said gently. 'Let's do what the doctor says.' Taking his hand, she led him, meek as a child, down to the waiting room.

*

'I don't know what to do.' Matthew moved towards the sash window. The darkness outside was punctured only by the orange street lights, their harsh colour dissipating in the onslaught of the rain. Helplessly Anna watched as he leaned his forehead against the cool glass of the window.

'All we can do is wait,' she said softly. 'She's in the best hands, with the best doctors.' She felt utterly helpless in the face of Matthew's fear and uncertainty.

'If anything happens to her... if she... if she dies... I swear—' Matthew's hand pressed up against the window and balled into a fist in an attempt to keep control. He turned further away, burying his face into his arm.

'We have to trust the doctors. They won't let her down.' Anna could feel her heart beating wildly, full of fear and horror at the situation they found themselves in. Memories were washing over her of the night of James' death, and the sensations were dizzying.

'Anna,' it was barely a whisper. 'Oh God, Anna.' his eyes were two dark caverns of fear and grief as he turned back to look at her. 'I can't lose her. Not after fighting so hard to keep her for all these years...'

'Matthew...' Anna moved across the waiting room, aching to take him in her arms and soothe away the pain and horror. 'I'm here.'

Just as she reached him, the door to the waiting room opened and a doctor appeared. Instantly, Matthew's shutters seemed to come down again. He crossed the small space, moving past Anna to get to the doctor.

'Mr Carter? I'm Ms Burke. The team and I have just finished operating on Meredith and she's in recovery.'

'How is she?'

The doctor gestured to one of the chairs and Matthew sat.

'She's in a critical but stable condition. We had to operate to repair an extradural hematoma – a tear in the artery – from where she hit her head in the collision. We're going to keep monitoring her over the next twenty-four hours to see how she's responding. We'll be watching closely to ensure that the bleeding has stopped, and to minimise any risk of further damage.'

'When will she wake up?'

'She was unconscious when she was brought in, and she may continue to be so for some time after the anaesthetic wears off. If we feel she needs it, we'll keep her in an induced coma. She's young, so we're optimistic she'll come round of her own accord, but she might need to stay asleep for a little while longer.'

'Did she have any other injuries?'

'Cuts and bruises, nothing more. In physiological terms, she escaped fairly lightly.' Ms Burke noticed the bleak expression on Matthew's face, and her expression softened. 'She's in one of the best neurology units in the country, Mr Carter. We will be doing everything we can to ensure she makes the fullest recovery possible.'

'And will she... make a full recovery?'

'As I said, it's early days. There are a number of longer term symptoms that can arise from this type of injury; I'll make sure you have as much information as possible as to the kinds of issues with memory and cognition that can occur. But for the moment, we need to treat her immediate injuries. If she needs any kind of rehabilitative treatment, we can assess that over the next few days and weeks.'

The doctor stood back up and consulted her notes. 'You can come through to recovery and see her.'

Matthew swallowed and nodded. 'Thank you.' He stood up. 'Oh Christ. I'd better contact her mother.' He cursed as he realised he'd left his phone in the car.

'Don't worry,' Anna said. 'I'll pop out and get your mobile.' She was grateful to have something, anything, to do in the face of so much fear and grief.

Matthew pulled her to him in a rather clumsy embrace. 'Thank you. And thank you for coming with me.'

As Anna wandered down the corridors and back to where Matthew had parked the car, a creeping sickness in her stomach began to rise. By the time she reached the entrance to the hospital, it had reached her mouth. Rushing for the nearest hedge, she threw up and up and up.

After a few moments, she composed herself. This was not the time to break down. Even two and a half years on, the sight, smell and sounds of a hospital, and the context of her visit, brought back so much from the night of James' death. She prayed that Matthew wouldn't have to go through what she went through, and that Meredith would recover. She had no idea what Matthew would do if she didn't. As the sliding doors of the hospital entrance parted to admit her once again, she felt as though she was entering the gates of hell.

*

Carrying two strong coffees and Matthew's mobile phone, Anna made her way up to where Meredith had been put in recovery. The eerily silent corridors, strip lighting glaring off polished floors and disinfectant smell all contributed to the grimness of the situation. She passed weary-looking medics on their way, no doubt, to break different kinds of news to other anxious relatives.

Eventually she reached the right room. Peering through the small window inset into the door, she saw Matthew sitting by a stark white hospital bed. He looked blasted to stone, much older than his years. Leaning forward in the chair by the bed, one hand on his thigh, his gaze was fixed on its occupant. In that bed, wearing a neck brace and attached to all manner of machines, was Meredith. Anna drew a sharp breath. Meredith looked so small, so vulnerable, so different from her normal vibrant self. The bandage around her head, and the white hospital sheets looked warm in comparison to her skin. Her dark hair fell lank on either side of her face. Even her lips looked pale. Matthew was gently holding her right hand and, sensing Anna's presence, he shifted his gaze from his daughter to where Anna was standing. With a superhuman effort, he released his unresponsive daughter's hand and walked to the door.

'Do you want me to sit with Meredith while you phone Tara?'

Matthew looked long and hard at her. 'Will you be all right?'

Anna smiled, touched by his perception and his concern. 'I think so.'

As he passed her, he touched her cheek with the hand that had been holding Meredith's. 'I'm so sorry, Anna. This must be the last place you want to be.'

'Don't be silly. I'm here for you. And for Meredith.' Anna reached up and touched Matthew's hand. 'For as long as you need me.'

'No. You should get home. You've got to work in the morning.' Matthew's voice trembled. 'I'll be all right.'

'Just let me stay until you've phoned Tara,' Anna said. 'And then I'll get home.'

Matthew dropped his hand from her cheek, and nodded. 'All right.' He wrinkled his brow, as if remembering something else. 'I'd better ring Pat, too, get her to nip round and let Sefton out. Excuse me?'

'Of course. Take all the time you need.' Passing him one of the coffees, she waited for a moment as he walked down the corridor, then entered the small hospital room. Bracing herself, she sat down in the seat Matthew had just vacated. For a moment she didn't dare to breathe. Then, slowly, she reached out and took Meredith's left hand.

'Hey, lovely,' she whispered. 'I'm here. Your dad's just gone to phone your mum. He'll be back soon.'

For a split second, she genuinely believed Meredith would answer, but as her ears became attuned to the steady beep of the heart monitor, and the rise and fall of the ventilator, she realised, to her horror, that she might never hear the teenager's voice again.

Matthew returned to the room a few minutes later looking even grimmer than he had when he'd left. 'She's coming on the next flight she can get.' Gesturing to Anna to stay put in the chair, he pulled a hard-backed wooden seat towards Meredith's bed. 'This is all my fault,' he said softly. 'I should never have agreed to her going out in that car with him so soon after he'd passed his test.' Balling the fist of the hand that wasn't holding his phone, he drew a deep breath.

Gently, Anna placed a hand over his clenched one. 'It was an accident, Matthew.' She gave his hand a tentative squeeze. 'You couldn't have known this was going to happen.'

'Then *he* should have!' Matthew snapped. He slumped back in his seat. 'I'm sorry. I shouldn't be taking this out on you. This must be hell for you, after what happened to James.'

Anna felt a sting of something she couldn't identify as Matthew mentioned her dead husband's name. 'It's not me you need to be worrying about, honestly.'

'Do you know if they brought Flynn in?' Matthew asked.

'I haven't heard,' Anna said. 'But if they did, I'm sure the police will want to speak to him.'

'He'd better keep his distance from here.'

The beeps and lights from the various monitors stationed around Meredith's bed kept their counsel for a minute as both Matthew and Anna were lost in their own thoughts. Eventually, Anna went to move. 'I'd better get going. If you're sure you'll be all right. Can I bring you anything in when I come back?'

Matthew rubbed his eyes. 'I... I don't know.' He looked back at Anna through tired, bloodshot eyes. 'What do I need?'

Leaning forward, she wrapped her arms around him and pulled him close. 'It *will* be all right, Matthew, I promise,' she whispered into his hair. Expecting to feel his arms around her in reciprocation but instead feeling his body go rigid in her arms, Anna broke away from him again. 'I'll see you soon. Ring me if you need anything. Or if there's any change.' Unsure of what more she could do or say, Anna looked back at the bed. Not for the last time, she prayed the Meredith would wake, and soon.

Chapter 34

The next morning, Anna felt as though she'd aged a hundred years. She'd taken a taxi back from the hospital and crashed into bed, only to wake three hours later from a fitful, restless slumber. Waking to unseasonably dreary weather, she watched the rain dripping down the leaded windowpanes. She resisted the urge to phone Matthew straight away since he might have managed some sleep, too, in the intervening hours. Stretching, she pulled the duvet back and padded into the bathroom.

Gloomily aware of her imminent shift at the tea shop, she forced down a cup of coffee and ran through her checklist of tasks. Fortunately, she'd pre-baked the scones for the cream teas before Matthew had arrived last night, and loaded them in the containers, and she always made sure Friday's bread order from the village bakery was enough to cover the Saturday trade as well, so it was just a matter of making sandwiches to order. Deciding that there was no point hanging around an empty house any longer, she slung on her fleece against the early morning chill.

As she passed Pat's, she saw the older woman was also up and about, and since she had a bit of time before she had to open the tea shop, she decided to whip in and update her on Meredith's condition. She was surprised to be met at the door not just by Pat but by Sefton.

'I thought I'd better bring him home with me,' Pat said,

handing Anna a cup of strong tea. 'He was fine when I went round last night, but he's an early riser.'

'Thanks, Pat,' Anna said. 'Is it all right if I borrow your key to Matthew's? I said I'd go over later and get some stuff for the two of them.'

Pat nodded. 'Of course.' She went to the dresser in the hallway and grabbed the key. On her return, she gave Anna a brief hug. 'This must be very difficult for you. You bearing up OK?'

Anna nodded, unable to speak. With an effort, she cleared her throat, and broke away gently from Pat's embrace. 'Tara's apparently flying in as soon as she can.'

Pat looked wary. 'Well, I suppose she was bound to.' She looked as though she wanted to comment further, but seemed to think better of it. 'Send our love to them both. I can't imagine that lively girl lying in a hospital bed.'

'She's in the best hands,' Anna said automatically.

'Drop the key back in when you have the chance and I'll nip round and spruce up the house for them.'

Anna managed a smile. 'Thanks, Pat. I'm sure Matthew'll appreciate it.'

The Saturday morning shift at the tea shop was, thankfully, busy enough to keep Anna's thoughts from straying too often to Frenchay. At around eleven o'clock a fifteen strong group of Strawberry Line cyclists, all requesting cream teas, cleared out the batch of scones she'd cooked and her Saturday morning regulars more or less finished the cakes.

At midday, Anna's mother Julia wandered in with Ellie, who, despite refusing to eat Anna's strawberry cake from the tin at home, seemed to have developed a taste for it at the tea shop, and installed themselves at the table by the window.

'Everything all right, Mum?' Anna asked as she put the cake down in front of Ellie.

'Fine,' Julia Clarke replied. 'Just thought we could do with some air, since your dad's gone out early to play a quick nine holes.' She took a sip of her tea and smiled at her daughter. 'Did you have a nice time last night?'

Five minutes later, thankful that all of her other customers seemed to be either engrossed in their conversations or their cakes, Anna had filled Julia in.

The older woman's face registered horror, then disbelief. 'That poor girl,' she said, reflexively reaching over and giving Ellie a cuddle. The toddler looked surprised, but then tucked back into the remains of her cake. Julia's attention shifted back to her own daughter. 'How are you holding up, darling?'

'OK,' Anna swallowed hard, affected by the concern in her mother's voice. She stuck her hands in the front pocket of her green apron to hide them in case they started to shake. 'No, honestly, I'm fine.'

'You don't have to be brave.'

'I know, Mum, but if I start crying now, I don't think I'll ever stop. If she doesn't pull through...'

'You mustn't think like that.' Mindful of where they were, Julia just reached out and squeezed Anna's forearm. 'She's made it through the first few hours; that can only be a good thing.'

'I was going to go back up there when I finish here with some stuff for them both,' Anna said. 'Would you mind keeping hold of Ellie for a bit longer?'

Julia smiled. 'Of course. Take as long as you need. I might pop back to yours with her tonight, though, and stay there, rather than risk her waking Dad in the middle of the night again.'

Anna grimaced. 'Sorry about that – she must have been a bit disoriented.'

'It's no trouble, but if she's in her own bed, she'll settle better. I'll just crash out in the box room if you're late back from the hospital.'

Anna gave her mother and daughter a final smile before carrying on with her shift. Her phone was still in the front pocket of her apron, but it had been unsettlingly silent the whole morning. She hoped that no news was good news.

At close of business, Anna didn't dawdle. She cashed up as soon as she could, locking the takings securely in the tea shop's safe, and then walked briskly home to get her car. Giving herself a quick once-over in the hall mirror, she chucked on a new T-shirt and then headed back out of the door.

After a few minutes she pulled up in the drive of Cowslip Barn. The house looked cold, empty and uninviting. She let herself in, and, taking a wrong turn into Matthew's study, she was brought up short by a couple of new pictures in a silver frame on his huge mahogany and leather desk. One was of Meredith, obviously taken at some point the previous summer; she looked so vibrant, so alive. The other, tucked into the corner of the same frame, Anna was shocked to see, was of herself and Ellie. It was a shot that Anna remembered being in the local weekly newspaper, taken at the May Fair. They were both smiling at the camera, Ellie in Anna's arms. The newspaper had focussed on the 'young mother takes on new business challenge' angle in the accompanying caption, which Anna had found alternately embarrassing and hilarious at the time. Now, reminded of happier times, it made her draw in a sharp breath.

Heading up the creaky stairs, she navigated her way to Matthew's bedroom at the back of the house. Despite their closeness, she hadn't actually been into his bedroom before. The scent of his cologne and the rumpled bedsheets caught her senses. Chucked over the button backed chair by the window that overlooked the back garden was a pair of blue jeans and a checked blue and white shirt, and hung up behind the door was his suit jacket. Feeling like an intruder, she opened Matthew's wardrobe and pulled out what she hoped was a suitable shirt and a fresh pair of jeans. Then, she pulled open his chest of drawers to find some new underwear. She allowed herself a brief smile as she noticed how neatly folded everything was; Pat obviously had no qualms about arranging the more intimate areas of her employer's life as well as doing the dusting.

Meredith's room was exactly as she had left it. Make-up spilled across her dressing table, and too many tops, skirts and pairs of jeans to count lay abandoned on her bed and over the floor. Anna felt a lump rise in her throat. She grabbed a pair of pyjamas that were, at least, neatly folded on the bedroom chair. As she moved towards Meredith's dressing table, her heart skipped a beat; there, between the make-up tubes and general cosmetic detritus was a small, wrapped present, with a card attached. Meredith had been so proud of the cufflinks she'd found for Matthew for Father's Day, which was tomorrow. The thought that the teenager might not pull through to give them to him was too much to bear. Suddenly desperate to get out of the house, Anna glanced at the bed and saw an old, tatty stuffed toy rabbit propped up against the pillows. With a trembling hand she picked it up and put it on the pile of clothes she was holding. Returning down the stairs, she grabbed a plastic bag from the storage container in the kitchen, then, breathing a sigh of relief, locked the front door behind her.

*

In the daylight, the drive to the hospital seemed less terrifying, but the destination had lost none of its fear and uncertainty.

Pulling into the car park Anna saw that the Land Rover was still in the same space as Matthew had left it. As she locked her car and hurried through the hospital entrance, she prayed there had been a positive development in Meredith's condition.

As she reached the floor where Meredith had been the previous evening, she suddenly wondered if the teenager had been moved. She paused briefly to try to locate the information desk, but before she could ask, a voice, deep but with an unmistakeable West Country burr, raised but not yet shouting, caught her attention.

'You've got a bloody nerve turning up here!'

Anna hurried in its direction. Her heart sank as she rounded the corner to the next corridor.

'Please, Mr Carter, I came to see how Merry is.' Flynn looked pale, his long dark fringe not quite long enough to cover the livid purple bruise on his forehead. The colour was matched by the shadows under his red-rimmed eyes, and even from a few metres away, Anna could see his hands were shaking wildly.

Matthew moved closer to the boy. Flynn was touching six feet but he was still in the gangly, skinny phase of his adolescence. Matthew, in contrast, despite the traumas of the past few days, was three inches taller and twice as broad. It was like seeing a young pretender squaring up to an old buck.

'Get out!' Matthew growled. 'I, and my daughter, don't want to see you.'

Flynn took a step back, obviously afraid. 'Mr Carter, I need to explain...'

'I said get out!' Matthew was trembling as much as Flynn, his rage threatening to boil over.

Anna had seen enough. Matthew was exuding such menace, such pent-up rage. 'I'd do as he says, Flynn,' she said. 'Speak to Mr Carter another time.'

'I just need to know she'll be OK,' Flynn said, almost in tears. Anna surmised, by the look of the boy, that he'd been crying a great deal.

'It's early days, Flynn,' Anna said. 'Please, go home and get some rest yourself.'

Flynn looked helplessly towards Matthew again, but Matthew had turned away, dismissing the boy as much with his body language as he had with his words. Lowering his gaze, he turned and walked back down the corridor.

'How dare he show his face here.' Matthew began to pace up and down. 'He walks away from the smashed up wreck of that car virtually unscathed while my daughter ends up comatose.'

'He must be thankful to be alive,' Anna said softly.

'He should be more than bloody thankful,' Matthew snapped. 'And he'd better stay out of my way.'

Anna drew closer to Matthew, mindful of his explosive mood. 'He's obviously terrified, and desperately wants to know about Meredith. I know you're angry; you've got every right to be, but for Meredith's sake, please, try to stay calm.'

'And how would you react if the kid who killed your husband had turned up at the hospital?'

Anna took an involuntary step back as if Matthew had slapped her. Horrified, she gaped at him. Her knees went weak in the face of his rage, and she understood exactly why Flynn had been so terrified.

'Christ, Anna, I'm sorry. That was completely out of order.' Matthew pulled Anna to him, but for a moment Anna felt more claustrophobic than comforted as his arms wrapped around her. Steeling herself not to struggle away from him, she was relieved when he moved away again.

'Is there any change?' Anna asked, trying frantically to regain her equilibrium. She felt as though the floor was moving beneath her feet.

Matthew shook his head. 'If you mean has she woken up, then no, but her vital signs have stabilised over the past few hours so they're going to move her to intensive care later this morning.' He reached out a hand, trying to take one of Anna's, but she retreated slightly, denying him the contact. A look of irritated incomprehension crossed his features before he composed himself again.

'That's good, though,' Anna said. 'Have they said anything about... long term damage?'

'Too early to say.'

An uneasy silence fell between them. Anna took a moment to look at Matthew. Grey-flecked stubble peppered his face and his eyes were dark and cavernous. He looked as if he'd fall apart if he didn't get some rest soon.

'I've brought some fresh clothes for you, and a few things for Meredith.' Anna passed Matthew the bag.

'Thanks. I take it Pat gave you the key?'

Anna nodded. 'She says not to worry, she's going to pop in later today and give the place the once-over.'

Matthew gave the ghost of a smile. 'Thank her for me.'

'Have you eaten?'

'Didn't want to leave her.' Matthew swallowed. 'I'd love a coffee, though.' He rummaged in the pocket of his jeans for some change, but Anna shook her head. 'It's OK, I've got it.' Desperate to get away from him, she walked back down the corridor.

Anna stepped out of the lift on the ground floor and headed towards the hospital shop. Drawing closer to the coffee machine, she saw Flynn hovering by the entrance. He caught sight of her immediately and wiped his eyes before meeting her gaze.

'Please, how's Meredith?' His voice trembled.

'She's still unconscious, Flynn,' Anna said gently.

Flynn bit down hard on his bottom lip. 'If I could, I'd swap places with her.'

Anna's heart went out to the frightened boy. 'I know. But the best thing you can do at the moment is to give her and her dad some space.' He looked so young, so defenceless. She'd never met the boy who had been driving the car that killed James, but, faced with Flynn now, she could imagine how haunted and terrified he must have been after the events that took her husband from her.

'Can you tell her...' Flynn swallowed. 'Can you tell her... how sorry I am. That I never meant... that if I could go back I'd...' he blinked furiously.

Anna nodded, impossibly moved by his vulnerability. 'Go home and get some rest. Matthew's staying here at the hospital with Merry until she's strong enough to leave, and he's not going to let you near her at the moment. Perhaps when she wakes up...'

Flynn nodded. 'I understand. Thank you. For listening to me.' Wiping his eyes with the back of his hand, he stumbled from the hospital.

Anna watched him cross the car park and get into one of the parked cars. As the car pulled away, she saw that it was his mother who had come to collect him. Her perception of him as terribly young stayed with her long after they'd left the hospital.

Chapter 35

The hours crawled by. Anna persuaded Matthew to rest in one of the family rooms that backed onto the intensive care ward, while she sat by Meredith's bedside. Strictly speaking, she shouldn't have been allowed, but the nurses showed compassion and discretion in the face of Matthew's exhaustion.

'You will wake me if she opens her eyes,' he said. Matthew's habit of stating rather than questioning made an answer unnecessary.

Time's relentless march became something of a threat. Meredith still looked as though she was sleeping, especially now the ventilator had been removed, but Anna knew, from the regular checks that were made on her by the medical staff, the levels of concern were increasing. Snatched conversations about 'alpha waves' and 'brain activity' were taking on an altogether more sinister feel.

Anna began to imagine she saw Meredith moving; a flicker of an eyelid here, the twitch of a finger there. But, in truth, it was more in her mind than in the room itself.

At around nine o'clock, Anna slipped out of Meredith's room to grab another coffee and splash her face with water. She decided to give Matthew another hour or so before going to wake him, and then head home to relieve her mother of babysitting duties. Walking back out of the visitors' bathroom, on her way to Meredith, she caught sight of a figure striding down the corridor. Too far away to be seen clearly, something about the gait and bearing of the new visitor caught her eye. As the figure drew closer, the clack of her heels on the tiled floor becoming more distinct, Anna felt a shiver of apprehension.

Fashions might have changed in the intervening years between her wedding photo and the reality, but Tara Carter was still beautiful. The once long, lustrous blonde hair was now cropped short, framing slanting clear blue eyes in a heart-shaped face. An all-American tan accentuated her looks, and, despite the fact she'd just stepped off a seven-hour flight, she looked icily calm, composed and extremely glamorous.

Before Tara reached her, however, Matthew appeared from the family room. Tara didn't miss a beat.

'Where's Meredith?' Tara asked. 'These damn British hospitals are like rabbit warrens. It's taken me ten minutes to get any sense out of Reception.'

If Matthew was shocked by the abrupt entrance of his ex-wife, he did his best to hide it. Walking up to her, he kissed her guardedly on her rigid cheek. 'I've just spoken to the consultant. They're moving her to run a few tests, and then they'll keep her down there for the next few hours.'

'Tests? What tests? Matthew, what the hell happened here?' Tara's voice was brittle, frantic. Despite everything, Anna's heart went out to her. She couldn't imagine the horror of having a child in this situation.

'We'll know more about her prognosis after they've done the tests. We just have to wait and see.'

'If anyone tells me it's early days one more time, Matt, I swear I'll—' Tara trailed off.

'Well, I'm afraid that's the way it is,' Matthew said bluntly.

At that moment, a trolley came out of Meredith's room. Tara stifled a cry. Automatically, Matthew put an arm around his ex-wife as she covered her mouth with her hand. Tara leaned into him; she looked small and frail beside him. As the trolley passed, Tara reached out a not entirely steady hand and touched one of Meredith's.

'How can this have happened to you, baby?' she whispered.

The porter stopped briefly, and then, with a sympathetic look, continued to wheel the bed to its destination.

They must have made quite a sight, Anna thought, after the event. Two parents, united in fear and grief, and her; close, but not close enough. She observed, from the outside; all of the experiences of the past few months counting for nothing compared to the fact that the two other adults in the corridor had created the child who lay in the hospital bed between them.

As Meredith vanished round the corner to her next destination, Matthew broke away from Tara and moved back towards Anna. 'I'm sorry, I should have introduced you two.' He glanced from one woman to the other. 'Anna, this is Tara.'

'I wish we were meeting under better circumstances,' Anna said, extending a hand.

Tara glanced at Anna's hand, but didn't take it. 'Quite.'

Anna couldn't help but notice the way Tara looked her up and down, assessing, measuring. She was uncomfortable under the scrutiny. 'Well, I'd better get going,' she said finally.

'I'll walk you to your car, once I've seen Meredith down,' Matthew took the hand that Anna had offered to Tara, as if in mitigation.

'No, really, it's fine.' Anna suddenly needed to put some distance between herself and the formerly married couple. 'I can see myself out. You should go... you should *both* go.'

Tara gave the slightest of nods, and Matthew, unable to keep up with the cross-currents, acquiesced. Alone, Anna exited the building, the feeling of unease growing ever stronger.

'I remember the day you were born,' Matthew whispered, still holding his daughter's hand. 'You were so tiny – only six pounds, and you fitted into the palms of my hands.' He swallowed hard. 'Your mother and I were so proud of you. Of the fact that we'd created you. And I loved you from that moment. I will always love you, Merry.'

The door to Meredith's room opened slowly and in slipped Tara. There were dark shadows under her eyes, partly from jetlag and partly from worry about her daughter. She took a seat on the hard wooden chair on the other side of Meredith's bed.

'Any change?' she asked softly.

Matthew shook his head. He felt weak from exhaustion, and apart from those few hours in the family suite, he hadn't left Meredith's bedside since she'd been brought in.

'I wish...' Tara twisted the large white gold diamond solitaire that adorned her left hand round and round. 'I wish I'd been there for her.'

'No point looking back,' Matthew said gruffly. 'What's gone is gone.'

'She was – is – my baby, Matthew. If she doesn't...'

'She will wake up, Tara. I have to believe that.' Matthew ran a hand over his achingly tired eyes.

'Why don't you go and get some coffee? I'll sit with her for a while.'

'Making up for lost time?' Matthew said bitterly.

'Please, Matt, don't,' Tara said. 'Not now. Not here.'

Matthew felt a prickle of shame, but couldn't quite let the anger go. 'You being here. It changes nothing,' he said flatly. 'But while you are here, you should make the effort to spend some time with her. Just in case—' he trailed off, fighting with his emotions again. 'I'll go and get that coffee.'

Out in the hallway, the strip lighting cast a greenish glow, making the faces of the medical staff seem even more drained. Matthew nodded to a couple of House Officers he recognised and headed off down the corridor to find yet more coffee. Never had he missed Anna's presence more. Checking his phone, he was gratified to find a text message from her.

Miss you. Love to Merry. Don't forget to eat! A xxx

Swiftly, while the coffee was being dispensed, he replied:

Miss you too. No change with Merry. Wish you were here. M x

Matthew wanted nothing more than to rest his head on Anna's shoulder and make this whole situation go away, but for the moment he had to be strong. Meredith needed him. As much as he hated the thought, Tara needed him. Sighing, he grabbed the polystyrene cup of what passed for coffee in the hospital and took a gulp. Then, automatically, he selected another cup to give to Tara. He hoped she still took it black with one sugar.

Returning to Meredith's room, looking in through the glass window in the door, he saw Tara was also texting someone. He felt a surge of anger. Couldn't she have waited until she got out of Meredith's hospital room? Swallowing back the bile that rose in his throat, he opened the door and placed Tara's coffee on the cupboard next to Meredith's bed.

Tara looked at it, surprised. 'Thank you,' she said.

'No problem.' He sat down in his chair again. 'Anything

important?' He gestured to Tara's phone, trying to keep the edge out of his voice.

'Just checking in,' Tara said. 'Todd wants to know when I'll be home.'

'Doesn't he know how sick our daughter is?' Matthew's voice was low, but dangerous.

'Of course, Matt, but, not being a parent himself he doesn't quite understand. Not like your sweet little widowed single mother, I suppose.'

'Leave Anna out of this.' Matthew snapped. 'She's got nothing to do with you.'

'But she's clearly got plenty to do with *you*!'

'You know nothing about Anna, and nothing about me anymore, Tara, so don't presume that you do.'

'Oh, I know plenty about you, or have you forgotten? Meredith's been emailing me quite a bit since we arranged for her to spend the summer. And I know for a fact you'd never have let her go out with that boy in his car so soon if that tragic little housewife hadn't got your attention. What the hell were you thinking?'

'You forfeited the right to ask when you walked out on us.' He started to shake. 'She's not a child any more. She needed some freedom.'

'And look what happened, Matt!'

It was at this point that a passing Sister, hearing raised voices, opened the door to Meredith's room. 'Mr and Mrs Carter, can I suggest you take your "discussion" outside of this room, and preferably away from this hospital? Now is not the time or the place for raised voices.'

Matthew dropped his head. 'You're right. I apologise, Sister.' He turned back to Tara. 'I'll wait outside until you're ready to leave.'

Tara nodded, smiling apologetically at the senior nurse. She settled back down in her chair, phone in hand.

Matthew, shaking from exhaustion and rage, walked out of the room and slumped in a chair in the hallway outside. Shame washed over him as he realised he'd once more allowed Tara to get the better of him. He thought about texting Anna again, but he didn't want to inflict his black mood on her. Glancing back through the door pane, he saw Tara finally put her phone away.

Chapter 36

The next few days ran into one another in their monotonous regularity. Matthew reluctantly allowed Tara to take some solo shifts at the hospital when he realised work was piling up at the farm, although he managed, for the first time in his life, to delegate a great proportion of it to his second and third in command.

Although Matthew had felt uneasy, he'd allowed Jonathan to take over his office and manage the rest of the FastStream process. Exactly a week after the accident, when he knew Matthew was still at the hospital, Jonathan decided to pop in on Anna and see how she was. They'd spoken a few more times when he'd been basing himself at the tea shop, and, with Matthew spending all the time he could at the hospital, Jonathan hoped Anna would be pleased to see him. He also sensed she might be feeling a bit pushed out of the equation with Tara's arrival. He hadn't wanted to come face to face with Tara himself, so although in his darker moments he cursed his cowardice, he'd stayed away from the hospital. Leaving Matthew's office mid-evening, he swiped a couple of bottles of sweet cider from the shelf in the on-site shop and headed round to Pippin Cottage.

'I see you've not bothered fixing the doorbell then,' Jonathan grinned. He handed Anna the bottles and stepped into the hall.

'What are you doing here?' Anna's mind began to race. What if Matthew turned up out of the blue and found Jonathan in situ?

'Thought you could do with the company,' Jonathan said, walking down the corridor to the kitchen. 'And I know Matthew's staying in one of the family rooms again tonight.' Tara had taken up residence in another, although her complaints about the state of them had not endeared her to the hospital staff. 'Bottle opener?' Jonathan asked, rifling through the kitchen drawers.

'That one under the bread bin,' Anna breathed a sigh of relief at the news that Matthew wasn't likely to drop in.

'So, how are you bearing up, darling?' Jonathan asked once they'd sat down at the kitchen table.

'Oh, I'm all right,' Anna said. 'It's just frustrating being out of the loop. I want to be able to help but I kind of feel like I can't go up there too often without stepping on toes.'

'Tara's toes, presumably?'

Anna nodded. 'She is Meredith's mother, after all.'

'And Matthew loves you,' Jonathan said softly. 'Don't forget that, while you're "out of the loop", as you put it.'

'I know,' she said sadly. 'It's just—'

'What, darling?'

'I hadn't expected Tara to be so stunning. I mean, in my head she became this evil, twisted monster. And she's...'

'Gorgeous?' Jonathan grinned ruefully. 'It's not particularly fair, is it?' He took another sip of his own bottle of cider. 'But don't let it get you down. She's hard as nails and twice as bitchy.'

'I gathered that,' Anna said. 'That's why I'm staying out of her way.'

'So, I can guess that you know why they split,' Jonathan said, 'but do you want to know how they met? I'm guessing my brother hasn't exactly been forthcoming on the information front in that regard.'

Anna regarded Jonathan warily, and was somewhat surprised that he'd want to discuss it so openly. 'I'm not sure. Do I really want to know?'

'It's a great story,' Jonathan grinned. 'And it might give you a bit more of an insight into what became of their relationship.'

'Oh, go on then.'

Jonathan leaned back in his chair and stretched. The hours behind Matthew's desk had taken their toll. 'The sparks that flew when Matthew and Tara met would have burned down the main barn. And no, I'm not being melodramatic.' He sipped his cider. 'They met at university. Rather aptly, Tara was studying Drama, and Matthew was finishing his Law degree. He'd taken a year out to help Dad, so he was nearly twenty-three when he graduated.'

'He really was going to break away from the business, wasn't he?' Anna said wonderingly. 'What changed his mind?'

'I'm getting to that, be patient, darling,' Jonathan smiled and picked up one of the crisps from the bowl Anna had dug out to go with the cider.

'It was, as they say, a *coup de foudre*. Matthew was set for a First, graduating top of the year, you name it, he'd won it. I always wonder if he was so determined to succeed at the law because he knew, deep down, he was never going to be able to practise it. The cider business is ingrained in all of us; as the elder son, it was his destiny, really.'

'It never occurred to you to step in?' Anna asked.

'We're not talking about me, and anyway, I've always been the prodigal. Dad might have liked me better, but he trusted Matthew more.' Jonathan's light tone, for a moment, had an undercurrent of bitterness.

'Two weeks before the end of his finals, Matthew had, uncharacteristically, taken the night off. There was a student pub in the University village. It was the kind of place that pretended, back in the early nineties, to be a proper boozer, while lapping up all the readily available cash that students had. It would put on the odd theme night, karaoke, that sort of thing. Tara was there with a group of her Drama friends. They'd commandeered a table and were drinking terrible American lager and rehearsing for their end of first year exams. Tara, in her inimitable way, was holding court – you couldn't look anywhere else. Matthew was drawn into the performance. Tara clocked him straight away. Once she found out a little bit more about him, she set her sights on him. Two weeks later he'd moved into her student digs. He lived with her all through his internship.'

'You sound like you saw it happen,' Anna said.

'I did. I was visiting Matthew for the weekend. I've never seen him react that way to a woman. He spilt his pint, stumbled over his words; he didn't know what to do with himself.' Jonathan smiled. 'He'd had girlfriends before, but Tara hit him like a falling tree branch. I didn't think I'd ever see it again… until now.'

Anna blushed. 'Anyway…'

Jonathan grinned. 'After she graduated, they got married. Matthew was preparing to start his first proper job. His internship was horribly gruelling but the firm he was with had offered him a really decent package. He'd have been set for a few years, until Dad handed the business over. He kind of knew it would come, but he desperately wanted a career he could call his own first.'

'So what happened?'

Jonathan shuddered; the memory was still fresh. 'A week before he was due to start the job, Dad had a massive heart attack. Matthew had no choice – he had to go home.'

'God,' Anna whispered. 'Talk about timing.'

'Quite.'

'And Matthew just went?' Anna said. 'Dropped everything? The job, the prospects?'

'Family's always come first for Matthew,' Jonathan replied. 'That's why what happened between him and I was so hard for him to take. He could no more have ignored the business than stopped the sun from setting.'

'Couldn't you have—'

'No,' Jonathan said firmly. 'I was still at university myself, and I knew fuck all about running a business. The idea was that, eventually, I'd come in as equal partner and we'd run it together. As you know, things didn't quite work out that way.'

'What about Tara? Did she put her degree to good use?'

'She tried to get a few roles with a local theatre company but she wasn't wildly successful. I think she resented Matthew for that. The problems pretty much started then.' Jonathan sighed. 'Matthew didn't believe in divorce; he'd have doggedly kept on until the end, but Tara wanted out. She loved him, in her way, but being the wife of a Somerset cider maker, especially back when the business wasn't what it is now, wasn't part of her life plan. When he just dropped his legal career to run what was, essentially, two barns and a shop, she couldn't really take it.'

'So he's turned the business around, then?' Anna asked.

'You know he has. This deal with FastStream is nothing compared to what he had to do just to get it breaking even again fifteen years ago. He had Cowslip Barn mortgaged as collateral at one point.'

'I had no idea it was that close to the edge,' Anna said. 'From the outside it always looked so effortless.'

'My father knew about apples, but he wasn't too hot on

the finances,' Jonathan said. 'He refused to admit that, come the 1990s, he needed to move with the times. When Matthew took the helm, he dragged Carter's kicking and screaming into the digital age. But it took a while. By the time Meredith was conceived, Tara was already getting restless.'

'Why didn't she just walk?' Anna said.

'Nowhere to go,' Jonathan replied. 'She had no job, and pride wouldn't let her go back to Pennsylvania with her tail between her legs. When Meredith was born, things settled for a while, but Matthew was still working every hour of the day. He couldn't cope with Tara's demands when he walked in the door after an eighteen-hour stint.'

'The workaholic and the drama queen – an explosive combination, especially with a baby, too.'

'You're right. Well, after Meredith things did calm down for a while, but Tara was used to better things – and Matthew couldn't provide them. He didn't draw a salary on the business until late 2001, so they were asset-rich but cash-poor. Tara took Meredith to her family's place for a few months. That was the first time they split.'

'How did Matthew take that?'

'He got on the next plane after her, but she sent him packing. Eventually, when her family got too much, she brought Meredith back home. Matthew was shit-scared she'd walk out for good, and devastated at the thought of losing Meredith, whom he loved to absolute distraction.'

'So they sorted things out?'

'For a bit, but really, they were into injury time. He tried to get home earlier, to give Tara a break from looking after a toddler, but there was too much to do.'

'I hate to ask, Jonathan, but where were you when all this was going on?' Anna looked him directly in the eyes. 'It sounds like Matthew was desperate for some help.'

'You're right, of course,' Jonathan said. 'And you're ahead of me. I finished university and came home when Meredith was about three. I took on some of the business, but I had a lot to learn, and Matthew didn't have time to train me. We muddled through for about six months before... well, you know the rest.' Jonathan hung his head.

'So you and Tara ran off, and left Meredith with Matthew.' Anna said flatly.

'You don't need to pass judgement,' Jonathan said wearily. 'I've done that enough myself over the years.'

'I'm trying not to, but I'm still struggling with the fact that Tara left Meredith, more than anything else.'

'I know, darling, but in fairness to Tara, Matthew made absolutely sure she couldn't leave the country again with Meredith. After she went back to the US the first time, he locked Merry's passport away in the work safe to stop Tara taking her again. In the longer term, Tara agreed to him getting full-time custody.'

Anna was shocked, but not entirely surprised, to hear about Matthew's ruthless streak. 'Hence why he's so protective of her.'

'Absolutely. Tara tried to fight it, but she settled for visits in the holidays in the end. She knew it was a massive concession getting the divorce in the first place, and in reality, with an affair with me under her belt, she realised she couldn't expect too much. Of course, we were completely unsuited to each other, and she dumped me pretty swiftly when she got back to the US. I was actually relieved – I didn't have the bollocks to walk out on her, being not quite then the man of substance you see before you today.' He gave a wry smile.

'And Matthew turns the business around, raises Meredith and generally gets on with his life?' Anna finished.

Jonathan nodded. 'Got it exactly. He's spent so much time

being a father and an MD, he's not really had any time for another relationship. From what I can gather, he's had a few encounters, but never really found anyone who can handle him, Meredith and the business. Until now, of course.'

Anna blushed. 'We've only been together a few months.'

'I know, darling, that's what makes it all the more amazing. You've turned him on his head. Got him thinking with his heart again after years of pretending he didn't have one. And what's more, Meredith adores you too. That's no mean feat. If she's decided she likes you, that's more than half the battle.'

'What happens if she...' Anna couldn't finish the thought.

Jonathan's warm hand crept across the table to cover her own. 'She won't. She'll wake up and get over this. She has to.'

'I hope you're right.' Anna gave a slightly watery smile. 'If it was Ellie lying in that bed, I wouldn't want to leave her side for a second.'

'That's why you and Matthew are so good together. Your children mean the world to you. When Meredith comes home, I hope the four of you will be able to make a fresh start. Together.' There was the barest of breaks in Jonathan's voice.

'Thank you,' Anna said softly. 'And perhaps in time...'

Jonathan shook his head. 'Let's not run before we can walk, darling.' Giving her hand a final squeeze, he stood up from the table. 'Anyway, I've spent enough time gossiping. I'd better get back to Dad's and make sure he's not ransacking the drinks cupboard in my absence.'

'Does he make a habit of it?' Anna asked.

A shadow passed over Jonathan's face. 'Since Meredith's been in hospital, he's been taking solace in the bottom of a whisky glass rather regularly.' He gave Anna a sardonic grin. 'Kind of goes with the territory, I'm afraid.'

'I'll bear that in mind,' Anna said gently. Raising her eyes to meet Jonathan's, she gave him a small smile. 'Thanks for coming over tonight.'

'A pleasure, darling. Now go and get some rest. We all need as much energy as we can get at the moment.' He leaned forward and kissed her on the cheek. 'See you soon.'

Just as Anna closed the front door, her phone buzzed. Wandering over to the sofa where she'd left it, she was glad to see it was a text from Matthew.

Miss you. No change. Talk later. X

Texting a quick response, Anna decided to get an early night. She slept more soundly than she expected.

Chapter 37

The next day, when Tara had left the hospital to get some fresh air, Matthew took the comfortable chair alone by Meredith's bed. The beeps of the machines had become so commonplace he didn't notice them, and, although Tara had very gently combed Meredith's hair back from her face, the girl still looked blanched, small, defenceless.

'Meredith,' Matthew tried again, willing his daughter to wake up, 'if you can hear me, please, try to open your eyes, squeeze my hand, anything, my darling.' He took her hand, feeling it cool and soft in his own. His head ached, his eyes felt heavy, and, against every fibre of his being, his mind began to drift, until he was falling into the first vestiges of a troubled sleep. The hospital sheets made a starchy pillow as he rested his forehead where Meredith's hand lay. He knew he'd give anything, anything at all, for Meredith to wake, and in his exhausted state, his mind started to play tricks. He imagined he could see her eyes opening, her breathing becoming deeper, the beginnings of some sarcastic comment or other on her lips. He was hoping so desperately for it, he could almost hear it.

'D-Dad? Where am I?'

Her voice was barely a whisper, and in the semi-darkness of the hospital room, Matthew couldn't even be sure he'd heard her. Days of wakefulness had given way to exhaustion and he hovered between sleep and waking. But at the sound of his daughter's voice his head snapped up.

'Merry? Meredith? Can you hear me?'

'Dad?' Confused tears began to slide down her pale cheeks as she tried to grasp where she was. 'What happened? Where am I? Where's Flynn?'

'Don't worry about that now – or him,' Matthew murmured. Gingerly he put out a hand to stroke a strand of dark hair away from Meredith's forehead.

'What happened, Daddy?'

'You were in an accident, my love. You're in hospital.' Matthew choked on the last words, and swallowed hard.

'I want to go home.'

'You will soon, I promise.'

'Where's Flynn? Is he OK?'

Matthew considered the question for just a split second too long.

'Daddy? Please tell me Flynn's OK. Please!' She tried to sit up but was thwarted by the many wires and tubes.

'He's fine, Merry.'

'You're not just saying that?'

Matthew shook his head. 'I promise you... he's fine.'

Meredith sank back against the pillows again. 'It wasn't his fault. Please, Dad, it wasn't his fault!'

'Ssh, sweetheart. Not now. Let me go and get the doctor.' Matthew stroked Meredith's forehead gently. 'We'll worry about that later.'

'But Dad, please. Listen to me.' Meredith groaned as the headache made stars shoot across her vision. 'How long have I been here?'

'Long enough, my darling.' Matthew went to stand up, but Meredith grabbed his hand in a surprisingly strong grip.

'When can I go home?' she asked.

Matthew smiled slightly. 'Soon, my darling, I promise.' He

kissed the back of her hand. 'Mum's come over to see you.'

Despite everything, Meredith looked wary and a flicker of humour crossed her face. 'No way. Did I nearly die or something?'

Matthew couldn't speak. He cleared his throat. 'Something like that.'

'Well, for god's sake, keep her away for a bit,' Meredith replied. 'Or I might change my mind about recovering!'

'Don't you dare!' Matthew groaned. He desperately wanted to take his daughter in his arms but, mindful of her injuries, settled for kissing her hand again.

'Can I see Anna?'

'Soon,' Matthew said. 'She's dying to see you.' He winced at his poor choice of words.

'Dad,' Meredith's voice cracked. 'Don't leave me... please.'

'I promise I won't,' Matthew's own voice trembled. 'Just let me get the doctor.' He stood up on legs that threatened to collapse and walked for the door of the small hospital room. As he left, Meredith closed her eyes again, exhausted.

Dazed, Matthew wandered from Meredith's room and out into the corridor. His daughter, his precious, darling child had woken up, and his head and heart were in a whirl. Immediately, he whipped out his phone and started to punch out Anna's number. As he was pressing the last digit, a waft of the sharp, tangy scent in which Tara habitually drenched herself reached him. He shoved his phone away.

'How is she?' Tara asked. 'Any change?'

Matthew swallowed hard. 'She's awake.'

'Oh, my god!' Even under her tan, Tara paled. Dashing past him, unsteady in her high-heeled boots, she burst through the door of Meredith's room. As the door closed behind her, Matthew heard one of them crying. For a split second he debated whether or not to go into the room and check

Meredith was all right; but he stopped himself. Tara might have her faults, but she was still Meredith's mother.

Reaching into his pocket for his mobile, he once again keyed in Anna's number. She answered on the second ring. Sinking down onto one of the plastic chairs in the corridor, he told Anna the news, and then the exhaustion finally took him. As he ended the call, he looked up to find Ms Burke, Meredith's surgeon, staring down at him.

'I think it's about time you and Meredith's mother got some proper rest,' the doctor said gently, but firmly. 'Go home and get some sleep tonight.'

'I can't leave her,' Matthew said flatly. 'What if she wakes in the night and I'm not there? What if she's frightened? What if—' his mind finished the thought, even though his voice couldn't.

Ms Burke gave a small smile. 'She'll be checked on every half an hour now she's awake, and they'll move her down to a general ward when we're happy with her progress. She's come through the worst of it, Mr Carter.' She looked down at her clipboard briefly and nodded. 'The most important thing now is that you're in a state to support her over the next few days. Go home. Get some sleep and a hot shower. Come back in the morning.'

'Doctor's orders?' Matthew said wearily.

'Yep.'

As the doctor moved away to check on her other patients, Tara came back out into the corridor. She looked red-eyed but hugely relieved, and for the first time since she'd arrived, Matthew realised how hard it had been for her.

'Her surgeon's told us to go home and get some rest,' Matthew said as Tara reached him.

'I want to stay with her,' Tara replied quickly. 'One of us should.'

Matthew glanced at Meredith's door to make sure it was closed again. 'I think the doctor might have a point. I don't want to leave any more than you do, but for tonight, I think we will need to.' Fighting with himself for a moment, he eventually continued. 'You'd better come home with me. It's too late to go trailing round Bristol for a hotel room.'

Tara looked surprised. 'OK. But we'll be back first thing?'

'Of course.' He smiled bleakly. 'But let's stay with her as long as they'll let us. I'd like to see her safely off to sleep, at least.'

Chapter 38

Almost blind with exhaustion, Matthew drove himself and Tara back to Cowslip Barn. It didn't escape either of them, as they turned into the driveway, that this was a jaundiced replaying of the first few days of their marriage.

'I'll make the bed up in the spare room,' Matthew said as he turned the engine off. 'I take it you can still remember where that is.'

'Of course.' Tara pushed open the Land Rover's rickety door. 'And don't worry, I'll be out of your hair tomorrow, just as soon as I can book into somewhere nearer the hospital.'

Matthew hoped his sigh of relief wasn't too obvious. On legs that felt too tired to carry him, he walked up and opened the front door. Good sense told him to go straight to bed, but the craving for a stiff whisky overrode that. Wandering into the living room, he went straight to the bottle on the sideboard and poured a large measure.

Following him into the room, Tara looked around. 'Just as I remember,' she said, picking up a bundle of *Mendip Times* magazines and shifting them from the armchair to the already crowded coffee table in front of the fire. 'I see you've got rid of Aunt Maria's sideboard, though.' She gestured to where the whisky bottle sat. 'What's that, Ikea?'

'She was your aunt, not mine – didn't seem relevant to keep it after you walked out.'

'Oh, Matt, don't be tetchy,' Tara chided. 'Surely we can suspend hostilities now Meredith's out of danger.' She eyed the proofs of the latest marketing literature for the company that were spread out on the overcrowded coffee table. 'You've done well, these past few years. Jack must be proud.'

Matthew said nothing, just took another gulp of his whisky.

Tara stood still, eyes roving over the room. 'This brings back memories,' she said eventually.

'Old memories,' Matthew said gruffly.

Slowly, deliberately, Tara approached him. She reached a lazy hand out and touched Matthew's fingers that were clenched tightly around the whisky glass.

'Certain things never really die,' Tara murmured.

This time the silence between them was heavy, expectant. Matthew could feel the tension coursing through his body. In the dim light he could see the sharp contours of Tara's cheekbones, a little too close to the surface these days. As she edged closer to him, tilting her head upwards so her lips were a whisper from his, he could feel her breath against his jaw.

'If you're thinking what I think you're thinking, you can stop right now,' Matthew said. 'We're done. Over. Were a long time ago.'

'Is that what you *really* want?' Tara was undeterred. 'After all, it's been so long.'

'Believe it or not, it took me a long time to get over you,' Matthew growled. 'I can forgive you for leaving me; God knows you had good reason to at times, but to leave Meredith...' Deliberately putting some distance between them, he walked over to the living room window.

'Oh, spare me the emotional blackmail!' Tara retorted. 'You were always her favourite – my leaving just cemented that cosy little setup. And now it seems that you're busy sorting out a replacement mommy for her with that dowdy little tea shop owner of yours.' Turning away from him, giving him the full benefit of her long, lithe figure in profile, she walked to the sideboard and poured herself a generous whisky.

'And why shouldn't I be happy?' Matthew's voice raised. 'You destroyed me when you left! You chose the one person to sleep with who would cause maximum damage both to me and the rest of the family.' Slamming down his glass on the windowsill, he fought to compose himself. 'In all this time, in all these years, I only ever wanted to ask you one thing, Tara. Why? Why him?'

'Who could blame me, when all I ever saw of you was your back as you walked out of the door?' Tara closed the distance between them again. 'What kind of a marriage was that? And don't even think about trying to pull Meredith in on your self-righteous guilt trip. I'm surprised you even knew who she was by the end of our marriage.'

'I was working!' Matthew yelled. 'Everything I did, all the hours I put in, were for you and Meredith, to keep this roof over our heads, to guarantee our future together. Can't you see that?'

'Bullshit. It was never about me and Meredith and you know it.' Tara slammed back her whisky. 'The only reason you worked so hard was to prove to your old man that you could do the job. Let's face it, we both know Jonathan was your dad's favourite, and you went out of your way to try to prove you could run the business better than he ever would.'

'And let's not forget how much of a favourite of yours he was, too.'

The sound of Tara's long-nailed fingers making impact on Matthew's cheek resonated off the cottage walls. Before she could drop her hand, Matthew had grabbed it.

'That's typical of you.' Still holding her hand, he brought his face in close to hers. 'I'm glad you left me and Meredith.

If you'd ever tried to hit her like that, I'd have sent you packing anyway.'

Before Matthew had a chance to exhale, Tara pulled his face to hers. The kiss was enough to take them to the bedroom, where years of separation were stripped away in a matter of moments. Their coupling was as frenzied as it was passionate, and as Matthew came, he felt a wave of darkness and desolation. It was a union riddled with a horrifying inevitability.

'What have we done?' he muttered, pulling away as Tara tried to reach out for him.

'I would have thought *that* was obvious.' Rolling over, trying to regain the ascendancy, Tara ran a lazy hand over Matthew's bare chest.

'Fuck...' Matthew moaned, throwing an arm over his face. 'Fuck, fuck, fuck.'

'Well, I'd have preferred making love, but whatever.'

'Love?' Matthew chuckled humourlessly. 'Don't make me laugh.'

'You loved me once,' Tara said softly, though her voice had a dangerous edge. 'Enough to marry me and create our daughter. Does that count for nothing?'

'It did. A long time ago. But it's over, Tara.' Even as he said it, he could feel the prison doors clanging shut as the guilt hit him.

'You've got a funny way of showing it, if that little performance was anything to go by.'

'Consider it a proper goodbye,' Matthew replied, disgusted with himself.

'Is that what you want?'

'It's the choice you made when you left me. And yes. It is what I want.' Matthew threw the bed sheet aside, pulled on his jeans and with shaking hands buckled the belt. 'I'll be in the spare room. I want you out of here tomorrow morning.'

'You could stay,' she purred, trying to regain the ascendency. 'After all, it's hardly gentlemanly to leave a lady alone after making love.'

'I don't see a lady,' Matthew said. 'Just an expert at pushing my buttons.' Feeling a wave of dizziness, and nearly knocked sideways by revulsion, he contemplated his ex-wife.

'You weren't complaining ten minutes ago,' Tara retorted. She raised her arms above her head so Matthew could see her full, still pert breasts.

Matthew averted his eyes. 'I should have known better.'

'Really, Matt, it's a little late for that,' Tara replied. But the bleak look on Matthew's face was enough to make Tara realise Matthew was serious. 'We'll talk in the morning.'

'I don't think so.' The bile rose in Matthew's throat as the full realisation of what he and Tara had done hit him square on. 'I'll take you back to the hospital with me in the morning, but then I suggest you make alternative arrangements for the rest of your time here.'

As he left the bedroom, he felt a chill wind slip through the open window and wrap itself around his bare flesh. If Anna had been the summer breeze in his life, Tara was the hurricane bent on total destruction.

Chapter 39

That night, the relief Anna felt at hearing Meredith had awoken was only slightly tempered by the fact that, as the sound of the church clock striking eleven drifted through the air, she realised Matthew hadn't replied to the goodnight text she'd sent him. She'd grown accustomed to a late night exchange of messages, and she felt the faintest prickle of unease as she pulled back her bed sheets and tried to surrender to sleep.

In truth, Anna was having a conflict of her own. She still couldn't quite shake the feeling of disquiet that had dogged her since Matthew had confronted Flynn. She'd never met the boy who had been driving the car that killed her husband, but she imagined Matthew's reaction to Flynn was not so far off the mark of what hers would have been. But the ease at which he'd thrown that at her, the starkness of his accusation, made her feel nauseous.

And then there was Tara.

Anna had tried to steel herself against the inevitable feelings of jealousy that being in the vicinity of Matthew's ex-wife would bring, but she couldn't help comparing Matthew's past love to his present one. And no matter how much she tried to ignore her misgivings they always came back stronger. Knowing Matthew loved her, and feeling secure in that love were evidently two very different things.

'He was so blunt,' she'd said to Charlotte, over a glass

of wine earlier that evening. 'I know he was angry, and god knows he had provocation, coming face to face with Flynn so soon after the accident, but, I don't know, I guess I expected better of him.'

Charlotte had smiled ruefully and topped up their glasses. 'You're the one who's always saying you'd prefer people not to pussyfoot around the subject of James,' she'd said. 'Can't you just chalk it up to massive amounts of emotional stress and move on? I mean, his daughter *was* lying unconscious in a hospital bed at the time, and the boy who put her there *was* right in front of him. Frankly, Flynn's lucky Matthew didn't deck him.'

'I know it sounds like I'm being oversensitive,' Anna took a sip of her wine, 'but I can't shake this feeling of... I don't know, does dread sound a bit melodramatic?'

Charlotte raised an eyebrow. 'There's something else you're not telling me.'

'What do you mean?' Anna studiously avoided Charlotte's gaze.

'Oh, come on, Anna, you can't tell me that Tara turning up here hasn't got you a little flustered. Christ, if it was me, I'd be sticking pins in a Chanel-dressed voodoo doll by now!'

'Well, she's going to be here, isn't she?' Anna replied, trying to sound more reasonable than she felt. 'After all, she *is* Meredith's mother.'

'Just because Merry's a sweetheart doesn't mean you have to like her mother.'

'I've not really had enough contact with her to form an opinion,' Anna hedged, trying to forget Tara's calculating gaze, her effortless elegance.

'Oh, please!' Charlotte rolled her eyes. 'You really expect me to believe you're not at all bothered that your new boyfriend's ex-wife and the mother of his beloved child turning up here doesn't make you, at the very least, a little bit tetchy?'

Sometimes Anna cursed Charlotte's ability to read her so accurately. 'Well, maybe it *is* a bit weird,' she conceded. 'But we're all adults, we can cope.'

'And now that you've got the standard, *I'm down with it all* response out of the way, would you care to tell me how you're really feeling?'

Anna sighed. 'You're not going to let this go, are you?' She picked up her own wine glass. 'OK. Perhaps I am a little bit... uneasy... about Tara being here.'

'Well, no one can blame you for that,' Charlotte said stoutly. 'It's bound to throw even the most secure woman to have the ex turning up on the doorstep.' She paused. 'How did Matthew react to being in the same room as her again?'

'I'm not sure. She arrived as Meredith was being wheeled down to have some tests done. He kissed her on the cheek and then I just, sort of, left.'

'So far, so civilised,' Charlotte said. 'I suppose they've both been staying at the hospital, have they?'

Anna nodded. 'Neither of them wanted to leave while Meredith was still unconscious. Now she's woken up, perhaps...'

'Perhaps the Bitch Queen might bugger off?'

'I was actually going to say, perhaps Matthew might be able to come home and get a bit of proper rest,' Anna countered. 'I'm worried he's going to lose his mind, being cooped up in the hospital for so long.'

'And the fact he's been in close quarters with Tara isn't bothering you at all?'

'They divorced years ago; there can't be anything left between them, surely.'

Charlotte refrained from commenting.

'What?' Anna replied to the unfamiliar silence. 'Come on, spit it out. What are you thinking?'

'You've spent months now telling me Mr Broody has been coming over all passionate and actually communicating with you, and now he seems to have clammed up again now the ex-wife's back on the scene.'

'Well, as you just told me, he *has* been through a hell of a lot over the past week or two.'

'So he hasn't said anything to you about being forced to spend so much time with Tara, then?' Charlotte looked at her best friend. 'Nothing at all? No bitching about her, no moaning about her bad habits, no overcompensating for the trickiness of the situation by trying to reassure you he's not going to fall back in love with her?'

'No.' Anna felt vaguely irritated by the line of questioning. 'Do you think I should ask him? Call him out on it?'

'Well, darling, honesty is the best policy... except when it isn't.'

'Meaning what?'

'Meaning that, if you push him for an explanation, you might not like what you get in return.'

'You think he's still in love with her?'

'Not if he's got any sense, but, in my experience, sense rarely comes into it.' Charlotte gave Anna's hand a squeeze. 'It's up to you, really. If it were me, I'd give him a bit of breathing space, let him work out what it is he really wants. If it's you, he'll make it plain soon enough.'

'So in the meantime I have to sit tight and act like the dutiful little woman?' Anna drained her glass of wine. 'I'm not sure I can do that.'

'Then put some distance between the two of you,' Charlotte said. 'Let him come to you when he's ready.'

'I'm sorry. I shouldn't be snapping at you. Just when I feel like I'm finally getting my head around my life, something like this happens and I'm back feeling like the world's most emotionally illiterate moron.'

'No harm done, lovely,' Charlotte said. 'If love was easy, we'd be doing it all the time, wouldn't we?'

As Anna heard the clock strike the half hour, she reached back over to her bedside table and turned her phone off.

Chapter 40

Matthew woke with a headache that was only marginally worse than the thumping guilt in his gut. Blearily, he staggered out of the uncomfortable spare bed, feeling a wave of nausea. He'd brought the rest of the bottle of whisky to bed, and he couldn't recollect exactly how much of it he'd consumed. Stubbing his toe on the empty bottle as he crossed the bedroom, the answer, as well as the pain, made him swear out loud.

Fiver for the swear box, Dad! He could hear Meredith's voice in his head as he walked down the creaking stairs and into the kitchen. The cottage felt cold and charmless without her. By now, she'd have been rattling a cereal bowl in the kitchen, clicking on the kettle for a cup of instant coffee and pouring biscuits into Sefton's metal bowl. The dog, still residing at Pat's, would doubtless miss his mistress on his return.

The quiet was oppressive as Matthew waited for the kettle to boil. Glancing at the kitchen table, he saw a note propped up on an empty milk bottle.

Matthew,

I've got a cab back to the hospital. I'll be staying at the Coach House nearby if you need to reach me, but I daresay I'll see you at Merry's bedside.

Yours ever,

Tara.

Matthew felt a churning sense of relief. At least he'd have time to gather his thoughts before he encountered Tara again. Unable to stomach a solid breakfast, he gulped back the still scalding cup of instant coffee. *Yours ever* – that was a joke, surely. Tara had never really been his, even when she had been married to him. He might have given his heart to her, but he had never felt he'd had hers fully. Last night had, undoubtedly, been a monumental mistake, but it had given Matthew a sense of clarity about his ex-wife he'd never really had before.

This realisation did precisely nothing to alleviate the situation he found himself in. He'd done the one thing he swore he never would; he'd gone back to Tara. Albeit for a few, reckless moments, and under great stress, but he'd done it. While their daughter was lying in a hospital bed. He'd betrayed his own heart, and, worse, he'd potentially broken someone else's into the bargain.

Anna.

The thought of her, lying in bed at Pippin Cottage, her pretty face peaceful in an unknowing slumber, unaware of what the man who claimed to love her had just done, was enough to make the bile rise. He felt the distance between them already becoming insurmountable, and for a second he entertained the notion that he just wouldn't tell her what had happened. He'd close his eyes to the events of last night, and they would go away, like everything else he found difficult to manage.

But this was different.

As he pictured Anna's face again, tired and vulnerable as she had been the last time he'd seen her at the hospital, fear like he had never known curled itself around his gut, making his stomach churn and his hands tremble. The hell of eternity without her loomed large, and all for a few moments of sex that had been more like a battle. Bolting for the sink, he retched, bringing up coffee and bile until he had nothing left.

As she started her morning shift at the tea shop, Anna tried to ignore the fact that three texts she'd sent Matthew had yet to be answered. She stuck her phone resolutely into her handbag.

The tea shop was busy with a group of walkers who had started from the Congresbury end of the Strawberry Line. After an hour and a half of walking, they were all gagging for a cuppa and a fruit scone, so by the time her break came at just gone eleven o'clock, Anna was more than ready for it. She avoided checking her phone while she drank her own cup of coffee, and when she noticed there was one last slice of her own carrot and orange cake left on the display, she broke her own rule and tucked into it. But, eventually, she couldn't avoid it any longer. She reached into her bag for her phone, steeling herself for yet another blank screen. When she saw the envelope icon, her heart lurched.

Merry wants to see you. Visiting hours 2-6pm.

Anna felt her stomach join her heart. It didn't take a genius to work out that something was amiss. The question was, what the hell was it? Texting a quick, neutral affirmative, she shoved her phone back in her bag and restarted her shift.

As fate would have it, 'Fudge Cake and Fiction' were meeting at half past five when the tea shop closed. It was their second official book club meeting, and Anna didn't have the heart to cancel it. She'd even changed the time to ensure a bit more take-up on the feedback from the first meeting. Her mum was picking up Ellie from nursery and would keep her until the meeting was over at about six thirty. Guiltily aware that she hadn't had the chance to read anything she could swap this month, except for a few pages of Meredith's copy of

The Hunger Games that she'd left in the tea shop a couple of weeks ago, she hoped she'd be able to make up for it with slices of actual chocolate fudge cake. Perhaps the discussion about books would go some way to taking her mind off the horrors of the present, at least.

*

After the book club meeting, Anna arrived back at Pippin Cottage to see a carrier bag hanging over the door knocker. Inside it was Meredith's phone charger, which Pat must have unearthed from the teenager's bedroom. Anna knew Meredith lived on the phone, and she had no doubt the girl would be most grateful for the opportunity to reconnect with the outside world. Grabbing the bag, and adding it to the leftover cake slices that weren't going to last another day on the counter, she and Ellie headed up to the hospital. She'd decided to take Ellie with her this time, feeling as though she needed the moral support for facing Matthew, and still at a loss about his abrupt text message. Somewhere in the back of her mind she worried that Matthew might be blaming her for Meredith's accident; it was she, after all, who'd encouraged him to allow Meredith to start seeing Flynn in the first place. Perhaps Matthew felt that this terrible situation was partly her doing? She tried to dismiss it; Meredith was strong-willed enough to defy her father if she wanted to, but she couldn't quite shake off the thought.

When they arrived at the hospital, Anna automatically found herself scanning the rows of parked cars for Matthew's Land Rover. The car park, however, was crammed, and entirely too big for a casual glance. She'd know if he was here soon enough, she thought.

As Anna and Ellie boarded the lift up to where Meredith was residing, Ellie kept up an endless stream of chatter. Anna, trying to appear as though she was listening, nodded and murmured affirmatives where necessary. The lift juddered to a halt. The doors opened, and Anna couldn't help the breath that hitched in her throat as she saw Matthew stepping in through the rapidly closing doors of the other one.

'Matthew!' she called out, but it was too late; the doors had closed again.

'Come on, Mummy!' Ellie squeaked, grabbing Anna's hand once more. 'Want to see Merry.'

'All right, hang on a second,' Anna said, a little more sharply than she'd intended.

Working her way down the corridor, she eventually found Meredith's ward, and plastered the brightest smile she could muster to her face.

'Thank god you're here, I'm, like, so bored of Mum and Dad checking my eyes aren't rolling back in my head every second. And they won't tell me when I can go home.' Meredith smiled down at Ellie, who was looking very unsettled. 'It's all right, titch, I'm fine, really.'

'The doctors have to make sure you're really better, Merry,' Anna said. She was pleased to see Meredith had much more colour in her cheeks, and life in general.

Meredith's eyes lit up as Anna produced first the leftover cake and then her phone charger, and she wasted no time in plugging her phone in. Immediately, it started to beep. At least twenty of the received messages were from Flynn. Meredith alternated between tears and excitement as she read them, a look of increasing desperation on her face.

'He must feel so awful,' she whispered. 'I can't imagine what he's been going through.'

'You've been very ill, Merry, everyone who cares about you has been worried.'

'I need to see him,' Meredith said, sitting up suddenly in

bed. 'Please Anna, please get him in here to see me.'

'Merry, you know I can't go behind your dad's back. He doesn't want Flynn within fifty miles of you right now.'

A tear trickled out from under Meredith's lashes. 'It's so unfair. The accident wasn't his fault.'

'Merry—'

'Anna, please listen to me,' Meredith said. 'Honestly, it really wasn't Flynn's fault what happened.'

'He was driving the car, Merry, and there were no other cars involved. Ultimately it was his responsibility.'

Meredith looked guilty. 'Yes, he was driving, but it was my fault he hit the tree, I'm telling you. It's well unfair of Dad to blame him for the accident.'

Anna sighed. 'Why don't you tell me what happened?'

Meredith began pleating the top of the hospital sheet that lay across her thighs. 'We were going to be late. Flynn knew Dad would chuck a mental if we got home after my curfew – it took me long enough to convince him to let me go out with him in the first place. We left the ski centre in a rush, and as we were coming back down Church Road, I was teasing Flynn for wanting to suck up to my Dad. I was messing about a bit, and I started blowing in his ear, trying to get him to lighten up. He turned to look at me, and out of nowhere this massive deer appeared, right in the middle of the road.' Meredith shuddered at the memory. 'Flynn swerved to avoid it, but he didn't realise how close we were to the oak tree outside the church. The next thing I knew, I was waking up here.'

Anna drew in a sharp breath. Meredith had a very matter-of-fact way of speaking, but as she finished, tears took over and splashed onto the back of her hands.

'Oh, lovely,' Anna said gently. 'Your dad's bound to want to murder Flynn for what happened, regardless of who did what. Yes, you were a bit daft, and yes, he should have kept his eyes on the road, but everyone is so thankful you're alive. Give your dad time – he'll come round.' She reached out and put a gentle arm around Meredith's shoulders.

'Even if he does, I'll be grounded for, like, the next fifteen years!' Meredith said gloomily. 'And I'll probably never be allowed to see Flynn again.'

'Let's cross that bridge when we come to it,' Anna said. 'It might be easier if you kept your distance from Flynn for a while, though, just to be on the safe side.'

'But it's the Harvest Ball at the end of September!' Meredith groaned.

'Concentrate on getting out of here, first,' Anna said, smiling again. 'And perhaps by the time the ball comes, we'll have worked on your father.'

Meredith smiled, and for a moment she looked like her old self again. 'I knew I could count on you,' she said. 'Now why don't you just get on with it and marry my dad, too?'

Anna felt a stab of unease at the yearning in Meredith's tone. 'Let's not get too carried away, Meredith – we've got a long way to go.'

'Yes, but at your age you can't afford to hang around,' Meredith replied. 'And you do like him, right?'

Anna blushed, shaking her head. 'Sometimes I think you're too nosy for your own good, young lady.'

'See, you're talking like my stepmother already!'

'I'll go and get you some more water,' Anna said firmly, grabbing Meredith's hospital issue water jug and standing up hastily.

'So I take it I can start planning the wedding, then?'

Anna fled from the room, before the tears that were prickling at the back of her eyes spilled over.

Chapter 41

'But Matthew, it makes perfect sense!' Tara replied, turning the same blue eyes on him that had captivated him when they'd first met. After a week of trying to avoid her at the hospital, Matthew had cursed inwardly upon opening the door to his ex-wife. She was now standing in his living room, her face betraying nothing of what had happened between them the night Meredith woke up. 'I have the best health insurance, and Meredith will have access to the best doctors, should she need them. She's already had a clean bill of health from the medics, and she should be cleared to fly soon. Why shouldn't she come home with me?'

'Home?' Matthew said. 'This is her home, Tara, or have you forgotten? She's spent the whole of her life here. A life you walked out on.' Abstractedly he got up and went to refill his mug, not even realising he was filling it from the tap and not the teapot.

'This isn't about us... this is about our daughter's physical and mental health.'

'You didn't think of that when you left, did you?' Matthew snapped, determined to keep his guard up this time. The guilt over their liaison churned in his stomach. 'Why, all of a sudden, are you so concerned?'

'You're right,' she said gently. 'I don't deserve her. You

picked up all of the pieces when I… went away. But Matthew, please let me help now. She had a terrible accident, and she needs time to recuperate. A change of scene would do her good.'

'What about school?' Matthew said, starting to feel as though he was clutching at non-existent straws. 'She's halfway through her GCSE courses, and doing bloody well.'

'School's nearly out for the summer – and if she decides to stay with me a little longer, I'm sure we can arrange a tutor or something.'

'And what makes you think I'll be happy to let my daughter go and stay with you and your latest boyfriend when she needs to be recovering?'

Tara rolled her eyes. 'Please. I am her mother; I know how to take care of her. And Todd and I have been together for four years. As it happens, he's going to be away on business in Europe for the next few weeks. She'll be company for me, and we'll get to spend some quality mother-daughter time together.'

As if you ever cared about that, Matthew thought.

'Give me some time to think about it,' Matthew finally said. 'She's still so fragile from the accident.'

'Then the Florida sunshine will be just what she needs,' Tara said firmly. Draining her cup, she put it down in the sink.

Matthew felt his head start to swim, as he realised he didn't really have a leg to stand on. 'All right,' he said. 'I'll let her stay with you on one condition. You need to go, and soon. She's on the mend now, there's no reason for you to stick around. I'll talk to the doctors and get her over to you as soon as I can.' He turned to face her again. 'And I'm warning you, Tara, if you fuck up, I will do everything in my power to make sure that seeing her again will be extremely difficult. She's too vulnerable for you to decide to give up on her again.'

'I know that,' Tara said quietly. 'Nearly losing her was a wake-up call.'

'And as for what we did, as far as I'm concerned it didn't happen. It was a mistake.' As the words came out, he hated himself for acknowledging his deception.

'If that's what you want,' Tara said flatly. 'It's a shame, though. All that history, and you're putting your head in the sand again.'

'I'm not interested in history,' Matthew snapped. 'I only care about the future.'

'What's the matter, Matt? Worried your precious little widow will dump you if she finds out the truth?'

'I don't want her hurt,' Matthew snapped. 'She's been through too much already.'

'Shame you weren't thinking about that the other night.'

'I made a mistake,' Matthew deliberately moved away from Tara. 'In the heat of the moment. I should have known better.'

'You didn't think that at the time!'

'Well, I do now. It meant nothing. And if you're being totally honest, it meant nothing to you either. So why don't we chalk it up to experience and move on?'

'I'm sure Anna would be more than willing to "chalk it up," as you put it, as well, don't you think?' Tara's eyes were alight with menace. 'Why don't we ask her?'

'You wouldn't.' A cold finger of dread ran down Matthew's spine.

'Oh, Matt, have you really learned nothing about women after all these years?' Tara held his gaze, unafraid.

Matthew's pent-up rage boiled over. Grabbing Tara by the arm, he frogmarched her to the front door. 'If you so much as breathe in Anna's direction, Tara, I will make sure that you never see Meredith again. And don't think I won't.' He let go of her arm as she started to struggle like a cat. 'Do you understand me?'

Tara, frightened by Matthew's anger, nodded.

'I'll see you on the other side of the water,' he said, by way of parting.

As he closed the door on his ex-wife, Matthew put his head in his hands. He felt as though he was drowning. A terrible tale pervaded the Carter family business, a kind of ghost story that, through its telling, had got more and more visceral down the generations. It was said that, on the night the newest of the oak cider vats was filled with fermenting apple juice, one of the workers, drunk on too much of the finished version of the product, had fallen head first into a vat. He'd flailed for some time before, exhausted, he'd drowned. Four generations on, gasping for air in the aftermath of his conversation with Tara, Matthew had never identified with the unfortunate soul so strongly. He knew full well he couldn't trust Tara to keep her mouth shut, and threatening her with Meredith had been lower than low. He was going to drown.

Chapter 42

With Tara so much in evidence at the hospital, Anna was glad of the tea shop. The reassuring repetitiveness of serving customers, combined with the sight of unfamiliar tourist faces, as well as those of the locals, was enough to keep her from brooding too heavily on the sudden distance from Matthew. She realised she was going to miss the tea shop when Ursula and Brian returned from Italy. Even though her initial contract as manager was only for a year, she couldn't help but hope it might be extended. It gave her a much needed anchor.

Meredith, driven to distraction by the bedrest, had been texting Anna regularly, and was clearly getting stronger by the day, which Anna appreciated as, in a move to give Matthew some space, she hadn't visited her since she took Ellie up to the hospital. The doctors were sufficiently reassured by her vital signs that they had allowed her down onto the children's ward for the duration. Anna greeted the news that the doctors hoped to discharge Meredith, and even clear her to fly, with a mixture of relief and apprehension. Anna knew, of course, that Meredith hoped to spend time with Tara over the summer, but she still worried for her.

Through Pat, Anna also knew that Matthew was back at home, though he hadn't graced her doorstep once. She guessed he must be exhausted by his trips to and from the hospital as well as catching up on the work that had piled up during his absence, but she wished he'd confide in her, lean on her a little. She still couldn't shake the feeling that he might be blaming her for the accident. After all, she'd been the one to encourage him to allow Meredith to see Flynn in the first place. She knew it was irrational to think that way, but in the absence of clear answers, her mind whirled.

Putting on her green apron for another shift at the tea shop, Anna was grateful for the distraction. There was always someone to talk to, and many of the customers were bringers of intriguing titbits of information. As she checked the small wooden tables for any stray cups or cutlery, she wondered if she'd switched off her phone.

Turning back to the counter from the coffee machine, she noticed that Jen, Matthew's PA, had walked in. She felt the familiar lurch in her stomach that signalled her reaction to anything even vaguely connected to Matthew. Steeling herself, she forced a smile. 'Hi Jen, what can I get you?'

Jen smiled back. 'Just a flat white to take away, thanks.' She paused for a moment, as if wondering whether or not to continue the conversation. 'How are you? How's Ellie?'

'We're fine, thanks,' Anna replied automatically. 'She's busy at pre-school and things have been pretty hectic here because of the tourists, so...' she trailed off, unsure of how to proceed. She and Jen had never spoken more than a few words, and most of those had been over the telephone.

'It's great that Meredith will be allowed home in a few days,' Jen said. 'We've all been worried about her.'

'Yes, it is,' Anna replied. 'I'm sure Matthew will be pleased to get her back home.'

Jen gave her a curious look. 'I'm sure he will. Any messages for him, as I'm going that way?'

Anna shook her head. 'I'll see him sometime.' She turned away to make Jen's coffee before the other woman could see her flaming cheeks. Well-intentioned as Jen was, Anna couldn't handle the possibility of being cross-questioned at the moment. When she turned back again, Jen was holding out a five-pound note.

'Take care, Anna,' Jen said, as Anna gave her the coffee and her change.

'You too.' And with that, Jen walked back out of the tea shop. Anna had to fight every instinct she had not to race after her and get her to tell Matthew how much she missed him. She remembered what Charlotte had said; Matthew would come to her in his own time. She was amazed at how hard she was finding the wait.

'Everything all right?' Lizzie, who'd popped in to pick up her mobile phone that she'd mistakenly left out the back the day before, asked as she came back through.

'Jen always seems a bit scary,' Anna replied. 'She seems to know more about anything than anyone!'

'Hmm,' Lizzie replied. 'Are you sure that's all?'

'Honestly, I'm fine,' Anna said. She couldn't bring herself to discuss things yet; after all, she wasn't even sure what there was to talk about. Turning back to the cool cabinet, she busied herself with adding last night's baked goods to the display.

*

Another week on and still with no contact from Matthew, Charlotte's advice was proving impossible to stick to. Leaving the tea shop the moment she'd cashed up, Anna hurried round to Cowslip Barn, unable to wait any longer.

Matthew, when he opened the door, looked like he hadn't slept in at least a week. 'Anna, hi,' he said guardedly.

'Hi,' Anna replied. 'Have you had your phone switched off?'

Matthew looked quizzical. 'Um, no, I – er – just...' He shifted on the spot, like a naughty schoolboy caught scrumping apples.

'Can I come in?'

'It's not really a good time.' Matthew refused to meet her gaze.

'Please?'

Conceding, Matthew opened the door wider and let her in.

'So I've sent you a few messages,' Anna said, when they'd gone through to the old parlour.

'I know. I'm sorry, I should have replied...' Matthew went to stand by the bay window. The white light pouring in to the room cast his face in shadow.

'Is everything OK? I mean, I know everything's not OK, it's just...' Anna cursed herself inwardly. Matthew kept his gaze firmly on the garden outside. She so desperately wanted to cross the room and hold him, but the tension that emanated from him held her back.

'Have I done something to upset you?' Anna asked.

There was a pause; Anna couldn't read his expression against the light from the window.

'If it is something I've done...' Anna could feel the panic rising within her, and the frustration at the brick wall Matthew had put up around himself.

Matthew's hands were clenched by his sides. 'I can't do this right now, Anna.'

Anna took a step nearer to him and raised a hand to his cheek. 'Do what? If it's me, please, tell me what I've done and we can sort it out.'

'It's not that,' Matthew deliberately stepped away, turning his face to the window so she couldn't see his expression. 'I need a bit of time to get my head around some things.'

'Anything I can help with?' Anna asked.

'Not really,' he said evasively. 'Look, I'm sorry, but can we talk later? I'll give you a ring.'

Anna took a step back, stung by the offhand rebuttal. 'OK. If you're sure. But you know where I am if you need to talk.'

Matthew nodded, but showed no sign of moving.

'I'll see you soon,' Anna murmured. When Matthew gave no further response, she took it as her cue to leave.

Blinking back sudden tears, she hurried to the hallway and back out of the front door. As she closed it behind her, she looked automatically at her watch. She was already five minutes late picking Ellie up from nursery. She hoped the rather formidable leader of the group wouldn't castigate her too strongly; she wasn't sure she'd keep it together if she did.

Chapter 43

With a heavy heart, Matthew watched Meredith walk through the departure gates at Bristol Airport. She'd agreed that she would still go and stay with Tara for a couple of weeks. She looked frailer than she actually was, and it had taken a good deal of soul-searching for Matthew to finally agree to let her go to America without him. But once Meredith had been cleared to fly, Tara had been adamant. She and Tara had built some bridges and both were keen not to let this new relationship lapse.

In two weeks' time, Matthew would fly out to Florida to collect her. He was dreading the trip; he didn't want to come face to face with Tara again, and the thought of being four thousand miles away from Anna, even though his exile from her was self-imposed, was tearing him apart. Somehow, being in the same village made things easier. Putting an ocean between them should have seemed helpful; instead it made him yearn for her all the more.

Even back in his darkest days when Tara had left, he'd never felt such a physical sense of loss. He'd met Tara's desertion with anger; it was as if he'd always known she'd betray him, even when she'd said 'I do'. He'd been angry at himself for allowing things to get so far; for blindly clinging on to a relationship he knew couldn't be saved. Much as he hated to admit it, it was his total inability to communicate with Tara that had been the final nail in the coffin of his dead marriage; her affair with Jonathan had been mere earth on top. He couldn't maintain his rage with them both indefinitely; but he'd been too proud to admit he'd had as equal a part in it as they had. It was easier to continue to be angry; to deny responsibility.

But losing Anna was like losing a limb. After years of protecting himself, of shielding his heart and using his head, he'd let himself love again. He'd come to life. Anna had shone a light on him that had ripened his shrivelled heart, and for the first time since Tara, he'd felt something so beautiful, so special, he'd questioned the reality of it on many occasions. And just as he was allowing himself to think of the future, he'd destroyed it. The scars, so newly healed, had been ripped open again; and what was worse was that this time he had to accept total responsibility for the pain. Even more difficult to bear was the knowledge he'd not only broken his own heart, but Anna's as well.

At a loss as to what to do with himself after he'd returned from the airport, Matthew decided to bury himself in paperwork. Today had brought another bombshell; the FastStream deal had been all but signed off at the end of last week, but now, regardless of the time and money that had been spent, the American company were looking to pull out and set up a new deal with Carter's arch rival, Simpsons Cider. Based in Norfolk, their ethos was apparently 'more in line with FastStream's core values'. To Matthew, it sounded like the biggest pile of bullshit this side of the local mushroom farm, and, despite his best intentions not to let it get to him personally, he couldn't help mentally reviewing everything he knew about corporate law, which, after twenty odd years, was neither extensive nor current. In despair, he'd called in his legal advisor, and, almost as an afterthought, Jonathan, for crisis talks that afternoon.

In the end, it was Jonathan who'd suggested he had a quiet word with FastStream's Head of Distribution, Chris McIvor, who was on business in the UK this week. Despite Matthew's reservations, he'd agreed to let Jonathan investigate in his own way. Now, all he could do was wait; something he wasn't particularly good at.

But even this crisis couldn't take his mind off Anna. Chucking down the contents of his in tray in frustration, he'd locked his office and headed home via the chip shop. But he couldn't settle in the house, and Sefton was agitating for his evening walk, so he'd grabbed his coat. Automatically, he'd found himself heading towards Flowerdown Lane but, steeling himself, he turned away, back in the direction of the farm.

For once, Matthew broke his own self-imposed rule and grabbed a bottle of 'Red Rover,' the strongest variety of cider Carter's produced, from the shelf in the shop. It was long past midnight, and he knew Anna would be in bed by now. He pictured her as she might have been earlier that evening, holding a little, forlorn hope he might make a detour on his way back from Sefton's late walk, then sitting in front of some mindless television. Eventually, she'd resign herself to the fact he wasn't going to call in, and head off to bed. Then, he castigated himself for the self-indulgence; more likely, she'd be sharing a bottle of wine with Charlotte and cutting her losses.

He knew it was unfair to her; everything that had happened had been painfully unfair, but he was at a loss as to how to make things better. Instead of levelling with her, he'd buried himself deeper, pulling away from anything that reminded him how to feel. And yet, all the time he had been trying to convince himself of his own emotional numbness, the wounds he had inflicted on himself were festering, until he felt like he was decaying inside. There was a swarm of wasps in his heart, feeding on it until there was nothing left but rotten pulp.

And now, here he was. Pulling out the penknife from his pocket, he flipped open the bottle opener and popped the cap off the cider. At just over eight per cent it was the kind of cider you only drank a bottle of; three or four would probably have knocked out a carthorse. Matthew grabbed a second one, and a third, to be sure.

As he had done back in February, under much happier circumstances, he wandered across the courtyard to the barn where the cider vats were. He didn't bother to turn on the lights. The night was clear and there was the first hint of autumn in the air. The moonlight shone brightly as he opened the heavy barn door. Pausing for a moment, he took a deep pull of the bottle of cider and then stepped inside.

Silent, sentinel, eternal, the vats stood watch. Only marginally darker than the night outside, the wooden barrels had seen so much in their time at the farm. They didn't care about pain, betrayal, heartbreak; they helped to create something that contributed to them all.

The memory of kissing Anna in the presence of these same vats was so strong, Matthew could still taste her on his lips, feel her in his arms. Knocked almost sideways by longing, he sat on one of the steps leading up to the gantry. He took another drink from the bottle, tasting the sweetness of the cider and beginning to get the hit from the alcohol. He wondered what Eli, the nightwatchman, would make of it if he found him passed out next to the vat when he finished his patrol in the small hours. Eli was another old village character who should have been pensioned off years ago, but who Jack couldn't bear to let go and Matthew retained out of affection. He knew he'd be round on his checks in the next half an hour or so before settling in at the small office front of site until dawn broke.

How had it come to this? He'd allowed himself to feel for the first time in years, his heart had blossomed like one of those damned trees on which he built his empire. And then, when he thought it was safe to take a risk on the future, he'd blown it all for a few, tawdry moments in the past. He couldn't entirely blame Tara, either. He'd fallen for it, hook, line and sinker, and now he'd broken Anna's heart, Meredith's, and his own into the bargain.

'I'm sorry.' His voice sounded raw in the darkness. The vats stood impassive. He knew, long after he'd departed this life, they would still be watching over the trials, tribulations and traumas of his family and their descendants. It was about all he could be sure of. With the careful consideration of a man who already knew he'd had too much to drink, he put the cider bottle down beside him and buried his head in his hands.

AUTUMN

Chapter 44

Anna had virtually given up hope of ever hearing from Matthew again by the time September arrived. Although she couldn't quite bring herself to delete his number from her phone, she was reluctantly coming to the conclusion that their relationship had run its course, although for what reason she still didn't know. With Meredith away for another week, despite the commencement of a new term, and even Jonathan being elusive, the whole Carter family seemed to have faded from her life.

It had, in fact, been a very busy week. The start of the new school year had brought the school run parents back in force, and now that Anna knew some of them a lot better, due in part to 'Fudge Cake and Fiction', she always enjoyed catching up with the gossip. Only this morning, Sarah and her friend Adele had enlightened her, over a couple of lattes, about the plans for the PTA quiz night. Seen as a way to help introduce parents of the new intake to each other, it involved ten rounds of general knowledge and a bucket of booze. The end result was never short of hilarious, and often raised a few eyebrows the next morning at the school gate. Had she still been seeing Matthew, Anna thought ruefully, she might have asked him if Carter's could supply some of the drink to oil the wheels. As it was, she suspected the PTA would have to make do with their usual cheap, but surprisingly palatable after the third glass, Côtes du Rhône and Chardonnay.

That evening, just as Anna was clearing up the detritus of Ellie's dinner, the cottage doorbell clanked. Her heart lurched, even though she knew it was more likely to be Christian Aid collectors than Matthew.

'Hello, darling,' Jonathan said as he stepped through the door. 'Sorry I've been a bit lax in the visiting department – stuff came up at work that we're still in the midst of sorting.' He leaned forward and kissed her cheek. 'How are you doing?'

'Oh, you know, bumbling on,' Anna replied. Pleased as she was to see Jonathan, she'd have given anything to have answered the door to his brother.

'Glad to hear it.' Jonathan looked wryly at her. 'Any chance of a quickie? Drink, I mean!' He meandered through to the kitchen, with Anna following in his wake.

'Mummy get you one,' Ellie said, stuffing the last bit of cake into her mouth.

'What brings you to my door?' Anna asked, determined not to broach the subject of Matthew unless he decided to.

'I've come to ask you something,' Jonathan replied, turning his best blue-eyed stare on her.

Anna raised an eyebrow. 'Does it involve money? Because if so, it's a definite no.'

'What do you take me for?' Jonathan replied in mock outrage. 'I keep telling you, I'm a reformed character.'

On cue, his mobile phone chirruped, and Anna was a quick enough reader to see the name *Vicky* popping up on the screen before he switched it off and pocketed it again. She refrained from comment and passed him a wine glass.

'Listen, darling, I know you've had a bit of a tough time lately, what with my big brother being a pain, so I wondered if you fancied coming to the Harvest Ball with me next Saturday.'

He grinned at her. 'You know the kind of thing, posh frock, marquee, speeches, cheesy disco.'

Anna shook her head. 'Thanks for the offer, but I don't think so. Not sure I can face a night out just yet.'

'Oh, come on,' Jonathan wheedled. 'You haven't been out since my brother started behaving like an arse, and I know it's not exactly a night on the tiles, but it'll be a giggle.'

'I don't think I'd be much of a giggle at the moment,' Anna replied.

'Would it make any difference if I told you Meredith's Model UN team was going to be there to accept an award from the Head of the Rotary Club and she's got to give an acceptance speech?'

'When she was in hospital she mentioned she was hoping to go, but she didn't mention the award.'

'She doesn't want to ask you to come herself,' Jonathan said. His voice was suddenly a lot more serious. 'But she really wants you there.'

'I don't know,' Anna said. 'I'd like to, but I'm guessing Matthew'll be there too. I don't know if I can handle that.'

'That's exactly why I want you to come with me!' Jonathan had a glint of devilment in his eyes. 'He needs a bit of a shake-up, to make him realise what an idiot he's being. How do you fancy being my date?'

Anna shook her head. 'Supporting Meredith is one thing; going purely to wind Matthew up is quite another.'

'Oh, come on, darling,' Jonathan urged. 'Isn't there just a little tiny part of you that wants to stick two fingers up to my big brother?'

'I'm not like that,' Anna replied. 'I've never been a game player.'

'Well, it's a good job that I can play enough games for the both of us, then!' Jonathan couldn't stop the mischievous smirk that twitched at the corners of his mouth. 'If it makes you feel better, why don't you pretend you're only going along to support Merry, and let me be the smug bastard who will hang off your arm all night?' He picked up one of Anna's hands in his own, turned it upwards and tickled her palm playfully. 'Go on, say yes. You know you want to.'

'If I promise to think about it, will you stop going on?' Anna, exasperated but strangely flattered, snatched her hand back.

'No.' Jonathan grinned. 'You've got to give me an answer before I'll leave.'

'Oh, all right then!' Anna replied. 'If it'll get you out of my house any quicker, I'll go with you!'

'Excellent! You won't regret it, I promise you.' Jumping up from the table, he dropped his now empty glass into the sink. 'And I know Meredith will be chuffed you're going to be there to support her.'

'I'm not so sure Matthew will,' Anna said darkly, wondering why the hell she'd allowed herself to be so easily convinced. Was there a part of her that wanted to see Matthew again so desperately she was prepared to face a confrontation?

'Don't worry about Matthew,' Jonathan said breezily. 'It'll do him good to see you out and about without him; perhaps it'll make him realise what he's missing!'

'That's not my intention,' Anna replied.

'I should hope not, when you're on a date with his far better-looking and much more fun younger brother.'

'Oh, get out!' Anna gave in and had to laugh. 'What time does this thing start, anyway?'

'I'll pick you up at seven. Can Pat babysit?'

'I should think so,' Anna replied. 'Mum probably would have but I know she and Dad fly out to New Zealand on Wednesday until Christmas.'

'That's settled then.' Jonathan walked towards the kitchen door. 'Oh, and darling...'

'Yes,' Anna said warily.

'Wear a nice dress.'

'Out!' Anna barely restrained herself from throwing Ellie's now discarded lump of angel cake at Jonathan's departing back.

Chapter 45

'Come on, darling, try to relax and enjoy yourself.' Entering the marquee for the Harvest Ball, Jonathan smiled at Anna, took her hand and kissed it playfully. 'Imagine how much it's going to wind my big brother up to see you on my arm tonight.'

Anna shook her head. 'You know that's not why I agreed to come.' She glanced over to where Meredith was standing. It was the first time Anna had seen her since she'd been discharged from hospital. Dressed in rose pink chiffon, she looked fragile and beautiful beside Flynn, whose nerves were palpable.

'I know.' Jonathan was suddenly all seriousness when he saw the direction of Anna's gaze. 'But she needs all the moral support she can get.'

'And Matthew's going to put in an appearance at some point?' Anna asked, her voice shaking slightly.

'He can't get out of it,' Jonathan replied. 'He promised the Rotary Club he'd be here to present the special team award for Young Speaker of the Year, so he really had no choice.'

'Anna!' Meredith had spotted her. As she hugged her, Anna could feel how much weight Meredith had lost during her recuperation and a shard of concern worried at her heart. 'Thanks for coming.' Meredith had thrown off most of her jetlag, having only returned to the village a couple of days ago, and had spent most of the time on the plane back to the UK practising the speech she had to give tonight.

'I wouldn't miss it,' Anna said quickly. 'You look gorgeous.'

'So do you,' Meredith replied, but Anna could tell she was trying to cheer her up. Anna knew she didn't look her best; she'd had too many sleepless nights for that, but she'd tried to paper over the cracks as best she could. The red dress was one of Charlotte's, and wasn't really Anna's shade, but at a pinch it had had to do.

'Are you ready to give your speech?' Anna asked, noticing the cue cards in Meredith's right hand.

'No!' Meredith grimaced. 'But Flynn's been helping me to practise, and I think I can pronounce all of the place names now.'

Anna smiled weakly. 'You'll be fine.'

'So… Dad'll be here later,' Meredith said, searching Anna's face hopefully for a positive response. 'He's skipping the dinner but he'll be here to award the prizes during the coffee.'

'I know,' Anna said guardedly.

'He's not exactly happy about having to come face to face with Flynn again, but he's going to have to suck it up tonight for the sake of the Rotary Club!' Meredith gave a nervous smile. 'Flynn's bricking it.'

'I'm sure it'll be fine,' Anna thought, feeling no such thing. Matthew's volcanic rage when Meredith had been unconscious in hospital had stayed with her, and she knew from Meredith's texts that a certain uneasy peace had been brokered between Matthew and Flynn, after the cause of the car accident had become clear, but there was still a long way to go before either would be truly comfortable in the other's presence.

'Do you think that maybe you might… you know… have a chat with Dad tonight?' Meredith bit her lower lip.

Anna sighed. 'I don't know, Merry. I think it might be best if we kept our distance from each other. And anyway, this is your night.'

'But he misses you so much!' Meredith's eyes were glistening in the soft lights of the marquee. 'Please, just talk to him.'

'Merry, my darling,' glancing at Anna, who was temporarily incapable of speech, Jonathan stepped forward and put his arm around his niece, 'let your dad and Anna work things out in their own time. They will when they're ready, I'm sure.' He placed a kiss on the top of her head. 'Just enjoy tonight. After all, you should make the most of the fact that you're here with Flynn.'

Meredith nodded, and, stepping forward to hug Anna again, she then wandered off, hand in hand with Flynn.

'Are you OK?' Jonathan turned back to Anna.

Anna nodded. 'She's gutted about Matthew and me, isn't she?'

'You don't need me to tell you that, darling. I think she'd feel better about it if she knew why the two of you had got so distant.'

'I wish I knew that myself,' Anna suddenly felt exhausted.

He snaked an arm around her waist. 'He'll come round in time, I'm sure. But for now we'd better grab our seats for this rocking gig.'

*

When dinner had been served and the gathered Rotarians and local dignitaries were satisfied and settled in their seats, it was time for Meredith to speak. As she stood up at the table, Anna saw her knees shaking underneath the hem of her dress, and her heart went out to her.

'Rotarians, Ladies and Gentlemen,' Meredith began. 'Thank you for hosting this dinner tonight.' She took a moment to look around the marquee at the assembled, mostly old, but kindly faces that looked benignly back at her. 'I am here this evening to talk to you about the way that the Model United Nations can have a positive impact on not just young people, but on the world around us...'

And all of a sudden, Anna lost track of what Meredith was saying, as, out of the corner of her eye, she saw Matthew slipping in through the tied back door of the marquee. The sun was setting behind him and for a moment Anna couldn't see the expression on his face. But the curve of his head, the set of his shoulders in his dinner jacket and the uncompromising nature of his presence still took her breath away.

Matthew took a seat against the wall of the marquee, just out of Anna's field of vision. With an effort, she turned her attention back to Meredith. She was currently thanking the Rotary Club for their part-funding of the trip to Belfast. A round of applause greeted the rest of the team as Meredith introduced them, and then it fell to the head of the Rotary Club to speak.

'It gives me great pleasure to introduce the man whose company has so generously funded this year's award, and someone who has a very personal interest in the success of the team of young people you see in front of you. Rotarians, Ladies and Gentlemen, I give you Matthew Carter.'

There was a smattering of further applause as Matthew stood up and walked towards the front of the marquee. He paused for a moment to survey his audience; did Anna imagine it, or did his gaze linger a fraction longer in the area where she was sitting? Then, that rich, deep, heartbreaking voice with its seductive West Country burr began, and the sound was enough to make her face flush and her mouth go dry.

'I can't tell you how pleased I am to be here tonight,' Matthew began. He spoke without notes, the force of his personality holding everyone in the room captive. 'As many of you here know, the past few months have been very difficult for at least one member of this very impressive debating team, and, although Meredith will make me pay for it later if I embarrass her too much during this speech, I tell you that to remind you of the odds that they have had to overcome to win this award.' Matthew cast a quick glance at his daughter and her teammates. 'On behalf of Carter's Cider, I would like to present the award for Young Speaker of the Year to Flynn O'Connell, team captain of the St Jude's Model United Nations delegation.'

As the audience applauded once more, Flynn, looking like he'd rather be anywhere else than accepting an award from his girlfriend's father, walked up to Matthew. There was a brief hesitation from both, and, although it wouldn't have been obvious to anyone else, Anna, whose knowledge of Matthew's mannerisms and physicality was intimate by now, noticed his back stiffen and a split-second hesitation before he shook Flynn's hand.

'I'm pleased Matthew didn't punch him!' Jonathan whispered as the applause started again. 'But then I suppose it wouldn't have done much for his reputation.'

Anna shook her head, quite unable to speak.

As the team sat back down again and the head of the Rotary Club brought the formal part of the evening to a close, Jonathan caught Anna's eye and gave her his trademark wicked grin. 'That's the boring bit over. Now we can misbehave!' He gave her hand a brief squeeze, but Anna was too distracted by Matthew to notice. If she never saw him again in her lifetime, she'd still be able to recall exactly the curl of his hair over his collar, the arrangement of the crows' feet around his eyes, and the fall of those long, lithe limbs. 'He told Meredith he was going to skip off after the presentation,' Jonathan murmured. 'So you don't need to worry about talking to him.'

'I don't think he'd make a beeline for me, anyway,' Anna said. 'He's hardly gone out of his way to see me over the past few weeks.'

'Well, in that case, there's no need to worry then. Shall I get you another drink?'

In dire need of one, Anna nodded. Jonathan wandered off to the bar in the corner of the marquee in search of a couple of glasses of champagne.

'What did you think? Was my speech OK?' Meredith asked as she came back up to where Anna was sitting.

'You were great,' Anna replied, giving the happiest smile she could. 'Your dad must be very proud of you.'

'Difficult to tell, these days,' Meredith snorted. 'He's not saying much. Well, even less than usual, I mean!' She turned to Flynn, who was stood behind her. 'At least he managed to shake your hand without ripping your arm off!'

Flynn gave a smile that was more of a grimace. 'Can't say I'd blame him if he had, really.'

'So have you talked to him yet?' Meredith demanded. 'I mean, you might as well, seeing as you're both in the same – er – room.' She grinned as she looked around at the tented walls of the marquee.

Anna shook her head. 'Not tonight, Merry. It's not the time or the place.'

Merry rolled her eyes. 'I wish I knew when the right time or place *was*.'

Anna was about to reply when she felt the hair on the back of her neck rise.

'I was just saying, Dad, it's about time you two talked.' Meredith's voice gave only the slightest waver as Matthew drew closer.

Anna didn't dare to turn around, sensing Matthew was barely a foot from her.

'I'm going to head off, Meredith,' Matthew said gruffly. 'You'll be home by eleven?'

Meredith nodded. Something in Matthew's tone brokered no disagreement.

'See you later.'

With that, Matthew turned and walked out of the marquee. Anna felt relieved, but strangely deflated. So much for Jonathan's big plan.

'You two are going to have to talk,' Meredith said softly.

'We will,' Anna replied. 'Soon. I promise.' But even as she said it, she wasn't so sure. Matthew had, after all, just completely blanked her.

Before Meredith could respond further, Jonathan returned with two glasses of champagne. 'Here,' he said to Anna. 'Get that down you, and then we'll have a quick dance.'

'I'm not sure I'm in the right frame of mind for dancing,' Anna replied, taking a hefty slug of her champagne.

'Drink faster then!' Jonathan quipped. 'Well done on your speech, darling.' He leaned over and kissed Meredith's cheek.

'Thanks, Uncle Jonno,' Meredith replied. 'I'll see you later – the rest of the team are outside getting some fresh air. Thought we'd join them.'

'Fair enough,' Jonathan gave Meredith a wry glance. 'Just no nicking any champagne bottles on the way out!' He turned back to Anna as Meredith and Flynn left. 'Come on, finish that glass and let's get on the dance floor.'

Anna smiled, in spite of herself. 'Won't that cramp your style a bit, dancing with the Merry Widow?'

'I think the wives of the venerable Little Somerby Rotarians can do without me for one night.'

In the end, it was better to acquiesce than to argue, and Jonathan was fun to be with. Anna could certainly see his appeal; Jonathan was handsome, witty and charismatic, but at the end of the day, he just wasn't Matthew.

'Now doesn't that make you feel better?' Jonathan grinned several songs later as he flung her around the dance floor.

Anna nodded, too out of breath to comment. Then, without warning, Jonathan drew her in closer to him as a rather more sedate tune came over the system. Swaying together, Anna took the opportunity to recover, but after thirty seconds, she stiffened in Jonathan's arms.

'What is it, lovely?' Jonathan turned slightly on the dance floor so he could see the direction of Anna's gaze. There, on the other side of the marquee, distant and unapproachable, his hand closed around a glass of whisky, obviously having thought better of leaving the party early, was Matthew.

'I can't do this.' Anna struggled in Jonathan's arms.

'Not so fast!' Jonathan whispered. 'You've got nothing to be ashamed of. Just relax.'

Conceding reluctantly, Anna moved closer to Jonathan and continued to sway to the music. She was aware, all the time, of where Matthew was in relation to her; to whom he was speaking, his body language. Every so often she knew he was glancing over at her, and his awareness of her, in Jonathan's arms, made her feel like she was standing naked on the dance floor.

'You're doing nothing wrong,' Jonathan said. He kept up a reassuring undertone as they moved around the floor, until the song came to an end.

'Can you get me another drink, please?' Anna asked, hands shaking uncontrollably.

'Of course, lovely. I'll be back in two shakes of a lamb's proverbial.'

Anna immediately felt the loss as Jonathan strode off. She scuttled to the side of the dance floor, trying to disguise herself in the shadows.

'Not with Matthew tonight?' The braying voice of Lando

Statham-Smythe, Rotarian, smashed into Anna's conscious-
ness like a cricket bat to the head.

'Um, no, not tonight,' Anna mumbled, instinctively pulling
her pashmina a little closer across her chest. The dress she
was wearing was hardly low-cut, but something about Lando
made her feel as though he was mentally undressing her.
Watery blue eyes bulged out from under a heavy browline as
if his collar was squeezing the life out of them, and he cupped
a slightly lukewarm glass of cava in one of his clammy paws.

'Trouble in paradise?' Lando leered, taking a sip of his
drink.

'Not at all, old chap, she just thought she'd hang off my
arm tonight instead of my brother's!' Jonathan, smooth as silk
dipped in gloss paint, glided up to Anna's side and handed her
an alarmingly large glass of white wine. 'OK, darling?'

Anna nodded, thanking whatever god happened to be
looking down at her.

'Shall we?' Taking Anna's free hand, he led her to a
secluded table and pulled out a chair for her.

'Seriously, you've turned a rather less than fetching shade
of grey,' Jonathan said softly. 'Is Lando really that awful?'

'Charlotte said he groped her bum so badly at the carol
service last year, she had a bruise for days,' Anna grimaced.

Jonathan tried, unsuccessfully, to smother a bark of
laughter. Anna felt a sting as she realised how much his laugh
resembled Matthew's.

'Well, if I was married to Sally, I'd take any opportunity
I could get!' Jonathan grinned at her. 'Of course, if I was
married to you, on the other hand...' he cocked his head and,
deliberately to throw Anna off balance, he glanced up at her
from under his lashes.

'Don't you ever stop flirting?' Anna asked, shaking her
head in exasperation.

'Only when I'm asleep,' Jonathan kept smiling. 'And sometimes, not even then.'

'You're incorrigible.'

'And encourageable, sweetheart, so go on, encourage me.' His eyes widened and he assumed a serious expression.

Anna couldn't help smiling back. 'Give it up, Casanova. You're not my type.'

Jonathan clapped a hand over his heart. 'You injure me, my lady.'

'I'm sure you've had worse,' Anna was grinning now, despite herself.

'On the contrary,' Jonathan said. 'No woman has ever been able to resist my charms.'

'Let's not go *there*,' Anna shot back. Much as she liked Jonathan, there was still his past to consider, after all. She couldn't write off the hurt he'd caused Matthew quite so easily.

'Fair enough.' Jonathan shook his head. 'But at least you're smiling again.' He picked up Anna's right hand and traced a playful pattern on her palm. 'And it's bound to really be annoying my brother, seeing you smile because of me.'

Anna's stomach fluttered again. 'I keep telling you, that's not why I'm here.'

'I know, darling, but it can't hurt, knowing he's going to be really jealous of me right now.'

'I just wish he'd talk to me. I don't want to have to force a reaction out of him.'

'Sometimes he needs to be forced,' Jonathan said gently. 'Over the years he's got so used to burying his head in the sand whenever something happens he can't handle. He's got to learn to face up to things.'

'I'm not sure if this is the way to do it,' Anna said doubtfully. She glanced around the marquee until her eyes came to rest on Matthew's dinner-jacket clad back. The memory of his naked shoulders under her hands, his muscles moving in rapturous ecstasy as they made love, was so fresh it made her fingertips tingle.

'He'll come round.' All levity was gone from Jonathan's voice now, and as Anna's gaze returned to him from his older brother, she saw in his face that he was sincere.

'I wish I knew what I'd done wrong,' she said. 'But he won't even level with me.'

'Now's definitely not the time, darling,' Jonathan said gently. 'You've had the best part of a bottle of champagne and Matthew's been on the Scotch since he got here.'

Anna nodded. 'You're right. Perhaps I've done my bit for tonight. Will you take me home?'

Jonathan smiled, and again, Anna understood why he was irresistible to most women. Impossibly good looks combined with the ability to make you feel as if you were the only interesting person in the world were a seductive combination. But it was a studied seduction; while Matthew seemed oblivious of the devastating effect of his charisma and striking looks, Jonathan knew all too well the way he could turn women to liquid in his palms.

'Everything all right, lovely? Within reason?' Jonathan had noticed her studying him, and put a gentle hand on her arm.

'Just thinking,' Anna replied.

'About what?'

'About how you're so not my type, but I like you anyway!'

Jonathan looked affronted. 'I don't know which way to take that.'

'Just take me home,' Anna said. 'And if you're lucky, I'll make you a cup of tea.'

'How could I refuse such an offer?' Jonathan looked skywards for a second, then quickly scanned the marquee. 'I can't see Meredith, but I don't think she'll miss us if we slope off. I'll just nip outside and see if she's about. Back in a tick.' Jonathan headed off through the marquee.

Grabbing her handbag from where she'd dumped it on the nearest table, Anna wondered if Pat would be surprised she was back home so early; Jonathan had been breezy in his assurances that it would be midnight before they returned. Anna was sure she hadn't misinterpreted the look of concern on Pat's face when she'd seen Jonathan at the cottage door earlier that evening, and Anna hoped she'd get the chance to clarify things with the woman who'd been so kind and supportive of her. After checking her phone for any messages, she zipped up her bag, turned back around and went slap into Matthew.

Close up, Anna could see how the granite had eroded. The dinner jacket looked too big for him, and his eyes were shadowed. But the anger he exuded was enough to make up for any diminution; it gave him an air of menace that unnerved Anna and made her want to bolt like some terrified animal.

'I suppose you're proving a point tonight,' he said gruffly. 'By parading around with my brother.'

Anna swallowed. 'I wanted to be here to support Meredith. I promised her I would be.'

'How very noble of you.' Matthew took a sip of his fast-emptying whisky glass. Anna could see his eyes were darkened from the effects of the booze, looking almost black in the dim light of the marquee. 'There I was, thinking Jonathan had put you up to it.'

'I can't do this now, Matthew,' Anna said wearily.

Finishing his glass, Matthew shoved it away from him on the table. 'Heaven forbid we should upset the applecart on a night such as this.' He looked around, the scorn evident in his eyes and his voice. 'I mean, what would people think?' The throng of braying villagers, all in various states of inebriation, continued about their business, but one or two glances were thrown their way from time to time. Never had village life felt more claustrophobic.

'I should go before we both say something we might regret.' Anna's voice sounded braver than she felt.

'Oh, please,' Matthew said. 'I think we're long past the *saying something we might regret* stage of things.'

'Believe me, I've wanted to talk, and to listen,' Anna's temper flared, despite the fact she knew that Matthew's words stemmed from having at least one drink too many. 'And I've tried to understand until my brain has tied itself in knots. But you know the one thing I don't get, Matthew? How you could just close off from me, when all I wanted to do was be there for you.'

'Oh, Christ, Anna,' Matthew's eyes were cavernous, tortured, and as Anna met his gaze, full on, for the first time in weeks, she was sure she could see conflict and uncertainty. Then, as quickly as it had happened, Matthew seemed to close off from her again. 'I wish you well of Jonathan,' he said brusquely. 'Perhaps you'll be able to hold onto him longer than Tara did.'

'Wh-what?'

'If you get lucky, he might even stick around in the morning.'

'I just wanted to come for Meredith tonight,' Anna stammered, at a loss as to why Matthew's mood had switched back so suddenly.

'I'm sure you did.'

'Why are you doing this? You know how I feel about you. Please...' Anna's frustration turned to anger as she saw Matthew's lip curl in scorn.

'I'm sure Jonathan will provide you with a more than adequate shoulder to cry on. And whatever else you want.'

'Poor show, big brother.' Jonathan's voice broke through their exchange. He handed Anna a glass of champagne and took a swig of his own. 'You know as well as I do it's not like that.'

'I don't know anything anymore.' Matthew turned abruptly, knocking over a chair to the right of him. 'And I'll thank you to stay out of situations that don't concern you.'

'No can do, I'm afraid.' Jonathan interposed himself between Anna and Matthew. 'Anna came here with me tonight, and I'm going to make sure she gets home without incident as well.'

Matthew snorted. 'That would be a first. You'll be telling me next you're going to walk her to her door and then leave.'

'And what's it to you, anyway?' Jonathan's voice raised a notch. 'You're the one who fucked up your own relationship, Matt, you didn't need me to do it for you this time. Why the hell should you care?'

'You know I do! That's precisely why you brought Anna here tonight.'

'That's as maybe, but you're hardly making things better, are you? Now if you don't mind, I need to get this lovely lady home before I turn into a pumpkin.'

'We're not finished,' Matthew growled.

'We are,' Jonathan countered. 'Come on, lovely, let's get your coat.'

'Oh, fuck off, and leave us alone.' Matthew took a step towards Anna, but Jonathan stood his ground.

'I don't think so.' Taking Anna's arm, Jonathan went to lead her away. As he did so, Matthew's fist swung towards him. Without missing a beat, Jonathan stepped out of the way. Matthew overbalanced, righting himself just in time before he hit the ground.

Beckoning to Patrick Flanagan, who was hovering like a guard dog a few feet away, Jonathan put his other arm around Anna. 'Paddy, can you get Matthew home before Meredith has the misfortune of seeing him?'

'Will do. Come on, old chap. Time to call it a night.'

'Anna, I'm sorry, please, listen to me.' It was as if all the fight had left Matthew as he realised what he'd done.

'Not tonight.' Patrick guided Matthew away.

'I knew I shouldn't have come,' Anna whispered.

Jonathan gave her a wry smile. 'It won't hurt him to be reminded of what he's lost. He needs to learn he can't keep making decisions for everyone around him. And he's going to have a terrible headache in the morning.' He squeezed her shoulder and pulled her close for a second. 'As for whether or not you see him again after this, that's up to you, darling. Shall I walk you home now?'

Anna nodded and allowed herself to be escorted from the marquee.

Ten minutes later, when they arrived at the doorstep of Pippin Cottage, Jonathan gave her a light-hearted bow. 'My lady.'

'Thanks for seeing me home.'

'A pleasure, as always.' Gently, he leaned forward and kissed Anna on the cheek. 'You might reconsider about *really* giving Matthew something to be jealous about. It'd be great fun, I promise you.' He gave her a wink.

'You're sweet, Jonathan, but I prefer my men darker and a little more brooding.'

'I could always dye my hair,' Jonathan quipped.

'Just be my friend,' Anna said. 'You're good at that.'

'Really? That's the first time I've heard *that* from a woman.'

'You should try it more often,' Anna replied. 'You might get to like it.'

'For you, anything. Sweet dreams.' Smiling down at her, his face suddenly seeming much younger in the moonlight, he kissed her hand and headed off into the night.

Chapter 46

'Haven't I said goodbye to you once already?' Matthew growled as he opened Cowslip Barn's front door. 'I thought it was Meredith.'

'Well, you'd better let me in and give me some of that Scotch,' Jonathan replied tersely. 'Otherwise I'm going to camp out on the doorstep until my niece does get home.'

Saying nothing, but opening the door to admit his brother, Matthew walked unsteadily back to the living room. Jonathan pushed the door closed, putting it on the latch in case Meredith had forgotten her key.

'So why are you being such a total twat, then, big brother?'

'I'm not the twat making moves on his brother's woman again.'

'Oh, come off it,' Jonathan snapped. 'You know it's not like that so stop acting like a kicked puppy. It doesn't suit you. Now answer the fucking question.'

'You wouldn't understand,' Matthew replied.

'Try me.' Jonathan helped himself to a glass of Scotch.

'Not a chance. And if all you're going to do is grill me, you can bugger off.'

'Don't you think it's about time you talked to someone?' Jonathan took a gulp of his whisky.

'Nothing to talk about,' Matthew grunted. 'And if I was going to have a cosy chat, it certainly wouldn't be with you.'

'Well, Dad did volunteer to come over a couple of days back, but I didn't think he'd get much out of you.' Jonathan positioned himself in the other chair by the fireplace.

'I warned you,' Matthew growled. 'This is not the time for a reconciliation.'

'I'm not here on my own behalf. I know better than that.'

'Then why *are* you here?'

The silence hung between them. Matthew's hand was clenched so tightly around his Scotch tumbler that the crystal creaked in protest.

'Anna doesn't know what she's done wrong, Matthew. All she knows is that since Meredith was in that accident, you've backed off from her, and she's confused. She thinks... she thinks you blame her for Meredith being injured.'

Matthew drew in a sharp breath. 'That's madness.'

'Mad or not, that's how she sees it. She thinks if she hadn't persuaded you to let Merry see that boy, Merry would never have been in that car.'

'And how the hell do you know?'

'I've mastered something you never quite got around to,' Jonathan shot back. 'I actually learned to talk and listen to women.'

'And we all know that talking's only the start of it.'

'Anna's not Tara,' Jonathan said flatly. 'She's better than that. We're mates, that's all. For some unfathomable reason, right now there's only one man on her radar, and he's currently drinking himself into an early grave.'

'And I suppose you've been having all kinds of cosy chats about my inadequacies as a father, brother and lover, have you?' Matthew said as his temper, ignited by exhaustion and too much whisky, began to flare. Standing abruptly, he swayed slightly from the head rush.

'Not at all,' Jonathan replied, staying seated. 'She just needed to sound someone out who knows you well.'

'You hardly fit the bill,' the sarcasm was dripping in Matthew's voice. 'The last time we had a cosy tête-a-tête was well over a decade ago.'

'Some things, and some people, don't change, and some do, Matt.'

'Oh, and I suppose you're now Galahad rather than Lancelot, are you? Forgive me if I'm not entirely convinced.' Despite his exhaustion, Matthew started to pace the parlour.

'Spare me the histrionics, Matt, I'm not here to go over old ground. It's your future I'm here to talk about.'

'Your concern for my welfare is touching but totally un-necessary. I don't need your advice on my love life, or any other aspect of my life for that matter.'

'Anna just wants to know why you've put so much distance between you. You owe her that, at least.'

'It's better that she... that she just thinks it fizzled out.'

'You mean it's better that she carries on blaming herself for Meredith's accident?' Jonathan, alert, stood up. 'You're just going to wash her away like the barrel dregs?'

'I'm warning you, Jonathan,' Matthew's voice was stronger, but it was born of anger rather than assurance. 'You don't want to push this. Anna's better off this way.'

'Better off? Matthew, she's dying of guilt. Can you live with yourself, knowing she'll hold that forever?'

'It's not what you think. I need time to get to grips with it all.'

'You've had time,' Jonathan said brutally. 'It's been weeks since you've spoken properly to her. If you want to end things, for god's sake have the balls to do it properly. Don't leave her hanging on. You lost one woman because you refused to acknowledge there was a problem; are you prepared to lose another?'

'Leave it,' Matthew snapped, but the fight was going out of him.

'Why don't you try levelling with me, first?' Jonathan said, his tone suddenly much gentler.

Matthew refilled his tumbler and then gulped back a large mouthful. Taking a deep breath, he looked Jonathan straight in the eye. 'I can't argue any more,' he said, his voice raw. 'Please, Jonathan, just go.'

'Tell me why you're doing this.' Jonathan desperately wanted to reach out and put a hand on his brother's shoulder, but he was still wary of the maelstrom of emotions between them, and even more wary of a punch in the face.

'I've been such a fool.' Matthew held Jonathan's gaze, struggling to focus. Shaking his head, he continued, 'I've been sitting here for weeks, trying to get my head around what's happened, and I still end up tied in knots.'

'Tell me,' Jonathan said gently.

Matthew leaned forward in his seat, hair falling over his eyes. He heaved a great, resigned sigh. 'The night Meredith woke up, Tara and I slept together.'

Jonathan choked on his mouthful of whisky.

'I know.' Matthew, at last, put his head in his hands. 'It was a stupid, irresponsible, destructive thing that achieved nothing. The minute it was over I regretted it. But because of that, I've ruined everything I could have had. It was an act even you'd have thought twice about.'

'Were you totally out of your mind?' Jonathan took a last gulp of his Scotch, then immediately filled his glass again. As he put the bottle back down, he paused as the sound of a door closing caught his attention. For a moment he assumed it was

Meredith coming home, but when she didn't materialise, he figured it had just been the wind.

'I've really fucked up, haven't I, Jonno?'

Matthew hadn't used his brother's nickname for years, and Jonathan's throat tightened. 'It's not over, Matt. Not unless you want it to be.'

'How can you say that? I did the one thing I swore I never would. For eleven years I kept that promise; now, when I've got the chance to be happy, and to make someone else happy, I end up throwing it all away.'

'So just don't tell Anna,' Jonathan said. He reached out and tentatively put a hand on his brother's shoulder. 'You don't have to be honest about *everything*, you know.'

Matthew's head snapped up. 'That's always been your philosophy, hasn't it? Don't say anything and hope you don't get caught.'

'Fair point, but on this occasion, why the hell not? She doesn't know. All she thinks is that you've distanced yourself from her. You can tell her what you like. Tell her it's work, Meredith, fucking hell, tell her that you haven't been able to get it up and you're feeling intimidated. It doesn't matter.'

Matthew shook his head. 'You know I'm not like that. I can't get any deeper with Anna unless I'm prepared to be completely honest. And at the moment, I don't have the strength. I know what it'll do to her if I tell her.'

'So don't tell her,' Jonathan repeated patiently. 'Just go and apologise for being a distant idiot and pick right up where you left off. She'll never know.'

'I can't do it. I wouldn't be able to live with myself.'

'You're seriously thinking of going in there and telling her you shagged your ex-wife, aren't you?' Jonathan was incredulous. 'She'll kick your arse from here to Bristol.'

'Then it'll have to end,' Matthew said. 'Tara lied to me once and it nearly destroyed me.'

'Even if you know that telling her the truth will probably destroy her too?'

It was Matthew's turn to take a deep slug of his whisky. For a while he didn't speak. Eventually, he responded. 'If I don't level with her, then I'll have no choice but to end it.'

'You've got to do what you think is best,' Jonathan replied. 'But remember, some things are bigger than truth. Think about the future you have, you *should* have with her. Isn't that worth one little lie?'

Matthew shook his head. 'I can't do it.'

'On your head be it, brother dear.' Jonathan finished his whisky. 'Much as I'd love to hang about and debate your moral fortitude versus my distinct lack of same, I need to get going. That fucking cockerel of Sid Porter's will be squawking the dawn in a few hours.'

'I still can't believe you've dragged it out of me.'

'Really?' Jonathan raised an eyebrow. 'I would have thought, given our history, that you'd have expected it.' Standing up, he gave his brother a last pat on the shoulder. 'Don't spend the next few hours stewing, Matt. If you're going to come clean, just go and bloody do it. She deserves that, at least.'

'You're right. For once. But don't let it go to your head.' Standing up to see his brother to the front door, Matthew's expression was thoughtful. 'I should be feeling like utter shit,' he said. 'And I should have punched your lights out at least a dozen times over the past few weeks.'

'So?' Jonathan prompted.

'So I just can't work out why I feel so bloody optimistic all of a sudden!' Matthew shook his head. 'For the first time in a long time, I know what I want. And she's sitting in a cottage next to the west orchard.'

'It must be spending time with your all-round fantastic younger brother,' Jonathan said sardonically.

'Don't push your luck, Jonno.'

As Jonathan left, Matthew, despite his better instincts, smiled.

Chapter 47

Anna was about to turn in for the night, relieved that it was, at last, all over. Her shawl was flung over the back of the sofa, and her handbag was chucked on the desk near her computer. Ellie was sound asleep upstairs and as Pat had left there was a look of concern etched on her features at Anna's wan appearance. Pat was desperate for Anna and Matthew to work things out, and, much as she liked Jonathan, she was wary of him.

Realising she hadn't checked her phone for a little while, she walked back over to the desk and reached into her handbag to get it. As she checked missed calls and read messages, including a belated text from Charlotte wishing her luck, from the corner of her eye she saw a movement outside the cottage. Feeling her heart lurch, she hoped it wasn't Jonathan, deciding to try to persuade her again to make a whole night of it. Peering through the murky, mullioned front window, she made out a shape scuttling up the garden path. Flying to the front door, slipping in her stockinged feet, she flung it open and Meredith collapsed into her arms.

'Sweetheart, what's the matter?' Anna noticed the girl's desperate thinness, her frailty, and her heart broke again. 'Is it your dad? Is he OK?' She had a sudden, horrific vision of Matthew falling down the stairs drunk.

For a few minutes, Meredith couldn't speak, she was heaving and sobbing so much. Gradually, as Anna held her, murmuring soothing nonsense into her ears and stroking her long black hair back from her face, she began to calm down.

'Come into the lounge,' Anna said gently. 'And tell me what on earth's happened.'

Half carrying Meredith, she managed to get her onto the sofa, and wrapped the shawl she'd slung on the back of it around the girl. Meredith's sobs had slowed to hiccups now, and she wiped her nose on the back of her hand, a peculiarly childish gesture that broke Anna's heart.

'When I got home, the door was on the latch,' Meredith said. 'So I crept in, because I was a bit past my curfew and I didn't want the aggro.' She took the tissue Anna offered her and blew her nose loudly.

'Anyway, I heard Dad talking to someone in the living room, and when I heard the other person too, I was so shocked, I just froze.' Meredith put her head in her hands.

Suspecting she already knew the answer, Anna asked anyway. 'Who was your dad talking to, lovely?'

'It was Uncle Jonathan.' Meredith hiccupped again. 'And I was, like, so pleased they were actually talking to each other, I stood there, listening. I just wanted to hear them chat for a bit. And then...' Meredith started to cry again.

'What is it, sweetheart?' Anna took Meredith's hands in hers.

'I guess I sort of knew Uncle Jonno had something to do with Mum and Dad splitting up, but I didn't realise... how could they? How could they both do it? Dad must have been so hurt.' She trailed off again, unable to speak for a few moments.

Anna let her cry, stroking her hair until Meredith calmed down again. She'd always known Meredith would find out about the reasons for her parents' divorce at some time, but she knew Matthew, and Jonathan for that matter, would be devastated when they realised how she'd found out.

'And it gets worse,' Meredith sniffed.

'How, lovely?' Anna asked, wondering how much worse it could, conceivably, get.

Meredith shook her head. 'I can't tell you.'

'It might help,' Anna said gently. 'Your dad wouldn't want you worrying about things you'd overheard.'

'It's not that,' Meredith sniffed. 'I can't tell you because it's to do with you and him.'

Anna went cold. Was she about to find out why Matthew had distanced himself? Was Meredith going to confirm her worst suspicions; that he did, indeed, blame her for the car accident? Bracing herself, she turned to face Meredith. 'I understand,' she said. 'And you don't have to tell me if you don't want to. After all, things you overhear can often be wrong, or misinterpreted. Perhaps I can help you to work it out.'

'This was pretty clear,' Meredith said quietly. Taking a deep breath, she looked Anna straight in the face, her eyes a combination of apprehension and doubt. 'But if I tell you, please don't blame me. I couldn't handle it if you stopped talking to me.'

Anna gave Meredith a sad smile. 'I won't hold it against you, I promise.'

'Oh, god, Anna...' Meredith's voice trembled.

Anna's heart thumped.

Eventually, fists clenched tightly, Meredith spoke. 'He said,' she swallowed hard. 'On the night I woke up in hospital, he and mum went to bed together.'

The world seemed to slow down to an agonising, grinding halt. Anna's stomach lurched as she tried to digest what Meredith had said. So *that* was what was behind Matthew's sudden change in affections; the weeks and weeks of silence;

that awful, stilted conversation at Cowslip Barn. Now it was becoming achingly clear. But this was not the time to give in to her own personal brand of heartbreak. She had to get Meredith calm enough to go home.

'Let's talk about this in the morning,' she said gently, helping Meredith to her feet. 'Your dad's going to be panicking, wondering where you are.'

'I doubt it,' Meredith sniffed. 'He and Uncle Jonathan were pretty well stuck into the whisky when they were talking. I doubt either of them know what year it is by now.'

'Even so, I should get you home.'

Anna managed to hold herself in check until she'd calmed Meredith down enough to walk her home. Whatever her feelings about what she'd just heard, she knew she couldn't burden Meredith with them; the poor girl had been devastated enough already.

She risked leaving Ellie for the ten minutes it took to ensure Meredith got to the bottom of her own drive, and then she fled back to Pippin Cottage, hoping against hope she'd make it to her bedroom before the tears came. As she dashed up the garden path, she heard a barn owl hoot somewhere in the trees above her. She'd always associated that sound with the passing of someone, or something. Was it hope she was losing?

Only when she was sure she was alone did she give in to her own emotions. As the early grey fingers of a murky, late September dawn clawed through the night sky, she felt sick to her stomach. Not only had Matthew slept with Tara, but he'd also allowed Anna to believe she was responsible for the sudden distance between them. For weeks he'd been evasive, perpetuating the illusion he blamed her for Meredith's accident, when all along he'd been harbouring secrets of his own. Hurt and anger mingled in her stomach, curling around her heart. With a shaking hand, she sipped the cup of tea she'd made for herself and nearly gagged as she realised it was stone cold.

Shivering uncontrollably, she mounted the cottage stairs on shaky legs and collapsed into bed, pulling the duvet up to her chin. Ellie would wake her in a couple of hours' time, and she prepared herself for a long day. But no matter how hard she tried, sleep wouldn't come.

Chapter 48

'I'm sorry, *what* did you just say?' Charlotte grabbed her coffee mug with both hands as it nearly came crashing down on the kitchen table. Still in her dressing gown, her hair in a loose plait, her eyes slightly bleary from a disturbed night with Evan, she was instantly alert. The church bells for the Sunday dawn Eucharist were tolling as the two women sat down at Charlotte's cluttered kitchen table, and Charlotte winced at their pitch.

'I think you heard me,' Anna said flatly.

'With *Tara*? Darling, are you absolutely sure?'

Anna nodded, unable to speak for a moment.

'The bitch! The bastard!' Charlotte put her mug down and jumped up. Crossing to the kitchen cupboard, she pulled out a bottle of brandy and unscrewed the cap. She poured a generous measure into both hers and Anna's mugs. 'Don't look at me like that – if I need a slug of this, then you must need the whole bloody bottle!' Before putting the cap back on, she took a nip from the neck before sitting back down.

Anna sipped her now enriched coffee. The brandy warmed her a little, but she could still feel the sickness in her stomach.

'I trusted him, Charlotte. I opened myself up to him, body and soul. And now this.'

'And I presume you haven't spoken to him about it?' Charlotte asked gently.

'No. I couldn't face him. Although, frankly, he was so drunk at the Harvest Ball, I don't think he'd have noticed if I'd gatecrashed his bedroom and started throwing crockery at his head.' Her attempt at humour surprised her, but was swiftly replaced by another wave of desolation. 'But if Meredith hadn't come round last night... do you think he'd ever have told me himself?'

'Who can say, darling?' Charlotte took another gulp of her coffee, winced and put the mug back down. 'Matthew always seemed so straight. So honest. I can't believe it. I mean, Jonathan's one thing, but Matthew?'

'What am I going to do?' Anna said, taking a more moderate sip from her own mug. 'It's so humiliating.'

'You have done *nothing* wrong,' Charlotte said furiously. 'You are not to blame in this. If Matthew Carter wants to shag his ex-wife then that's up to him. You have nothing to feel humiliated about.'

'When I met her, I could tell she didn't think I was much competition,' Anna swallowed hard.

Charlotte jumped up again and put her arms around Anna. 'Don't you dare take any notice of that bitch. She might be Meredith's mother but that doesn't make her a decent human being. And Matthew knows that. He's made a colossal cock-up but he will realise what he's lost.'

Anna winced at Charlotte's choice of words.

'What do you want to do?' Charlotte rubbed Anna's shoulders.

'I don't know. I don't want to see him right now. If it wasn't for the tea shop I'd take Ellie away for a few days, try to get my head straight. I don't feel like sticking around and stewing.'

'Then do it,' Charlotte said. 'I'll fill in for you, and if you don't trust me alone, get Lizzie to keep an eye on me. I think

I can vaguely remember how it works in there.'

'Are you sure you've got time?' Anna asked. Charlotte had a habit of taking things on breezily, and then realising too late she'd overstretched herself. It was her rather haphazard bookkeeping that had rendered the local toddler group in need of a professional accountant last year.

Charlotte smiled sheepishly. 'Well, it's been a few years, but I did do that summer in there back before I had Evan.' She rolled her eyes. 'As I remember it was actually rather fun, but I was so crap at it that Ursula had to check virtually everything I did. She put up with it, but it eventually came to an end when I got too pregnant to fit between the tables. I think my skills might be better when I'm not up the duff!'

'Are you sure you'll be OK?' Anna asked. 'I mean, will you be able to work around Evan's nursery hours?'

'Oh, Simon's not too busy at the moment so he can always do some childcare for once,' Charlotte replied. 'And I promise I won't do a runner with the takings, either.' She glanced back at Anna. 'And it'll only be for a few days, so not even I can trash your profit margin in that time.'

'We've got a backup supplier for the cakes, who usually stepped in when Ursula and Brian took their holidays, so I'll give them a ring, but Lizzie's more than able to monitor the stock.' She started suddenly. 'I was going to take a few days off soon anyway, so it shouldn't come as too much of a shock to Lizzie to see you on Monday morning. I'll call her to let her know I'm bringing it forward, but I can't face going into specifics, so could you not say too much?'

'That all sounds fine,' Charlotte said. 'And it'll give you a bit of breathing space. Things might look different in a few days.'

Anna hugged Charlotte and then finished her coffee.

Getting rather unsteadily to her feet, she gave her a watery smile. 'Thank you. You're a star.'

'Rubbish. Now get going before you make me cry, too.'

As Anna went to retrieve Ellie from Charlotte's lounge, she wondered where the hell she was going to go.

Chapter 49

Later than he'd intended on Sunday morning and feeling slightly the worse for wear, Matthew put the lead on Sefton and pulled the front door closed. Meredith hadn't surfaced when he'd left the house, which was just as well as he didn't want to have to explain exactly why he was looking, and feeling, so apprehensive. Nor did he want the third degree. The only person he wanted to talk to was Anna. And after his chat with Jonathan last night, he knew he couldn't hold out on her any longer.

Sefton ambled alongside his master, barely requiring the lead. Although ordinarily Matthew would have taken the dog through the orchard and come down Flowerdown Lane on the way back, today he decided to head straight for Pippin Cottage. What he had to say to Anna wouldn't wait.

The drizzle that had started as he'd left the house had intensified into a dirty autumn rain as he drew closer to his destination. He pulled his tweed cap a little further over his forehead, zipped up his Barbour and picked up the pace a little. How could he not have levelled with her? His actions had caused the wound that Tara's return had reopened to fester, and that had infected his good sense and judgement to an unforgivable degree. He'd wasted so much time wallowing in resentment and guilt; now he needed to clear his conscience with Anna. He only hoped she'd still want to know him once he'd done so.

Turning down Flowerdown Lane he could see lights on in Charlotte and Simon's cottage. As he passed the front of their house he could see Charlotte putting the kettle on and toast on a plate for her son. Pat was visiting her sister in Whitby, so her house was quiet. Passing by, giving Sefton's lead a little tug as he started to sniff around the hedge, he came to the wrought-iron gate of Pippin Cottage.

From first-hand experience he knew Ellie was an early riser, and at this hour he'd expected to see her through the living room window, well into some complicated game or other. Yet this morning the whole cottage was in relative darkness. Stopping at the gate, Matthew listened, trying to work out if he could hear any movement. Opening the gate, wincing at the creak of the rusty hinges, he headed up the garden path, on the alert for any signs of life.

There was no reply to his first knock, so he tried again. Still nothing. He knew that Anna's bedroom was at the back of the house, so, heedless of being seen, he tied Sefton up on the porch and walked around to the rear of the cottage. There were no lights on at the back, either. The kitchen was deserted, although he could see a batch of Anna's most recent cakes still sitting on a wire cooling rack on the kitchen counter. The sight of them gave him hope that she couldn't have gone too far. Anna's bedroom curtains were open. If she wasn't in bed, and she wasn't downstairs, then where was she?

He walked back around to the front of the cottage. It was only then that he realised Anna's car wasn't in her parking space. Deflated, he headed back down the front path, Sefton at his heels. He resolved to ring her the moment he got back to Cowslip Barn, and not to stop until he got an answer.

Walking into the kitchen ten minutes later, he saw Meredith

had finally surfaced. She was sitting ramrod straight at the kitchen table, still in last night's dress.

'Did you fall asleep in that frock?' Matthew said. 'Or have you been out all night?' He walked past her to the kettle, picked it up, filled it and flipped it on.

It was only when she failed to respond that he stopped and looked properly at her. Meredith's face was pale, but her eyes flashed with barely suppressed anger. Matthew was reminded of Tara's cat-like rage when he had thrown her out of the cottage a few weeks ago. A shiver ran down his spine.

'What's the matter? Did Flynn do something to upset you?' He approached the table, and went to sit down, but at the last minute he stopped.

'Dad... how *could* you?' Meredith whispered. 'You and Mum... after all this time.'

Matthew took a step backwards, as if Meredith had slapped him. '*What*?'

'Don't try to fob me off with some story,' Meredith's voice got a fraction louder. 'I heard you talking to Uncle Jonathan last night.'

Matthew felt his stomach fall through the floor. 'Oh, Christ.' He moved towards her, but she stood abruptly, nearly knocking over the wooden kitchen chair.

'No. Don't, Dad. Just don't.' She grabbed the back of the chair and righted it, but her hand stayed there, gripping it for dear life.

'It was a mistake,' Matthew said, trying desperately to keep calm in the face of Meredith's rising emotions. 'It never should have happened.'

'All the years I prayed that you and Mum would get back together, all the nights I cried and cried because I wanted her to come back so much, and now, when all I want is for you to marry Anna and live happily ever after, you've done this.' Her voice was so low he could barely hear her, her eyes large and vulnerable framed in her tired face.

Matthew couldn't bear it any longer. He stepped forward and tried to put his arms around his daughter. 'Meredith, please. You don't understand,' he tried to keep his voice calm, despite the rising panic inside. 'Mum and I thought we were going to lose you. When you woke up, there were so many things going around in my head. We were terrified for you, but I was still incredibly angry with her. I realise how destructive that is now. I made a huge mistake. She did, too. Please, darling, listen to me.'

'Why should I listen?' Meredith said flatly. 'You betrayed Anna's trust, and mine. And Mum doesn't want to come back and live with us, does she? She's quite happy with her new life and her new boyfriend. She doesn't want boring old us back. So what was it all for?'

'It was a mistake,' Matthew tried again to make his daughter see. 'And no, Mum doesn't want that. Neither do I. Despite our differences, your mother and I never intended to hurt you. You were always our top priority, in everything we did, everything we decided. I know it wasn't easy for you, and I know that you're hurt, but please, try to calm down and understand. Things happen in the heat of the moment, my darling. Things that in the cold light of day mean something entirely different.'

'That's such a crap excuse!' Meredith's upset turned to anger in an instant. 'You're always telling me to think things through, not to dive in and do something I'll regret. You've been telling me my whole life, *be careful, Meredith, think about it, Meredith*. And then you go to bed with Mum and blame it on the heat of the moment?'

'It's no excuse,' Matthew said, trying to hold on to his last vestiges of calm. 'But it happened. And I've got to try to deal with it as best I can.'

'So that's it?' Tears started to slide down Meredith's cheeks. 'That's all you can say? Christ, Dad.' As Matthew tried to come towards her again, she dashed across the kitchen and headed for the stairs. 'I can't believe you've done this. After everything we've been through. And Anna's gutted, too.'

'Meredith, please!' Matthew shouted after her, but she'd bolted up the stairs. A few seconds later he heard her bedroom door slam. Slumping against the kitchen worktop, his head started to thump. Slowly, his addled brain processed the last thing Meredith had said.

Anna's gutted, too.

His stomach lost the battle and the bile rose. He swallowed. How the hell had Anna found out? Had Jonathan ratted him out after their late night conversation? Had his brother decided to make a night of it with Anna and filled her in during some post-sex pillow talk? Somehow, he doubted that. Jonathan had been so sincere in his desire to help Matthew make things better, and, even given his past actions, Matthew knew instinctively that his brother wouldn't have betrayed his trust again. Suddenly, heartbreakingly, it all fell into place; Meredith's exhausted look, the dress from last night.

Christ.

Anna knew because Meredith had run to her. After everything he'd done to Anna, after the way he'd frozen her out of his life, she had still been there for his daughter. He struggled for breath against the rising tide inside him.

That's why Anna hadn't opened the door this morning. That was why her car wasn't in its parking space. He had to find her; he had to explain. But what was the use? She'd never give him the time of day now. He looked longingly at the half-drunk bottle of Scotch on the counter; the temptation to chase oblivion was overwhelming. But there had been entirely too much of that of late.

Closing the back door quietly behind him, he dropped the bottle into the recycling bin as he passed it. He knew that Anna's parents were still abroad, and would be until nearly Christmas, and Pat was away. The only option he had left was Charlotte, and even he wasn't brave enough to risk talking to her so soon. Her temper, and her loyalty to Anna, would be a lethal combination, he suspected. There was one other person, however, he really needed to see, although it surprised him to admit it. It was yet another conversation that was long overdue.

Chapter 50

'I miss you.'

Everything else seemed so inadequate, so unnecessary. What more needed to be said, after nearly three years without him? When Anna had married James, she'd assumed they'd be together for life. In a way, they had been; but she'd never thought she'd be the one left alone. At least, not until she was old and grey and had a gaggle of children and grandchildren to keep her company.

'What should I do, James?'

The macabre absurdity of standing by the graveside of her dead husband, asking for advice about how to proceed with a new love made her give the ghost of a smile.

'I wish you were here.'

Even that wasn't entirely accurate, she realised. When they'd met, she and James had been convinced they were immortal; finding out the hard way that they weren't had been the worst lesson she'd ever had to learn. But, much as she'd loved the man, she couldn't love a ghost. Matthew wasn't a ghost; although the spectre of his actions haunted her.

'I've met someone.'

Somehow, saying it out loud made it more real.

'But it's complicated. I don't know what to do. Stuff happened. I don't know how to deal with it.' She leaned over and adjusted one of the red roses she'd brought with her where it sat in the headstone's steel vase.

'I thought… if I came to see you, things might become a bit clearer. I know that's stupid.' Her hands flapped helplessly at her sides. 'I miss you. And I will always love you. But I love him too. Despite everything.'

She thought she'd cry, but tears were for the living, and James had been beyond them a long time ago. She'd driven straight here as soon as Ellie had woken up, stopping briefly to buy them both breakfast at an old haunt on the Salisbury-Chichester road. The three of them, when there were three of them, always stopped there when they drove back to visit her parents. The proprietor had looked curiously at them both when they'd arrived, and Anna had waited for the inevitable question, relieved when it hadn't been broached.

As a result of this early start, she and Ellie had arrived at the old country churchyard just outside the village where she and James used to live before the Sunday morning service had begun. Ellie was sound asleep in the car, which Anna could see from this spot in the graveyard. Above her head, in the ancient yew trees, she heard a song thrush practising its call, and the hedgerow on her right obviously housed several sparrows who were chattering merrily, strangely at odds with their sombre surroundings.

Anna turned away, and there was a fluttering of wings behind her. Hardly daring to breathe, she froze. She had never been a believer in omens, being entirely too much the agnostic realist, especially after the past couple of years. Turning round to face James' gravestone once more, she saw a tiny, red-breasted robin perched on the top of the marble. Her late grandmother had always said robins carried the spirits of people who'd passed on, and although the pragmatist in her refused to believe it, she could have sworn the robin looked her straight in the eye at that moment. The question was, what, if anything, was it trying to tell her?

Chapter 51

To say Jack was surprised to see his elder son was an understatement.

'Can we talk?'

'Of course. Come into the parlour.' Jack, still straight-backed and debonair, even in his checked shirt and tan cords, led the way. Once they had both settled themselves in the two wing-backed chairs, Matthew spoke.

'I need to ask your advice, Dad.' Matthew shook his head. 'I can't quite believe I'm here.'

'I'll do my best,' Jack said. 'I'm not very good at these father-son chats. You of all people know that.' He gave a small smile. 'But then, you were never very good at confiding in me.'

'Difficult to confide in someone who doesn't want to listen,' Matthew said.

'Oh, don't start all that again!' Jack said. 'Jonathan's given me enough grief already.'

Matthew, ashamed, felt his face burn. 'Sorry.'

Jack gave Matthew a wry look. 'I suppose it's too early for a drink?'

'A bit,' Matthew admitted. 'Perhaps afterwards.'

'What can I help you with?' Jack asked gently.

'I've fucked up, Dad. And I don't quite know how to get out of the mess I'm in.' He gave a hollow, mirthless laugh. 'I was hoping you might be able to shed some light on the situation.'

'I'll do my best,' Jack replied. 'Would you like to start at the beginning?'

Matthew took a deep breath, and the long, tortuous story of his lapse with Tara poured out. As he finished, he looked back up at his father. 'And now I just don't know what to do.'

There began a pause between them that seemed to last an eternity. Eventually, Jack spoke. 'Matthew, my boy, what do you take me for?'

'In what sense?' Matthew's own voice was perfectly neutral, betraying no trace of the emotions that were running so close to the surface. He had got so used to hiding things from his father, this current situation shouldn't have presented any issues for him.

'You've given so much of your time to the business, and to raising my granddaughter, isn't it time you stopped treating your father like the fool you clearly think I am, and were honest with me? You know full well you've only given me half the story.'

Jack, heedless of the fact it was barely eleven in the morning, reached out to the occasional table by his chair and poured a glass of apple brandy from the decanter. He looked at Matthew, then quickly poured another glass and passed it to his elder son. 'I know about your brother and Tara,' Jack said. 'I've always known.'

Matthew nearly dropped the tumbler on the hearthstones. 'Wh-what?'

'Oh come on, Matthew, don't keep taking me for a fool!' Jack's voice hardened slightly. 'There was no way I couldn't have. We were lucky that by the time it all happened, your mother was too ill to realise.'

'But you never said… you never let on in any way that you knew.'

'Of course not!' Jack said impatiently. 'I know you've always thought Jonathan was my favourite, and that I wouldn't be able to cope with the truth, but once you've seen someone you love diminish and die before your eyes, you become harder. What Jonathan did was unforgivable, but you should have trusted me with the truth.'

Matthew hung his head. 'I know. But you must understand, because of what he'd done it took me a long time to come out the other side of what happened. I thought I was protecting you. I didn't want to hurt you any more than Mum's death already had. Clearly it was all for nothing if you already knew.'

'I wanted to help you,' Jack's voice was rough with emotion. 'You're my son, Matthew, as much as Jonathan is. You spend your life shutting people out. That's part of the reason Tara couldn't stick it. If you'd let her in more, perhaps she wouldn't have found comfort elsewhere.'

Matthew felt a prickle of anger. 'She picked the one person she knew would cause me the most hurt. She knew what she was doing. She left *me,* Dad.'

'Of course she did, but it takes two to end a relationship. And two to keep one alive. Believe me, I know. Your mother had to do her fair share of forgiving, if not forgetting.'

Matthew was startled, although he'd often suspected as much. Jack might be more of a harmless flirt now, but thirty years ago it had been a different matter. He remembered, as a boy, seeing an unidentifiable darkness in his mother's eyes on more than one occasion, and feeling bewildered that he couldn't seem to make her smile.

'But she stayed with you,' Matthew said gruffly.

'She always knew I loved her best, despite my... ramblings,' Jack said, draining his glass. 'She was more than I deserved. And Anna's more than you do.'

'Apart from that stupid mistake with Tara, I've been rigidly faithful to Anna since we started seeing each other,' Matthew snapped. 'As I was to Tara when we were married. I am not a *rambler*.'

'That may be so,' Jack said. 'But you've committed a gross sin of omission with both of them. You've got to let people in, Matthew. It's not a weakness; quite the opposite, in fact. Your brother, for all his faults, was always better at doing that.'

Matthew shook his head. 'Jonathan is my brother. I trusted him more than anyone. I loved him. And he betrayed me. He tore my life apart. And you knew. All these years, you knew. Why didn't you tell me?'

Jack's gaze, when it met Matthew's, was bereft. 'I was afraid,' he said softly. 'I was afraid I'd lose you both. I hoped that eventually you'd move past the betrayal, but the years passed and you were still so far apart. When this FastStream deal came up, it was a way to try to reconcile you. I'm sorry that I never told you the truth.'

'You should have told me, Dad,' Matthew said, but the sadness in his father's eyes almost derailed him.

'You're right,' Jack replied. 'But let me now tell you this. Anna's a good girl. Don't let your fear of the same thing happening again drive her away.'

Matthew's neck stiffened. 'I'm not afraid. I can't afford to be. I've made the firm what it is today by taking risks. How can you sit there and tell me that was wrong?'

Jack sighed. 'I'm not talking about the business, son. What you've accomplished will never be anything other than hugely impressive. But you made a terrible mistake with Tara, and an even bigger one by not telling Anna about it. You didn't allow her the freedom to decide for herself whether or not she wanted to see you again. You just assumed you knew what she thought and felt. And then, inevitably, she found out what had happened another way.'

'Oh, come on, Dad, do you honestly think she'd have

welcomed me back with open arms if I'd actually told her first?'

'Perhaps not, but it was her choice to make, not yours. You denied her that choice by keeping silent. That Meredith told her was deeply unfortunate, but the bigger sin was taking that choice away. I'm telling you, son, you have to stop believing that you know better than everyone else in your life, or it'll destroy any chance of happiness you have left.'

The gentleness in his father's voice disarmed Matthew and dissipated his anger. He put his head in his hands. 'I can't help it, Dad. Since Meredith's accident...' his voice caught in his throat.

'Meredith's fine. A little wiser, and a little more cautious perhaps, but fine. You can't protect her from the whole world. She's as stubborn as you and she'll go out and find danger if you don't allow her to court it occasionally. And if nothing else, she's learned not to listen at keyholes.' Jack reached forward and patted Matthew's shoulder with a gnarled, arthritic hand.

When Matthew looked back up at his father, he saw tears in Jack Carter's eyes.

'Listen to me,' Jack said gruffly. 'Go and find Anna, wherever she is, and tell her you love her before it's too late. Don't let this one get away from you.'

'How can I find her if she doesn't want to be found? She's gone, I don't know where and I don't have the first clue where to look.'

Jack shook his head. 'For an intelligent man you really are stupid sometimes. Take a leave of absence. Find her. Don't mess this up, Matthew. You might not get another chance at happiness.'

Matthew shook his head. 'Why did we not do this years ago?'

Jack looked wryly at his son. 'Would you have listened to me?'

Grinning ruefully, Matthew conceded that perhaps the old man had a point, picked up the decanter and poured them both another drink. 'Don't worry, Dad, I'm not driving anywhere today. I'll take your advice first thing tomorrow.'

When they parted, Matthew felt that, for the first time in years, he'd actually communicated with his father.

Chapter 52

Cowslip Barn was quiet when Matthew walked back through the front door, and he hoped that Meredith hadn't decided to skip out in the time he'd been with his father. Feeling a real flutter of nerves in his stomach, he mounted the stairs and drew a deep breath before knocking on her bedroom door.

'Come in.'

He still didn't quite know how to start the conversation, but, bracing himself, he opened the door. Meredith was lying on her bed watching the latest episode of an American high school drama, the remains of a cheese sandwich on a plate beside her.

'Pat'll moan if she finds more crumbs in your bed sheets. She almost went on strike when she found most of the kitchen crockery under your bed.' Matthew gave a faint smile.

'I'll take it down when I'm done,' Meredith replied, glancing at him. 'Did you go out?'

'Yes.' Matthew sat gingerly on the edge of Meredith's rumpled bed. 'I went to see Granddad.'

'Did he give you a bollocking as well?'

'You could say that.' Matthew shook his head. 'Not that I don't deserve one.'

'What are you going to do?'

Matthew ran a hand abstractedly through his hair. 'Firstly, I'm going to apologise to you. You don't deserve this, and I know how hard it's been for you. I gave you the hope that Anna and I would be together, and now it doesn't look like that's going to happen. I can't imagine how you feel.'

'Gutted, mostly,' Meredith said. 'I really thought you and Anna had a chance to make each other happy. Angry with you for being a dick. Angry with Mum for ruining everything again. And really, really sad for Anna.'

Matthew swallowed hard. 'You articulated that extremely well. Better than I could.'

'Must have inherited that from Mum.'

'I just wish I knew what to do next,' Matthew shook his head. 'Any ideas?'

'Talk to Anna. She's the one who deserves your apology.'

'I know.' And in that moment, a wave of desolation washed over him; it wasn't the first, and it certainly wouldn't be the last. 'She won't listen to me.' He ran a hand over his tired eyes.

'Daddy,' Meredith whispered. She moved towards Matthew and put her arms around him. 'I'm sorry I shouted at you earlier. You and Anna will work this out, I know you will.'

Matthew pulled Meredith close and clenched his jaw. 'We might not be able to.'

'Talk to her, please.' Meredith looked up at her father, and in her face were traces, still, of the hopeful child she once was. She was on the brink of so many things, so many new experiences; it made Matthew's heart ache to look at her.

'I can't.'

'Yes, you can! You just go round there, knock on the door and refuse to go away until she lets you in.' Meredith's voice carried more than a hint of desperation. 'You have to make her listen to you.'

'I can't.' This time there was no mistaking the tremble in his voice. He tightened his embrace.

'Please, Dad.' Meredith's voice was so full of hope. Matthew could hardly bear it.

'I can't, Meredith.' He closed his eyes briefly and tried to breathe. 'Because she's not there.'

'What do you mean?' Meredith pulled back so that she could look her father in the eye. 'Where is she?'

'I don't know.'

'Dad, you've got to find her!' Meredith was alert, despite the fact she'd had very little sleep. 'She must have told someone where she was going – she wouldn't have buggered off without telling at least one person. She's got the tea shop to sort out, for a start. She wouldn't just have left that.'

'Her parents are out of the country, so I doubt they'd be any the wiser.'

'What about Pat?'

'Gone to her sister's.'

'She wouldn't just have walked out on the tea shop without telling *someone* where she's going. Anna's not like that.'

'She must have been in a pretty poor state of mind,' Matthew said. 'She might just have gone without thinking.'

'No.' Meredith was adamant. 'Someone knows. And if I know Anna, she'll have told Charlotte. Why don't I go round there and find out?'

'Leave her be for today,' Matthew said. 'If she does know what happened, she'll be pretty angry with anyone by the name of Carter at the moment, and she's got good reason to be. I'll go and see her tomorrow.'

'No offence, Dad, but you're the last person she's going to want to see. Why don't you let me try?'

Matthew rubbed a hand over his tired eyes. 'Not today.'

'OK,' Meredith conceded reluctantly. 'I'll pop round after school tomorrow and see if I can find anything out.'

'Don't give her a load of grief,' Matthew warned. 'She's

Anna's best friend and she only wants to protect her.'

Meredith gave a small smile. 'Understood. For what it's worth, Dad, you've been a prat, but I think you're worth a second chance.'

Matthew pulled Meredith close again. 'Thanks.' As her arms curled around him, a small amount of the anxiety he'd been carrying since his ill-fated night with Tara started to dissipate. He had a long way to go before it was all gone, but reconciling with Meredith was a good first step.

Chapter 53

'So let me get this straight,' Jonathan said. 'One minute you're desperate to get after Anna and plead with her to take you back, and the next you're flatly refusing to go because a bunch of middle-aged Yanks are flying in tomorrow?' He shook his head. 'I don't get you sometimes.'

Matthew had been greeted with the eleventh hour news that the FastStream reps were flying in on the redeye from Newark when he'd reached his office that morning. It was now getting close to lunchtime, and he was still at a loss as to how best to play it. He began to pace his office, agitated and conflicted beyond belief. 'I can't just swan off at a moment's notice and leave this place in the lurch. There's too much at stake.'

'Then let me handle it,' Jonathan replied. 'Some things are more important than the business. I know you find that hard to believe, but in this case it's true. I can do this. You know I can. I've proved it to you by getting the buggers to agree to come in the first place.'

'I need to be here at the table with you,' Matthew snapped. 'And you still haven't told me exactly what you said to McIvor. The about-turn FastStream have done on this deal is nothing short of miraculous.'

'It'll keep,' Jonathan said hastily. His brand of business was, he imagined, a little less strait-laced than his brother's on occasion, and he didn't want to get into a conversation about principles, especially when they involved a lot of alcohol and several promises he probably wouldn't keep. 'I can handle the Americans,' Jonathan continued. 'Now for once will you follow your heart instead of your head and get down to Hampshire and bring Anna home.'

Matthew's head snapped up. 'She's in Hampshire?'

'Yes.'

'How do you know?'

'Charlotte fessed up in the end, but to be honest, it wouldn't have taken a genius to work it out. Even I knew where she and James lived before she came here, and her grandfather still lives there.'

'And Charlotte told you this, when?'

Jonathan grinned. 'Earlier this morning. I went to see her at the tea shop and charmed it out of her. But I wanted to make you sweat a bit before I told you.'

Matthew's patience snapped. Before he could even think, he'd grabbed hold of his brother and thrown him back against the wall. 'You can presume to tell me how to run my business, Jonathan, and you can even manage to get Dad back on side, but don't you *ever* tell me how to conduct my relationships.' His face was close to his brother's and he could feel Jonathan's shortening breaths.

'Forget about me for a minute, will you? Anna's gone, and she's taken Ellie with her, and unless you get after her and tell her how you really feel, she won't be coming back. She's one step away from putting Pippin Cottage back on the market and getting the hell out of here for good.' He reached up and pulled Matthew's hand away from his collar. 'Don't let your own pig-headedness lose you the one person who can make you truly happy.'

Matthew froze for a moment, lost, angry and afraid.

Then, slowly, he dropped his hand from where it had balled in Jonathan's shirt. Taking a step back, he bowed his head.

'I can't lose her, Jonno. She's what makes me draw breath.'

'I know.' Jonathan's voice was gentle. 'Let me handle the Yanks tomorrow, and get yourself after her, quickly.'

When Matthew raised his head again, his eyes were full of desolation. 'You are not off the hook,' he said bleakly. 'But I will trust you this time. Don't fuck it up.'

'You either, big brother.' Jonathan replied. 'Now you'd better take me through this presentation of yours so you can shoot off as soon as it's light tomorrow.'

'I need to go now.'

'You can't,' Jonathan replied. 'The Land Rover's in bits on Patrick's driveway, again, remember? He promised to have it back to you, good as new, early tomorrow morning. And Dad's Jag is in for its MOT so you can't nab that. Wait one night, and then you can get your stubborn, pathetic backside down to the commuter belt and win back the woman you love.'

Matthew shook his head. He still couldn't get that same head around it all. How, over the space of so short a time, had he become so remarkably illiterate in the ways of the world?

Chapter 54

Anna knew she couldn't stay with her grandfather indefinitely, much as her instinct was to hide out with him for the foreseeable future. She knew that, by returning to Hampshire, returning to where she and James had spent their married life, she was looking for something, hoping for something she was never going to find. She was running away from the present in search of her past; a past that was, literally, dead and buried.

That Tuesday morning, the low autumn sun cast Ludshott Common in a strange, golden light as Anna and Ellie meandered over the slight inclines at the heart of the Hampshire-Surrey border. It felt more like a day in late summer than mid-October. The sepia light and the birds singing in the trees made the atmosphere warmly electric. Though the pine trees still held their needles, many of them were brown from the lack of rainfall, and a carpet of dropped shards crunched beneath their feet as they walked.

'We going home soon?' Ellie asked as she picked up yet another fallen gorse spike.

'Why?' Anna replied. 'Don't you like staying with Great-Granddad?'

'Yes,' Ellie said. 'But I miss Evan. And Merry.'

Anna swallowed hard. She knew she couldn't hide forever. 'Just a few more days, darling.'

Satisfied, Ellie upped her pace, toddling ahead on the

path and chasing falling coppery beech leaves. The scent of approaching winter was in the air, but the warmth counteracted it. Anna was bombarded by sense memories of blissful, humid summer nights in Matthew's arms, and a fresh wave of longing threatened to overwhelm her. Would she ever feel whole again?

Glancing back towards where the footpath led from the main road to the common, Anna blinked in the sunlight. When they started the walk, they'd been alone; it being too late for the dog walking stockbrokers and too early for the lunchtime pensioners taking a constitutional. But there was someone else striding down the pathway. Someone who was tall, broad, and walking with a slightly uneven gait. Someone she'd know anywhere, but who seemed strangely out of place striding across this common, in this unusual light.

It couldn't be.

Could it?

Was she hallucinating? Anna froze in her tracks. The figure came closer, pace picking up as he gained ground.

A confusing maelstrom of emotions overtook her. Matthew, in his fallback blue jeans, and a crumpled checked shirt, his hair looking as though it hadn't seen a brush in a week, grey stubble peppering his face, was striding towards her. He looked tired but elated that he'd finally found what, or whom, he was looking for.

'I thought I'd never find you!' The voice, the sheer power of his presence was unmistakeable.

'What are you doing here?' Anna blinked furiously, still not convinced she was actually seeing straight.

'I came after you as soon as Jonathan told me where you'd gone.'

'Jonathan? But how did he know?'

'He wheedled it out of Charlotte.'

'Of course he did.' Anna sighed. 'But it's still no good. I can't handle it right now.'

'Handle what?'

'You, life, anything, really.' Anna reached out and plucked a spike of gorse from a nearby bush. It gave her something to focus on, something to ground her.

'You're not making any sense,' Matthew said.

'Well, why don't *you* talk?' Anna flared up. 'Don't you think it's about time you levelled with me?'

Matthew looked long and hard at her 'All right.' He took hold of Anna's shoulders and turned her to face him. 'When Tara left me, I was a mess,' he said. 'I was angry, scared, I had no idea what to do with Meredith, the business was about to go under and to cap it all I'd not only lost my wife, but my brother.' He shook his head. 'It took a long, long time for me to get back on an even keel, and some people would say that I'm still listing a bit, even now.

'Anna, when you came to the village, it was as if a whole lot of things that I'd been unsure about, afraid of, suddenly stopped being so frightening. I looked at you and I realised that it was time to stop being angry, to stop holding on to the hurt and to start living my life again. And that, in itself, frightened the hell out of me.' He slid his hands down Anna's arms to hold her hands. 'And I'll admit, I could never have worked that out by myself. Meredith knew before I did that you were someone special. It took her nearly dying for me to realise that she was absolutely right. And even that didn't stop me from making the second most colossal mistake of my life. And then, by not levelling with you, I made the biggest one.'

'Matthew...' Anna whispered. The hurt of finding out about Matthew and Tara's encounter threatened to engulf her again and she wasn't sure she could handle it.

'No. Let me finish, please. I need to say this. And I need

to know you've heard it. What you choose to do with that knowledge is entirely down to you.' He drew a shaky breath, and his hands started to tremble in hers. 'I will never be able to express how much I regret that night, and how sorry I am that it happened. It was the lowest point of my entire life, and what Tara and I did will haunt me until the end of my days. I hate myself for what I did. But I love you, Anna, and I never, ever, want to risk losing you again. I can't imagine my life without you, and if you choose to live yours without me, if you can't find it in your heart to forgive me, I'll deal with that, somehow, but I want you to know that the fact of my loving you will never change.'

The birds in the trees above their heads chirruped softly, and that was the sound that Anna would forever associate with what happened next. Slowly, gently, she raised her hands to Matthew's face. She felt the tautness of his jaw under her fingertips as he struggled not to lose control, and saw him blinking furiously. She increased the pressure of her fingers and brought her lips to his. His mouth was warm and soft, and trembled as it met hers. Tentatively, she deepened the kiss, until both of them were shaking so much they had to break apart again to breathe. Anna noticed the wetness under her fingers as she moved to look at Matthew again, but wasn't sure if it was caused by her tears or his. When they parted, they were both gasping and Anna was grateful for Matthew's arms around her.

'I can't help it,' Anna whispered. 'I've tried to tell myself I'll get over you, that I can walk away from this if only I kept reminding myself of what you and Tara did, but I never believed it. You made a stupid mistake, in horrible circumstances, and grown-ups are allowed to make mistakes sometimes, if only to learn from them.' She willed herself to take the next step. 'I knew that from the start, really, but I tried to convince myself it was over between us so that I wasn't the one who'd end up letting you down. I love you too, Matthew, and I always, always will.'

Matthew, the haunted expression still evident in his eyes, couldn't take it in. 'You love me? In spite of everything?'

Anna nodded. 'Always.'

And in that moment, as his arms wrapped around her, both of them knew their future could only be together. Matthew was still shaking so badly he could barely stand, and Anna clung onto him as if she was drowning, but in a sense they were both just coming to the surface.

As they parted, Matthew looked down at Anna wonderingly. 'I'm not angry anymore.' He traced Anna's lips with his fingers. 'You give me such peace. I've never felt so calm as when I'm with you.'

'Really?' Anna hiccupped, realising that, to any onlooker, peaceful was the last thing they looked. Even as she brushed the tears from her eyes she couldn't help saying. 'And you make me so happy.' Somehow it seemed right that this had happened in a place that had meant so much to her and James. It signified the coming together of two parts of her life.

'So… time to go home?' Matthew said.

'Yay!' Ellie, bored of chasing beech leaves, pulled at Matthew's jeans-clad legs until he gathered her up in his arms.

Anna gave the first laugh she'd managed in many weeks. 'I think so.'

Hand in hand, Matthew cradling Ellie in his free arm, they strolled back over the common.

TWO MONTHS LATER

Chapter 55

'Where do you want all this?'

Anna looked up from counting the till float and laughed. 'When I said I wanted some mistletoe, I wasn't quite anticipating that much!'

Matthew nudged the front door of the tea shop shut with his elbow, walked over to the sofa in the corner and dumped the huge armful on the coffee table. 'It's rather fond of apple trees, and although we need to keep the commercial stock parasite-free, I couldn't quite bring myself to have it all cut out of the show orchard.'

'You old romantic,' Anna smiled. 'There I was, thinking you ran the business with your head.'

'Most of the time I do,' he said. 'But somehow, lately, I've been persuaded that my heart occasionally has to have a say.' He drew closer to her. 'I can't think what's changed my mind.' He brushed his lips against Anna's. Deepening the kiss, she slid a hand through his silver black hair and allowed herself to luxuriate in the sensations for a moment or two.

'What time's kick-off?' Matthew asked as they broke apart.

Anna tweaked her ponytail and smiled. 'Six o'clock. Ursula and Brian's flight lands at three thirty, so hopefully they'll make it on time.'

'Meredith's coming with – that boy,' Matthew still couldn't bring himself to mention Flynn's name, despite their tentative rapprochement, 'and Dad's asked Miss Pinkham.'

Anna raised an eyebrow. 'Oh yes? He said he was bringing someone, but was cagey about exactly whom. That's a turn-up for the books!'

'Do you want a hand hanging some of this stuff?' Matthew gestured to the mistletoe, which was already shedding berries on the sofa.

'Haven't you got to get back to work?' Anna asked. 'I thought things were always hectic before shutdown.'

'Jonathan's tying up a few loose ends for me before he flies back out to the US tomorrow,' Matthew said.

'He's not here for Christmas?'

'Nope. Got a better offer, apparently.' He raised his eyes heavenwards. 'I should imagine it's got a woman on the end of it.'

'We really need to get him settled down,' Anna laughed. 'He's getting too old to fly halfway around the world for a date.'

'Don't let him hear you say that,' Matthew grinned. 'As far as Jonno's concerned, he's still in the prime of his adolescence.'

'I'm glad you two are managing to run things OK, though,' Anna said. 'I never thought I'd see the day.'

'Me neither.' Matthew gave a strange smile. 'And neither did Dad. Speaking of whom, I should probably go and check on him before this party kicks off. Do you mind?'

'Not at all,' Anna said. 'Lizzie's coming in at five, and between us we'll get this place sorted.' She smiled. 'So get going and I'll see you later.'

A couple of hours later, The Little Orchard Tea Shop Christmas party was in full swing. Paperchains hung from the ceiling, made by Ellie and Evan the night before, and tea lights glowed in festive-coloured glasses on the tables. Despite the small floor space, Anna had managed to cram in her parents, Ellie, Charlotte, Simon and Evan and the book club. In the other corners of the room, Jack Carter and Miss Pinkham raised a mug of mulled wine together and Ursula and Brian were sipping Scotch-infused coffee and sampling some of Anna's Christmas-inspired cinnamon and almond cupcakes. As Anna approached their table, her godmother looked up at her.

'Well done,' she said, putting her cake back on the plate. 'This place is looking busier than ever. I knew I left it in good hands.' Struggling to get up, she enfolded Anna in a warm embrace. 'I'm proud of you. And James would have been, too.'

Anna hugged Ursula back. 'Thank you for trusting me.' She closed her eyes; the changes in the past year suddenly leaving her awash in another emotional sea. 'I like to think he would be, too.'

'We need to talk about what happens next at some point,' Ursula said when they broke apart again. 'After all, it looks like you're pretty settled here.'

'I am,' Anna nodded. 'And it looks like you're pretty settled in Umbria.'

'Let's get together and discuss it over the holiday, shall we?'

Meredith and Flynn were tucked out of the way at the table near the back of the tea shop with a large group of their St Jude's friends, and, as Anna broke free from Ursula, she was sure she didn't imagine Flynn trying to make a bolt for the kitchen when the tea shop door opened to reveal Matthew as he stepped in off the street.

'Sorry I'm late,' he murmured as he walked straight up to Anna, cutting through the other party guests like a cake knife. 'Something came up at the last minute.' He leaned down and kissed Anna briefly.

'There's always something,' Meredith said, leaving Flynn at the table and joining them. 'What was it this time?'

'Oh, nothing,' Matthew said hurriedly. 'It'll keep.' He pulled a hand out of his coat pocket. 'Need any help handing things around?'

'I think we've got it under control,' Anna said. 'Just grab some mulled wine and a sandwich and relax.'

Meredith grinned. 'Great party, Wicked Stepmother. These cheese and pickle sarnies are lush.'

'Glad you like them,' Anna said wryly as Meredith sneaked one from Ellie's plate, who squealed in protest until Meredith pinched a cupcake from the nearby cake stand and put it on her plate instead.

About half an hour into the party, when everyone was suitably relaxed and the mulled wine was starting to take effect, Anna glanced around at her guests. The tea shop was packed with most of her regulars and quite a few droppers in. Groups of people congregated around tables and it wasn't just the children who were enjoying pulling the mini crackers.

She headed over to the counter and cleared her throat. 'Thanks, everyone, for coming tonight to celebrate my first year, almost, of running The Little Orchard Tea Shop. And Christmas, of course.' She looked around at the gathered friends, family and clientele and smiled. 'When I first came back to Little Somerby, I had no idea that managing the tea shop would involve so much hard work, but also so much fun and laughter. I hope that this party has gone some way to show how much I appreciate your support.' Her gaze lingered on Matthew and Meredith. 'So much has changed for me, in ways I never thought possible; and you've all been such a huge part of that. Thank you.' She swallowed hard. 'And have a very Merry Christmas.'

Sometime later, after the guests had left, Anna wiped her last table. Lizzie had also left, and her parents had taken Ellie home for the night. Jack had left with Miss Pinkham and

Meredith and Flynn had also wandered off. Matthew had vanished earlier, but had promised he'd be back to walk her home. She looked at her watch on the way back through to the kitchen. As she was hurriedly washing and drying up a couple of stray plates, she heard the bell ring above the tea shop door.

Wandering back through, she stopped in her tracks. Matthew was in the doorway, a look of uncertainty on his face. Snowflakes shimmered around him, backlit by the white streetlights, and a few had settled in his hair. She was taken back to the day she moved into Pippin Cottage, and he'd stood in her kitchen doorway. So much had changed since then.

'Everything OK?' she asked, wiping her hands on the tea towel she was still holding.

Matthew looked at her long and hard. 'Just taking a moment.'

'For what?' Anna dumped the tea towel on the counter and walked towards him.

Matthew smiled and glanced upwards at the sprig of mistletoe that Anna had hung above the tea shop door. 'I don't think you've made use of any of that cursed plant yet, have you?'

'Well, Jack did catch me as he was leaving.'

'You'd better come here, then.' Pulling her towards him, he captured her mouth in a passionate kiss.

Breaking apart some moments later, Anna caught her breath. 'Crikey,' she said. 'I've completely forgotten about the cold.'

Matthew grinned. 'Perhaps this might also help to take your mind off it.' Rummaging in his jacket pocket, he withdrew a small, midnight blue velvet box.

Anna's heart stopped.

Matthew took a step away from her, and with a slight grimace at the action, gently got down on his good knee.

'I've been waiting for the right moment since that day on the common,' he said. 'But between the kids, the tea shop and the cider farm, there never seemed to be one. So now seems as good a time as any.' A lock of hair fell over his forehead as he looked up at her, a look of intensity in his eyes that she'd seen so many times before. 'So will you be my own Wassail Queen, Anna Hemingway, and also do me the honour of becoming my wife?'

Anna, struggling suddenly for breath, could think of no other words but 'I will.' She opened the jewellery box and her heart thumped. Lying on the velvet cushion was a gold band set with five antique diamonds. 'It's so beautiful,' she whispered, blinking furiously as her vision blurred.

Matthew's face, so serious during his proposal, relaxed into a grin. Rising to his feet again, he drew Anna closer once more, and kissed her; a kiss that was long, sweet, and laden with the promise and hope of a lifetime. 'I'm glad,' he said as he released her. 'And I can tell Meredith she was right.'

'No need, Dad,' Meredith called from across the street. 'I knew that already.' Sliding back into Flynn's protective embrace, she waved and headed off home.

Anna laughed. 'One step ahead, as ever,' she said. Then, looking back up at Matthew. 'Walk me home?'

Matthew smiled back. 'Always.'

Acknowledgements

First and foremost, huge thanks to Caroline Ridding and Sarah Ritherdon and the team at Aria for their enthusiasm for this story and its characters. Many, many thanks also to my wonderful agent, Sara Keane, who showed me just how amazing literary agents can be.

To my husband Nick, whose apparent indifference to the whole process was at times infuriating and at others motivating. The gift of the 'book signing pen' was truly wonderful, though. To Mum and Dad for always encouraging me to write, and to Mum again, and Helen and Penny for being perfect proof readers and having eagle eyes. To Luke for filling me in on Police procedures after car accidents and Michael for listening to the ramblings. To Flora and Roseanna, of course, for making writing my guilty pleasure between refereeing their sisterly squabbles.

To Backwell School, especially the English Department and library, who put up with my nonsensical ramblings about imaginary people for the best part of three years. You're all wonderful and I couldn't imagine working with a more brilliant, compassionate and indulgent bunch of people. Especially Steph Hollington, who listened, read and humoured me throughout.

To Vicky Bagley, who was my first editor for this project,

back when it was at first draft stage. You believed, and I needed that!

To the fabulous friends who read, critiqued and suggested – especially Carly Kilby, who while we swam was a sounding board for a lot of plot points. Also Dee, Beth, Sarah, Bex, Anna, Kate and the rest of the yummy mummies for reading and encouraging, and all those who have supported my writing in one way or another.

To the wonderful writers I have met in real life and online. Lynn Kendal, your friendship, support and encouragement over more years than I care to count has got me to this point; ditto Rhianna Pratchett. To Bristol University Teachers As Writers group for all the encouragement. Also, the ladies of the South West Chapter Romantic Novelists' Association for allowing me to hang out with you. To Sue Wilsher and the talented and lovely ladies of the Mumsnet Get Published Facebook group for all of your support and encouragement.

Thanks also to those whom I've asked random questions over the past few years; Sam Burke for the medical advice and Matt at Thatchers Cider for giving me a tour at the early stages of writing.

And finally, to you, the reader, for reading this novel. I hope you've enjoyed it!